# NO COMFORT IN
# VICTORY

# NO COMFORT IN
# VICTORY

## GREGORY BEAN

ST. MARTIN'S PRESS 🐾 NEW YORK

Library of Congress Cataloging-in-Publication Data

Bean, Greg.
    No comfort in victory : a Sheriff Harry Starbranch mystery
  / Gregory Bean
      p.    cm.
    "A Thomas Dunne Book."
    ISBN 0-312-13133-X (hardcover)
    I.   Title.
  PS3552.E1525N6   1995
  813'.54—dc20                          95-8569
                                               CIP

A Thomas Dunne Book

First Edition: July 1995

10 9 8 7 6 5 4 3 2 1

*In memory of my father,*
*Keith Bean*

# ACKNOWLEDGMENTS

I don't know how it is for most first-time novelists, but for me, the process of getting *No Comfort in Victory* to print was more a team effort than a solitary pursuit. I owe lots of people my heartfelt thanks, beginning with Red Garretson, the Wyoming brand inspector who shared his expertise on rustling, and Gary Puls, sheriff of Albany County who helped me fill in the empty spaces in my knowledge of Wyoming law enforcement. Thanks also to Melissa "Sam" Sherman, who read my rough manuscripts, kept me honest, and came to know Harry Starbranch as well as I do; to Sherie Posesorski, my editor through two drafts and one of the best editors I know; to Nancy Thompson and Oliver Coolidge, who both know and love mysteries and gave me great encouragement; to my agent Helen Rees, who never gives up; to Joan Mazmamian, who brought my manuscripts to Helen's attention and has believed in them all along; to Peter Wolverton, my editor at St. Martin's; to my sons, Coleman, Padraic, and Nick, whose love gives my work meaning. Most of all, thanks to my wife, Linda, who not only shamed me into beginning this novel, but gave me the time, the wise advice, and, when necessary, the confidence to see it through.

"A fanatic is a man that does what he thinks th' Lord
wud do if He knew th' facts iv th' case."
—Mr. Dooley (Finley Peter Dunne)

# NO COMFORT IN
# VICTORY

# ONE

Ralphie Skates was a nasty, leather-necked son of an oil-patch whore who once served ten years in the state pen at Rawlins for beating his wife's lover to death with a lead-weighted baseball bat. But for all his mean and swagger, he wasn't tough enough to stop the bullet that had torn off the bottom half of his face and driven most of his teeth out the back of his neck.

Lying on his side in the dust of Tess McAfferty's corral, the fingers of his right hand rested in a pile of cow shit. His left arm, pinned beneath his heavy body when he crashed to the packed ground, was twisted at an unnatural angle. His pants bagged around his knees, and a couple of shiny green bottle flies snacked on his flaccid penis. A puddle of black blood congealed beneath his shattered head.

Across the corral, two attendants from the county's ambulance service fitted Colleen McAfferty's sixteen-year-old body into a rubber body bag, carefully tucking the last wisps of her silky blond hair in so it wouldn't get stuck in the zipper. When we found her, she was almost naked, her buttocks and back scratched and scored by the cactus and prickly pear that grows at the corral's edge, her light cotton shift ripped open at the bosom and bunched around her hips, her robin's-egg blue panties stuffed in her mouth to keep her from screaming.

For a good part of my working life, I was a homicide detective in Denver, Colorado, and I've seen more than my share of corpses in various stages of mutilation. I've seen them hewed, carved, chopped, cleaved, and split. I've even seen them melted down with acid. But I've never gotten used to it. Never gotten over the queasy feeling that begins to bubble in the pit of my stomach every time I have to look violent death in the face, have to stare at the hunks of meat that used to be parts of a living human being—especially when those parts represent the earthly remains of somebody's kid.

It had taken every ounce of my self-control to leave Colleen the way we discovered her until Jim Bowen, the Albany County coroner, who'd been called a little after 7:00 A.M., could drive thirty miles to the McAfferty ranch outside Rock River, Wyoming, and pronounce the victims of this double homicide officially deceased. Nearly impossible to keep from removing the panties from her mouth, pulling her shift down to cover her nakedness. To stop myself from closing the blue eyes that still reflected the terror of her final moments.

Bowen wasn't ready to put anything in writing yet, but to him it looked like she'd been sexually assaulted, most likely by Skates and maybe others, before someone wrapped his hands around her windpipe and broke her neck. The bruises on her rib cage, breasts, and cheeks made it clear that the bastards who raped her punched her plenty before they got around to killing her. There were smears of crusted blood on the insides of her thighs.

"Well, Sheriff Starbranch, here's the way I see it," Bowen said somberly. An undertaker by profession, he only works part time for the county as coroner. Not yet 10:00 A.M., and his business uniform—coal black suit, starched white shirt, and spit-shined black wing tips—was already filthy. There was dust ground into the knees of his pants, flecks of blood on his shirt. His thinning brown and gray hair stood out in little wings, and a long smudge of dirt ran across his forehead. "Skates is on top of her, doing his business, maybe he's just finished, when something scares him. He starts hobbling across the corral. He can't go very fast because he hasn't had time to pull his pants up, and he only makes it this far before someone plants a slug in his mouth."

While he talked, Bowen poked around the raw meat of Ralphie's face with a long pair of stainless steel tweezers, smiled thinly when he found a small hunk of twisted metal embedded in the flesh.

"Bullet fragment?" I asked.

"Maybe," he said thoughtfully as he held it to the light. "But it could be part of a filling. I can't tell. Whatever it is, the sumbitch didn't suffer much."

"Too bad," I said.

"What'd you say, Harry?" he asked.

I nodded across the corral to where the attendants were lifting the collapsing metal gurney bearing Colleen's body into the back of the ambulance. Their young faces were grim, the fronts of their white uniforms covered with blood. "Too bad he didn't suffer more. It looks like whoever killed him let him off easy."

Bowen mumbled noncommittally, returned to his gruesome excavations, his brow wrinkling in concentration.

I stood up, my forty-something knees creaking with the effort, and leaned my weight on the blackthorn walking stick I'd been using as a cane since I blew out my knee in a skiing accident the winter before. I turned away from the coppery smell of blood and the foul stench of shit and sucked a deep lungful of high plains air into my chest. Heavy with the smell of sage, alfalfa, and alkali dust, the air was spiced with a hint of moisture from the Laramie River, which flows through the center of the McAfferty ranch.

Tess McAfferty's corral is probably fifty years old, its sun-bleached pine railings hobbled together in a bizarre conglomeration of improbable angles, the gates sagging on their rusty hinges and the loading ramp a federal safety inspector's nightmare. On the far side of the enclosure my crew, a half dozen deputies from the Albany County Sheriff's Office poked around the killing ground, carefully packing the bits of possible evidence into bags that would be sent to the state crime lab for analysis. Two others, on their hands and knees, poured plaster into the set of tire tracks we believed were made by the vehicle driven by Ralphie's cohorts, who had also helped themselves to the former occupants of the corral, three yearling steers and an eight-year-old quarter horse mare named Jezebel.

When Tess called us in a little past sunup after spending the night at her boyfriend's place in Laramie, she told the first deputy on scene that the mare was Colleen's best friend and gymkhana partner, raised from birth right there on the McAfferty's Rock River ranch, hand-fed and trained as one of the finest barrel-racing horses in the county. The steers, brought into the corral for a shot of antibiotics, were part of the McAfferty herd of yearlings waiting for shipment to the feed lots in Nebraska come October.

While my deputies continued their crime scene investigation and Bowen picked at and prodded the remains of Ralphie Skates, I hobbled over to the edge of the corral and let myself through the creaking gates. About thirty yards up the hill, I could see the McAfferty's old two-story ranch house, the bright yellow light from the early morning sun dancing off the big picture window that looked out over the corral and the little valley that comprised maybe a third of their three-thousand-acre ranch.

On a clear day, you could see snowcapped peaks of the Snowy Range from the window. It would be nice to stand in front of it come evening with a cup of coffee and watch the mule deer and pronghorn antelope creep down to the banks of the tiny stream that ran through the sagebrush for their nightly drink and a bite of the hay scattered in huge cylindrical bales across the brown fields. Knowing that the earth of the valley was now stained with her daughter's blood, I wondered sadly if Tess McAfferty would ever enjoy that view again.

There were four vehicles parked in the gravel driveway, one of them a blue and white sheriff's department cruiser driven by Larry Rawls, the deputy who'd been interviewing Tess McAfferty. There was also a battered old Jeep, the springs poking through both of its cracked leather seats, a new mud-splattered Chevy pickup with a heavy-duty livestock rack, and the light green Honda Accord Tess had been driving when she came back from Laramie.

As I picked my way up the hill, my boots kicking up billowy little clouds of dust in the still August air, I tried to decide what I'd say to Tess, a woman I'd met only a couple of times in Laramie but who is something of a legend in the local ranching community.

Widowed about six years ago when a tractor toppled down an embankment and crushed her husband to death, she surprised both the Laramie bankers who held the mortgages on the property and her own parents, a couple of Ohio suburbanites who wanted Tess to gather up her young daughter and move back to the Midwest, by declaring that not only did she intend to keep the struggling ranch that had been her husband's dream, she intended to run it. And run it she has, with all the tenacity and strength it takes to keep a working ranch in operation, which only someone who has plunged their own arms elbow-deep into a heifer's vagina in order to hook a chain to the leg of a calf who's having trouble being born can begin to appreciate.

I didn't know what had happened in the McAfferty corral, but I had little reason to believe Tess responsible for either of the bodies we'd found there. I'd listened to the tape of her emergency phone call to the sheriff's office when she discovered the carnage, heard the hysteria in her voice as she begged the dispatcher to send help immediately. My gut told me the voice on that tape didn't belong to a murderess. Bobby Condon, the deputy stationed in Rock River and the first person on the scene, said he'd found her kneeling in the corral, tears rolling down her cheeks as she gently cradled Colleen's head in her lap, reassuring her dead daughter that everything would be fine if she could just hold on until help came.

"She tried to hit me when I pulled her hands away," Condon said sadly, "wouldn't leave Colleen alone until a long time after the ambulance got here and she knew there was nothing we could do."

By the time I arrived at the ranch, about two hours after the call came in, Tess had been coaxed back to the house, and she'd been there with Rawls ever since.

At the top of the hill, I walked through the little gate in the fence that separated her well-tended yard from the prairie and caught the earthy scent of the banks of marigolds, mint, and daisies that bordered her walkway, along with the smell of freshly mown grass. A bright Chinese wind sock dangled listlessly on a pole at the far corner of her porch, which was a jumble of garden implements, muddy boots, and mismatched lawn furniture. The white porch swing was outfitted with a half dozen fluffy pillows. Beneath it, someone had left a pair of pink running shoes and a copy of *Seventeen*. I didn't knock on the screen door, just pulled the sweat-stained Stetson off my head, wiped my feet on the welcome mat, and let myself in.

When my eyes adjusted to the change in light, I saw Rawls seated on an ottoman in the living room. Tess McAfferty sat on the couch, her arms wrapped around her body like she ached in every joint, rocking back and forth, her eyes red-rimmed and bloodshot from tears.

The room was bright and airy, the peach-colored walls lined with bookshelves and hung with family photographs: Tess and her husband at a Halloween party with a much younger Colleen dressed as a pixie. Colleen riding behind her father on a roan quarter horse, both wearing wide-brimmed cowboy hats and huge grins. Colleen dressed as a gypsy at a school play. A wedding photo of Tess and her husband sharing a glass of champagne. Tess and her husband on a beach, palm trees in the background, both of them in bathing suits, oversize sunglasses, and Mexican sombreros. When I came to a small handprint in a plaster disk, painted copper and inscribed with the words *For Mommy* in childish script, I felt my windpipe begin to constrict. I took a deep breath and cleared my throat.

Rawls, six three and pencil thin, looked about ready to cry himself. He was scribbling notes in the black notebook he'd consult later when he wrote his formal report, his long fingers clutching his pen so tightly it seemed it might snap. When he saw me, he flashed me a weak smile, an unmistakable look of relief on his narrow scarecrow face.

"Sheriff Starbranch," he said hopefully, nodding toward the corral, "anything?"

"Not much," I said. "Bowen isn't finished, and our guys haven't turned up anything definitive. How about here?"

"About the same," he said as he flipped the pages in the notebook. "Mrs. McAfferty came home a little after six, found the front door wide open. When she checked her daughter's bedroom and found it empty, she started looking around."

"I shouldn't have left her," Tess choked, fighting a new wave of grief. "If I'd been here they wouldn't have . . ."

Somewhere in her late thirties, Tess would be considered a beautiful woman if she fixed her light brown hair and wrapped her lean body in a nice black dress. Even with her long hair tied back in a ponytail, dressed in faded jeans, well-worn cowboy boots, and a chambray shirt, she was handsome, with high cheekbones, startling green eyes, and a patrician nose enhanced by the little bump about halfway up that kept it from being perfect.

I went to the couch and sank down beside her, looped an arm around her shoulders and drew her close. Shaking as if cold, she buried her face against my neck, and I could feel her warm breath as it came in gasps, the wetness of her tears as they soaked my collar. I held her tightly until the shivering calmed and her breathing became more regular.

"It isn't your fault," I told her softly. "The men who did this were animals. I doubt if you could have stopped them."

"Then I should have died trying," she whispered, digging her strong fingers painfully into my arm. Behind the heartbreak, I could hear the first faint stirrings of rage in her voice, rage and the strength I hoped would eventually carry her beyond her loss, beyond the memories of what she had seen when she peered into the abyss, and allow her to continue living.

"No, Tess, you should not have died trying," I said. "If you'd died, you'd have never had the pleasure of looking into their eyes when the judge hands down their sentence."

I hadn't thrown her much of a lifeline, but it pulled her, at least temporarily, away from the edge. She relaxed her grip on my arm—there'd be a bruise there later—nodded, and wiped the tears from her cheek with the back of her hand.

"We'll catch them," she said. It was not a question.

"I promise," I said. "But every minute that goes by makes it harder. I know you've told Deputy Rawls everything you know, and he can fill me in later, if going over it again is too painful. But if you think you could—"

"I can handle it," she said, reaching for a tattered tissue. "At this point, it's all I can do."

According to Tess, who told the story in quick, sharp bursts, she'd left home about three the previous afternoon and headed for Laramie, where she intended to have dinner with her boyfriend, Roy Hardy, an assistant professor of agriculture at the University of Wyoming, and spend the night at his house. Colleen, who liked Hardy, despite the fact that he wouldn't let her drive his new Mazda Miata convertible, usually came along on these excursions, but this time she'd pled cramps and asked to stay home. She said she was going to curl up on the sofa with some hot tea and a pile of magazines, call some friends, maybe watch a movie on the VCR later that evening.

"She was sixteen, so even though I don't like leaving her alone, I figured she'd be all right. I was coming home first thing this morning, and I'd done it once in a while before. She liked having time to herself now and then. Nobody to tell her what to eat, when to go to bed."

"Yeah," I said, thinking of my own teenage kid, the oldest of my three boys, who live in Denver with their mother, my ex-wife. "I know what you mean."

"When I came home this morning," she continued, "I could feel something wrong before I even got out of the car. The front door was open, and I could still hear the television going inside. Colleen isn't—"she faltered, corrected herself, stumbling over the terrible words—"wasn't one to get up that early in the morning."

I looked over at Rawls, who'd heard all this already. He quietly studied his notes, nodded in agreement when Tess told me something he'd written down, making a few additions. He was taking this hard, trying not to let it show. When his bottom lip began to tremble, he bit it so hard it bled.

"I hollered when I came in," Tess said, "and when she didn't answer, I looked in her bedroom. Empty. I found her about five minutes later. She was . . . already dead."

My hand went to my shirt pocket—for about the bazillionth time—for the cigarettes I hadn't smoked since I quit nine weeks before. I settled for a cinnamon toothpick, jammed it in the corner of my mouth.

"Was Colleen expecting anyone last night?" I asked. "Were you? Do you have any idea, any suspicion, who might have done this?" I watched her face for a reaction, and what I saw was genuine bewilderment.

She shook her head. "None at all. I know all of the neighbors around here, and get along with them. None of them would have . . ."

"How about people Colleen knew?"

"You think one of the kids she hangs around with did this?" Tess asked incredulously. "Christ, none of them is even allowed to drive out here after dark. And what about that—that . . ."

"Ralphie Skates," I said. "His name was Ralphie Skates. He's crossed paths with my department before. Assault, drunk and disorderly. Served time for second-degree murder."

"What would one of her friends have had to do with him? You think one of them brought him here?"

I had to admit she had a point, but I had to ask the questions anyway, even if I didn't expect them to lead anywhere.

"Nah," I said. "I don't think it was one of her friends, but I've got to figure out what happened down there."

"Well it's obvious isn't it?" Tess growled.

"You tell me, Tess," I said. "What's obvious?"

"Jezebel," she said as her voice began to crack again. "Rustlers have been hitting around this valley all summer, and some of them came out here to steal those damn sick cows and Jezebel. Colleen must have heard them and died trying to save her."

When I finished talking with Tess, I left her in the care of Rawls and her physician, who'd arrived and spent several minutes digging around in her black bag for some mild sedatives, a bit of pharmaceutical comfort that Tess loudly refused to take.

At the corral, Bowen had finished his examination of Skates, who was now bagged and resting—uncomfortably, I hoped—in the back of the ambulance that would take his remains to Laramie for an autopsy. Bowen and two of my deputies were on their hands and knees in the sagebrush at the side of the rutted road that meandered down the gentle hillside from the McAfferty house to the corral's loading ramp. From a short distance, it looked for all the world like someone had dropped a contact lens and they were all trying to find it.

"Hey Harry," Bowen called when he saw me trudging down the road toward the little group of archeologists. By now, the breeze had ruffled his hair until it was standing completely on end, and he had taken off his jacket. There was an inch-long rip in the knee of his suit pants. "Look what we found here!"

He held two fingers in the air to show me his prize, but it

wasn't until I was almost on top of him that I realized that the stuff on the tips of those fingers wasn't mud but thick, dark red blood. A gelatinous, platter-size spill of it had soaked into the ground at Bowen's knees, and more frosted the pungent green leaves of the closest sagebrush. Bowen's Polaroid camera hung from his neck, and four or five not yet developed photographs lined the top of his evidence case.

"Blood!" he said triumphantly, shaking those fingers at me like some macabre victory sign.

"Christ, I can see that," I said testily. "But whose is it?"

Bowen shrugged. "Fuck if I know. I can't even type it out here. But I can tell you this. It doesn't belong to either Colleen McAfferty or Ralphie Skates—they both died in the corral. Whoever this belonged to was shot and killed right near the loading ramp."

"How you know he was killed?"

Bowen tossed me a large plastic evidence bag filled with bits of meat, gristle, a couple fragments of bone. I caught it and looked at him, waited for the answer to the question I didn't have to ask.

"Just guessing," he said. "But that looks to me like a little hunk of heart, a couple globs of lung, and a few smidgens of rib bone."

He pointed at a spot about six feet in back of the bloody sagebrush. "I found those scraps over there. The bullet that hit the son of a bitch blew 'em right out his back. After that, he didn't go anywhere on his own hook."

After Bowen packed up his gear and drove away—his black Ford sedan sending up rooster tails of dust on the washboard road leading from the McAfferty ranch to the blacktop highway into Rock River and Laramie—I staked out a seat on the splintery planks of Tess McAfferty's livestock loading ramp and watched the progress of my deputies. Expanding their search in an ever widening circle around the corral, they now concentrated on the area directly south, the direction we figured the shot that killed Ralphie Skates had come from.

We already knew a few things about what happened in that corral and suspected others, but we were a long way from knowing enough. By late the next day, I'd have the results of Bowen's autopsy, and the state Department of Criminal Investigation's lab in Cheyenne might get me a report on the other evidence we'd collected a day or so after that.

In the meantime, I had to get things rolling on the little I had.

The bodies of both Colleen McAfferty and Ralphie Skates were in the advanced stages of rigor mortis, but because heat speeds that process and the night before had been uncommonly warm, the best estimate Bowen could make of the time of death was ten to eighteen hours before we found them. That would mean they died the day before, either in the late afternoon or early evening.

He didn't know whose blood had been spilled at the side of the corral, but we both knew that considering the vital organ debris, we were at least one body shy. That meant someone, or several someones, had carried it away.

Skates, Bowen said, had been killed by a single gunshot wound to the head, probably fired from some distance by a gunman using a high-velocity handgun or a rifle. Judging by the destruction of Ralphie's face, we figured the killer had used an expanding bullet, either a hollow-point or the kind of soft-pointed round favored by big-game hunters because the slug will mushroom on impact to twice its caliber. The Geneva Convention outlawed the use of bullets like that in warfare because they do so much damage they're considered cruel. In the West though, they're used in most gunshot deaths, because the people who own rifles and pistols for hunting don't think to load with more humane military ammo before they start shooting people.

If Ralphie's killer had used sporting rounds, the bullets might be so deformed after impact that we could never match them to the weapon they were fired from. That's assuming that we could find them—which, considering the fact that they had around a dozen square miles of open country to hide in, we had not been able to do.

Nor had we turned up any spent shell casings within a hundred yards of the murder scene. That meant the killer, knowing we might eventually be able to pull a fingerprint or match the ejector and extractor markings against his weapon, had probably been smart enough to collect his own brass after the shootings.

On the plus side, we had found and made casts of some fresh footprints that led up to and away from a small, rocky knoll about fifty yards south of the corral. Those prints might turn out to be the bit of evidence that broke the case, and then again, they might have been made by anyone, maybe even one of the hired hands Tess occasionally used to work cows or wrestle irrigation pipe. Certainly the gunman could have concealed himself behind that cover and had a clear shot at Ralphie and whoever else was in the enclosure. Then again, he could have stood right at the edge of the corral when he pulled the trigger. I just didn't know enough at that point to say for sure whether the bullets had been fired from ten or two hundred yards. And anyway, the trail away from the knoll disappeared within thirty yards as it crossed the small, rocky stream that bisects the ranch, still flowing with plenty of water despite the summer's drought.

I put my arms behind me on the rough wooden planking of the livestock ramp and lifted my face up to the sun, stretched my sore legs and the muscles in the small of my back. The temperatures might hit ninety or better in the afternoon, but at that moment the thermometer barely caressed eighty, and the warmth was luxurious, with just a hint of dewey moisture still lingering in the air.

Down the valley of the McAfferty ranch, the bright green of the irrigated alfalfa, the grasses and parti-colored wildflowers along the slender ribbon of the streambed—there'd be some big brown trout lurking in the deeper bends—stood out in stunning counterpoint to the nearly universal brown of the parched prairie.

In the distance I could see the cool, inviting, blue-green slopes of the mountains, their peaks capped with glacial ice. Somewhere beyond the far bank of the creek a couple of meadowlarks treated each other to a midmorning serenade.

This place, I thought, should have been the perfect place to raise children.

In general, Albany County is a safe place to live. We'd had no suicides in the last year, and only a handful of burglaries, rapes, and assaults. My small and underresourced department, in fact, spends most of its time doing search and rescue for the hikers and hunters who get lost in the mountains, serving civil papers, writing traffic tickets, and picking off drunk drivers. For the tough jobs, I've got myself, my undersheriff, a handful of deputies, and a drug dog that's a reject from the police department.

In the county's outlying communities—Victory, the small town at the foot of the Snowies where I live; Rock River; Bosler; Tie Siding—and on ranches like the McAffertys', life is even more Arcadian, and we take the honesty of our neighbors, and our own safety, for granted. People in towns like Victory are truly concerned with each other's welfare, close nearly every financial agreement with a handshake, leave their keys in the car, their front doors unlocked when they go to bed at night.

They do not come home to find their children raped and murdered.

The killing of Colleen McAfferty sickened me, saddened me, made me fear for the safety of my own children and my neighbors' children. But most of all it made me angry, filled me with the kind of rage that cries out for resolution. For justice.

The murders had been committed in my town, on my watch. That made it personal. I could hardly wait to get back to Laramie and begin kicking over the rocks of Ralphie Skates's life.

In the dark, vermin-infested places beneath those stones, I'd start looking for answers.

# TWO

I burned up the highway on the thirty-minute drive from the McAfferty ranch to my office in the basement of the county courthouse building in Laramie, checked with the dispatcher for messages, propped my feet on my desk, and dialed C.J. Fall's home number. The chief brand inspector in Albany County and the law enforcement officer charged with controlling the crime of livestock theft, I thought Fall might have some insight into the McAfferty killings.

I didn't expect to find Fall, a bachelor who spends most of his time in the field, at home, so it surprised me when he answered on the third ring. He was just having a bite of lunch, he said, before heading out to a ranch near Tie Siding, where he'd been called to check the brands on a couple of bulls the owner planned to sell to a buyer from Cody.

I told him about the murders at the McAfferty ranch, and the fact that it looked like the killings involved rustlers, a subject I knew very little about. I asked if we could get together soon so I could pick his brain.

"I should be back around five-thirty," he said wearily. "I'll be happy to talk to you then, if you come by the house."

"You ever eat dinner out?" I asked.

"Sure," he said. "Especially if somebody else buys."

I made arrangements to meet him for Mexican food at El Conquistador on Ivinson around six. Then I turned on my computer to see what we had on Ralphie Skates.

As I waited for the thing to warm up, I pawed through my messages—all of them from reporters—and threw them in the trash. I imagined the reporters had heard about the murders at the McAfferty place and wanted my comments. But since I knew next to nothing and wasn't ready to share what little I had, it seemed like a good idea to stall. Particularly since one of the calls had been from Sally Sheridan, the local reporter for the statewide newspaper, the *Casper Star Tribune,* and one of the many crosses I bear.

The computer quacked at me when it had retrieved Skates's file from electronic limbo, and I quickly scrolled through the scattered highlights of his career. Born in the Gas Hills outside Riverton in 1956, he'd been confined to the state reformatory in Worland in 1972 for motor vehicle theft and using a broken beer bottle in an assault on the highway patrolman who arrested him. Released on his eighteenth birthday in 1974, he'd celebrated by marrying the sixteen-year-old daughter of a local beet farmer. He killed her lover two years later in a fit of jealous rage, pleaded guilty to second-degree murder, and spent the next fourteen years in the state penitentiary. Since his release, his probation report said he'd been working as a laborer at the Mountain West Cement Company plant on the outskirts of town. He'd had a couple of beefs for drunk and disorderly, a couple of moving violations, and a bad-check complaint, but nothing serious enough to put him back in the slam.

All in all, Ralphie Skates sounded like your average run-of-the-mill white trash dirtbag, but there was nothing in his history to suggest he'd taken up a new career as a livestock thief. Still, crooks like Ralphie are nothing if not adaptable.

No next of kin or phone number was included in his file, but it listed an address about three miles south of Laramie on Highway 287.

I jotted it down on a slip of paper, buckled on the .357 Blackhawk hanging in a leather holster that dangled from a hook on the back of my office door, called the dispatcher to tell her my destination, and slipped out through the door to the motor pool to avoid whoever might be waiting for me in the reception area.

Ten minutes later I pulled off 287 and into the dusty drive of Ralphie Skates's house, a testament to rural poverty in America. I parked in the only place available, the front yard, which was nothing but an arid convention of crabgrass, oat grass, Russian thistle, and jimsonweed. Tumbleweeds clustered in a three-foot-high drift along the drooping wire fence. A dilapidated old barn, it's roof sagging dangerously and the front doors hanging loosely from sprung hinges, sat to the left of the house. Parked and forgotten in front of the barn was an old dented Chevy with four flat tires, a missing front quarter panel, and a WYOMING NATIVE sticker on the rust-pocked back bumper. The air smelled faintly of raw sewage, the result, I suspected, of a neglected septic tank.

The house itself was small, white stucco with great hunks of plaster falling away from the wood in several places. The windows were covered with plastic, which provided some insulation from the prairie wind in winter but would keep the summer heat inside as well. Through the plastic, I could see the dingy white shades Skates had pulled to keep anyone from looking in. On one near the front door, a marginally talented artist had drawn a corpulent naked woman holding her large breasts in her hands. Very classy.

A hook-and-eye latch held the wooden screen door shut from the outside, and when I banged on the door, I was answered by the bark of a dog. I waited on the small front porch for several minutes while the animal continued to yap, then, when I began to believe that no one else was inside, I slipped the latch, pulled the screen open, and tried the front door. It was unlocked, and when I cracked it open an inch, the animal Skates had left behind shoved his head through the opening, whining as he tried to force his shoulders through, his tail wagging like a metronome.

A full-grown black Labrador, he should have weighed sixty

pounds or more, but he looked barely half that, a canine skeleton with hide attached, his coat leaden and dull. He pushed through the open door and scrambled out into the sunshine, yipped weakly as he spun in happy circles, ecstatic at his escape from the confines of the closed house.

I'd feed and water him later, but first I unsnapped the Blackhawk and drew it. Its weight felt heavy and comforting in my hand. Then I kicked the door open with the toe of my boot, waited for a few seconds to satisfy myself that I was alone, then inched into the living room. The stench of sewer gas was even worse inside than outside. Gagging as my eyes swept the living room, I hoped the house didn't explode.

I don't think you could call the place where Ralphie Skates lived a home—*hovel* is a more accurate word. Every flat surface was littered with empty beer cans and the remains of molding TV dinners. Ashtrays overflowed with cigarette butts. There was grimy, sweat-stained clothing heaped in disgusting piles throughout the room. Ralphie had haphazardly tossed an impressive stack of reading material on the slipcovered sofa, and as soon as my eyes had fully adjusted to the murky shadows of his living room, I was treated to the page he'd apparently been drooling over last, a full-color photograph of a bottle blonde performing a very uncomfortable-looking sex act with a dildo the size of a summer squash.

There was a new-looking home entertainment center, complete with wide-screen color television, CD player, stereo, and turntable in a heavy walnut case on the far wall—equipment worth a couple grand at least. Ralphie might live like a pig, but at least he had good taste in electronics. I flipped on the TV's power and noticed the little light in the VCR that tells you there's a tape inside. I hit the play button and was treated to the sight of a large-breasted redhead with a shaved pubic area performing oral sex on a wide-hipped brunette stretched out on a lounge chair at the side of a backyard swimming pool. The brunette was bouncing around and moaning at the pleasure of it all but kept looking at the camera to see if it was still running. I turned the television off and popped the VCR tape out of the player—the movie was titled *Sisters in Sin*.

Ralphie's place was giving me the creeps, the same feeling I used to get when I'd patrol the twenty-five-cent peep show jack-off houses on East Colfax. I thought I could actually feel the crab lice crawling off the floor and up my pant legs. I fought back the urge to scratch my shins, put the tape back in the VCR, and picked my way through the living room to the kitchen, an even worse environmental disaster. Junk mail was stacked several inches high on the table and counter, sharing space with around a hundred dirty plates and pans, the debris, it appeared, of nearly every meal Skates had eaten in the past six months. At least a half dozen bulging black trash bags had been tossed in the far corner; most of them were ripped open—by the dog, I imagined—and leaked trails of garbage across the floor.

I held my nose and tried to ignore the smell of rancid meat as I poked through the mail, which Ralphie had had delivered at a post office box in town. There was the usual smattering of sweepstakes notices, a couple of unpaid utility bills, a thick packet of coupons, but no personal letters or notes. I threw the mail back on the table and started to look around for a phone and a personal phone book. Ralphie, who probably found the cost of installing a phone line in the sticks prohibitive, had neither that I could see. If he wanted to call anyone, he'd have to do it somewhere else. If anyone wanted him, they'd have to come to him.

A doorway led off the kitchen to what I figured was the bedroom, but the door was missing; Ralphie had closed it off with a tattered brown bedspread. I pushed it aside carefully and let myself into his bedroom, which smelled of body odor and semen and was as dark as a crypt. I fumbled around until I found a bedside lamp and switched it on, saw he'd put a thick navy wool blanket over the window to keep the sun out. This, I thought, was a man who liked to sleep in the daytime.

His bed was a riot of filthy sheets and clothing, the floor barely navigable, and the drawers of his dresser were open. I found nothing of interest on his nightstand or on top of his dresser, nor did his top drawer yield anything but the usual trash—nail clippers, tape, assorted tools, rubbers, a Buck folding knife in a black sheath. In the second drawer, along with his underwear and socks, I hit paydirt, a loaded Charter Arms .38—a definite no-no for an ex-con—and a thick wad of well-worn twenty-dollar bills.

I didn't touch the weapon, but I took the stash to his bed and sat there, counted until I came to the end of his bankroll. Seven thousand, four hundred sixty dollars. A lot of money, I thought, for someone who probably made eight bucks an hour tops at the cement plant. Gambling? Burglary? Stolen property? All of the above?

I dropped the money back in the drawer and looked in his closet, expecting to find it as sloppy as the rest of his house. To my surprise, it was nearly empty, except for a couple of heavy coats on wire hangers, a pair of ratty-looking jeans, two cracked and heel-worn pairs of cowboy boots, and a twelve-gauge Remington pump shotgun leaning in the corner. I stood on my tiptoes, searched the shelf with my fingertips until I found what felt like a full box of shells and pulled it down. They were twelve-gauge shotgun shells all right, loaded with double-ought buck, the kind of devastating load you'd use to hunt men instead of geese.

I slid the ammo back onto the shelf and walked through the living room and out the front door into the blinding sunlight. It was clear that Ralphie Skates had been involved in some lucrative illegal activity at the time of his death, lucrative enough to get him that space-age home entertainment system and a wad of bills thick enough to stop a toilet. But I hadn't found anything to tell me exactly what he'd been involved in, or with whom. Maybe it was there and I'd just missed it.

One thing was certain: someone needed to take the place apart from top to bottom. But if I did it myself it would take all day. I scuffed across the dusty ground toward my Blazer and my radio, where I planned to have the dispatcher send a couple of deputies out to toss Ralphie's crib while I worked another angle.

His skinny dog had jumped through the open window and was waiting in the back seat.

"Make yourself right at home, you slat-ribbed bag of bones," I grumbled, holding the door open for him to get back out.

The mutt did exactly what I told him to do, curled up in a ball with a contented little moan and fell asleep.

The receptionist at the cement plant offered me a soda and the dog a dish of water while we waited for Ralphie's boss to come in from the loading docks. We cooled our heels in silence, enjoyed the conditioned air and our drinks until he clumped in about ten minutes later, cursing the heat and brushing cement dust from his thinning hair. A well-built man on the short side of sixty, John Baker had the crinkly, calloused look of someone who's been around the block and intends to go around again. The look of a man for whom life holds few surprises.

He wasn't surprised to find a cop asking questions about one of his workers.

"Skates?" he said after I introduced myself and the subject of my visit. "Sure, I remember the squirrely bastard. Worked here for a few months after he got out of prison."

"Worked?"

"Yeah," Baker said. "He called in sick so often that I put him on probation last May. Told him if he called in sick again that month, I'd fire him."

"Did you?"

"Nah, I didn't fire him. Didn't have to. He just quit showing up. Called Irene here and told her to mail his final check."

"You never heard from him again?"

"No, and I didn't expect to. I go through laborers around here like Imelda Marcos goes through shoes. They don't last long, especially the ex-cons."

As he talked, Baker studied the dog, which had finished its

drink and was curled up on the floor, watching us expectantly. Baker frowned, shook his head and looked away. It took me a few seconds to realize he thought the abused animal belonged to me.

"Ralphie's dog," I explained. "He left it alone at his house. Doesn't look like he fed it much, either."

"You were there?" he asked. "His house?"

I told him about finding Ralphie's body that morning, told him about Colleen McAfferty. Explained that I was just starting to poke through Ralphie's life, trying to get a handle on something that would lead me to whoever else was on hand at the McAfferty ranch the previous evening when both of them died.

"Not a whole lot I can tell you," Baker said. "Except that he was lazy, and a troublemaker. Had a smart mouth, that boy. And he was always looking to bully someone with his fists, especially if they were smaller than him."

"You know anything about his personal life?" I asked.

"Nah," he said, a look on his face like he'd just taken a bite of poached rattlesnake. "To learn that I'd have to have a conversation with him. We only talked about work, and even then I was usually yelling at him."

"He ever try to bully you?"

"Not me," Baker said. He sounded more than a little offended. In the background, Irene stifled a giggle. "I can still handle the likes of Ralphie Skates, and he knew it."

I looked at the ham-size fists, took in his size-48 chest, the boxer's scars around the corners of his eyes, his linebacker's thighs, and figured old man or not, he was probably right. Ralphie Skates would have had his hands full with this one.

"Then how about friends? He goof around with anyone?"

"None of the regulars," Davis said as he reached down to ruffle the fur on the back of the dog's neck. The pooch liked it so much he rolled over and offered Baker his stomach. "Just one guy, an asshole buddy of Skates's who got out of the pen a little while after Ralphie did and came to work here. Name of Clarence Hathaway."

"He around today?" I asked hopefully.

"Fat chance," Davis said. "He liked it so much he quit the week after Skates. I haven't seen him since May either."

"Shit. You have an address on him?"

Davis looked at Irene, who shrugged her shoulders. "He was kind of a drifter," she said. "I don't think he ever gave me one."

"Is there anything you remember that would help me find him? How about his hangouts?"

Davis frowned. "Like I told you about Skates, we didn't have many conversations. I do know Hathaway used to hang out at one of the bars downtown occasionally. I heard him and Skates talking about going there once."

"The Buckhorn?" I asked. The Buck is an old-timey watering hole on Ivinson with lots of stuffed animal heads on the wall and at least one bullet hole in the backbar mirror. It's a favorite hang-out of the college yuppie crowd, and it wouldn't be the first place I'd think to look for an ex-con like Clarence Hathaway.

Davis shook his head thoughtfully. "No," he said. "His place is across the street. The bartender takes sports bets."

"Sinbad's?" I asked, naming one of Laramie's more notorious saloons, the kind of place where they give unarmed patrons their choice of knife or gun the minute they walk through the door, just to keep them on even terms with the rest of the clientele.

He arched an eyebrow disdainfully. "Yes," he said. "That's it. It's the only place in town they'll let a cockroach like Hathaway run a tab."

By the time I finished with Davis, the grumbling in my gizzard was reminding me that I had missed breakfast and was about to miss lunch. That being the case, the dog and I wheeled down Third Street to the Cowboy Bar & Grill, where I ordered a double bacon cheeseburger with Thousand Island and a side of onion rings. I thought about washing it down with a bucket-size gin and tonic with a thick wedge of lime and plenty of crushed ice, but I was still on duty and settled for a tall iced tea. Five sugars, no lemon.

After a quick peek in my wallet to make sure I wouldn't wind up washing pots and pans—my thirty-thousand-five-hundred-a-year salary doesn't leave room for meals out every day—I also ordered a half-pound slab of raw sirloin for the hound. Our waitress, a pleasant looker about fifteen pounds too Rubenesque for my taste, said she'd be happy to get the pooch his meat, but he'd have to eat it outside. Management's rules, she explained, not particularly apologetically. I, on the other hand, could certainly stay.

I obliged her by coaxing the dog through the front door and out to the car with the steak. He was so excited by the prospect of a square meal he forgot how much he hated being left in the car and jumped into the back seat. As I closed the door, he had the sirloin clutched between his paws and was gnawing it greedily, a contented look on his ugly dog face. A fine mist of pinkish saliva drifted down onto the upholstery. What the hell, I thought, it's the county's car.

Our bellies filled, I spent the rest of the afternoon stopping at all of Laramie's twenty-odd bars and saloons, and although the bartender at Sinbad's said he wished Clarence would come in since he owed close to three hundred dollars in bar bills and gambling markers, no one claimed to have seen him for the previous two days.

Around five, sweaty, tired, and footsore, I pulled back into the motor pool at the sheriff's office, checked with dispatch, and learned that Rawls and my undersheriff, Nicky Pajak, had radioed in from the McAfferty ranch and were expected at the office around quarter past. I needed to talk with them, so I bought a cola from the machine and retreated to my cool basement office to wait. The dog curled up in a cool corner of the office like he owned the place and fell fast asleep. Out the bank of windows along the far wall, I could see the legs of people walking past on their way into the courthouse, could hear the faint breeze rustle through the leaves of the maple trees on the big front lawn.

The sheriff's office is in the cellar of the town's old granite courthouse building, and we share space with the county court across the hall. The second floor of the homely, practical structure is given over to the county assessor and the county clerk. Third floor is the district court. Fourth floor is the public defender's office and the county jail, which is run by the sheriff's department. The place was built of huge chunks of native dung yellow granite, in the thirties by a man who designed World War I bunkers, and its walls are strong enough to withstand a direct hit from a nuclear bomb.

Since the behemoth will likely be standing long after the current generation of tenants and all of Laramie's 26,687 residents are returned to dust, there's never seemed a compelling reason to build a new courthouse, even though we're pretty crowded and there are some maddening drawbacks. In winter, the steam pipes rattle like big bags of metallic bones, and the old boiler breaks down every other day. In the spring and fall, the wind blasts unhindered through the poorly caulked windows, filling the whole building with arctic air and eerie moans.

While rising heat sometimes warms the upper floors a degree or two above freezing (we've got to keep the prisoners warm, or they'll sue us for cruel and inhuman punishment—again), it never gets warm enough down in "the tombs" where my office is to defrost the short hairs on an Eskimo's ass.

In summer though, the basement is the most comfortable hidey-hole in town—a good thing, since the skinflint commissioners who control the county's purse strings would never spring for AC. I always have lots of visitors in the summer months, most of them employees on the third and fourth floors, where it's so hot in August you could fry Spam on your forehead.

I rolled the icy soda can across my brow, took a long and satisfying sip, leaned back in my genuine leatherette swivel chair, and closed my eyes. In the outer office, I could hear the squawk and cackle of the radio as deputies called in, the easy laughter of the secretaries and dispatcher as they shared a joke with a couple of deputies reporting for end of shift. Someone had a desk radio tuned to the local country station, KOWB, and "Bubba Shot the Jukebox," my all-time favorite redneck song in the world, blared from the tinny speakers.

I guess I'd dozed off for a few minutes, dreaming I'd won a seat in the state legislature and showed up naked my first day at work, when Pajak woke me by banging on my door. His knock sounded like a three-hundred-pound woodpecker on steroids.

"Hello, Harry," he said grumpily in the backwoods cracker twang he picked up in Kentucky, where he was born and raised, "sorry to break your train of thought." With that, he shuffled in, followed sheepishly by Rawls.

Pajak, a short, muscular man who looks a lot like an oil burner, helped himself to the best seat in the house, an antique wooden bench rescued late at night from the Union Pacific Railroad depot. Rawls, who's so skinny he looks like he could be sucked down the drain along with the bathwater, made do with a folding chair.

Both of them had spent the day supervising the doings at the McAfferty ranch, finishing up the crime scene investigation and interviewing neighbors. Rawls looked like he'd been ridden hard and hung up wet. Pajak looked cantankerous and stormy. In other words, absolutely normal.

Nicky Pajak, as I tell anyone who asks, was born mad at the world and hasn't seen anything in forty-six years to improve his disposition. Unlike almost everyone else in the office, he's a career sheriff's department employee and has spent more than twenty years working for one elected sheriff after another, some of them so underqualified they wouldn't have known Miranda from mouse turds. He's kept his job by being a better organizer than most of the lunkheads he's worked for, and by being the only person who knows enough about administration to keep the place running on a day-to-day basis. Understandably, the experience has contributed to making him a sour person, and because of that he's hard to like.

I looked at the pair of glum faces inhabiting my office. "I take it things went poorly today," I said. "Otherwise, you guys would be in a more insouciant mood."

My attempt at erudition fell flat with Pajak, who grimaced at the word *insouciant* the way he would if he ate a worm. "No, Harry," he said. "Things did not go well."

I ignored the sarcasm in his blunt voice. "No new physical evidence?" I asked. Pajak answered me with a dismissive wave of his hand.

Rawls, meanwhile, knocked a Camel from his pack and lit up. A former English major at the University of Wyoming, Rawls has a graduate degree in seventeenth-century English poetry, but he applied for a job at the sheriff's department when he learned college had not prepared him for anything practical, like earning a living. He's spent his entire five-year career in the department trying to live down his expensive—and to his way of thinking, effeminate—educational background by attempting to isolate and assimilate the sort of ultramasculine personality traits found in classic cinema. A student of Humphrey Bogart movies, he'd most recently begun imitating Bogie's speech patterns, a fairly difficult enterprise considering his pronounced Western drawl, and smoking unfiltered cigarettes, although he never inhaled. All in all, he cuts a humorous figure. Imagine Ichabod Crane with a cigarette hanging from his teeth, squinting because the smoke hurts his eyes, and you have Rawls to a T.

"Nothing that would nail the case," he said earnestly. A wisp of smoke drifted into his eyes, and he waved it away miserably. Although Rawls looked ridiculous, the tobacco smelled so good I thought about bumming a Camel for myself. Resisted temptation. "We'll know a lot more when we get the lab and autopsy reports back, but we didn't find anything out there that would lead us to the bad guys."

"No shell casings?"

"Not one," Pajak broke in. He sounded vaguely offended

that I'd even asked, as if asking somehow brought his thoroughness into question. "I swept the whole area with a metal detector. Nothing."

"How about the neighbors? Anybody see anything?"

"No help there, either," Pajak said. "The closest neighbors are two miles away, and the women in the family didn't see a thing. The husband left for the hills this morning."

I looked up questioningly. "Bringing his cows down from the high country," Pajak explained.

"So we wait for the reports," I said. "And in the meantime, we keep digging into Ralphie Skates. I've had a couple of deputies at his place all afternoon. We'll see what they turn up."

I told them about the money I'd found at Ralphie's house and also filled them in on Clarence Hathaway, suggested we put out a call for both the sheriff's department and the Laramie Police Department to be on the lookout for him. Clarence was our best shot at getting close to the rest of Ralphie's associates. If we couldn't turn him up by the next day, I said, we'd widen the search to include the highway patrol and the state Department of Criminal Investigation.

"I don't get it," said Rawls. "Knowing what little we do about Skates, I can't figure him stealing livestock. Maybe burglaries. Auto theft. I can even see him doing rape. But what would he know about cows and horses?" As he talked, Rawls's huge Adam's apple bobbed in his wire-thin neck. "And who killed him?" he asked. "And whose blood was that at the side of the corral? Jesus, I hate shit like this."

"All good questions," I said. "And as luck would have it, I'm meeting someone in a few minutes who I hope'll help us answer a few of 'em."

"Who's that?" Pajak asked.

"C.J. Fall," I explained. "I'm taking him to dinner."

Pajak made a face, cracked his knobby knuckles and stood up to leave.

"Make sure you bring your checkbook." Rawls chuckled. "I hear the old man eats like a sumo wrestler."

# THREE

I was fifteen minutes late when I pulled into the parking lot at the El Conquistador, and I found C.J. Fall at a corner table, halfway through his first cold bottle of Corona and a basket of chips loaded with spicy salsa. A wiry old man whose longish white hair was a bit unruly from his wearing his hat all day, he still looked like the epitome of a western gentleman—a pleasant, weather-beaten face, clean white cotton shirt with pearl buttons, turquoise bolo, and brown, spit-shined cowboy boots. The short-barreled revolver he carried in a shoulder holster offset the grandfatherly image a bit, but not much.

When he saw me he waved me over to the table and motioned to the waitress to set me up with a Corona of my own. I poked the hunk of lime down the neck of the bottle and drank gratefully, finishing the beer in about seven seconds flat, and before I could even take the bottle away from my lips, the waitress came back with a frosty replacement.

Fall laughed. "I took the liberty of telling her to keep 'em coming'. That way, we won't be interrupted as often. I also ordered enough dinner to keep a whole passle of Mexicans fartin' a month. Tacos, enchiladas, rellenos, flauta, green chile . . . have I missed anything?"

"Only a little respect for my poor abused stomach," I said.

The corners of his eyes crinkled merrily. "Yeah, well, I told her to go light on the serranos," he said. "Me, I'm nearly at the end of my days. I can afford to live dangerously."

While we drank beer and waited for our food, Fall and I caught up on the county gossip, most of which centered around the rumor that Helene Stavros, mother of six, grandmother of nine, and secretary to the county treasurer, had left town in the company of someone other than her husband, namely Howard Banks, retired Marine Corps colonel and current administrative assistant to the county commission. The pair of them had reportedly been spotted locking their nearly geriatric lips in the coffee shop of the Virginian Hotel in Medicine Bow, where they were thought to be shacking up, since neither had reported for work in the past two days.

The conversation was pleasant and the beer tasty, so we didn't get to the real subject of our meeting until we were nearly finished with our main course. My late lunch still rested heavily at beltline, so I only picked at my dinner, but Fall destroyed tacos, rellenos, and everything else in sight. He looked so happy I didn't want to disturb him with business, although I was eager to pick his brain about the fine points of livestock rustling in my county, a subject I know painfully little about.

It's a simple fact that although I was raised in La Junta, Colorado, which is about as rural a place as you can get, I grew up in town, where the only cows in regular attendance were served on buns at The Dump, the local drive-in. Sure, I can saddle a horse and ride him, if I hang on to the saddle horn with both hands. I wear cowboy boots and a Stetson. I'm a good shot with a rifle and a pistol. My idea of formal attire is a fresh pair of jeans and a western-cut corduroy jacket. And I enjoyed the hell out of *Lonesome Dove*.

But I'm not, and never have been, a *livestock man,* which is a breed apart and a true minority, even here in the Wild West. That being the case, I don't know much more about their problems than what I hear around town and read in the papers.

I sure didn't get many rustling cases as a homicide detective in Denver, although I did once arrest a guy for sneaking into a meat packing plant and making off with a frozen side of beef, which he stuffed into the back seat of his Volkswagen. Later, as chief of police in the tiny hamlet of Victory, where the cows in the immediate vicinity outnumber the human population of 650 by about three to one, I never had a single case of rustling inside or even near the city limits. And even now that I've moved my base of operations thirty miles to the relatively cosmopolitan university town of Laramie and taken over law enforcement responsibility for the whole of Albany County, a rural county where beef is the number-one cash crop, no one in the sheriff's department knows any more about the prevention or investigation of this crime than I do. Nobody expects us to do much about it, either.

Not that we have to.

In modern-day Wyoming, rustling is controlled and investigated by state brand inspectors. They don't do it the way the old regulators used to, by lurking around a cattle ranch until they catch someone in the act of stealing a cow or a pony, sneaking up, then shooting him to death. These days, they work for the Wyoming Stockgrowers Association and their activities are reimbursed by the state.

Although not all of them are certified peace officers, they carry sidearms and can make an arrest on their own if they see a crime taking place. That doesn't happen often, though. Usually, when they make a case, they file their complaint with the county attorney, and then the sheriff's department makes the actual arrest.

We have a good working relationship with C.J. Fall and the half dozen full- and part-time inspectors under his supervision, in large part because he's so good at what he does he never bothers us for favors, or manpower I couldn't spare even if he asked. I like him. And based on what little I knew about Colleen McAfferty's murder, it looked like I needed him as well.

"So Harry," he said as he scooped a last spoonful of fiery green chile from the bowl, "I understand there was some real unpleasantness out at the McAfferty place this morning. You gonna fill me in?"

I motioned to the waitress for coffee and began to tell him what little I knew about the murders, and the way we planned to proceed with the investigation.

"The problem right now," I said, "is that I need to know more about Ralphie Skates and Clarence Hathaway. See where it leads."

He squirted about half a cup of honey onto an after-dinner sopapilla, stuffed the whole thing in his mouth, and chewed thoughtfully. "Can't help you there," he said. "Never heard of either of them."

"All the same, it looks like they were out there rustling cows, and Colleen McAfferty's quarter horse," I said.

"Lots of people into rustling these days," he said by way of explanation. "It's turning into a real growth industry."

I told him about the money I'd found in Ralphie's dresser, over seven grand. "He hadn't worked since May, and we don't think he's been into burglaries. You're telling me he could have made it rustling?"

"No problem," Fall said. "Hell, he could make that much in a weekend."

I must have looked skeptical, but Fall shook his head to let me know he was serious.

Finally finished with his dinner, he struck a match and held it to the tip of a small cigar. "Here's the deal, Harry," he said. "Right now, yearlings are bringing close to eighty cents a pound at the kill plant. You bring them an eight-hundred-pound yearling, and that's a pretty good profit, especially if you weren't the one who bought the cow in the first place or spent the money to raise him.

"Fill a truck up with fifty or sixty yearlings, and get 'em out of state as quick as you can—maybe truck 'em down to Oklahoma, North Platte, or Fort Worth, where they don't have brand inspectors—and you're talking money. The kind of money that attracts people like Ralphie Skates."

"No brand inspections in those places?"

"Nah," he said. "They only inspect brands at sale time west of the Missouri River. Sell your critter east of the river, and they don't give a damn whose brand it's wearing.

"We got maybe five thousand mother cows in Albany County year-round, and the ranchers bring in another hundred twenty-five thousand yearlings to fatten up on summer grass. With that many animals in that much area, it's pretty damn tempting to help yourself."

"Could Skates have gone into rustling without you being aware of it?" I asked.

"Sure he could have," Fall said. "We try to check brands every time we see a truck of livestock moving out of state, but plenty of 'em get through anyway. Maybe he's just been lucky so far. And maybe . . ."

"Yeah?"

"Maybe he was working for someone else. It takes some manpower to coax a bunch of scared cows into a crowded trailer. If you're taking more than one at a time, you need help to do it."

"You got any ideas who he might have been working with?" I asked.

"A couple," he said. "I've heard that Wayne Carney from over in Carbon County has been running a fairly big operation in the backcountry, around the county line. And I heard from one of my spies that Bobby Snow from your neck of the woods around Victory turned up at a Canadian kill plant a few weeks ago with a suspicious-looking load of horses. Either of them would be big enough to need the services of someone like Ralphie Skates. Why don't you let me make a few calls? See what I can turn up?"

"Thanks," I said gratefully. "But I don't understand something you just said. Why would Bobby Snow be taking horses to a kill plant across the Canadian border?"

"The Japanese," he said. "They eat 'em."

"Horses?" I asked incredulously. "The Japanese like horse meat?"

"Well," he said, "it isn't that they particularly relish horse meat. Most of 'em think they're buying beef. I mean, they don't get that much meat to begin with, so how they gonna know the difference?"

"I had no idea," I said. My stomach quivered a little with the thought. I've tasted horse meat on a couple of occasions, and it might be a little more palatable than road kill, but not much. It's certainly tougher.

"Most people don't," Fall said. "But right now, the market for horseflesh is higher than it's been in decades. It used to be that only the Belgians liked an occasional horse steak, but beef prices are so high in Japan right now that a lot of enterprising American and Canadian businessmen are selling them horseflesh for a bit less. The Japanese buyers turn around and sell it in the shops as bargain-basement beef. From what I hear, the market over there has really opened up."

"And rustlers around here are supplying it?"

"Why wouldn't they?" he asked. "A good fleshy horse brings sixty cents a pound at the kill plant, and for a thousand pounds of horse, that's good money. Besides, a lot of horses aren't branded, and they're easy to steal, since they generally trust people. Hell, I've seen expensive quarter horses with velvet ribbons in their manes waiting for the bolt at those kill plants, and you know that just a coupla days before, they were somebody's pet."

"So Colleen McAfferty's Jezebel . . ." I said.

"Will probably wind up in Tokyo," he finished for me, shaking his grizzled head sadly. "As the main ingredient in a Sony executive's stir-fry."

By the time I'd said good night to C.J. Fall, checked in with the office, and made the twenty-minute drive from Laramie to Victory that evening, the sun was settling behind the peaks of the Snowy Range, and its dying rays wreathed Medicine Bow Peak in a soft magenta glow. From the southwest a lead gray bank of heavy cloud scudded over the foothills, and the dry air held the promise of rain that might come before morning.

I'd followed a station wagon jam-packed with tourons from New Hampshire all the way out Highway 130, and it pleased me when they slowed to a sedate twenty miles per hour as soon as they passed the town's boundary line, which meant they'd seen the Harry Starbranch unmanned traffic-control device and responded accordingly.

The town has neither the inclination nor the manpower to keep someone on traffic duty all the time, or even most of the time. To compensate, a police chief in the 1960s painted a decrepit old Ford Fairlane black and white, bolted a couple of red coffee cans on top of it, and parked the bogus cruiser right off the highway at the edge of town, where it's done traffic duty since.

It never fools the locals and it doesn't even fool the tourons for long, but their involuntary speeding-ticket-avoidance-responses generally cause them to take their Birkenstocks off the gas and hit the brake as soon as their brains register the black-and-white. By the time they realize they've been hoodwinked and start hitting the gas again, they're all the way through town and heading into the Snowies.

I slowed down myself when I passed the entrances to the Trail's End and Gus Alzonakis's, the gargantuan, competing steakhouses that sit directly across from each other on Victory's main drag, at least long enough to note their nearly empty parking lots. This despite the $10.99 all-the-prime-rib-you-can-eat special at the Trail's End and the $8.99 cow-a-bunga rib-eye platter at Gus's establishment.

Down the block, the Silver Dollar Saloon, owned by Victory mayor Curly Ahearn, was apparently suffering through an equally grim Monday night. Three lonely-looking pickup trucks lined the curb in front of the Dollar, but not all of the vehicles belonged to patrons, since Ray Hladky and Harley Coyne stood on the sidewalk beside one of them, admiring a nice trout that Ray held on a stringer.

He probably caught it that afternoon on the Laramie River, I thought enviously. In the old days, when my only job was being Victory police chief, I had plenty of time to spend fly-fishing. Went nearly every evening all through the summer months, in fact. Since I became sheriff, though, I'd only wet a line once all season. And even that day, I had to take one of the county commissioners along. A worm fisherman, for Christ's sake.

I'd gotten the sheriff's job the previous winter after my predecessor, a fifty-six-year-old semi-alcoholic with a hankering for slab bacon and fettucini Alfredo, dropped dead of a massive heart attack on Main Street in Victory, where I was—and still am, incidentally—chief of the town's two-man police force.

As luck would have it, the county commissioners had to appoint someone to fill the remainder of the deceased sheriff's term, and since one of them owed me big-time—I pulled him from the car he'd rolled on the highway between Victory and Laramie after a long night of drinking at Curly Ahearn's saloon, just seconds before the car exploded in flame—he strong-armed the other two commissioners into agreeing to my appointment.

Since the first of the year, I've been acting both as county sheriff, operating out of the office at the county seat in Laramie, and police chief in Victory, where I'm officially on temporary leave of absence. Much to my surprise, and the surprise of everyone who knows me on more than a last-name basis, I found I actually liked being sheriff, at least liked proving to myself that I'm able to do the job. Which is why I decided to run as an honest-to-good Democratic candidate for the post.

If I win the election, I'll resign as chief of police in Victory, and Curly Ahearn will have to find some new middle-aged social misfit to keep the peace. If I lose, well, I'll tuck my tail between my legs and go right back to Victory, where I'll resume my illustrious career writing traffic tickets, baby-sitting the tourists who stop by on the off chance of seeing an actual cowboy, trying to keep the lumberjacks and barflies from tearing each other's livers out at the town's many saloons, and drinking with Curly.

Past the Silver Dollar, I wheeled around the block and pulled my sheriff's department Blazer to a stop in front of the Victory police station. Through the window, I could see Frankie Tall Bull, a three-hundred-pound, full-blooded Teton Sioux and Victory's lone police officer. His six-four frame was hunched over his desk, his heavy brow wrinkled in concentration. His huge fingers delicately clutched the orange stick he used for detail work on the clay model for his latest sculpture, a twenty-four-inch warrior on a skittery pony jamming his lance into the side of a raging buffalo.

Frankie Bull is not just your average International Harvester–size Indian. He's also a talented sculptor, and he told me when I hired him that police work wasn't his life's ambition, just something to pay the bills until the brain-damaged gallery owners of his acquaintance figure out what they're missing by allowing his work to remain unappreciated and unsold in the garage of the home he shares with his wife, Frieda.

Since he's entirely capable of keeping the peace in Victory and conscientious about doing so, I didn't mind him lugging his artwork to the office and even encouraged him to bring it along. He says he gets more accomplished at the office than he does at home, on account of the fact that it's usually quieter.

I'd hired Frankie Tall Bull the previous February, after interviewing about a dozen other candidates for the job, most of whom turned out to be drunks fired from other police departments in the region or would-be Dirty Harrys desperate to get their feet in the door of a small department.

Frankie showed up for the interview dressed in a black leather motorcycle jacket with eagle feathers in his long braided hair and a pigsticker on his hip big enough to chop wood. When I asked him about his background, he told me that after his discharge from the Marine Corps, he'd worked for three years as a tribal policeman on the Pine Ridge Reservation in South Dakota. It was about then, he said, that he met Frieda, a full-blooded Sho-shone from the Wind River Reservation in Wyoming, at the Miss Indian America Pageant in Sheridan, where she was a contestant.

"It was the Montagues and Capulets," he said, since the Sioux and Shoshones are hereditary enemies. At first, she refused to even talk to him. When she finally began to talk, she refused to date him. When she agreed to date, she declined to sleep with him.

Still, he'd persevered and finally convinced her to marry him, on condition that they move in with her family at Wind River. Where, he said unhappily, he'd been unemployed for the last two years, unless you counted the million and a half hours he'd spent sculpting.

"We moved to Laramie at the start of the semester so she could start working on her teaching certificate," he told me. "I've gotta find some way to pick up the tab."

Despite his limited experience, I went with my gut instinct and hired him two days later.

I've since discovered that in spite of his admittedly menacing appearance—even the lumberjacks are afraid of him—there's a side to Frankie Bull that few people ever see, since he's careful to hide it. For one thing, he's a gourmet cook, which I didn't learn until the first time I had dinner at his home, where he served me the finest coq au vin I'd ever tasted—okay it was the only coq au vin I'd ever tasted, but it was damn good. Second, he's a classical music fanatic, especially fond of Vivaldi and Ludwig Van. Third, he does all the housework, grocery shopping, and laundry. Fourth, he reads romance novels, although he'll claim they belong to Frieda if you see one peeking out his jacket pocket.

He's one strange Indian, if you ask me. Strange enough, in fact, to be chief-of-police material if I win the election and have to resign.

In the meantime, he fills in for me and does both of our jobs without complaint, and the 650 good citizens of Victory rest easy knowing that under his watchful eye, the crime rate has dropped to almost nothing. It's not that the drunks have quit drinking, the lumberjacks have stopped brawling, the cowboys have stopped riding their horses into bars, and the hormonally unbalanced high school kids have stopped statutorily raping each other in the steakhouse parking lots. It's just that most of the would-be debauchees are so afraid of what Frankie Tall Bull would do if he caught them—tie 'em to a chair and make 'em listen to the "1812 Overture"?—they're walking on eggshells.

"Hello, Chief," he said when I walked in. He swept his arm around the office, which looked cleaner than usual, with all the filing baskets empty, the coffee cups washed and stacked next to the automatic coffeepot. "I knew you'd be in this evening so I spruced the place up."

I hadn't been to the office in nearly a week and asked him how he figured I'd stop by.

"The owl told me," he said mysteriously. "Always listen to the owl."

"Bullshit," I said. "You've been watching too much *Dances With Wolves*. How'd you know?"

He shrugged his massive shoulders. "The phone," he admitted. "You've been getting more calls here the last hour than a damn bookie. Reporters from the *Boomerang,* the *Star Trib.* Nicky Pajak called to say he'd pick up the autopsy reports tomorrow morning and meet you at the sheriff's department around noon. I figured that since none of those people found you at the office in Laramie, you must be on your way home. And since it's been a while since you dropped in here to see if we can still manage in your absence . . ."

I rolled my eyes, made a gesture most Sicilians find offensive, and reached for the stack of mail and incident reports waiting on my desk. "That's just what this town needs," I said. "One more smart-ass."

"Okay," he said as he went back to his sculpture. "I heard from Pajak about your bad day. I guess I can cut you a little slack."

While Frankie etched out a strand of the fine fringe on his

buffalo hunter's shirt, I rummaged through the incident reports and caught up on the goings on in Victory.

On Thursday, there'd been a head-on collision on Highway 130 north of town between a bull elk and a Dodge Caravan driven by a family from Arkansas. Family fine. Caravan totaled. Elk deceased.

On Saturday, minor fistfights at both the Trail's End and the Silver Dollar. Drunken combatants separated and driven home. No injuries that required hospitalization. No charges filed.

On Sunday, there'd been a report of vandalism at the old Union Pacific Railroad depot, but it turned out to be a false alarm. The front window had been broken—not by drunken high school kids, as the librarian who reported the incident had suspected, but by a young golden eagle that must have been diving after a field mouse and neglected to pull up in time, a mistake that had proven fatal to the bird.

That day, Monday, Frankie had outdone himself, writing six traffic citations and chasing down Victory's only skateboarder, a fifteen-year-old orange-haired punker who'd tried to skip out on his tab at Mrs. Larsen's Country Kitchen. Again, no charges filed, since the skateboarder had agreed, at Frankie Bull's urging, not only to return to the coffee shop and pay his bill but to spend the afternoon washing dishes as an act of contrition.

"Looks like you've had a full week," I said, a bit too sarcastically. Fact is, we like it when nothing happens around Victory. "You doing anything tomorrow morning?"

He looked up from his clay. "I don't think so," he said. "Unless I have to chase down another skateboarder."

"Then how about taking a ride with me out to Bobby Snow's ranch? I want to ask him a couple of questions and—"

"And you need a bodyguard, right?" He chuckled. "A big, ugly one with a scalping knife and a .357."

I tossed the unopened mail and the reports back on the desk. "No, I don't need a bodyguard," I grumbled. "I'd just like a little company, that's all."

Acting like he believed me, he nodded agreement and went back to his artwork. "Around nine?" he asked without looking up.

"Eight-thirty," I said. I seated my hat and reached for the handle of the front door. "I'll pick you up here. And Frankie . . ."

"What is it, Chief?"

"Bring your pigsticker." I smiled. "Just in case."

The old farmhouse I rent from my octogenarian landlady, Edna Cook, is about three miles south of Victory, a five-minute drive from the police station. It was my intention to take my weary bones home, beat my muscles senseless with the shower massage, fix a peanut butter and Miracle Whip sandwich, pop a can of Coors, and find a ball game. After that, I might tie a few royal coachmen in case I ever got the chance to go fly-fishing again, then crawl into bed with a good mystery.

That plan disintegrated as soon as I pulled into the driveway and saw Curly Ahearn's old Jeep in my spot, leaking oil on the driveway.

I discovered His Honor in my living room, where he'd helped his bald-headed self to my recliner, my wide-screen television, my remote control, a six-pack of my beer, and a heaping plate of ham and cheese sandwiches from my refrigerator. On the tube, Boston's Roger Clemens threw 105-mile-per-hour rockets at a Yankee batter. Curly, naturally, showed support for the Beantown team by wearing my BoSox hat. Backwards.

The dog followed me in, looked warily around the living room and made for the plate of sandwiches.

Curly whacked the pooch's nose away. "You're late," he huffed. "And what the hell is this thing trying to steal my food? Some kinda genetic experiment?"

"The only thing I'm late for, Curly, is keeping you out of my provisions," I said. I tossed my hat on the rack, unbuckled my holster.

"And that," I said, pointing at the animal, which had retreated to the kitchen and was poking its head around the corner to see whether Curly would give chase, "is obviously a dog."

He moved the sandwiches to the safety of his lap. "Whose dog?" he asked.

I hesitated. "Mine, I guess. His previous owner cashed in his chips."

"Skates?"

I nodded.

"That's great," he chuckled. "Just what you need around here, another mooch."

He was still laughing as I made my way to the kitchen, pulled a can of beer from the fridge, and grabbed a stick of summer sausage and some cheese to snack on while we watched the game.

"Look who's talking," I said when I'd shucked my boots and gotten myself settled on the couch. "The man's married to the kind of woman buys him L.L. Bean hip waders for Christmas instead of ties, and where is he? Hiding out at his friend's house, drinking beer with a stolen hat on."

He laughed. "You know the old saying, absence makes the heart grow fonder. And by the time I get home tonight, that old woman is gonna love me to death. By the way, before you get too comfortable, you got a coupla calls while I was waiting. Nicole and that campaign manager of yours."

Nicole is Nicole Starbranch, my ex-wife and mother of my three children. We divorced over five years ago, after I left Denver. For the last ten months, we'd been having a kind of minireconciliation. At least we were dating—and getting along a lot better than we did when we were married.

Larry Calhoun, my campaign manager, likely wanted to discuss how we could use the murders to our advantage if I made a speedy arrest. As he had pointed out several times in recent weeks, my bid for election to the sheriff's office was in deep shit, and we might never pull it from the quagmire unless one of two things happened.

"Either a big case," he said, "or we catch Baldi shacked up at the Diamond Horseshoe with an underage hooker."

Baldi is Anthony Baldi, a former lieutenant in the Laramie Police Department and a law-and-order Republican who's running against me on the platform that he might not be a perfect human being, but at least he's moral and sober, which is more than he'll say for his drunken, fornicating opponent, yours truly.

In the old days, I could have followed the example of Aaron Burr, a great American, in my opinion, and challenged the miserable slanderer to a duel. Nowadays, though, it's considered very bad form to ventilate your political enemies, especially if there's a grain of truth to their charges, which in this case there is. It's common knowledge around here that I like an occasional jigger of mash and a cold beer come sundown. Nearly everyone knows I relish the company of women. And while I've never allowed either of those pleasures to interfere with the performance of my job, I haven't always enjoyed them in moderation.

Baldi'd been using those puny vices and Laramie's remarkable rumor mill to make me sound like the most deviant human being to hold office since Huey Long, but I'm not particularly ashamed of the way I've lived my life. And even if I was, I wouldn't feel the need to defend myself in public—a course of action that had become a frequent topic of debate between Calhoun and myself.

Calhoun is quick to point out that pride, stupidity, and stubbornness don't win elections. He says he sometimes thinks I'm trying to sabotage my own campaign, that I don't really want the job, at least not badly enough to do what it takes to win.

He's a nag, is what he is, and it gets tiresome. I had no intention of returning his call that evening. The next day would be soon enough.

"What did Nicole have to say?" I asked. "She want me to give her a buzz?"

"Nah. Just said to tell you the kids are spending the weekend with her sister, and she'll be up here Friday evening around eight. Said you should get the wine and she'll bring the green stuff."

The green stuff, I thought happily. Kama Sutra Pleasure Balm. Definitely something to look forward to.

"What was she talking about?" Curly asked. "Crème de menthe?"

"I haven't the faintest idea," I told him. "You sure you got the message right?"

"I thought I did," he said, "but who knows? It wasn't such a great connection."

Curly hit the mute button on the remote, put his plate on the coffee table, and turned my hat around until the bill was facing the proper direction. He leaned over and patted my knee. "Tough day, huh Harry?" he asked, a note of tenderness in his gruff voice.

I leaned back on the sofa, took a long sip of beer. "It was a nasty one," I agreed.

"I remember that girl," he said somberly. "Rode in the night rodeo a couple of times last summer. Barrel racer, wasn't she? Pretty thing."

I flashed on the way Colleen looked when the attendants were putting her body in a bag. She hadn't looked so pretty then. I didn't answer.

"Any chance you'll wrap it up soon?" he asked.

I shrugged, took another sip of beer. "I don't know," I said. "So far there's not a lot to work with."

"Too bad," he said. "It'll be harder for everyone if it drags on."

I assumed he was talking about Tess McAfferty. "Tess is a strong woman, Curly. God only knows what kind of pain she's feeling right now, but she should be able to get through it."

Curly smiled and shook his head gently to tell me I'd missed the point. "It's not just her, Harry," he said. "I'm more than a little worried about you. You look tired, podna."

I was tired, but so what? "I'll get a good night's sleep, Curly. I promise," I said, a bit testily. "Tomorrow, I'll get up and do my job. Don't worry about me, for Christ's sake. I'm not the one who got killed."

I finished the last of my beer and crushed the can. Curly took it from me and went into the kitchen. He came back with two fresh brews and handed me one, and I popped the tab. "Is that really why you came out here this evening?" I asked suspiciously. "Because you were worried about how these murders were going to affect me?"

"That's partly it," he said. "I thought you might need a friend to talk to."

"Thanks, but—" I halted. "Partly? What's up, Curly?"

He studied my face, his brow creased with concern. "You really don't know?"

I leaned forward anxiously. "Know what?"

Ahearn bit his lip, studied the beer can in his hands. "After the day you've had, I hate to be the one to make it worse."

"Cut the shit, Curly," I said irritably. "What's going on?"

He watched me for a long count, looking like he was trying to figure out how much bad news I could take in a day. "Jerry Slaymaker," he said softly. "He's out."

I don't know what I'd been expecting, but that wasn't it. His words took me by surprise, like a blow to the solar plexus. My chest felt tight, and I could feel my pulse throbbing in my neck at the simple mention of Slaymaker's name.

Curly studied my face. "You remember him then? Calhoun said you would, and none too fondly."

I nodded, drank half my fresh beer on the off chance alcohol would stop my heart from racing. Of course I remembered Jerry Slaymaker. He'd been a hotshot building contractor in Denver in 1984 when I arrested him for the rape and murder of a nine-year-old kid named Sean McDonald, whose naked and decomposing body had been discovered stuffed inside a fifty-five-gallon drum tucked in the corner of a warehouse owned by Slaymaker's cousin.

"I remember Slaymaker," I told Curly. "But what does he have to do with anything? The man's serving a life sentence."

"Not anymore," Curly said. "He's had an appeal pending for

months, and the Colorado Supreme Court overturned his conviction late this afternoon."

"On what grounds?" I asked, stunned.

"The clothes," Curly explained. "His attorneys got a court order to have DNA tests run on the clothes you used to convict him, and the DNA doesn't match McDonald's."

My mind refused to accept what I'd just heard. It was impossible. Inconceivable. Absurd. The blood on those clothes had belonged to Sean McDonald. No doubt about it. My brain reeled as I remembered that season, and the hunt that ended in Slaymaker's arrest and conviction.

In 1984, Sean McDonald had been a gap-toothed, tow-headed boy whose only concerns in life were getting stand-up doubles and earning his Bear badge in Cub Scouts. He'd been on his way to the neighborhood 7-Eleven for a Slurpee when he disappeared at a little after three o'clock one April afternoon. He was the fourth boy his age to go missing that year, and since the other three had subsequently turned up dead—all raped and murdered—we immediately feared the worst. We searched the neighborhood from top to bottom, brought in dogs, even a psychic. No luck. It was like Sean McDonald had fallen off the face of the Earth.

A week after he was reported missing, we got a call that a janitor at the warehouse had peeked inside the drum on account of the fact that it wasn't sealed and was leaking a foul odor.

Sean McDonald's corpse was curled up in the bottom.

The coroner's report said he'd been raped so brutally he would have probably died of blood loss from the damage to his large intestine and anal tissue. He'd also been stabbed at least thirty times, just for good measure.

The case was top priority, and my partner and I spent thousands of hours walking blind alleys, chasing phantoms. Separating wheat from chaff. Gradually, one name began to turn up more and more: Jerry Slaymaker.

Trouble was, we couldn't find a single piece of evidence that would nail him in court—no murder weapon, no physical evidence from Slaymaker's car, no trace evidence from McDonald's corpse. If the killer had left semen in McDonald's body, it had decomposed by the time we found him.

All we found was enough circumstantial evidence to convince ourselves Slaymaker was the killer. For starters, Slaymaker had been a friend of the kid's widowed father, had visited their home on a number of occasions. The kid wouldn't have been afraid of him. Slaymaker had been seen driving around the McDonald neighborhood on a number of occasions. One neighbor had even called in his license plate number while reporting a suspicious person a half a block from the McDonald's two-story ranch home a couple weeks before the disappearance.

Slaymaker had a key to the warehouse on his key ring. He had no decent alibi for the afternoon of the killing. In addition, I found two witnesses who said they saw the kid get in the car with someone fitting Slaymaker's description the afternoon he disappeared.

It wasn't enough, at least not enough to bring down a man like Slaymaker. The prosecutor said that unless we found something better, he'd probably walk. I couldn't let that happen, promised myself I'd do whatever it took to put him behind bars.

Finally, I got the hard evidence that nailed him, a pair of bloodstained men's trousers and a blood-spattered shirt. We didn't have DNA testing in those days, but Slaymaker had type O blood and the blood on the clothing was type B positive, Sean McDonald's blood type. The lab compared blood samples from the clothing and samples taken at McDonald's autopsy, concluded there was a ninety-seven-percent chance the blood on the clothing was Sean McDonald's.

I arrested Jerry Slaymaker at his office in front of his partners and clients. He bellowed and blustered while we were on his home turf, but as soon as we got in the car to head downtown for booking, his attitude changed. He was arrogant, smug, almost proud of himself. I asked him why he killed Sean McDonald, and he laughed out loud.

"Because I felt like it, asshole," he sneered. "It felt good."

The judge wouldn't allow that confession as evidence at his trial, but the bloody clothing was enough for the jury, who found Slaymaker guilty of murder. Life in prison. No chance of parole.

Six months after the trial ended, Sean McDonald's father stuck a .45 in his mouth and pulled the trigger. His suicide note explained it all. "He was my son," he wrote in a spidery hand. "I can't go on knowing I let his killer live."

The case was the beginning of the end of my career with the Denver Police Department. It haunted me still, but at least I'd taken some comfort in the knowledge that Slaymaker was being punished, would spend the rest of his miserable life in jail.

Now, if Curly was to be believed, he was out again. Someone had made a terrible mistake.

"Are they sure about those DNA tests?" I asked tautly. There was so much tension in my jaw muscles my whole face was beginning to ache. The room looked fuzzy.

Curly shrugged, fumbled around in his shirt pocket until he came up with a pack of cigarettes. He lit one, inhaled, and let the smoke dribble out his nose. "They say they're absolutely certain," he said simply. "The blood on that clothing did not belong to Sean McDonald. Ergo, the most compelling evidence against Slaymaker is useless. Ergo, Slaymaker gets a new trial."

And without that clothing, he would never be convicted a second time.

"If it wasn't McDonald's blood, then whose goddamn blood was it?" I growled. I stood up, began pacing the room. It seemed too small to hold me, the walls were closing in. The implications were all too clear. If it wasn't McDonald's blood, Slaymaker had killed someone else, someone we didn't know about. That brought his body count to at least five.

"Doesn't really matter," Curly said. "The court's ordered a new trial, but nobody thinks the prosecutor will choose to retry it. In the meantime, Slaymaker's lawyer is threatening a huge lawsuit against the Denver Police Department. Against you personally."

I stopped pacing, turned to face Curly. My fists were clenched at my sides, my nails cut into my palms. I wanted to lash out at someone. Anyone. It was grossly unfair. All I'd done was put a murderer in jail. "Me personally?" I spat. "For what? Doing my job?"

Curly shook his head to let me know he thought the whole thing was bullshit. "For manufacturing evidence," Curly said. "Slaymaker claims you planted those clothes in his trash can."

I felt something growing in my belly. Anxiety? A knot of fear? I tried not to let it show. "What does the department say?" I asked. "They're backing me, right?"

"Maybe. Maybe not," Curly said. "At this point, it looks like they're waiting to see which way the wind's blowing. Say they won't comment on a case that will probably wind up in court. They'll let you take the fall if they have to."

"Bastards."

"They're not the only bastards in this ball game," Curly said. "Somehow Baldi got the news about all this before you did, and he's using it to illustrate your incompetence. Says you're all right when it comes to traffic tickets and breaking up bar fights, but you can't be trusted on a big case. He plans to hold a press conference Wednesday afternoon."

This last bit of information tipped the scales. I was so outraged I couldn't even talk for a minute or so, and then I lost what little hold I had on my temper. I threw my beer against the wall, swept our banquet off the coffee table and banged my fist against the door so hard the top hinge popped out of the wood. "That miserable son of a bitch," I yelled. "I ought to go over to his house, drag his ass out in the street and—"

"Hold on!" Curly said urgently. He crossed to me quickly,

grabbed my biceps to prevent me from damaging something important, like the television. "That kind of attitude won't help you a bit."

I was beyond reason. I pulled free forcefully, pushed him away and banged out the front door, stood on the front porch and took deep breaths until my heart rate fell back under the red line. Then I sat down on the top step and hugged my knees to my chest.

Several minutes later I heard Curly come out behind me, saw him in my peripheral vision as he sat at my side. Together we watched some wispy clouds scud across the face of the moon, listened to the scree of a nighthawk hunting the prairie beyond the house. I was embarrassed that I'd taken my anger out on him, had nearly hit him.

"Curly, I'm . . ." I started to apologize, but it stuck in my throat.

He put an arm around my shoulders. "No contact, no foul, Buckwheat," he said. "I wasn't worried."

I nodded gratefully, went back to staring at my toes.

"I wouldn't worry about it," Curly said softly.

"Worry about what?"

"Any of it," Curly said. He reached down and picked up a handful of gravel, began chucking it into the driveway. "You solve the McAfferty killing and you'll take the wind out of Baldi's sails."

He made it sound so easy. "I'll get right on it, Curly," I snorted.

"I know you will," he said, ignoring my sarcasm. "And this lawsuit. That's bullshit, right? You didn't plant that evidence. And if you didn't plant it, you've got nothing to worry about. The whole fucking thing is a nuisance, but that's all it is."

I stood and stepped down off the porch, jamming my hands in my pockets, and walked to the edge of the light spilling through the open front door behind me. It occurred to me that if I just kept walking, the darkness would swallow me up.

"Harry?"

"What?"

"It *is* bullshit, right?"

I didn't answer. The prairie breeze felt good on my forehead. I closed my eyes and waited for the world to stop spinning.

"Talk to me, Harry. I'm your friend, remember?"

I was touched by the concern in his voice. I turned back toward him, saw the worry and uncertainty in his eyes. He is my friend, maybe the best I have. I owed him something. The truth. At least as much of it as I could give him.

"Slaymaker killed that little boy, Curly," I said quietly. "No matter what the evidence says."

# FOUR

I tossed and turned until around 2:00 A.M., so I was tired and cantankerous as Frankie Tall Bull and I drove up the dirt road that leads to Bobby Snow's T-Bar Ranch the next morning.

Overhead, a heavy cover of dun-colored clouds choked the sky, hanging so close to the ground it obscured the lowest foothills of the Snowies. So far the clouds hadn't delivered on their promise of rain, but they did a good job of holding the heat in the valley. The air was thick and humid, the temperature already at 85 degrees.

I'd let the shower blast me with cool water for at least a half an hour before I left home in a vain effort to drive the fatigue from my body and soul, but already my damp shirt clung to my back. We had the windows rolled up to keep out the haze of alkali dust kicked up by the tires, and I silently cursed my department mechanic, who had once again ignored my request that he fix the air-conditioning.

As we approached Snow's house, a ramshackle one-story affair tucked away in a small stand of aspens and maples near the banks of the Little Laramie River, I reflected on what I knew about him and his family.

The great-grandson of a Welsh homesteader, he was born on

the T-Bar and lived there until after he graduated high school. Then, like lots of other ranch boys, he left home to try his hand on the rodeo circuit. Unlike lots of other ranch boys, Bobby Snow was good at it, and he won enough money as a saddle and bareback bronc rider in his fifteen-year career to support his wife and keep up the payments on his fancy pickup trucks.

A contender for world champion bareback rider in the early eighties, his career on the circuit had come to an abrupt end in Salinas, California, when a sunfishing bronc came over backwards and broke his hip. After he healed, he scraped together enough money to get back to Victory, where he'd found the family ranch in serious financial difficulty and his father in the hospital suffering from a massive stroke. Old man Snow died three days later, and since he was a widower and Bobby an only child, his financial problems became Bobby's.

The word around the valley is that Bobby was ill-suited to the rigors of running a working ranch from the start, since it requires backbreaking physical labor from dawn to dusk, seven days a week, and doesn't allow much time for drinking and carousing, a rodeo cowboy's main recreational activity. Still, by supplying bucking stock to the rodeo circuit, he's narrowly managed to avoid bankruptcy and at least two attempts by the First Rocky Mountain bank in Laramie to foreclose on the heavy mortgages it holds on the place.

The effort apparently cost him his wife, who left him in search of greener pastures and younger cowboys in 1990. It also seemed to have cost him his self-control. Until Bobby Snow came back to Wyoming, he had a nearly spotless police record. The intervening years have fattened it with a dozen complaints for simple assault as well as a good number for drunken driving, disorderly conduct, and one for aggravated assault with a deadly weapon after Bobby pulled a rifle on a rig worker who cheated him at a game of eight ball. He didn't shoot the oil-field hand but wound up bashing him in the head with the butt of his .30-06. When the roughneck woke up and got over his headache, he pressed charges, but he disappeared before he could testify in court. It was the one complaint on which Bobby walked, the only one that could have meant hard time.

We found him and a couple of his hired hands at the corral trying to convince an 1,800-pound Brahma bull to scoot up the rickety stock ramp and into the livestock carrier that would transport the murderous animal to its destination. A number of bulls had already been loaded; their heads and long horns were visible through the sides of the carrier, which shifted on its axles as the drooling, sweaty monsters stomped, snorted, and butted their massive heads against the sides of the stalls. At the front of the carrier, a bored-looking truck driver sipped coffee from a stainless steel thermos cup, a lit cigarette in his off hand.

Snow's hired hands, both of whom had been absent when the Lord gave out necks but present when he gave out pecs and deltoids, saw us before their boss did and gave us a pair of scowls.

The elder of the hands was about thirty-five, six-two, 190 pounds. A rough scar across the top of his forehead looked remarkably like a zipper, the kind of stitches taken with a livestock awl.

The second man, ten years younger and twenty pounds heavier, was a study in malevolence. For starters, the pug's nose had been broken so often that the cartilage had been entirely destroyed, leaving him with two upturned nostrils in a mass of drooping flesh. His eyes were small and heavy-lidded, his lips pulled back in a grimace around the stub of a cigar his brown teeth clenched in the corner of his porcine mouth. On his belt he wore a long folding knife and a snub-nosed revolver in a holster on his hip. He carried a short whip in his right hand and an electric cattle prod in his left. He looked like the kind of man who enjoyed using both.

His eyes lighted briefly on my uniform and badge, but he dismissed me quickly as inconsequential. He took more time with Frankie Bull, whom he studied with professional interest, working his gaze up Bull's thick legs to the big knife on his belt, to his barrel chest and heavy arms. When he got to Frankie's braid, his hammered silver ear cuffs, and the wide hand-beaded band on his hat, his lips curled in a sneer and he raised his eyebrows in an obvious, unspoken challenge.

Frankie's face around his mirrored sunglasses remained impassive, but I could feel him stiffen, sense the anger and hostility that bubbled beneath the surface. Men like this were more than familiar to him, Western racists who waited in dark alleys behind saloons for the Indians drinking inside to emerge and stumble into their clutches. The thugs would beat them brutally, steal the money remaining in their wallets, rape them if they were women, and leave them broken and bleeding in the mud and garbage. Most of them were too stupid to imagine that their victims would ever fight back, but I suspected that more than a few of these prairie crackers had come away from encounters with Frankie Bull wishing they'd never been born.

"What can we do for you, Cochise?" the man asked. He didn't look at me but at Frankie Bull, his voice a low rumble that came from the pit of his abdomen. "You forget the way to the reservation?"

When his hired hand spoke, Bobby finally looked away from his labors at the loading ramp, first at the speaker, then over his shoulder at us.

"Shut the fuck up, Ray," he snapped, a look in his eyes that would melt copper. For a short count, it looked like Ray wanted to argue, but he came to his senses and took a step backwards, humiliation and resentment plastered on his ugly face.

"I'm sorry about that, Officer," Snow said to Frankie Bull. "Ray runs off at the mouth."

When Frankie didn't answer, Snow shrugged his shoulders and turned his attention to me. "Sheriff Starbranch," he said. "What brings you out here? Some kind of trouble?"

A tall man with a running back's lean, tightly packed frame, Bobby Snow wore badly scuffed boots with riding heels and stubby spurs, torn blue jeans, and a Western shirt with the sleeves cut off. His arms were well muscled, particularly the forearms, developed in countless eight-second rides aboard a thousand pounds of bucking, writhing fury. His salt-and-pepper hair was cropped close beneath a sweat-stained, short-brimmed Stetson. His eyes were veiled behind expensive Ray-Bans, but the colored glasses didn't hide the menace in his face.

It was the face of a big cat, a predator in search of raw meat.

I closed the distance between us, my hand straying to the grip of my sidearm. "I don't know if it's trouble for you or not," I said. Behind me, I could feel the comforting presence of Frankie Bull, matching me step for step. "But I need to ask you some questions about a couple of your friends."

Bobby Snow smiled, gave me a what-now? shrug. "Just out of curiosity," he said, "you got a warrant?"

"No," I said. "This is a murder investigation, and all I want to do is talk. Don't need a warrant for that. Of course, if you'd rather talk at the office . . ."

He motioned in the direction of the loading ramp. "I'm real busy right now," he said sarcastically. "I pay these guys by the hour. Who ya wanta know about?"

"Ralphie Skates," I said, watching his face for a reaction. "Clarence Hathaway."

Snow's face was a mask of indifference. "Don't know 'em," he said, his voice even and strong. "Should I?"

I shrugged my shoulders noncommittally. "One of 'em's dead. The other one's missing. I hear talk that you might know 'em. That's all."

"Well, I don't," he said. "What are they, ranchers?"

"Nope. Ex-cons. From Laramie. Lately it looks like they may have been doing a little rustling."

"Can't help you." He chuckled. "I try to run with a better class of people."

At his side, Ray and the other muscle head laughed. Frankie Bull snorted in derision.

"I can see that," I said. "I just hope for your sake that I don't find out different."

We stood there for a moment, the implied accusation hanging between us. Bobby's jaws bunched tightly. Then he slapped his gloved hand against his thigh.

"You think I might be in with them?" he asked angrily. "Is that what this is about?"

"Just curiosity," I said cordially. "Like I said, I heard you knew 'em."

"Well, like I said, I don't. And I'll tell ya somethin' else. If you and your friend here don't have a warrant, I think it's time for you to get the hell off my place."

As Snow spoke, Ray and his compatriot moved away from Bobby and fanned out to the sides. The older man came to a stop about four feet from my left elbow, Ray within reach of Frankie Bull. If worse came to worst, I thought I could take my man with the blackthorn walking stick. That would leave Bobby and Ray to Frankie's ministrations. No matter the outcome, it was a situation to avoid.

"Okay," I said. I brought the blackthorn stick up, held it in both hands like an overgrown billy club. "We're leaving. But I'll be back with a warrant.",

I turned my back on Bobby Snow, caught Frankie's mirrored eyes and nodded toward the Blazer.

"Time to fly?" he asked.

"Time to fly."

With a nod, Frankie wheeled toward the car, closing the distance between himself and Ray. One of them would have to give ground.

"See ya around, Geronimo," Ray mumbled. He'd dropped the whip but was ready for business with the prod, bringing it upward, into position.

From my vantage point, I didn't see Frankie's fist as it slammed into Ray's belly, but I heard the air whoosh out of the big man's lungs, saw his mouth drop open, his eyes bulge like a landed carp's, saw him sink almost gracefully to his knees.

We left him there, retching, while his friend tried to lift him to his feet. Bobby Snow did nothing to help. He watched the two of them with open disgust and finally stomped off in the direction of the loading ramp, cursing as he went.

"Care to explain that?" I asked Frankie when he'd folded his long legs into the vehicle and belted himself in, a self-satisfied grin on his brown face.

"Old Sioux proverb," he said. He pulled his hat down on his forehead until the brim rested atop his thick, black eyebrows, settled back in the seat. "Spare the rod, spoil the asshole."

By the time I'd dropped Frankie Bull at the office in Victory and made my way back down Highway 130 to the sheriff's department in Laramie, the skies had opened up and dumped a microburst on the county. On the outskirts of town near the old Wyoming Territorial Prison, water was an inch deep on the roadways, and because the ground in this country is incredibly slow to absorb water, the runoff had already turned the dry streambeds that feed the Laramie River into boiling, coffee-colored torrents choked with driftwood, tumbleweeds, and odd bits of garbage.

The top floor of the elderly courthouse, of course, was leaking worse than Ronald Reagan's cabinet, and I found the deputies who run the jail scurrying around trying to collect enough slickers and plastic drop cloths to keep the twenty prisoners currently incarcerated in our ancient lockup from complaining to the ACLU.

I pulled a stack of messages and mail from my in-basket, poured a cup of sludge from the communal coffeepot and carried it to my office, working my way through the correspondence as I went.

At the top of the stack was a manila envelope from the coroner's office: copies of the autopsy reports on Colleen McAfferty and Ralphie Skates.

According to Bowen, who had finished the paperwork that morning, Skates had died as the result of a single gunshot wound to the head at approximately 5:00 P.M. on Sunday. The bullet, fired from a high-powered rifle or pistol, had entered his upper lip on the left side of his face, dislocated his jaw, knocked out several teeth, and severed his tongue before it cut a devastating swath through the rest of his skull. The report said his medulla oblongata was completely destroyed, along with his cerebellum and pons Varolii. The round exited the base of his skull, carried with it a good deal of brain matter and a saucer-size chunk of his occipital bone.

Death, Bowen wrote needlessly, was instantaneous.

The fatal wound, he said, was not a contact wound, and there was no powder residue on the body, so it had not been fired at close range.

There was no way to identify the precise type of weapon used in the killing, since we'd been unable to find the spent bullet. A fragment of lead plucked from the back of Ralphie's oral cavity, however, suggested that the round had partially fragmented upon impact. This led Bowen to conclude that his initial impression had been correct. It had been a sporting round, probably a soft- or hollow-point.

Semen and vaginal fluid on his genitals, pubic area, and thighs indicated that he had engaged in recent sexual activity. There were three two-inch scratches on his left shoulder.

As an aside, Bowen noted that Skates was suffering from what must have been a painful outbreak of herpes at the time of his death.

The report on Colleen McAfferty indicated she had been sexually assaulted before she died at around 5:00 P.M., although until the lab reports were completed there was no way to determine if the semen in and on her body came from more than one individual. There were large bruises on the insides of her thighs, and considerable vaginal tearing.

There were also large bruises on her left cheek, left shoulder, upper arms, forearms, throat, and abdomen. Her right eye had been blackened and her buttocks were scraped raw in several places.

Although she was in considerable pain before she died, Bowen reported the actual cause of death as strangulation. Whoever did it crushed her larnyx in the process and left deep palm-size bruises on her mastoid and trapezius muscles.

The movies make it look easy to choke someone to death with your bare hands, but I knew from my experience in homicide that it's very difficult. For one thing, it takes several minutes. For another, it's hard to keep your victim from squirming free long enough to take another breath.

Whoever killed Colleen had strong hands, large enough to encircle her entire neck, squeeze off her air supply, and hold her down until she died, an outcome she desperately tried to avoid. Many of her bruises appeared to be defense wounds, suggesting she fought her attackers and her killer hard. Bowen found material beneath the fingernails of her right hand he said was probably human tissue.

Perhaps the lab would match it to Skates. Maybe it would tie someone else to the crime, if and when we started to make arrests.

I leaned back in my chair and thought about what I'd read, put mental images with the words. And the longer I let my imagination run, the angrier and more impotent I felt.

Once a cop gets a murder case, he's too late to do the victim any good, and the best he can hope for is to wrest a measure of justice by catching the killer and hoping the judicial system works. That's not ever enough though—at least, not for me. So I often find myself fantasizing that once, just once, instead of turning up too late to save the victim's life, I show up while the crime is in progress, guns blazing like Roy fucking Rogers, and we walk off into the sunset happy. We being me and the victim, stepping over the bodies of the bad guys I've just slaughtered.

The little movie playing on the back of my eyelids had me walking up to Ralphie Skates just as he wrapped his hands around

Colleen's throat, laying the barrel of my Blackhawk right up against the back of his skull, and savoring the look of recognition and fear in his eyes in the split second before I sent him to hell and saved the young woman's life.

It was a satisfying fantasy, but not particularly productive, so I forced the images of Colleen and Skates out of my mind and tried to concentrate on quieter things—a burbling stream, the sound of the evening breeze in the pines—and took deep, rhythmic breaths until my fury had subsided and my heart rate was back to normal.

Then I opened my eyes, tucked the autopsy reports back in their envelope, and sorted through the rest of the mail and messages.

A call from the chairman of the county commission about the latest cost overrun estimates at the new $9-million-plus jail under construction across the street.

That one went in my to-do-later pile.

One from Sally Sheridan regarding the follow-up story on the killings for the next morning's edition of the *Star-Tribune*.

Round file. Two points.

One from the cop reporter at the *Boomerang*.

To do later.

One from Tess McAfferty, asking when her daughter's body would be released for burial.

Fifteen rings. No answer.

And one from C.J. Fall, along with the number where he could be reached, a ranch outside Woods Landing. I dialed and waited, watched fat raindrops trickle down the dirty office window, while Sonia Whitman, the rancher's wife, went to fetch Fall from the loading chutes.

"Harry?" he asked when he came on. His voice rose and fell as it traveled the ancient phone lines, and it struck me that for such a skinny guy, he sounded a hell of a lot like Wilford Brimley. "Thanks for getting back to me. Gives me an excuse to come inside for a minute and dry off."

"No problem," I said. "What can I do for ya?"

"Nothin'. It's what I can do for you. I checked on those two names we discussed yesterday, and it looks like you can forget about Wayne Carney. He's been in jail in Norman, Oklahoma, for the last two weeks. Drunk driving, resisting arrest."

"And Snow?" I asked hopefully. "How does he look?"

"Pretty good. My people say they've been hearing about him for the best part of the summer but haven't seen any hard evidence yet. Still, the rumor is he's dirty. Very dirty."

"Is it worth asking for a warrant?" I asked. "See if the missing cows and Jezebel are out at his place?"

"I doubt it," Fall said. "If he's the one who took 'em, he's smart enough to have gotten 'em out of state as quick as he could. Maybe he had someone else take 'em, but I'd bet anything you won't find those critters on the T-Bar. Serving your warrant would just tell him we're on his tail."

I drummed my pencil on the metal desktop, silently cursed my overzealousness. "I think we may have already queered the surprise," I said finally, then explained what had happened at Snow's ranch that morning. "He's expecting me to come back."

"You got any way to tie him in with Ralphie Skates or that other fella you're lookin' for?" he asked.

"Clarence Hathaway? Not yet."

"Then don't bother going," he said. "Even if he had stolen livestock on the ranch this morning, it's long gone by now. I'll see if any of my people've heard anything about who might be working with Snow, see if Ralphie's name pops up. In the meantime, just let it rest, will you Harry? Maybe he'll think we forgot him."

"Nah," I said. I remembered the look of loathing on Snow's face when Frankie and I drove away, Ray still on his hands and knees, dry-heaving like he might actually lose a lung. "He ain't gonna forget us. And I don't think he'll believe we forgot him, either."

Larry Calhoun jammed a plum-size hunk of blood-rare steak in his mouth and smacked his lips in savage delight. Like a starving man, he'd downed about half his mesquite-grilled London broil in three bites. So far, I hadn't touched mine.

A sturdy, stern-visaged specimen, Larry is a brutally honest, fifty-six-year-old widower who spent most of his life as a drill instructor in the Marine Corps. When he retired a decade ago, he moved his hormone-ravaged teenaged daughter, Tina, to Laramie, bought a little house on Lewis Street, ran for county assessor, and won the job by a landslide. The assessor is the guy who sets the property valuations upon which taxes are based, so his popularity didn't last long. For most of his last term, in fact, there'd been talk of a recall petition from a bunch of spoilsports who claim he set their valuations at twice what they should have been, just because they were Republicans.

All of that is bad for the county Democrats—whose valuations have remained very low during his tenure—because Larry finally told them they could find some other chump to run for assessor in the coming election. He planned to retire again, this time forever.

It's good for me, because he's the only friend I have, besides Curly, who's ever won an election and one of the few people around here I trust to tell me the truth, although I don't always like it. I asked him to be my campaign manager last spring after I bought him at least four doubles of Jack Daniel's, and he reluctantly agreed. His price: two dozen royal coachmen, a dozen golden ribbed hare's ears and six dozen Starbranch special stonefly nymphs, a trout fly that fish find so irresistible it ought to be illegal.

"Somethin' wrong with the grub?" Calhoun mumbled around a mouthful of food. "Wanta send it back?"

"Nah, nothin' wrong with the meat," I said distractedly.

Calhoun shrugged his shoulders. "Well, I can't make you take nourishment, Harry. But if you won't eat, you're just gonna have to sit there and watch me. Hope you don't mind."

Before I could answer, he renewed his attack on lunch, using a piece of thick bread to sop up the blood and juices from his steak. I looked away to avoid staring.

We'd come to the restaurant ostensibly to discuss campaign strategy and take advantage of the Cowboy Bar & Grill's $4.95 London broil special, but I wasn't particularly hungry, and I couldn't concentrate on political intrigue because I was preoccupied with the McAfferty investigation. Since my conversation with Fall before lunch, I'd thought about Bobby Snow and the best way to find out what he was up to. Although I had no concrete reason to believe it, I had a strong hunch he'd been involved in the murder of Colleen McAfferty, maybe of Ralphie as well. I also suspected he knew where we could find the reclusive Clarence Hathaway. While I agreed with Fall that we had no reason to push him very far just yet, certainly no grounds for a warrant, I decided that as soon as I got back to the office, I'd pull a couple of deputies off road duty to watch his ranch from a distance. Maybe we'd get lucky.

"Earth to Harry. Come in."

I snapped out of my ruminations, looked quizzically at Calhoun, who was holding a bottle of steak sauce over his plate and tapping the bottom. The sauce spilled out, and he used a knife to spread it over the remainder of his meat. "You were a million miles away, podna," he said. "You okay?"

I shrugged my shoulders, tried a weak smile. "It's just this McAfferty thing, Larry. That little girl out there got some hard treatment before she died. It shouldn't have happened anywhere . . ."

Calhoun's expression turned grim. He speared a hunk of meat savagely with his fork. "Especially your county," he said quietly, finishing my thought.

I nodded in agreement, threw my napkin over my plate, and pushed it away. Maybe I'd feel like dinner later.

Calhoun popped his last bite of steak in his mouth, used his own napkin to wipe the juice from his chin. "Ya'll have anythin'?" he asked, all business.

"Not a hell of a lot," I admitted. "We won't get the lab reports back until tomorrow. In the meantime, we're looking into a couple of people."

Calhoun unwrapped a toothpick, used it to remove a bit of steak from his back teeth. His smile when he spoke was a thin one. "Yeah, well, I'm already hearing rumblings from your competition that you're dragging your feet."

"Baldi?"

"None other. Told a bunch of people in the county clerk's office that you should have called the DCI in right away, since your boys don't have the experience for this sort of thing. Said crime around here is getting out of control and you obviously can't handle it."

Calhoun's voice was flat, without inflection. He was just passing information, and it tweaked me a bit that he wasn't as pissed off about Baldi's complaints as I was already beginning to feel. God damn all Monday morning quarterbacks. "Now why would I have called the DCI?" I asked. "We're plenty capable of handling a crime scene investigation."

"I know you are. You know you are," Calhoun said patiently, in the same tone of voice you'd use to explain a difficult long-division problem to a third-grader. "But this is politics, and politics don't have nothin' to do with fact. In politics, all that matters is what people believe, and if Baldi keeps yappin' about the way you're bunglin' and stallin' the investigation of this 'heinous atrocity,' they're gonna start believin' it. Any chance you'll make an arrest in the next week or so? That'd shut him up."

I didn't give him an answer because I didn't think his question deserved one. It's a law of murder investigation that the majority of killings are carried out by the most obvious suspect. You find a woman with a history of infidelity stabbed to death in her living room: the husband probably did it. You find an abusive goon full of nine-millimeter holes lying dead in his ex-wife's driveway: chances are good she finally got tired of his bullshit and served a permanent restraining order.

It doesn't take a mental gymnast to make a quick collar in cases like that, and the arrest looks good in your year-end statistics. Unfortunately, the murders of Colleen McAfferty and Ralphie Skates didn't fall into that category. With good police work and a little luck, we'd probably eventually make an arrest. But we might never bring the perpetrator to justice. It's those cases that haunt lawmen for the rest of their careers.

"Well," Calhoun said matter-of-factly. He opened two packets of sugar and dumped them in his coffee, stirred it angrily, his spoon clanking against the side of his cup. "I hope you break it pretty damn quick. With this Slaymaker business, we're gonna need somethin'."

The rational part of my brain told me that Calhoun wasn't completely insensitive to the human suffering and tragedy that had occurred at the McAfferty ranch, he was just being practical and realistic. The emotional part of my brain was pissed off that he'd even think about using those events to our advantage. "Come on, Larry," I said indignantly. "A murder investigation takes as much time as it takes. Sometimes it's years. It's not a brake job; you can't rush it. And who's gonna take Slaymaker seriously anyway? My opinion? I think we should just ignore the whole thing."

Calhoun wiped his face with a napkin, laid his knife and fork crosswise on his plate. The foreboding frown on his face made him look all the more military and severe. He was obviously struggling with a little anger of his own. I just couldn't tell whether he was mad at Baldi or at me.

"This ain't Nicaragua, Dorothy," he said, his voice low and tight. "This ain't fucking Mexico. This is Wyoming, maybe the most conservative goddamn state in the Union. And around here, voters still care whether their lawmen play by the rules and get sound convictions. You wanta cut your own throat? Fine. Ignore Baldi. Then you might as well start packing the crap in your office, because you're on your way back to Podunkville."

I dismissed him with an exasperated wave of my hand, rolled my eyes. "You may be overstating the case a little, don't you think?"

"Here's what I think," he said. "I think that with the demographics around here, a Democrat is in deep shit from day one. There are only about twelve thousand registered voters in the county, and sixty percent of the full-time residents are old, Republican, and suspicious. The only thing Democrats have going for them is the liberals at the university, and once in a while that's enough to get one of us elected, as long as it's too cold on Election Day for the old folks to get to the polls. If they get interested in an election, though, they'll vote, come hell or high water. And you can be damn sure they'll be interested in voting an incompetent cop who tampers with evidence out of office."

"I'm not incompetent!" I said, loudly enough to draw stares from diners at most of the nearby tables. "The son of a bitch was guilty, Larry. He raped that little boy. He stabbed him. He stuffed him in a damn barrel. Do you understand what I'm saying?"

"Doesn't matter," Larry said. He threw his napkin on the table and stood up. "It's what people believe that matters. That's my whole point. Unless there's some part of you that just doesn't give a shit whether you win or lose, you gotta deal with this, Harry. Go to the people. Make an explanation. Blame it on somebody else, if you have to. But I'll tell ya this: it isn't gonna do you a damn bit of good to keep insisting Slaymaker's guilty when the courts and the evidence don't agree. If I was you, I'd keep that opinion to myself."

I ignored him, looked down at my coffee.

"You do want to win, don't you?" he asked angrily.

I was quiet for several long seconds. "Yeah," I said quietly. "I want to win."

"Why? Just to prove you can? To make up for past sins? To prove to Nicole that you've grown up? That you're more than an ex-drunk, small-town cop? If that's it, it's a pretty piss-poor reason."

I didn't answer, shrugged my shoulders.

"Well," he said, pushing himself away from the table, "you'd better figure it out pretty damn quick. Let me know when you do."

With that, he turned on his heel and clomped out of the restaurant, his heavy jaw as tense as a spring-loaded trap.

I was still sitting there ten minutes later, drinking a second glass of iced tea, trying to figure out how I'd gotten myself in this mess, when a long shadow fell across the table. It belonged to my undersheriff, Nicky Pajak.

"Somethin' stick in your craw, Harry?"

"I'm fine," I snapped. "Why?"

"Your face is all red," he smirked. "Sort of looked like you were choking."

I gritted my teeth, stood and dropped a twenty on the table to cover the check. "You here for lunch?" I asked finally. My tone made it obvious I was unhappy he'd interrupted my privacy.

"Nah," he said. "I'm here lookin' for you. I just got a call from the highway patrol over in Carbon County. They found Clarence Hathaway about a hundred yards from a rest stop out by Elk Mountain."

"Hathaway? They found him?"

Pajak handed me my Stetson. "Well . . ." he said, "they found a body, and they think it's Hathaway."

"Think?"

"Coyotes," he explained simply. "They been at it pretty good."

# FIVE

Fatty Winston, sheriff of Carbon county, stood at the edge of the pavement, a short-barreled pump shotgun in one hand, poking his stubby finger into the chest of a highway patrol captain. The captain had twenty-five pounds and six inches on Fatty and looked like he wanted to break the sweaty little troll in half.

I opened the door of the Blazer and rolled out, smelled the cool, pine-scented breeze as it snaked down the flanks of Elk Mountain. Once again, I was stunned by the beauty of the place—a huge hunk of the Medicine Bow range, jutting up from the Laramie plains like the knuckle on an Irish giant's hand.

A hundred yards beyond the blacktop parking lot I could see three Carbon County deputies and a couple of highway patrol officers gathered in a tight knot around something hidden from view by the banks of sagebrush. The object that held their interest, I imagined, was the body. A few other lawmen combed the immediate area, and their perambulations occasionally disturbed some of the magpies and crows lurking around in hopes of cashing in on the unexpected surfeit of carrion. The birds flew off, piercing the sultry afternoon quiet with their angry, raucous caws, only to land again a few yards away and resume their vigil.

When Fatty heard the door of the Blazer slam and saw us

shuffling in his direction, he forgot the highway patrol captain long enough to wince in irritation, spitting a long stream of brown tobacco juice from the huge wad that bulged his cheek to punctuate his display of displeasure.

"I wondered how long it'd take you city boys to show up," he said. His gravelly voice dripped with sarcasm. "Make sure we aren't standing around out here with our dicks in our hands."

"Hello Fatty," I said. I didn't offer to shake hands. He didn't have his dick in his hand at that exact minute, but it probably hadn't been long. Instead, I nodded to the patrol captain, whose name tag identified him as Alvin Sharps, and introduced myself and Pajak.

"One of your men found the body?" I asked Sharps.

"Well," he said, "a couple of bird watchers actually found it. They were on their way to Salt Lake and stopped here at the rest stop because they saw all those birds swooping around. They took a closer look. Found more than they intended."

"It looks like the body's been out there for a while?"

"Day or so," Sharps said. "It's not in very good shape. We got an ID from his driver's license, remembered the be-on-the-lookout call your folks put out last night—"

"And called you before they even thought of calling us," Fatty broke in. He scowled at Sharps. I understood then at least part of the reason for Fatty's ill temper. As the popularly elected sheriff, he's the highest law enforcement authority in Carbon County, and calling my department before his own had been a minor breach of protocol. Knowing Fatty, I'm sure he imagined the slight as a deliberate and malicious attempt to subvert his authority, make him look bad in the eyes of his men.

Not that anything Sharps did could make him look worse than he already does. Winston has been sheriff of Carbon County for over thirty years, and in that time he's managed to carve himself a reputation as the most thickheaded, backward, intolerant, and ruthless lawman in the state. It's a reputation he's proud of, and he'll be the first to tell you the only reason Rawlins isn't a worse hellhole than it already is is because nobody wants to mess with him or his dragoons.

I spoke to Fatty but looked at Sharps, who didn't seem particularly apologetic. "Well," I said, "it looks like the SO's deputies got here before we did anyway."

Fatty grunted, let fly with another stream of juice. It hit less than an inch from the toe of my boot. I ignored the insult, pointed in the direction of the officers gathered around Clarence Hathaway's body. "Mind if we take a look?"

"Fine by me," Fatty rumbled, and jammed a pair of mirrored aviator sunglasses on the bridge of his pudgy nose. "But I better go along with ya. Make sure ya don't do nothin' to contaminate the scene."

With that, he lumbered off in the direction of the body, leaving the rest of us to follow. I bit my tongue and fell in with Sharps, far enough behind Fatty Winston that he couldn't hear our conversation.

"Nice fella," Sharps said, a thin smile on his lips.

"A real prick," I agreed. "What's his beef?"

"Jurisdiction," Sharps explained. "By the time he and his deputies got out here, we'd already started a crime scene investigation. He couldn't wait to take charge, let us know who was boss."

"You find anything?"

Sharps shrugged his broad shoulders. "Not much," he said. "Looks like somebody just dumped the body off. Whoever did it didn't spend a lot of time. Left some tire tracks. Coupla footprints close to the body."

"What kinda tracks?"

"Double-wheel," Sharps said. "A trailer of some kind. The trailer's prints were over top of the tracks of the vehicle pulling it, so those were obliterated. But we got some good photographs and casts of the trailer tires. Wheelbase measurements, that sort of thing."

"Let me know what you find out?" I asked.

"You bet," he said, then shook his head in disgust. "But that may be the only evidence we get. Fatty's boys waded in there like a herd of buffalo. Pawed the body. Poked around. Hell, he hasn't even called a coroner yet."

When we reached the small covey of deputies around the body, they parted to let us through. Winston led the way, happily pointing to the carcass, grinning and watching our eyes for a reaction. I took a deep breath of air, smelled the sickly-sweet scent of decay and rotten eggs, forced my face into an expressionless mask. Behind me, I heard Nicky cough, force down a gag.

I knew exactly how he felt. Clarence Hathaway may have been a murderer, a rapist, and a good-for-nothing horse thief. He may have even deserved to die in the electric chair. Still, nobody deserved the treatment he'd received.

His corpse had been tossed atop a mature sagebrush, and his body was bent backward in an unnatural-looking bow over the inch-thick branches. Prairie scrub supported the middle of his back, but his legs splayed out in a wide V, and his right leg was twisted backwards, the heel of his boot nearly touching his buttocks. His head hung upside down, his empty, magpie-picked eye sockets staring directly at the sun, the muscles of his face constricted in a demonic rictus grin. His blackened tongue lolled thickly from one side of his mouth, and maggot larvae crawled in the mucus of his nostrils, slithered up the sides of his nose.

Something—coyotes or badgers, most likely—had chewed a big enough hole in his abdominal cavity to pull most of his large intestine free, and a six-foot section of the organ trailed away from his body into the tangled underbrush. Something else had bitten through his blue jeans and torn away three or four pounds of thigh.

His chest was a crusted breastplate of purplish, dried blood, and another colony of lively maggots slithered at the edges of the obvious bullet wound located just above the left pocket of his cream-colored shirt.

I knelt down at Hathaway's side, peered under his body to

see beneath it, but Winston grabbed hold of my shoulder and pulled me to my feet.

He grinned as he took a sixteen-inch wooden dowel from his back pocket. "Look at this," he said.

I watched in stunned horror and disbelief as he grabbed the front of Hathaway's shirt and lifted the corpse a few inches away from its bed of sage. His lips pursed like he was ciphering a difficult math problem, Winston stuck the dowel into the opening of the wound in Hathaway's chest and pushed. The wooden rod slipped easily into the dead man's chest cavity, met no obstruction until at last the bloody end of the stick protruded from a point just below Clarence's left shoulder.

"It went through," Winston said, smiling wickedly, "and fucking through."

Late that afternoon, I sat across from Rawls and Pajak at one of the three redwood picnic tables scattered under the maple trees on the front lawn of the county courthouse. We'd come outside to discuss our progress on the case without the distraction of the office clatter, and of our phones, which were ringing off the hook with calls from reporters who wanted someone to fill in the details of what looked like the beginning of a major crime spree.

Even as we spoke, one of the department secretaries was putting the final touches to a written statement I'd have Pajak release in time for the evening news. It didn't provide much detail, but it implied that we had plenty of evidence and were closing in on a possible suspect. It wouldn't keep the media off our backs for long, I knew. Nothing ever did.

It felt good there in the shade, the air perfumed by the smell of rich earth and cut grass. I rolled a soda can between my palms, enjoyed the icy condensation on the outside of the can, squinted beyond the shade to watch the moderate afternoon traffic roll down Grand Avenue.

Rawls's legs are so long he looked uncomfortable sitting on the picnic bench. His knees kept bumping the underside of the table. "So how do you see this, Harry?" he asked.

"I don't know for sure," I said truthfully. "But at this point, there's no reason to think our initial reading was very far off base—as far as it goes. Skates, Hathaway, and persons unknown dropped by the McAfferty place very late Sunday afternoon or early Sunday evening to steal the livestock in the corral. We're pretty sure they traveled in a big pickup, maybe a fifth-wheel, and pulling a stock trailer.

"They didn't see Tess's car in the yard, so they might have assumed nobody was home. They drove down to the corral and started loading."

"And they were surprised by Colleen," Rawls broke in, interrupting my train of thought.

"Right," I said. "She might not have heard them drive in, but she must have heard or seen something once they started loading the stock and went down to check it out."

"So she was a bonus for these bastards," Rawls said.

I crushed the soda can, flung it at a trash barrel. "It looks that way," I said. "We're pretty sure that at least Skates raped her, maybe some of the others did too."

"But why kill her?" Pajak asked. There was a note of challenge in his voice. Maybe he thought I knew the answer and just wasn't telling.

"Who knows how their minds work?" I said. "Maybe she was fighting them, maybe they didn't want to leave a witness. Maybe they just like rough stuff, and this time it got out of hand."

Pajak shook his head in dismissal and turned around on the bench to sit with his broad back to us. Rawls and I were quiet for a spell, each of us imagining the scene in our minds, trying to see it through the perpetrators' eyes.

I couldn't do it with any success though. I kept seeing it through Colleen's. Saw their leering faces. Smelled their fetid breath. Felt the shame and humiliation as they tore my clothes, grabbed at me with rough, calloused hands. Felt the cactus score my bare flesh. Felt their weight as they pressed down on top of me. Felt strong hands around my windpipe.

I know some cops who can show up at a crime scene and within minutes put themselves right inside the killer's skull. They intuitively sense his motivation, his desire, his psychosis. They feel his finger on the trigger or wrapped around the hilt of a knife. They share his jubilation, his almost sexual sense of excitement as he watches life drain out of his victim's eyes.

If they stay on his trail long enough, they come to know him even better than he knows himself, can often second-guess his next move.

And for them, that psychic ability sometimes pays off. By becoming their quarry, they catch him.

It's never worked that way for me, though. No matter how hard I try, I can't establish a real empathic connection with a cold-blooded killer. Instead, I empathize viscerally with the victim. It's a curse I've borne since my first day on the job, and perhaps—I admit when I'm being particularly honest with myself—one of the reasons I left homicide investigation.

Pajak turned on the bench to face us again, brought me back from my brooding with a question, the one we'd all been asking ourselves again and again.

"So who shot Skates and Hathaway?" he growled. "One of the other rustlers? And if that was the case, why did they carry Hathaway off and leave Skates there for us to find? I'm assuming, of course, that the blood we found at the side of the McAfferty corral came from Hathaway. With Fatty in charge of the Hathaway killing, we won't have a lab report for a couple of days, if then, but still . . ."

"I think that's a safe assumption," I said. "I think we know that Hathaway was shot and killed at the corral. We are certain Skates was killed there. Now we've just got to figure out who did it and why."

"I don't know about you," said Rawls, "but Bobby Snow is

my pick in the who sweepstakes. If we could only tie him to Skates and Hathaway . . ."

"Yeah," I said skeptically, "that'd be nice."

It would have been nice. Trouble was, there was something off plumb in the theory that Snow had killed Skates or Hathaway. For starters, it didn't seem there was a good reason for him to have shot them. He didn't shoot them to take their money, since both men had been found with several hundred dollars in their wallets.

If he was angry about the rape and the murder of Colleen, why wait until after it was over and shoot Skates with his pants down?

And even if he shot them for some other reason, why did he leave Skates for us to find? Maybe he panicked, but I doubted it. Leaving Ralphie's corpse was sloppy, and while Bobby Snow seemed like a man who'd have few second thoughts about taking human life, he didn't strike me as a slob.

At that point, though, he was the best suspect we had. And if he'd been involved, it made sense that he'd want to distance himself from those crimes as quickly as possible.

"Did you assign deputies to watch his place?" I asked.

"Yeah," Rawls said, "starting about one thirty this afternoon. They say they haven't seen a livestock trailer on the ranch, or anything else that looks suspicious. But maybe something will turn up tonight."

I wasn't overly optimistic. If I was Bobby Snow, I'd have done exactly what Fall suggested—order someone else to drive the stolen livestock and the trailer out of state. I'd have them dump the body on the way. After that, I'd tell the driver to run like hell for Canada or somewhere with no brand inspection to sell the stock. I wouldn't let him come back until the evidence was at the slaughterhouse and the livestock trailer was as clean as an operating room.

"I'm gonna phone C.J. Fall again," I said. "See if he can get some people to keep an eye out for Jezebel at the kill plants. If we miss our driver there, we'll just have to hope we pick him up when he brings the trailer back across the county line. At that point, we'll try for a warrant and have the DCI's lab guys look it over. I don't give a shit how thoroughly he cleans that trailer, they'll find something if it's there.

"Hell," I said, "maybe we'll get lucky. Maybe a day or so from now, a livestock trailer will turn up at Bobby Snow's ranch and the tires and wheelbase will perfectly match the impressions and measurements Alvin Sharps took out at Elk Mountain. Maybe they'll also match the prints and impressions we gathered at McAfferty's. Maybe we'll discover that trailer belongs to Bobby Snow. Maybe he'll admit the whole damn thing. Maybe this stinkin' case will turn out to be a grounder after all."

"That's a lot of maybes," Pajak said dryly.

"I know it," I said, and heaved myself up from the table. "Maybe while we're waiting, you could drop by the county clerk's office, see if Snow was issued a license plate for a livestock trailer. See what other kinds of vehicles he's been issued licenses for. Maybe I'll drop by Bobby's house on the way home. Maybe he's got no goddamn alibi for Sunday night."

I drove out Highway 130 toward Bobby Snow's ranch and Victory in the growing dusk. With the windows down, the warm air rising from the blacktop whipped through the Blazer, created a miniblizzard of papers that had been tossed atop the dashboard, cigarette ashes from the opened ashtrays, and bone dry bentonite-laden dust. I ignored the irritation, settled back in the seat, and turned the radio up as far as it would go. Pounded my hands on the steering wheel in time to Travis Tritt, who sang about adultery in the Bible Belt, the guitars full-blooded and insistent.

A few miles from Victory, I crossed over the Little Laramie River, a slender ribbon of sparkling turquoise in a sea of browns and dull prairie greens. Down the waterway to the north I could see a lone fly fisherman along the bank, knee-deep in grass, the arc of his line a graceful bow as he laid the fly gently on the current.

In the green alfalfa fields to the south, the first mule deer of evening ventured out of their day beds, their huge ears cocked, taking one tentative step at a time toward the water. Small herds of pronghorn antelope stopped their browsing to watch me pass.

At the turnoff to the T-Bar, I eased across the cattle guard and stopped to wait while a fork-horn buck who'd been nibbling timothy along the edges of the hayfield bounded off down the middle of the road. After twenty yards, his haunches bunched and he took one gigantic bounce to the left, launching his body into the air like a huge four-legged kangaroo. He soared over the sheep-tight fence on the left side of the road, landed in mid stride, and disappeared into a dry streambed leading back toward the river.

Three vehicles were parked in front of Snow's house, a fifteen-year-old green Ford four-wheel-drive pickup, its sides and oversize tires caked with dried mud, a half-ton utility truck, and a compact Honda with Illinois plates. No lights were on in his barn or near the corral, and only one dim light burned in the house. I shut the engine down and stepped out, listened to the electronic sputter of the yard light, the chirp of crickets, the tick of the engine as it began to cool.

I didn't see evidence that either Bobby or his hired goons were in the house, but I still felt uneasy. Straightening my tie, I threw my hat on the front seat and unsnapped the safety strap on my Blackhawk. Then I climbed the porch steps and hammered on the screen door. The front door was open, and the quiet murmurs of a radio turned low and the smell of fried meat drifted through the screen. Through the door I could see into Snow's living room and beyond that, a dark hallway I imagined led to the bedrooms. There was a half-empty wine bottle and three empty beer cans on a coffee table in front of the couch, a pair of blue jeans in a heap in the middle of the floor. At the side of the couch, a pair of black pumps had been left atop a stack of newspapers. A pair of pink panties were draped over the arm of the couch.

When I'd waited for thirty seconds without an answer, I

pounded the screen again, stepped back from the door.

"Tell me sheriff," a voice called from the stand of aspens about twenty feet from the porch, "are these visits gonna be a regular thing?"

Startled by the noise, I went to the side of the porch and strained my eyes into the darkness of the grove. When they began to adjust, I could make out the pale outline of a hammock stretched between two trees. I came down off the porch and walked in his direction, my hand on the butt of my revolver, my heart beating a little irregularly from the surprise.

Snow was sitting up, bare-chested, and had one muscular leg thrown over the edge of the hammock, his foot on the ground. Although I hadn't been able to tell it from a distance, I now saw he wasn't alone. His companion was a pretty brunette whose disheveled shoulder-length hair curled up at the ends. Snow's movement had pulled the afghan away from her small breasts, and she giggled softly as she pulled it back up, snuggled down in the hammock, reached out to touch Snow's back.

I tried without much success to avoid her eyes. "Guess I came at a bad time," I mumbled. She looked to be in her mid twenties, considerably younger than Bobby Snow, but she didn't seem particularly embarrassed by her circumstances. The half smile on her full lips suggested that she was having fun with this, enjoying my discomfort.

"Nah," Snow laughed. He reached for his shirt hanging over the edge of the hammock, fumbled with the garment until he'd found his cigarettes. He lit one, passed it to the girl. "Twenty minutes sooner would have been a bad time. Now, it's just irritating." The woman chortled again, took a deep drag on the cigarette, and raised herself up on one elbow. The afghan fell away once more. She ignored it.

I tried to ignore her.

"Listen, Bobby," I said. "I came out here—"

"Because you wanted to punch Ray around a little more?" he interrupted. "Sorry, he's gone for the day."

"He had that coming," I snapped. "The man has a big mouth, Bobby."

"And a long memory," he said. His voice had turned to ice.

I took a step toward the hammock. "Is that a threat?" I asked.

He held up a hand, palm out. "No, Starbranch," he said. "Just an observation. Listen, is there something we can do for you? Or did you just come to throw cold water on our afterglow?"

"Yeah," I said, "there is one thing you can do for me. You can tell me where you were between four P.M. and around nine P.M. Sunday evening."

Snow's hard eyes locked on mine at the question and held for a five count. The muscles on his forearms were knotted, his jaw tight. Then the corners of his mouth turned up in what could loosely be described as a smile, and he reached over to pat the woman's thigh. "Well one thing's for sure, podna" he said. "I wasn't with her. Just met this'n last night at the Cowboy Bar in Laramie. Out from Decatur, Illinois, on vacation she is. But you do like your cowboys, don't ya darlin'?"

The woman nodded in agreement, bent over to kiss him between the shoulder blades, snaked her arm protectively around his midsection.

"Let's cut the crap, Bobby," I said. "I don't like this any more than you do. Just tell me where you were, and I'll be on my way."

He ran a hand across his brush-cut hair. "Well, if you must know," he said, "I was right around here. Spent the night looking for my new pickup and stock trailer. Some son bitch stole it right off the place Sunday afternoon, and I ain't found it yet. Hope I do though. We're talkin' over thirty-thousand worth of rolling stock."

The lie came easily, and when he finished Snow threw the afghan completely aside and stood, stretching his arms above his head, and reached down for his shirt. I looked away from his naked body, but I could feel the color rise in my face. When he'd had time to pull his shirt on, I turned back, saw the woman bite her knuckles to keep from laughing. The shirt was too short to cover Snow's penis, still in what you'd call a state of excitement, pointing right at my belt buckle.

"You didn't mention a stolen pickup and stock trailer this morning," I said peevishly. I've never been too gracious when it comes to being the butt of someone else's joke, and these morons were beginning to piss me off.

He casually fumbled with his bottom button. "You didn't ask," he said, simply. "I went into town and reported the thefts to that big Indian cop this afternoon. He said ya'll would do your best to find 'em. Nice guy, that Freddie Bull. Real helpful. And you know what?" He smirked. "Ray doesn't think much of 'em, but *I* really love those earrings."

I was in a rank mood when I wheeled into the driveway of my farmhouse twenty minutes later, so rank that I'd driven right past the Silver Dollar on my way through Victory without stopping for a single Coors. I'd slowed down near the open front door just long enough to look inside the smoky barroom and see Lou McGrew, the ripe Clairol redhead who tends bar for Curly in the evenings, lean over to set a round of boilermakers on a table crowded with young, tanned cowboys. Her more than ample front stretched the capacity of her low-cut cotton blouse, and there was a toothy smile on her powdered face. There are lots of nights when thirty minutes of Lou's well-divided attention and shameless flirtation can cure whatever ails a man—but that night I just wasn't fit for human company.

I'd decided the best remedy for my humiliation-induced funk was a couple of fried egg and onion sandwiches smothered in picante sauce, followed by at least half the cherry cheesecake I'd been saving in my refrigerator and a double snifter of warmed brandy. After that, I'd put a little Van Morrison on the stereo, soak myself in a hot tub, smear my bad knee with Bag Balm, slip on my Wyoming Law Enforcement Academy sweats, and crawl into bed.

With any luck, I wouldn't have to speak with a living soul for at least twelve hours.

That plan went straight to hell the moment I turned off the ignition and saw Edna Cook, my eighty-three-year-old widowed landlady, sitting in a lawn chair on my side porch. Even in the relative dark, I could make out her shriveled form, see the wreath of smoke from the slim brown cigar she was puffing floating around her head.

Edna, who owns the 160-acre tract of land we live on, has been my neighbor and friend since I first moved to Victory. Her house is right next to mine, and she allows me to rent my two-bedroom abode for the paltry sum of $250 a month. In return, I run occasional errands for her and help feed the two geriatric quarter horses she treats better than her human relatives.

It's a great deal for me, since I have free run of the farm and plenty of room for a target range right out my back door.

For her part, Edna likes the setup because she can use my proximity as ammunition against her kids and grandkids, who think she ought to give them the farm, which they desperately want to sell, and spend her golden years in a nursing home with people her own age. Although she's a spry old bird and plenty capable of looking out for herself, Edna likes to remind her acquisitive heirs that because there's a cop living right next door, they needn't worry about her safety.

I shuffled up to the porch and took a seat on the wooden step. My back door was open and the kitchen light was on. They hadn't been that way when I left the house that morning, so Edna must have gone inside while I was away. She'd been waiting to tell me why.

"Was there some problem out here?" I asked. I pulled a beer from the six-pack at her feet, twisted the screw-off cap.

"Nothing that a shotgun wouldn't cure," she said between puffs on the cigar. "Since when did you have a dog, Harry?"

"Since yesterday," I said. "Belonged to a guy who turned up dead. Kind of adopted me, I guess."

"You gonna keep him?"

"I guess I haven't thought about it. Why?"

"Because if you do, I think you should take him to the vet and have his teeth pulled."

"His teeth? Why? Did he bite you?"

"Hell no," she said, "he didn't bite me. Tried to hump my leg, though. Chased him off with a broom."

"He got out?"

"Nope, he stayed in, just where you left him. Amused himself by destroying your throw pillows. I saw him standing in the window with a hunk of stuffing in his mouth and came over to see what was going on."

"Shit," I grumbled, standing. "Thanks for coming over, Edna. Guess I better go in and clean it up."

She flipped the butt of her cigar into the gravel driveway. "I already did that," she said.

"And the dog?" I asked, sitting back down.

"In the barn," she said. "Chained to an anvil. If you're gonna adopt him, he's gonna need a kennel. And food, Harry. You gotta remember to leave him food. A dog can't live on pillows alone, although I suppose it's a fair source of fiber." She cackled.

"It's not all that damn funny, Edna," I said grumpily. "I loved those pillows."

"The dog did too," she wheezed. "Especially the pizza stains." By this time, she was laughing so hard it brought on a coughing fit. I offered her a sip of my beer, and she accepted, drank a third of the bottle in a single gulp. I let her keep it, opened another for myself, and sat back down on the step. "I'm beginning to think your daughter has a point," I grumbled. "Not only are you getting senile, you're getting mean. Maybe you oughta be in a home."

She rested her hand on my shoulder. "And then what would happen to you, Harry Starbranch?" she asked. "Lord knows you need someone lookin' after ya. I figure I gotta hang around, at least 'til you find yourself a wife."

I gave her gnarled hand a friendly squeeze. "Speaking of which," I said, "Nicole's coming up this weekend. You mind if we take the horses for a ride?"

"Nah," she said. "The exercise will do 'em good. You let her have the mare, though, and take that gelding. He's grown old and cantankerous, and I don't want him buckin' her off."

We sat for twenty minutes in companionable silence, sipped our drinks and counted stars in the night sky, watched the contrails of jets passing overhead on their way to Stapleton International in Denver, spotted an occasional bat flitting through the bluish beams of the yard light as it scooped up another insect.

I'd almost finished my second beer when Edna dropped the bombshell she'd apparently been working up to, her voice serious, filled with honest concern. "What's this I hear about you lyin' to put an innocent man in prison, Harry?"

For a moment, I didn't think I'd heard right. I shook my head in confusion, the muscles in my chest beginning to constrict. "What?" I stammered. "Who said I did that?"

"The meter reader," she explained. "He was out here this morning. I talked to him, and he said he'd heard at the office that you were being sued for one hundred million. Said everyone in Laramie is talking about it."

"You didn't believe him?" I asked. "You know me Edna. Do you think I'd do something like that?"

She studied my face. "I don't know, Harry," she said softly.

I glared at her angrily, tossed my beer bottle at the trash can and started to stand up. She put her hand on my shoulder and guided me back down. "I know this. You're a good lawman. It's what you are. If you did what they say, you musta had a damn good reason."

I sighed heavily and rubbed my forehead with my fingers. "Do other people believe it?" I asked.

"Apparently they do," she said, pulling a fresh stogie from the box in her apron pocket. "And what's worse, Harry, they wonder what else you've been lying about."

# SIX

I slept fitfully again that night, my brain refusing to accept the warnings from my body that unless it closed down the circuits, there'd be a heavy penalty to pay come daybreak. I couldn't get the images of the bodies I'd seen in the last two days out of my mind, and every time I'd shut my eyes and drift off into half sleep, the corpses would be right back there on the movie screen of my eyelids in all their gory splendor. I was awash in blood, paralyzed by the kind of unspeakable impotent terror that always lurks just below the surface of our conscious minds.

Several times I pulled myself awake and attempted to derail that train of thought by conjuring up a hopeful vision of Nicole and me in bed. Dreams like that are my own personal favorite, and I've found that I can sometimes guarantee myself a whole night of them just by thinking erotic thoughts about my lovely paramour as I drift off to sleep. Even that failed to do the trick, however, because without my consciously noticing the shift, Nicole soon became Tess McAfferty, and instead of making love, I was holding her in my arms, mute and helpless, while she cried inconsolably, begged me to find her daughter's killer.

I gave up around four thirty, showered, dressed, and fixed myself a thermos of strong black coffee. If I was going to spend a night without sleep, I decided, at least I'd harvest a little good from the ordeal. In the weak light of the fluorescent fixture above my kitchen sink, I grabbed my graphite fly rod and my comfortable old fishing vest, fed and watered the dog, and pulled the door closed on the way out.

Twenty-five minutes later, in the first gray light of the morning's false dawn, I stood on the bank of the Little Laramie making an expectant cast into the top of a fifteen-yard riffle that ended in the calmer water of a bend in the stream. The current grabbed the fly, and the tip of my rod twitched gently as the rushing water pulled the bait through the run.

Although it was still too dark to see my bait, I knew when it reached the deeper water at the bend because the tension on the line eased almost imperceptibly. I raised the rod tip as the fly drifted along the surface of the water toward the bank, my left hand holding a length of line, my breath caught in my chest.

The first trout hit a second later, grabbed the fly from the surface of the water, and dived. Instinctively, I pointed the rod tip up and gave a gentle tug to set the hook, began to coax the small fish out of the calm water and into the riffle. I pulled him in an arm's length at a time, holding the line in my teeth as I drew in another length of it. When he was in the water directly below me, I held the rod tip straight up with my right hand and felt along the line with my left until my fingers closed around the wriggling trout.

I lifted him out of the water and carried him to the bank. He was a twelve-inch brook trout, his blunt black snout and back speckled with white dots, his sides splashed with extravagant scarlet and deep forest green. Carefully, I held his body and slipped the barbless hook from his mouth. After that, I cradled him in my hands and walked him back to the river, pulled him back and forth in the water until he had his bearings. Then I let him go, and the fish disappeared into the black current with a single flick of his tail.

The second cast a minute later produced a similar result, as did the next.

By the time the sun had crested the Medicine Bow range to the east, a red ball of flame behind the black quills of the forested slopes, I'd pulled fifteen brookies from the hundred-yard stretch of water, each smaller than the last. Happily, I moved thirty yards downstream to another fast run of water.

My fingers stiff from the chilly water of the river, I removed the mosquito that had been so successful on the brookies and replaced it with a hellgrammite. I tied the small fly to the leader, and looked behind me to make sure my backcast wouldn't be caught in the chokecherry bushes along the bank.

Small trout fed at the top of the run and a couple of medium-size brookies rose in the middle, but in a deep hole at the bottom, the surface rippled with the feeding of a larger fish. I stood still, watched intently as the big brown rolled to the surface, his rise so slow and confident I could see the bright red splotches of color on his thick sides.

I laid the fly into the top of the run, felt the line tremble as it navigated the current, felt the slack as it hit the calmer water of the hole, watched as the fly drifted over the spot where the brown had risen. Nothing happened, but I still felt a rush of anticipation as I retrieved the line for another try.

My second cast brought the fly too far to the left, and as my third drifted through the slow water, the brown rose to gobble a real insect.

I took a deep breath to steady my nerves and made a fourth cast. As soon as I released the line, I knew it was perfect, that it would take the bait directly over the spot where the fish had risen. I pulled the rod tip up, took hold of the excess line in my left hand, and watched as the fly drifted into good water.

He hit so hard I thought my rod would snap. The line burned through my left hand as he dived and began a powerful downstream run. I held the rod straight out as he swam, and the line cut my fingers as it raced off the reel. If I didn't stop him soon, he'd have all my line, but I couldn't check him by applying more drag. Recklessly, I stumbled downstream after him, tripping over downed trees and roots, my clothing catching on the sharp underbrush.

I hobbled after him for twenty yards, fell twice but managed to keep him on. The air burst from my lungs in great, burning gasps. The fish, meanwhile, was as strong as ever, and with only about ten yards of line left on my reel and a muddy, impassable bog before me, I realized I'd have to take a stand, grab the line, and try to stop him short. I was only using two-pound leader, so there was a better than even chance I'd lose him. A strong fish could break two-pound without missing a stroke, and this was a strong fish.

I brought the rod tip up, wrapped my bleeding fingers around the line, and waited for the fish to hit the end. But before that happened, he leapt straight out of the water, a long and graceful lunge that showed me his entire eighteen-inch body before his nose sliced the surface and he dived again.

I hate to admit this, but at that second I panicked, brought the rod above my head and held on tight. I felt a muscular tug as the fish reached the end of the line . . . and then he was gone, my slack line and torn leader floating on the surface in a gentle S shape, my heart pounding like a Marine Corps drum.

Retrieving the line, I dipped my bloody hand in the current and then took my time walking back to the Blazer, a happier man than I'd been in two days. Since I always release the trout I catch, unless I want one or two for breakfast, being emptyhanded doesn't bother me. I'd caught a few fish and lost a big one, but the process for me was better than a month of analysis.

To the east, the sun was fully above the mountains, the air fresh and sharp, my sense of smell tantalized by a symphony of fragrance, the high notes provided by Indian paintbrush, prairie gentian, bluebells, forget-me-nots, and evening stars, the pungent sage an ever present bass.

I poured myself a cup of steamy coffee from the thermos in the Blazer and sat with my back against the front tire, sipping, listening to the murmur of the river, the songs of meadowlarks and sparrows, watching a golden eagle ride the air currents above the river, his wings motionless and ramrod straight.

It was just after seven and I needed to be at the office in Laramie around eight, but I didn't want to leave, thought how wonderful it would be to sit right there for an entire day, dawdle over a good mystery and watch the ebb and flow of the prairie.

At moments like that, I often indulge myself in my favorite fantasy, the one where I quit my job, drop out of society, and build myself a comfortable cabin with huge stone fireplaces in the foothills of the Bighorns, where my family and I would live for the rest of our lives in splendid isolation. We'd all get along, a regular little Norman Rockwell family. In summer I'd teach the boys to fish and grow vegetables. We'd raise horses, cattle, goats. In winter I'd build Nicole a kiln. She'd spend her days throwing beautiful pottery. I'd write a book, work as a fishing guide.

Come evening Nicole and I would drink wine, make leisurely love on a thick sheepskin rug before a crackling fire.

The fantasy includes no telephones, no televisions, no newspapers, and only a few select visitors. In the towns and cities there'd still be rape and murder. There'd still be horrible poverty and ignorant discrimination. There'd still be brutal child abuse and criminal neglect and rampant corruption.

Even in my fantasies, I've been a policeman long enough to know that evil will flourish as long as the human race survives.

But while the daydream lasts, my family is happy and safe.

We never feel its icy touch.

Ken Keegan was waiting in my office when I arrived a little after eight, drinking coffee from my favorite mug and resting his size 10 wing tips on the top of my desk, the morning's *Casper Star Tribune* folded sloppily in his lap. His suit coat, as always, looked as if he might have slept in it, and the knot in his tie was already loosened. His jacket had fallen open far enough to give me a clear look at the 9-millimeter SIG-Sauer in his brown leather shoulder holster.

I was surprised to see him there, but immensely pleased. It had been several months, and I'd missed him. Smiling broadly, I hurried across the room to grab his big paw in both my hands and gave him a sloppy bear hug.

I pushed myself away to look at him, and as usual, the sight was amusing. An investigator for the state Department of Criminal Investigation in Cheyenne, the only word that adequately describes Ken Keegan is square. His square head rests on a stocky, square body, which he drapes with baggy, square clothing. He's got a short, square haircut. His ears are square. Square white teeth. Even his nose is square.

We'd crossed paths many times during my years in Victory, worked a few investigations together, began socializing and eventually became close—at least, as close as a couple hoary old dinosaurs like us ever get. I think he respects me, because at one point, he'd even offered me a job at the DCI, a position I told him I'd have to think about.

"How do, podna," I said happily. I vaguely remembered he'd been away tracking a suspected killer in the northern part of the state. "Looks like you've kept your topknot—what's left of it."

He blushed and ran a ham-size fist across the top of his head. He's incredibly self-conscious about his receding hairline, and it tickles me to remind him of it at every opportunity.

"Up yours, Starbranch," he said, laughing. "If you want to use all your manly hormones growing hair, I guess that's your business. Me, I'd rather save 'em for pleasures of the conjugal variety."

He nodded at the newspaper, now lying in a crumpled heap on the floor. I could see a front page story about the murders at the McAfferty ranch, the discovery of Hathaway's body at Elk Mountain, and a sidebar that outlined my sinking campaign and Baldi's charges of incompetence in the sheriff's office. My picture was in the sidebar box with a drophead stating that, "Starbranch refuses comment on charges he planted evidence in the murder case." The photograph was several months old, and I wondered if they'd used a special lens to make my jowls so droopy.

"I guess I don't have to ask how you are, Harry," he said. "Jesus, trouble follows you like a redbone hound on a heated bitch, don't it? I bet you're wishin' you'd taken that job."

I motioned him back to the seat behind my desk. "Hell yes," I said. I settled myself heavily on the railroad bench, bent down to scrape a gooey glob of river mud from the toe of my boot. "Public office isn't quite the madcap adventure I expected. The offer still stand?"

"Nah." He laughed. "We kept it open as long as we could and ended up hiring some twenty-eight-year-old yuppie from Portland. So far, he's taken more than four weeks off to stay home with his wife and be a 'quality parent' to his eighteen-month-old kid. Not a single arrest, either."

"The new breed of lawman," I said. "Emotionally sensitive, knee-jerk liberal, politically correct."

"And a royal pain in the ass if you ask me." Keegan scowled. "It's like working with Phil Donahue. Guys like you and me, Harry, our days are numbered."

"Yeah, that's what the graybeards said when we picked up a badge too, Ken, and as far as I can see, nothing's changed a hell of a lot since. Give this kid ten years and he'll be just another thickheaded, right-wing flatfoot, worried about living long enough to collect his pension and complaining about the eager young punks who came in after him."

"I suppose you're right," he said. He swirled the dregs of his coffee around in my mug and stared into the brew, making a face like he'd seen something disgusting in the bottom of the cup. "I think it's the coffee that does it, Harry. It's the same in every cop shop I've ever been in, and god only knows what drinking it for twenty years will do to the arteries that supply your brain cells, let alone your Johnson. It's probably worse for you than rubbing alcohol. At least with alcohol you don't have to worry about worms."

We sat for fifteen minutes, made small talk, caught up on each other's families, people we'd worked with, and mutual friends. The phone rang several times, but I ignored it, asked the secretary to take messages. Finally, there was a lull in the conversation and Keegan sighed, massaging his temples with his fingertips. For the first time I noticed that the lines around his eyes had deepened since I'd seen him last. He looked like he could use a decent night's sleep.

"You remember why I went up north to the Meeteetse country last winter?" he asked.

"You were looking into some murders up there, weren't you? Coupla bodies somebody found out in the bush? You find out who did it?"

"Oh yeah," he said. "I know who did it. Never any question, really."

"So it's over? You made the arrest?"

"Nah," he said. "That's the trouble. I know who did it, but I can't prove it. Not a single fucking shred of evidence in eight months of work."

There was a clear note of bitterness in Keegan's voice, and I pondered it while he pulled a rumpled pack of smokes from the inside pocket of his suit coat and fired one up with his ancient Zippo. When he had it going, he sucked in a deep lungful of smoke and held the cigarette between his teeth while he shucked his jacket and draped it over the back of his chair. His wilted white shirt bloused out around the straps of his shoulder holster, which looked about three sizes too tight for his frame. He slipped out of the holster and laid the weapon on my desk. It smelled of leather and oil, a pleasant combination.

I waited while he smoked and made himself comfortable, which I figured he'd accomplished when he leaned back in the chair and rested his feet on the rim of my desk. There was a small hole in the sole of his shoe. "Anything you can talk about?" I asked. "Sounds like a good story."

He nodded, finishing the butt and grinding it out in the glass ashtray, immediately lighting another. "It is a good story, Harry," he said. "But so far, that's all it is. A good story."

I had time to listen and told him so, then got out the makings for a fresh pot. When the machine started to gurgle, I sat back down on the bench, leaned back, and folded my arms behind my head. Listening mode.

Keegan didn't seem to know quite where to begin. He watched tendrils of smoke from his cigarette drift toward the ceiling, rubbed his forehead with his free hand. I waited patiently, using an unbent paper clip to clean the gunk from my fingernails.

"You recall reading about a guy named Saul Irons, used to be the chief of police down in Flagstaff?" Keegan asked finally.

The name rang a bell, but I couldn't place it. I shrugged my shoulders and sniffed the air, which was filling with the steamy aroma of fresh coffee. Couple more minutes and it'd be ready to drink. I threw the paper clip at the trash can and it went in without touching rim. Two points.

"Sorry, pal. Should I remember?"

"Nah," Keegan said. "No reason you would. The guy was big news in the late seventies. Had some high-powered program going to crack down on drugs. But then he caught one of his own patrolmen selling heroin from his patrol car and shot the bastard dead. Maybe it was self-defense, like he claimed. Maybe it wasn't. Whatever, the district attorney never brought a case."

"And Irons?" I asked.

"He walked, but there were enough questions it ruined his career," Keegan said. "He resigned in Flagstaff and moved around for a couple of years, looking to hire on with another department. Had doors slammed in his face every place he applied." He shook his head. "It was too bad. The guy was a hell of a cop."

I began to recall Irons and his story—it had been the talk of nearly every department in the Rocky Mountain West for a few months—dragging bits and pieces of memory from the dusty storage boxes in my brain. Still, I couldn't imagine what he had to do with Keegan or the reason for his visit to my office. I poured us both a cup of coffee, took a sip, and balanced the cup on my knee.

Keegan left his cup sitting on the desk and stood up, the cartilage in his knees snapping like popcorn. When he'd worked the kinks out of his leg muscles, he went to the window and looked outside.

"That's where the tale starts to get strange," he said. He turned around to face me again, pointed across the room at his briefcase. "I've got it all in there," he said. "You can read the details later, but here's the thumbnail."

I nodded my agreement, and he continued.

"About eight years ago, we started hearing rumors that since he couldn't find work as a cop, Irons had taken up a new profession. With rustling on the increase and not a hell of a lot of interest in controlling it, a bunch of ranchers down in southern Colorado decided they needed to hire a modern-day version of the old range regulators."

I knew what he was talking about, but I let him go on.

"The old-time regulators were private detectives, sort of, except those guys didn't play by normal rules," he said. "If they were smart, the crooks moved somewhere else. If they weren't, they often just disappeared. Quite a few of them eventually turned up dead. And the regulators—"

"Like Tom Horn," I said, cutting him off.

He nodded. "Exactly."

Like almost everyone around these parts, I know Horn's story well. An ex-lawman turned professional killer, he was hired by the Wyoming Stockgrowers Association in 1894 to bring down the rustlers who were stealing livestock off the open ranges with joyful abandon. Horn made his employers happy by stalking the hated rustlers with almost supernatural patience and trail savvy, catching them in the act of stealing cattle or horses and killing them on the spot with a .30-30 Winchester rifle, a gun he fired from ambush, blowing holes the size of saucers in the miscreants.

He signed his work by placing a rock under the heads of his victims and leaving their bloating bodies for someone else—often their families or friends—to find. And while there's no way of tallying Horn's actual body count, since there's lots of room for bodies around here and not many people to discover them, he's credited in some circles with killing as many as fifteen stock thieves and scaring off all but the most foolhardy survivors.

The scourge of the rustler class in southeastern Wyoming, the darling of the stockgrowers, and a man who claimed to be a personal friend of the governor, the lean and taciturn Horn was a law unto himself on these windblown plains. At least until July 1901, when he made an error in judgment in the Laramie mountains and dry-gulched Willie Nickell, a thirteen-year-old boy he mistook for a rustler, a slaying so cowardly that even his pals in the powerful Stockgrowers Association couldn't protect him.

After an emotional trial, he was convicted, sentenced, and executed for murder in Cheyenne in November 1903. But even as Horn's neck was snapping at the end of a hangman's rope, the controversy over the events leading to his demise was gathering a full head of steam. Did he really kill young Willie Nickell, or was he framed? Was his cause noble, just, and true? Or was he simply a bloodthirsty and lethal bully with a good rifle, a steady hand, and an itchy trigger finger?

Get more than two people together in Wyoming even today, and chances are that none of them will agree on the answers to any of those questions. As a matter of fact, the only thing they will generally agree on is the fact that Horn is dead, has been for ninety years.

"Everybody remembers Horn," I said smugly. "I've read books about him. Seen his damn movie. Steve McQueen. He worked this country."

Keegan scowled at the interruption, lit another cigarette while he tried to regain his train of thought. Chagrined, I sat back and kept my mouth shut.

"He worked this country until he got himself *hanged,*" Keegan said. His emphasis on the word implied approval, but the look of challenge in his eye discouraged argument on the matter. Not that I had any intention of arguing. With Keegan, I've found arguing an entertaining diversion but fruitless on account of his general muleheadedness. I grinned to let him know I wasn't interested in debating Tom Horn and took a long sip of coffee.

"Anyway," Keegan said, "the word in Colorado was that the man those ranchers hired to control rustling in the early eighties was Saul Irons, and in six or seven years he pretty much eliminated livestock theft in a big part of southern Colorado." Keegan turned away from the window and sat back down in the chair. "There was a lot of talk about missing rustlers, but no bodies were ever found, and the guy was very cooperative with the local police and sheriff's offices. There were never any charges. The locals didn't have much to do with him personally. They were afraid of him. But they felt better having him around. He probably could have stayed on there as long as he wanted."

"But?"

"But he didn't. He moved to Meeteetse last summer," Keegan said. "And right away, we started hearing the same sort of things. People missing who never turned up, talk that Irons was being paid five thousand dollars for every rustler he put out of commission, permanently or otherwise, rumors of a secret group of ranchers who were funding his efforts under the table. The DCI sent me up there to take a look in November."

Keegan rubbed the bags under his eyes. Those things got any bigger, he could use them for overnight cases. "And?" I asked.

"And nothing," Keegan said angrily. "I came up dryer'n fifty miles of dirt road. I probably spent a total of a hundred hours talking to Saul Irons, but we both knew I was just pulling my own dick. I had nothing. Not even any evidence that a crime or crimes had been committed. We ended up spending most of our time together playing poker."

"How'd he say he made his living?" I asked.

"Said he was looking for historical artifacts," Keegan explained, rolling his eyes. "That's why he spent most of his time in the bush. And in fact he'd sold a few things to the Buffalo Bill museum in Cody, and some pieces to a couple Indian museums in the area. Didn't make much money, but it was enough to get by, the way he was living."

"Maybe he didn't do anything, Ken," I said, playing devil's advocate, just to keep myself in the conversation. "Maybe the guy just wanted to go off by himself and start over."

"Oh he did it, all right," Keegan said emphatically. "All that was rumored and more. I know a killer when I see one, Harry, and the first time I saw him, I knew Saul Irons was a stone killer. Felt it in my gut. Saw it in his eyes, the way he moved—like a cat, you know. A leopard maybe, a panther. The guy's a black belt in some kind of kung fu shit, an expert marksman, tracker, horseman, survivalist. Used to teach hand-to-hand combat at the Arizona Police Academy. He spends three hours most days practicing karate, two hours loading his own ammunition, and another two hours shooting it at paper targets. Throws a Bowie knife at a big hunk of tree stump in his back yard."

Keegan leaned forward and rested his arms on the edge of my desk. The muscles in his thick forearms were bunched and his square jaw was as tight as spring steel. "Does that sound like an amateur archaeologist to you?" he challenged. "Sound like the kind of guy who wanders around with a little shovel digging up arrowheads and pottery?"

He had a point. "None I'd want to meet," I said placatingly. "But what does that have to do with today, Ken? What does it have to do with why you're here?"

Keegan must have realized that he seemed a bit too tightly wrapped, because he took a deep breath and laughed self-consciously. I wondered how many times he'd had a version of this same conversation with his bosses at the DCI. Keegan hates being on the defensive.

When he spoke again, his voice was softer and had lost its edge. "Maybe it's coincidence," he said. "Maybe it's not. All I know is that a few months ago, the rumor mill had Irons leaving the Meeteetse country and moving south in this direction to work for some local stockmen. I know for a fact he moved because I watched him go, but I don't know why he moved with any certainty. He said he was gonna come down here and pan for gold. But now I read in the paper where these bodies—bodies of people suspected of rustling—are turning up around Albany County."

"Skates and Hathaway?" I asked.

He nodded grimly. "I think Saul Irons may have finally screwed up by leaving bodies where they'd be found. I think it's time to make him as uncomfortable as a pair of cheap shoes. I think it's time to prove this son of a bitch is a criminal. I think your current cases and mine may overlap."

He let that sink in. "I think we oughta work together," he said.

I didn't have to consider his offer for long. It made sense, since his department's resources are larger than mine. Besides, we make a good team. "You think we can find him?" I asked.

"No problem," he said smugly. "He's living in a cabin out on the North Fork near Bosler. I can take you out and introduce you two this afternoon. I've got a couple of errands to run first, but if you're not doing anything around twelve, twelve-thirty . . ."

My confusion and skepticism must have been apparent, because Keegan laughed. He reached for another cigarette, lit it, and inhaled happily.

A veil of exhaled smoke covered his face when he spoke. "He's not hiding, Harry," he said. "He even called me before he moved there to make sure I had directions in case I wanted to play a few hands of stud. I think he likes me."

"And do you like him?" I asked incredulously.

Keegan gave me a go-figure shrug. "What's not to like?" he asked. "For a cold-blooded killer, he's a hell of a nice guy."

At ten o'clock that morning, Coroner James Bowen sat on the railroad bench in my office, wiping his glasses with a handkerchief and sniffling from a summer cold. He'd dropped by because the DCI had faxed me the lab results from the evidence we'd collected at the McAfferty corral, and I thought he'd want to know what they showed as soon as possible, since Tess had been calling him every couple of hours to ask when he'd release Colleen's body for burial. He'd already officially ruled her death a murder, but he didn't want her buried until he knew there was nothing more to be learned from her corpse.

I'd read the reports while I waited for him to arrive, so as he began to peruse them, I chewed on what they said, tried to get beyond the anger and sorrow I felt so I could think objectively.

According to the DCI, it was impossible without expensive DNA testing to be one-hundred-percent certain whether some of the semen found in Colleen's vagina and on her thighs and pubic area came from Ralphie Skates, but since he was a secretor with relatively rare AB-negative blood and that corresponded with semen collected on and in her body, it was a good bet she'd been raped by Skates. Analysis of sperm diaphorase, an enzyme used to identify genetic markers in fresh secretions, tended to confirm this theory.

The skin and blood under her fingernails were also a match, and the lab was also able to match Skates's pubic hair with hair combed from Colleen's pubic area.

As troubling as those findings were, however, the lab report noted that pubic hairs from at least one other individual were discovered on Colleen's corpse, and there was a significant amount of semen from one or more nonsecretors found in her vagina, and on her body and clothing.

She was raped by more than one person, it appeared, but there was nearly conclusive evidence she'd been murdered by Skates. Although most people don't know it, you can get fingerprints from human skin, and prints taken from Colleen's throat were an exact match with Ralphie's.

Since Fatty Winston had custody of Clarence Hathaway's body and any lab testing would come at his request, if and when he got around to asking, there was no way for us to know whether the type O blood discovered by Bowen at the side of the corral came from Hathaway, or whether Hathaway had taken part in the gang rape of Colleen McAfferty.

Two additional items of interest were contained in the report, however.

First, examination of the bullet fragment found in Skates's oral cavity led the DCI's analyst to offer a preliminary judgment that although it was too badly damaged to link it to a specific weapon, Bowen had been correct when he said it had been fired from a high-powered hunting rifle of uncertain caliber. The shooter, the lab report confirmed, used expanding soft-point ammunition.

Second, the wheelbase measurements and tire casts from the murder scene had been matched with those of a Chinook livestock trailer, a big one that could hold up to a dozen animals. Judging from the lack of wear, the lab concluded that either the trailer was new or it had just gotten a new set of rubber. Those tires had obliterated the tracks of the vehicle pulling it.

As Bowen continued to read, I went next door to Pajak's office and found him huddled in conversation with T.A. Jacobs, a deputy who'd been on probation for the past two months for using his department vehicle on a fishing trip. The men looked up when I entered, Jacobs ashen and subdued, deep worry lines etched across his forehead and the corners of his mouth. Pajak looked stern and angry. He'd obviously been chewing Jacobs out for some new infraction, but I didn't ask about the nature of the beef, since Pajak would put it in writing before day's end.

Pajak's irritation at my intrusion was apparent. "What can I do for you, Harry?" he asked curtly.

I stood in the doorway and made no move to enter. "Real quick," I said, "did you check with the county clerk to see what vehicles were registered to Bobby Snow?"

Pajak sighed, doing me a big favor. "I did. I was gonna tell you first thing this morning, but you've been busy."

"And?" I asked expectantly.

"And he's got your usual collection of ranch clunkers, as well as a brand new fifth-wheel Ford truck," Pajak said smugly. "I expect he uses it to pull his new Chinook trailer. Or at least he did. I hear he filed reports that they were both stolen Sunday."

"Thanks," I said. I backed out, closed the door as I went. As I walked down the hallway, I allowed myself a small smile at this information, my first smidgen of evidence linking Bobby Snow to the killings of Colleen McAfferty, Ralphie Skates, and Clarence Hathaway. Granted, it was circumstantial, and not even particularly damning. Snow had taken steps to cover himself by filing the stolen-vehicle reports, and there was nothing to even suggest he'd been at the scene of the murders. But it was a start, and as the old saw reminds us, the longest journey begins with a single step.

By the time I returned to my own office, Bowen had finished with the lab reports. He stood at the windows with his hands clasped behind his back, like a sailor at parade rest. His chin was nearly resting on his chest. He turned around when he heard me enter, his face dark and brooding.

"You know Harry, it's been almost a decade since we had a murder in Albany County."

It was a statement of fact that didn't warrant a response. I let it hang in the air between us until he was ready to go on.

"But now," he said, shaking his head sadly, "I can't get over the feeling that things are changing for the worse."

"A couple of bodies will do that to you, Jim," I said softly, "especially when one of them is—"

"I haven't been able to get them out of my mind," he broke in before I could finish. "I see her face and it . . ."

I watched the emotions passing over his face, waited while he found words. "We have this idea that in Albany County, people are safe," he said finally. "We believe we're good people. We look out for our neighbors, for their kids. This sort of thing just doesn't happen here. You know what I mean?"

"I know Jim," I said. "We've been lucky."

"But it's slipping away," he said. "Tess lost a daughter out there, and it makes me sick. Hell, Harry, I've only done a few autopsies like that, ones where there was violence. And I knew this kid."

I crossed the room and put my hand on Bowen's shoulder, squeezed tightly to show I understood. He looked down, and when he looked back up, he was fighting tears, the moisture collecting in the corners of his brown eyes. He choked them back, took a deep breath, swallowed hard.

"You'll release her body today?" I asked.

He nodded.

"We'll go to the funeral together, Jim," I said.

He looked into my face, touched my arm with his strong hand. "Yeah, we'll go to the funeral," he said. "But Harry, when they put that little girl's body in the ground, they'll bury a big part of us with her."

I spent the rest of the morning at my desk, trying to move the investigation forward by telephone.

The watch commander in Fatty Winston's office said the sheriff had gone over to Old Baldy in Saratoga to play golf with a bunch of oil company executives and wasn't expected back in the office until the next morning. No, the watch commander said, he didn't know if the sheriff had sent evidence from the Hathaway killing to the state lab, and no, he didn't know when the coroner's report would be available, and no, he wouldn't call me even if they became available that day.

"You'd have to get that from Fatty," he grumbled. "We got a policy."

"Of course you do," I said sarcastically. "You'll have him call me?"

"I'll tell him you were looking for him," the watch commander corrected me. "After that, I guess it's up to him. I imagine he'll get back to you though."

"But I shouldn't hold my breath, right?"

"What's that?"

"Never mind," I snapped, and slammed down the receiver.

I didn't have any better luck connecting with C.J. Fall, who'd been in the field since before sunrise. After about a dozen dead ends, I did finally get hold of his number-two man, a lanky Texan named John Bell, whom I'd met a couple of times in the courthouse. I caught Bell at home on his lunch hour.

"What can we do for ya'll, Sheriff?" he asked, munching as he talked. In the background, I could hear a flock of kids arguing over a baseball game, one of them yelling that you could too go to base if the catcher dropped the ball on a third strike.

I explained that I was trying to link Bobby Snow to the murder of Colleen McAfferty and told him his boss had promised to let me know if any of his colleagues saw a horse like Jezebel at any of the kill plants under their observation.

"But what I want to know," I said, "is if there's any way to increase the surveillance? It feels to me like we're depending on luck here, and I don't like that much. I need to know for sure if that horse turns up and who brought it."

Bell was sympathetic, but not very optimistic.

"Usually, when we go to the plants ourselves," he explained, "we're following animals we know were stolen to a specific destination. In this case, we don't know where the McAfferty critters are being taken, so the only way we could be sure to find them is if we watched every likely destination point. And the only way we could do that is if some of our people, or some of your people, stay on the floor of each plant between Canada and Oklahoma for the next few days.

"We don't have the manpower for that sort of thing," he said apologetically. "Do you?"

I didn't, and even if I did, I didn't have the money to send deputies across state and national borders.

"Then what do we do?" I asked.

"We wait," he said. "It ain't the best approach, but you'd be surprised how many rustlers we've caught this way. Our people know to be on the lookout, and if that horse is sold somewhere where there's no brand inspection, we've got a fair to middlin' chance of hearing about it."

After I talked to Bell, I tried several times to reach Tess McAfferty but met a busy signal each time. On the fifth attempt, a man answered but said Tess had gone out and wouldn't be home until evening. I told him I'd call back and hung up.

A few minutes past noon, I put on my hat and sunglasses, and checked in with the dispatcher to let her know where I was going and that I wouldn't be back in the office that afternoon. Then I strolled out to the stone front steps of the courthouse to wait for Keegan, who'd promised to pick me up.

It was another hot day, the sunlight so bright it hurt my eyes. The skies were a vivid blue, empty of clouds from horizon to horizon. The harsh light flooded down on the city, brought out the luxurious colors of summer with stunning clarity, even the browns of the granite buildings and the dried flowers, but especially the emerald greens of the lawn and the shimmering leaves of the trees. The sun's heat rose in waves from the asphalt on the street and from the tops of the automobiles waiting for the light to change on Grand. A pair of long-legged brown young women in cutoff jeans and halter tops ambled down the sidewalk in the direction of the business district, their fluttering hands punctuating their animated conversation.

All in all, it was a fine summer afternoon, a day for the living, a day a kid on summer vacation would find filled with incredible promise. It was a day for thinking about love, about fun, about life. On that bright August afternoon, my recent conversation with Bowen and my own thoughts of death seemed oddly out of place.

I saw Keegan's black Ford a block away and started down the steps to meet him, but before I even reached the bottom step my campaign manager burst out the doors of the courthouse building behind me.

"Harry," Calhoun called as he bounded down the steps. "You weren't gonna go without me were ya?"

I was confused. "What?" I said.

"I'm your campaign manager," he said. "I need to be on hand to assess the damage."

I realized then why he was there. Baldi's press conference was scheduled to begin at one o'clock. Calhoun wanted to be in the audience when Baldi made his charges that I was a poor excuse for a law officer and probably a liar to boot. He wanted to help me craft a response, plot a strategy to save my campaign.

"I'm not going," I said as I turned away and steamed off toward Keegan's Ford. The metal tip of my walking stick tapped out an angry tattoo.

Calhoun had to run to catch up. "What do you mean you're not going?" he asked. He stepped in front of me to block my progress, moved with me when I tried to walk around him.

"It means what it means," I said angrily. "I'm not going. Baldi is bullshit. This Slaymaker business is bullshit. And I don't have time for it. You may have forgotten this, Larry, but I'm in the middle of a murder investigation, and that takes precedence."

He let me go, stood with his hands balled on his hips while I opened the passenger-side door of Keegan's car and eased myself inside. Keegan had his jacket off and the air conditioner blasting. Patsy Cline was on the radio.

"You remember this when Anthony Baldi is moving into your office," Calhoun yelled as I slammed the door. "Remember it when you're back in Victory writin' traffic tickets and that smug little prick is pinnin' on your fucking sheriff's badge."

As we drove away, I figured I'd remember it very well indeed.

# SEVEN

In the twenties Bosler, the little ranching community north of Laramie, was spicier than five-alarm chili, at least when your standard of measurement is towns of under a thousand residents located more than a thousand miles from the nearest major-league sports franchise. The hub of activity for the ranchers, railroad men, and bootleggers, it was served by at least two dance halls, a lively motel, one auto dealership, and a café where they served sixteen-ounce porterhouse steaks for under a buck.

The glory days ended along with Prohibition, however, and these days the place is almost a ghost town. The government keeps the post office open, and there's a working auction barn at the south end of town where nearly everyone from Bosler and neighboring Rock River congregates on Sunday. But for the most part, Bosler is just a depressing wide spot on the highway, overrun by tumbleweeds, littered with empty beer bottles and junked cars.

We turned northeast at Bosler on Highway 34, a picturesque road that follows the forks of Sybille Creek through the Sybille Canyon until it dumps you out on the dreary plains near Wheatland, the most boring community on planet Earth, unless you like polka music.

The heat rose off the scorched prairie grass and asphalt in

sweltering waves. I sat back in the comfortable seat, let the air-conditioning blow against my chest, and watched the canyon walls and bluffs roll by, the sun spilling down their sides like paint. To the left, I caught occasional glimpses of the cool blue waters of Sybille Creek, almost hidden in places by thick growths of willow, thimbleberry, ninebark, wild plum, and bitterbrush.

About halfway through the Sybille is the Sybille Research Unit where the state keeps a few scraggly bighorn sheep, elk, and deer, but we left the highway and turned south about three miles before we reached the facility, the car slipping and bouncing over the ruts of the rugged Jeep trail leading to Irons's cabin at the junction of Goat Creek and Berner Creek. Keegan grimaced as the front wheel on the driver's side dropped into a rocky eroded rut and the undercarriage banged against the top of a granite boulder protruding through the ground.

He sawed the steering wheel to keep the rear end of the car from slipping into the rut. "Damn," he swore. "I wonder if I've got an oil pan left."

I looked out the back window, squinted through our trail of dust, didn't see any oil slicks on the roadway. "City boys, city drivers" I grumbled, holding on to the dashboard with both hands to keep myself from being pitched into his lap. "If you'd like me to take the wheel, Ken, just pull over at the first wide spot. I don't think my body can stand much more of your navigation."

Keegan was still mumbling profanities when the front wheel popped out of the rut and we were able to continue at a breathtaking five miles an hour. He gripped the steering wheel so hard his knuckles turned white.

"Who owns this land?" I asked as we came to a relatively smooth stretch of road leading through a meadow choked with buffalo grass and blue gamma. We drove slowly into the middle of a herd of cattle congregated around a stock trough, Black Angus mixed with a few purebred Simentals. One of the animals sprawled in the middle of the road, and we waited for it to lumber to its feet and move a few steps off the roadside, slobbering profusely and glowering at us for disturbing its siesta.

"It's patented ranchland mostly," Keegan explained, "with a few sections of Bureau of Land Management and state land sprinkled in for good measure. Right now, you're on the old Wilbur Hardesty ranch. The cabin where Irons is living sits right along its southern border."

"You know Hardesty?" I asked.

"Never met the man." Keegan chuckled. "He's been dead for twenty years. These days, the ranch is owned by a group of Chicago investors. They bought it from his widow a couple years after he kicked off. Only people who live here full time are the foreman—fella named Barry Hart, his place is up on Prairie Dog Creek—and Irons, of course, at least for the time being."

Keegan's story about the Hardesty ranch is an all too common tale in modern Wyoming, where small livestock growers are rapidly becoming as rare as black-footed ferrets. These days, the only folk who can really afford to raise cattle are ultrarich tycoons and conglomerates who use the ranching losses as a tax write-off. It's a sad state of affairs if you ask me, the true end of a romantic era. And yet, I read every year where the eastern liberals and other people who've never seen a cow that isn't wrapped in cellophane at the supermarket want to increase grazing fees on public lands once again, which would make it even more difficult for the remaining family ranches to keep from sliding off the precipice of financial solvency.

Irons's cabin was a simple two-room post-and-beam affair built from rough-hewn pine logs, its sides a warm, deep brown from sealant and exposure to the elements. There was a wide front porch with a rickety breakfast table, and the high-pitched roof was covered with new tar shingles. At least a cord of split wood was stacked against the north wall of the cabin and the building's stone chimney.

The front door was open, and a well-kept blue and white Chevy four-wheel-drive was parked in the small gravel parking area off the porch. About twenty-five yards from the rear of the building, a small corral built of lodgepole pine and scrub held a fine-looking Appaloosa gelding and a couple scruffy packhorses, whose heads were lowered lethargically in the heat. A worn western saddle was draped across the top rail of the corral, and there was a small shed for pack gear near the gate.

The report of the first rifle shot cracked down the canyon from somewhere behind the cabin as soon as we'd gotten out of the car, the sound of lightning striking close enough to pucker your sphincter.

From reflex, I threw myself to the ground and rolled away from the vehicle, fumbling with the safety strap on my Blackhawk as I went. By the time I'd rolled a half dozen feet, I was able to draw the revolver, and I came up on one knee. I held the weapon in a two-handed shooter's grip as I swept the front of the cabin and the area near the corral with the muzzle. My heart hammered, my eyes felt wide as salad plates, and I spit dirt, but I didn't imagine for a second that I looked especially amusing.

That's why it took me a minute to realize that Keegan was still standing by the front fender of the Ford, laughing like a maniac.

When the report of the second round reached us a second later, he cackled even louder, and with the third, I thought he might actually do himself some serious internal damage.

He pointed to a small hillock about seventy-five yards behind the cabin. "Up there," he said. "I told ya, the guy spends every afternoon target-practicing."

I tried to focus my eyes against the glare and finally saw the shooter kneeling atop the hill at the base of a five-foot sage. He held a scoped rifle against his shoulder, pointed away from us at a target out of view. As I watched, he let go another round, and his upper body bucked from the recoil. He gave no indication he'd seen us, but something told me we hadn't escaped his attention.

I stood, jammed my revolver back in the holster, dusted the powdery soil from the knees of my pants and the front of my shirt. "That was real goddamn funny, Ken," I said.

"Yeah," he said. "It sure was. I especially liked the part where you rolled in the horseshit."

Cautiously, I ran my hand down the back of my pants and sure enough, there it was, still wet and fairly fragrant. I knocked the biggest hunks free, but I could already feel the dampness of the stain soaking through the cloth.

"On the way back home, you ride in the trunk," Keegan sniggered. Before I could think of a witty rejoinder he had turned away and was walking in the direction of the rifleman, laughing as he went.

I followed as best I could, picking my way through the minefield of manure around the corral, the cactus, and the slippery shale on the hillside. Irons didn't acknowledge us until we were less than six feet away, and even then he didn't turn around to say hello, simply grunted a greeting and continued to load copper hunting cartridges into the magazine of his 7-millimeter Remington. On a blanket at his side, there were two more rifles, a .30-06 Winchester and a custom model I didn't recognize, as well as a green army-issue metal ammunition case filled with boxed cartridges and a pair of high-powered binoculars.

About eight feet away in the sparse shade of the sage, a hungry-looking Doberman watched us warily, his tongue lolling from the side of his toothy mouth as he panted in the heat. The animal started to rise, but Irons stopped it with a quick hand command. The dog lay back down, but grudgingly, the muscles in its heavy shoulders bunched and tense.

Irons slammed the bolt home and carefully placed the rifle on the blanket. "Ken Keegan," he said finally. "To what do I owe the honor of this visit? You feelin' like a little poker?"

He stood to shake hands with Ken and looked questioningly in my direction. About fifty years old, Irons had the lean bow-legged body of a lifelong horseman. His stomach was flat, his thighs corded and muscular. His face, with its hawk nose and the widow's peak at his hairline, was all sharp angles. He wore a carefully groomed handlebar mustache and the kind of goatee made popular by Buffalo Bill Cody, just a narrow sliver of black hair bisecting his chin. His eyes, slate gray and piercing, provided startling counterpoint to the deep brown skin of his weatherworn face. At about six feet, he was a little shorter than me but not quite as heavy. I figured him for about 175, 180. Not bad for an older fella, I thought.

"I brought a friend, Saul," Keegan explained. "This is Harry Starbranch."

"I know who you are," Irons said as he reached to take my hand. His grip was rough and strong, the muscles of his forearms whipcord lean. "I keep meanin' to drop by your office and introduce myself, but I just haven't gotten around to it yet. At any rate, welcome. You gents feel like a beer? Some iced tea?"

"Nah," Keegan said, "we can't stay long. But thanks anyway."

I nodded at the custom rifle on the blanket.

"Nice piece," I said. "What is it?"

"It's a .22-.454 coyote rifle" he said proudly. "Dick Casull made it for me. You know him?"

I did indeed, as does anyone familiar with firearms in this part of the country. A Mormon gunmaker whose headquarters are in Freedom, Wyoming, Casull has made a name for himself as the designer and manufacturer of the world's largest handgun, a .454 mag capable of driving a slug completely through a sheet of quarter-inch steel, as well as the world's smallest handgun, a four-shot .22 derringer tiny enough to wear on your belt buckle. One round from the big .454 will do as much damage as six rounds from a .357, and the little buckle gun is the ultimate in lethal jewelry. Casull also designed the .290 carbine, which holds 290 rounds of .22-caliber ammunition in a carousel magazine and fires 1,300 rounds a minute when converted to fully automatic.

As far as I knew, however, the .22-.454 was something new.

Irons passed me the rifle and I admired the detail work on the breech, the buttery finish of the finely checkered walnut stock, the expensive German scope. When I finished, he handed me a cartridge that looked like some sort of bizarre experiment, the chunky brass over an inch long and tapered at the front to hold a small pointed slug completely out of proportion to the powder charge.

"It's a .22-caliber bullet powered by a .454 cartridge," he said. "Nearly flat trajectory for over a thousand yards. Develops a velocity of forty-two hundred feet per second, faster than the speed of sound. Like strapping a rocket to a BB. Coyotes are dead before they ever hear the sound of the gun."

I watched his face as I dropped the cartridge back in the palm of his hand. "People too?" I asked.

His gray eyes narrowed, but he didn't rise to the bait.

"I wouldn't know about people," he said flatly, "although I hear the military is interested in a modified version for snipers. Me, I only use it for varmints."

"Sure you do," Keegan said. "Two-legged ones, mostly. Who you workin' for these days, Saul?"

Irons smiled, pulled a pack of Blackjack licorice gum from his shirt pocket, folded a stick into his mouth, and offered the pack around. We both shook our heads. "I'm workin' for myself, like always," he said. "A little prospectin', coyote huntin', diggin' for fossils. Come winter, I might move on down to southern Arizona, see if I can't hire on as a ranch hand. Until then—"

"We've got bodies this time, Saul," Keegan interrupted. "Two of 'em. You care to tell us how it happened?"

Irons shook his head, tucked the back of his shirt in, and reached down for his hat, a short-brimmed sweat-stained Resistol.

"You know, I heard about those killin's on the radio yesterday mornin' and I said to myself, 'You better tidy the house, because you're about to get a visit from the law," he said. "We been over all this before, Ken. I ain't no damn murderer, and you've never had a scrap of evidence to suggest otherwise. I'm just an honest ex-cop tryin' to get by."

"An honest ex-cop who just happens to be around whenever rustlers start turning up missing, or dead," Keegan said. "That's too much serendipity for me."

Irons's eyes crinkled when he heard Keegan use the word *serendipity*. I guess mine did too. "You mean those guys up in Meeteetse?" Irons asked. "You never had a body, Ken. One day next winter, those two old boys will show up again, hale and hearty. Hell, you know how it is with that kind, get a wild hair and take off for Oklahoma. They'll turn up, you'll see."

"And what about Ralphie Skates? Clarence Hathaway?" Keegan asked. "They get a wild hair, too?"

"No," Irons said. "They got themselves killed. But I didn't do it. I was out here all day Sunday. You can ask the foreman if you want. We worked all afternoon and most of the evenin' tryin' to find a couple heifers that broke through the fence. Didn't get back here till after ten."

"We'll check," Keegan said. "But even if he verifies your alibi, it won't mean anything except you're on his payroll too. How many other ranchers are paying you to regulate their places, Saul? It's got to be a lot of ground for one man to cover."

Irons laughed. "You never give up, do you? You get one idea in your head and there's never room for another one. Take my word for it, Ken, you're wastin' your time. Wastin' the sheriff's time, too."

With that, he turned and walked off in the direction of his targets, which were lined up on wooden frames against an overhanging embankment about two hundred yards away. We waited in silence as his long legs ate up the ground, watched as he ripped the targets from their stands and sauntered back to us with the paper bull's-eyes in his hand. When he returned to his blanket and weapons, he threw the targets casually on top of the ammunition box, where they fanned open on impact.

"Listen guys," he said. "If you're not doin' anythin' Saturday, why don't you both come out here and bring your fishin' poles?"

Keegan mumbled a noncommittal answer, but my attention was on the targets Irons had been working when we arrived. The man had taken approximately twenty-four shots at the three targets, eight at each—and not a single round had hit more than an inch from the X marking the center of the bull's-eye.

I nodded appreciatively. "Not bad," I said. I fancy myself a decent marksman, but on my best day I can't approach that level of consistency. Certainly not at two hundred yards.

"It's not me," he said humbly, and pointed at the .22-.454. "It's the weapon. Like I said, the trajectory on that thing is as flat as my ex-wife's chest. You wanna give it a try?"

I grinned sheepishly. Made a stupid joke to get myself off the hook. "No thanks," I said. "I'd hate to outshoot a man with his own rifle."

Keegan rolled his eyes, but Irons didn't get the humor.

"Yeah," he said seriously. "I guess I'd hate that too."

"So what'd you think?" Keegan asked as we were turned back onto the blacktop of Highway 34, the nose of the Ford pointing toward Bosler and Laramie. We'd stopped by the foreman's house on the way out, and as expected, he'd corroborated everything Irons told us about their activities on Sunday afternoon. Saul Irons had an alibi for the time of the killings. At least for now.

"Two things," I said. "One, I think Saul Irons and Barry Hart are probably lying. Two, I think Irons is a hell of a marksman."

"That ain't all he is," Keegan said, obviously relieved to have his rubber back on smooth pavement. "Like I said, shooting is only part of his repertoire. Did you know he won the Rocky Mountain Full-Contact Karate Championships two years ago? Light heavyweight division?"

"No," I said, "it's not something I keep up with. But isn't he a little old? I mean, most of those guys are in their twenties, and he's got to be what? Fifty?"

"Fifty-three," Keegan said. "What does that tell you?"

"It tells me I hope I'm in that kind of shape when I'm his age," I said.

Keegan looked at the cute little roll of flab that's been creeping over my belt for the last year or so. It wasn't as big as his own, but it was gaining. "I don't think we have to worry about that, Harry," he said. "It tells me, however, that Saul Irons is one deadly individual. Maybe the best I've ever seen."

"Okay, he's got plenty of sand," I said. "But where does that get us? He's right, isn't he? We've got nothing to link him with any criminal activity whatsoever. Hell, did he act like someone who was worried he might get caught? No, Ken, he didn't. He acted like having the police show up on his doorstep was just about the best thing that's happened all week. You ever seen a murderer who was glad you dropped by to shoot the breeze, Ken? I haven't."

Keegan pushed the Ford up to seventy-five. "It's the game we play," Keegan said. "I know he did what I think he did, and he knows I know. But as long as I can't prove it, he pretends he isn't mad that I keep trying. And guess what, Harry, there are lots of times I find myself hoping I'm wrong. Saul Irons was a good cop in his day, and I happen to think he got a raw deal down in Flagstaff. There's a part of me that really wants to believe he's telling the truth, that he's just trying to live a quiet life, poking around for the odd gold nugget."

"But he isn't, Ken," I said. "Men like Saul Irons don't retire to become harmless old desert rats. They live by doing what they're best at, and since Irons can't be a cop anymore that leaves—"

"Killing," Keegan said sadly, finishing my thought. "That's why I gotta take him down."

Keegan parked in the shade outside the garage at the department motor pool a little after four-thirty, and we made our plans for the next day.

I'm pretty much a one-man show when it comes to investigators in the Albany County Sheriff's Office, so it would have been nearly impossible for me to carry on a two-front investigation, even if I'd been convinced that Saul Irons was somehow involved with the murders of Colleen McAfferty, Ralphie Skates, and Clarence Hathaway, which I wasn't entirely.

I had it in my mind that even though Ken Keegan was probably entirely correct in his belief that Irons was guilty of something, the best chance I had to close my own cases was to nail the lid shut on Bobby Snow. I didn't rule out cooperating with the DCI, and on the way back to town we agreed we'd keep in touch in case our investigations started to overlap.

For his part, Keegan would try and find out which local ranchers, if any, were paying Irons to regulate their grazing lands and attempt to tie down some of the rumors he'd been hearing about intimidation and murder. If any names turned up that might interest me, he'd be in touch.

Meanwhile, I'd pursue my investigation of the killings at the McAfferty ranch with special emphasis on Snow—an inquiry currently going nowhere fast. If I heard Irons's name mentioned anywhere along the line, I promised to let him know.

We said our good-byes and I got out of Keegan's car and watched him back out the driveway and into the street. He gave me a tired wave as he drove away, and I watched his car until it reached the end of the block, the engine stuttering as he gunned it onto Main.

Tell the truth, I was feeling a little run-down and puny myself. What I needed, I decided, was a healthy dinner and a good night's sleep. Which I'd get just as soon as I checked in at the office and checked out for the day.

When I turned around to go inside, however, I found my way blocked by Sally Sheridan, the Laramie correspondent for the *Casper Star Tribune*. She had positioned her roundish body smack in the middle of the doorway between the motor pool and the reception area, and her flame red hair billowed around her head like a cone of cherry cotton candy. Short of a cross-body block, not an especially intelligent public relations option when dealing with reporters, there was no way around her. I certainly couldn't go through her.

"Good afternoon Sally," I said cordially. "I'm glad you're here. I've been trying to reach you all week."

"You've been avoiding me like herpes, Sheriff, is what you've been doing," she snarled. "I know you got my messages. All twelve of them."

I tried to force my face into my best impression of innocence. "I don't think I did," I lied. "Maybe they forgot to put them on my desk. You know how Helene gets sometimes."

"Don't you dare blame that nice receptionist in there," she said, whacking her notebook with a ballpoint pen shaped like a Cuban cigar. "I watched her put most of them on your desk myself."

I gave her a sheepish grin, shrugged to show her I acknowledged my misdeed but wasn't ready to ask for atonement. "Oh, well Sally, I guess I've just been busy. You know how it is."

Her cheeks began to flush. "You weren't at Baldi's press conference this afternoon," she said accusingly.

"No," I admitted. "I wasn't. I didn't see the point."

"Then you haven't heard what he's claiming?" she asked incredulously.

"No," I said. "What's he claiming? That I go around looking for innocent men to accuse of murder?"

"No," she said. "He's not stupid. He's just claiming you're not a good enough cop to know the difference between an innocent man and a guilty one. He says he's withholding judgment on Slaymaker's claims you planted the evidence that convicted him—although he says other incidents in your past lead him to believe there might be some truth to the allegations."

"What?"

"Yeah," she said. She rifled through her notebook until she came to the pertinent notes. "He claims to have sworn affidavits from a couple of people who worked with you in Denver, both of whom say you were perfectly willing to bend the law on occasion if you thought it'd help you make a case. He says that with that kind of history, there's no reason to believe you've changed."

"And who are these affidavits from?" I asked as my ears

began their familiar slow burn, my stomach rolling like a loop-the-loop.

"Not saying," she said. "But he swears they're legit."

"My ass," I growled. "Where does he—"

"Is that a denial?" she asked, bringing pen to paper.

"You take it however you want," I snarled. "But if Anthony Baldi keeps up with this stinking slander, I'm gonna sue him so bad I'll own his goddamn dentures."

I pushed past her and stormed into the office, drawing startled stares from the assembled public servants and hangers-on.

"Is that last part a quote?" she hollered.

"Damn right it's a quote," I bellowed back. "So for God's sake, get it right!"

Trouble was, she *already* had it right. So did Baldi. And so did Slaymaker, damn his miserable hide. Not that I'd expect anyone to understand—with the possible exception of another cop.

All told, I worked for more than fifteen years as a policeman in Denver, but I hadn't been on the streets for more than a couple months before I learned a sobering truth: victims have no rights and the law usually works in favor of the criminals. Because of that, the worst crooks often walk. And once they're back on the streets, it isn't long before they find fresh victims. If you don't believe me, pick up a newspaper.

That being the case, I had a couple of choices: I could allow my disillusionment with the system to force me out of police work, or I could try to even the scales. Break the rules occasionally if I believed it would make the difference between the conviction of a man I knew to be guilty and his acquittal.

I broke the rules with Jerry Slaymaker. I didn't have a choice.

After months of building a circumstantial case that wasn't even strong enough to merit a search warrant on such an influential mover in the community, I was at the end of the line. My partner and I spent an average of fourteen hours a day on the case, and it was taking a toll on my personal life, as well as my professional life. In 1984 Sam hadn't been born yet, Robert was eight, and Tommy was three. I was away from home so much they called me Uncle Daddy, and I don't think I saw them while they were awake more than a few hours in seven months. I'd come home from chasing down another fruitless lead, sit at the kitchen table until I'd finished a six-pack. Then I'd lock all the doors, lie down on a blanket on the floor of their room, and fall asleep with my service revolver under the pillow, listening to the gentle breathing of my babies. Nicole thought I'd gone crazy, and maybe she was right. We fought about everything—money, sex, her shitty car—but we both knew the real reason for our arguments. I was obsessed with proving Slaymaker guilty but becoming more and more doubtful I had the ability to do it. I was a failure. Slaymaker was still free.

Meanwhile, another boy had disappeared. His dead body was found in a Dumpster ten days later. The child had been raped. Stabbed.

He'd also been decapitated.

There was no more physical evidence than we'd found in the McDonald case, but my gut told me Slaymaker killed him too.

My instincts told me he wouldn't quit there, would never quit. The man was just getting warmed up. He had to be stopped, and I didn't have time to play by the rules.

I broke into Slaymaker's home one evening when I knew he was attending a Homebuilders' Association banquet.

I found nothing upstairs. Nothing in his living room. Nothing in his kitchen and nothing in his garage.

After more than an hour of prowling his house in the dark, I found a plastic bag filled with bloodstained clothes hidden above a heating duct in his basement and made the only decision I could live with, since the evidence had been obtained illegally.

I made a quick circuit of the house to make sure I hadn't disturbed anything Slaymaker might notice when he came home. Then I slipped out the back door and dropped the bag of clothes in his trash, where I just happened to "find" it the next morning.

You don't need a warrant to look through garbage, after all.

That's one of the main reasons I was reluctant to answer Anthony Baldi's charges directly. I hadn't been asked about whether I'd broken into Slaymaker's house without a warrant on the witness stand, so I hadn't perjured myself. Which is a good thing, since I don't think I could have lied under oath.

I couldn't lie about it now, either.

Forced to answer the question, my conscience would dictate that I tell the truth. And if I admitted that I obtained critical evidence without a warrant, the chance of convicting Slaymaker on a retrial, if the prosecutors even decided to try again, would be zero. A killer would be set free to kill another child—the most heinous of all crimes—and it would be my fault.

Not to mention that the shitstorm immediately following any confession I might make regarding misconduct in the Slaymaker trial would probably prevent me from ever solving Colleen McAfferty's murder and finding some measure of justice for Tess.

And if that wasn't enough, on a purely selfish note, my career would be as dead as Elvis. And my chance of ever putting my family back together? *Nada.*

I couldn't let it happen.

But how to stop it? I had no fucking clue.

I wrestled with my dilemma for most of Wednesday evening after my conversation with Sally Sheridan, and I'm not especially proud to admit I did my wrestling in a bar while nursing more than a few double bourbons.

I'd stopped at Copper's Corners after leaving the office and arrived in the dark little saloon just in time for the start of an Atlanta Braves game on Ted Turner's network. I'm not a big Braves fan, and the team was having a miserable season, but the big-screen televisions around the room held the attention of the beery patrons well enough that nobody interrupted my brooding to chat. I sipped bourbon until around ten, then ordered a thick cheeseburger with a slab of fresh onion and another Jack Daniel's to wash it down. I ate greedily, the juice from the burger soaking through the napkin and trickling down my chin. When I finished, I sipped my drink with relish, smacked my lips in contentment.

It occurred to me that I'd had more whiskey in the past few hours than I'd had in one sitting for months, but I didn't feel drunk, just pleasantly mellow. Now, I thought, if I only had a cigarette . . .

"Hello Sheriff." The woman's voice came from behind my stool and took me by surprise. I swiveled around a bit unsteadily, found my eyes didn't focus quite as quickly as I'd anticipated.

It was Tess McAfferty, dressed in a knee-length black skirt, tailored black jacket, and white silk blouse. She wore an antique cameo brooch at her throat. Her butterscotch hair was pulled back and held in place by a black velvet bow. Her perfume smelled like fresh-cut flowers, and her makeup almost concealed the slight puffiness around her eyes. She looked around the room uncomfortably, taking in the tables full of construction workers and scroungy students, and placed her purse on the bar.

"Mind if I join you?" she asked, and nodded at the empty barstool beside mine.

"Of course not," I said. "Would you like to get a table?"

"No," she said. A glimpse of thigh as she hiked herself up on the stool. "This is fine."

When the bartender came she ordered a Sea Breeze, fishing around in her purse for a pack of Marlboro Lights. We didn't speak as she lit her cigarette and took a small taste of the icy drink. She glanced at the game, watched the people behind her in the backbar mirror.

"I've been making arrangements at the funeral home all evening," she said without looking in my direction. "After I was finished, I felt like I needed something to—"

"It's all right, Tess," I said, pushing the rest of my own drink away. "You don't have to explain. After what you've been through."

"It's Saturday, Sheriff. The funeral."

122

"I know," I said. "And after the service, where . . . ?"

"We're burying her on the ranch," she said. "There's a little meadow at the south end that she always liked, full of Indian paintbrush and bluebells."

"I'll be there."

She nodded gently, sipped her drink in silence.

On the outside, she seemed to be holding up as well as could be expected, but I could only imagine what she felt inside. Over the years I've dealt with too many people suffering the fresh wounds of loss, and it always affects me profoundly. But I'm most disturbed by those who have lost children, a nightmare so terrifying that only another parent can begin to imagine its unholy dimensions.

I knew from experience and instinct that there was nothing I could say that would help her find her way, nothing that would help to stem the bleeding in her soul. In the empty days after a loved one dies, even the most heartfelt words of support and condolence sound banal, hollow, and woefully inadequate. We didn't speak for more than ten minutes, and I believed that she needed it that way, needed time to sort through the emotionally charged events of the last few hours without interruption, time to soothe the frayed endings of her raw and battered nerves.

I respected that need.

I ordered a cola on ice from the bartender and asked him to total our tabs. In the reflection of the backbar mirror, I could see Tess staring down into the depths of her drink, her chin nearly resting on her chest. A single tear traveled the length of her cheek. I reached across the chasm between us and rested my hand on her wrist. "Tess . . ."

She flinched as if she'd been awakened from a dream, brushed the tear away with the back of her hand and shook her head in a vigorous no that said I'd overstepped some boundary.

Confused, I pulled my hand away. "I'm sorry Tess," I stammered. "I didn't mean to . . ."

She was looking at me, but it wasn't my face she saw. She

seemed to be reaching into herself to tap some inner pool of strength or will. When she found it, she took a deep breath and crushed her cigarette in the ashtray. "I didn't come here for sympathy, Harry," she said. "I don't need that "

"Then what do you need, Tess?" I asked gently. I laid forty dollars on the bar to cover my dinner and our drinks, pushed it toward the bartender. "I'll do whatever I can."

She paused before answering, but when she spoke she seemed stronger, more certain. There was flint in her voice that only moments before hadn't been there. "I need something that will really help."

"What?"

"Information, Harry," she said. "Just information."

I picked up the wad of damp bills the bartender laid down in change, counted off five for a tip and tucked them under my glass. "We don't know much at this point," I said halfheartedly. "But I'll tell you everything as soon as I—"

"Bullshit." She gave me a thin-lipped smile. "You'll tell me what you think I need to know. You'll tell me what you think will make all this easier. But that's not what I need. I need the truth."

She stared into my eyes, answered the question that was written there. "I can take it, Harry. I'm strong enough. You think I'm some poor, pitiful woman who needs your protection, but I'm not. If I was Colleen's father instead of her mother, would you treat me differently?"

I didn't respond. I guess I didn't have to.

"That's what I thought," she said angrily. "But remember this, Harry. Colleen didn't have a father. He was crushed to death on that damn ranch before he could get her raised. I'm all that little girl had, the only one left to do what needs to be done. So either you tell me—everything—or I'll find out what I want to know from someone else."

Getting down from the stool, she began collecting her belongings, jammed her cigarettes and lighter into her purse and fished around until she found her keys. She held them in her hand tightly, the keys pointing outward like weapons.

She was right, of course. She deserved to know as much as I could tell her. "I apologize, Tess," I said evenly. "I didn't mean to condescend—and I never thought you were weak."

She didn't answer, but her stare was hot and penetrating as she waited for me to go on. "What can I tell you?" I asked.

That was what Tess wanted to hear. She eased back onto the barstool. "Who killed Colleen?" she asked finally, her voice low and strained, her hands trembling slightly.

I took a deep breath, then told her about the lab report, that the tissue under Colleen's fingernails matched samples taken from Skates, and about the fingerprints we'd found on her throat. I told her it looked like Ralphie had raped Colleen before he killed her, and I told her we believed she'd been raped by at least one other person as well. I told her about the discovery of Clarence Hathaway's body, and our belief that he'd been tied in with Skates in a large-scale rustling operation. I told her what we were doing to find the people who'd murdered Clarence and Ralphie, but I didn't mention names.

She listened quietly, nodding occasionally. When I was finished, she let it all sink in. "Why did they have to kill her?" she asked.

I shrugged my shoulders sadly. "I don't know that, Tess. I wish to Christ I did."

"Do you know who else was at the ranch when she died?" she asked tightly. "Besides Skates and Hathaway?" A brief pause. "Is Bobby Snow a suspect?"

The directness of her question caught me off guard. "Everyone's a suspect, Tess," I said. "But yes, we're looking at Bobby Snow."

"Did he do it?"

"We're not certain," I said. "But we'll find out. It just might take a little—"

"What do you *think*, Harry?" she interrupted. "What does your gut say? Was he there?"

"My gut's been wrong before, Tess," I said, evading the question. "But if he had anything to do with Colleen's death, I promise I'll prove it sooner or later. We'll bring him in, put him in prison where he belongs. You just have to trust me."

She considered that, shook her head as if rejecting it. Looked down at her drink, then back at me again. A flush of anger was rising in her cheeks, and I felt I'd been given some sort of test and come up wanting. "Maybe it doesn't matter," she said dismissively.

"Well, it matters," I said. "The longer it takes to solve a case after a murder takes place, the more difficult it becomes. But there's no statute of limitations, Tess, and I'm not going to give up."

"That's not what I meant, Sheriff," she said. "Maybe it doesn't matter whether you prove it or not. It won't bring Colleen back, will it?"

"No," I admitted. "Nothing will bring Colleen back. But at least the other people involved would be brought to justice."

She recoiled as if she'd been slapped. Her mouth formed a tight line and her nostrils dilated. Her chest rose and fell in rapid, strained movements beneath the silky blouse.

"Justice?" she asked. "Will it be justice to put them in a safe jail with plenty of food, give them a lawyer and send them to prison, where they can take college classes and never have to worry about caring for themselves again? Will that be justice, Harry?"

"Not exactly, but—"

"Will it be justice to watch as their lawyers plea-bargain? Will it be justice when they get time off for good behavior? Will it be justice twenty years from now, after they've 'paid their debt to society,' when we let them out to live the rest of their lives in peace? Will that be justice?"

"Tess," I said. I reached over to lay my hand on her shoulder. "It might not be justice. Justice would be making sure they get exactly the same treatment they gave Colleen. But it's law. And law is what—"

126

She pulled away roughly. "Fuck the law, Sheriff," she hissed. She got down from her stool, grabbed her purse from the bar. "I don't give a damn for the law."

My knee cracked as I hobbled off my own stool, and I held on to the edge of the bar for support. "Tess, you can't—"

"They raped and murdered my daughter, Sheriff Starbranch," she said. Her eyes sparked with anger. "They left her body in the dirt. She was sixteen years old! Sixteen! For that—I don't care what the law wants—I want vengeance! I want to hold their hearts in my hands."

I should have followed her when she stormed out the door, but I let her go. If Colleen had been my child, I'd want a little vengeance too. No matter what I had to do. No matter the consequences.

And God help anyone who tried to stand in my way.

# EIGHT

By the time the jangling telephone woke me the next morning, the sun was well up, and an unmercifully cheerful beam of yellow early morning light spilled across the sheets of my rumpled bed and the untamed riot of clothing I'd thrown at its foot. My tongue felt glued to the top of my mouth and a dull pain throbbed at the back of my head, the kind of all-day headache no amount of aspirin will cure. I opened one sleep-encrusted eye, reached across the bed for the phone on the nightstand, felt a warm body under the sheets between the phone and my side of the mattress.

I hadn't been that drunk, had I? Not full-tilt coyote drunk. Not the awful brand of drunk where you wake up with your arm under a woman whose face and name you don't remember and chew your own limb off so you won't wake her as you sneak out of bed. No, I thought, I hadn't, even if this hangover said otherwise. Cautiously, I pulled the sheet back and the dog raised his square black head from the fluffy pillow to give me a soupy and foul-smelling lick on the cheek with his long pink tongue. I winced at his rancid breath, but I was still relieved to find myself in bed with a dog in the literal sense.

I pushed him out of the sack and lifted the receiver.

"Hullo?" I grumbled.

"Hi Harry," Nicole chirped. She always wakes in a better mood than I do, and there were times in our marriage when I hated her for it. "Were you still sleeping? You feel all right?"

I squinted at the digital alarm on the chest of drawers across the room. "What time is it?" I asked. I couldn't focus on my toes, let alone the clock.

"A little after eight," she said. In the background, I could hear a radio announcer reading the weather report—dry with highs near 85—the sound of the kids arguing over breakfast. "I'm just on my way out the door, but I thought I'd give you a call first."

"Shit," I growled. I sat up on the edge of the bed and the movement made my head spin like a ride on the Tilt'a'Whirl. I lay back down again, rested my forearm across my eyes.

She sounded hurt. "I'm sorry, Harry," she said. "I didn't mean to—"

"No it's not that," I said. I swallowed hard, pushed myself up again, reached for my watch. "I just overslept, that's all. Don't feel so good, either."

"Flu?"

"Maybe," I agreed. I remembered bringing a glass of soda with me to the bedroom, but I couldn't find it. Reaching under the bed, I found the glass on its side, mired in a dried puddle of sticky goop. I licked the congealed pop from my fingertips, ran my tongue around my front teeth. "I feel a little puny, tell you the truth. Maybe I'll be better after coffee."

"Yeah, I hope," she said, a note of worry in her voice. "I heard about the trouble you have up there. That poor girl. And those other killings."

"It's been pretty crazy," I admitted.

"Late night?" she asked.

"Yeah," I said. "I was talking to the mother of the girl who was murdered. She was—"

"I came in early to wake the boys for swimming lessons," Nicole interrupted, "and for a while I just stood there watching them sleep, and I couldn't help but imagine . . ."

"I know," I said. "I thought the same thing myself."

"About this weekend," she said tentatively. "Is this a good time for me to come?"

"Well, I hope you'll come," I said. "With any luck, more than once."

She giggled. "Darn you, that's not what I mean and you know it. I mean are you too busy with this murder investigation and . . . this other business."

So she'd also read about Slaymaker—and the ten-million-dollar lawsuit he'd filed against the Denver Police Department and my own self late the day before. Calhoun had left a message on my answering machine giving me the news about the lawsuit, to cheer me up when I got home.

"You mean am I going to be too busy to spend a little time with you?" I asked. "I don't think it'll be a problem. As long as you don't mind checking into a cheap motel so we can hide from the process servers."

She met my feeble joke with stony silence. "It's ridiculous, isn't it?" she asked finally. "How can they get away with saying things like that?"

"The fact is, Nicole, they can say whatever they want to say. Who's gonna stop 'em?"

"Do people believe it?"

"From what I hear, a lot of them do."

"It could cost you the election?"

"It could."

"Then you gotta do something, Harry. Soon."

I cleared my throat, stalled for a short count, then went on. "The way I see it, every option I have would be wrong for one reason or another."

"So what are you going to do?" she asked angrily.

I'd prepared myself for this reaction, and I hadn't looked forward to it at all. A big-city court stenographer whose career has taken off since our divorce, she'd made it plain after our reconciliation that she wouldn't mind living together again, but she damn sure wasn't about to try it in Victory, a place so small your neighbors excuse you when you sneeze. She likes Laramie, though, so my bid for election allowed her to hope for a sort of compromise. The county seat, she could work in either the district or the county court, and there were plenty of cultural and social activities connected with the university.

And besides, a man who becomes a county sheriff is demonstrating a lot more ambition and responsibility than a man who leaves career and family to be police chief in a town of 650 souls, if you take your soul count during the summer. My ex-wife has always considered ambition and responsibility important attributes in a spouse and father, but she found me sorely lacking in those virtues when we were married.

In those days, Nicole didn't object to my working as a cop per se, but she could never understand my complete and utter lack of desire to play the political games necessary to scramble my way up the career ladder, although everyone said I was being groomed for a captaincy, and someday might even be chief of detectives. Our definitions of success were basically incompatible, and while she never came right out and said it, I always knew she was a little embarrassed by what she believed was my complacency, my lack of ambition in advancing my career.

Truth was, I was having trouble maintaining emotional equilibrium where I was, didn't need the added pressure of office politics. And when I started coming unraveled psychologically toward the end of my tour of duty in Denver, started staying out later and later after my shift ended, drinking more and more, she could never understand that it wasn't her or my family responsibilities that were causing the problem, but the Job, always the Job.

She accused me of having affairs. I denied it. We fought.

She accused me of losing my desire for her, of ignoring her sexually. I denied it. We fought.

She said I'd abandoned my responsibilities to my children. I denied it. We fought.

She said I wished we'd never married, wished I could go

back to living alone. I denied it. We fought.

She said I was a borderline alcoholic. I denied it. We fought.

And the more we fought, the more I drank, the more reluctant I was to come home.

I considered her an unsympathetic, selfish bitch. She considered me an immature, lazy boozehound.

I suppose we were both right, up to a point. Our self-conscious efforts since the divorce to change and forgive have made our tenuous reconciliation possible, but there's a niggling part of our brains that still expects the worst.

Nicole was afraid that if I bungled the election and wound up back in Victory, I'd slip right back into my old inertia and bad habits. She wasn't about to let that happen.

"I don't know what I'm going to do," I said. "For the time being, I'm not doing anything."

"Damn it, Harry," she said tightly. "You can't simply ignore this. If you ignore it, people will think—"

"I don't really care what people think," I snapped. "You don't seem to understand, Nicole, that I've got other things on my mind right now than getting elected."

"I understand perfectly well," she said icily. "Everything comes before your family, Harry. That's the way it's always been, the way it always will be."

I fought down the wave of anger that was beginning to constrict my chest. It's amazing how quickly two people can revert to their old patterns of behavior, especially people who have been married for a while and know precisely where to find each other's hot buttons. Given the opportunity, this argument would escalate at the speed of light. I didn't think either of us really wanted that to happen. I took a deep breath, forced myself to speak calmly and rationally.

"That's not fair, Nicole, and you know it," I said. "You've read the papers. You know what I'm up against here. I don't have time to fight with both you and Larry Calhoun about a ten-year-old murder case when I've got another murder just days old to solve. You think I should just ignore Colleen McAfferty's death and concentrate on winning a damned *election*? I don't think you think that's the kind of man I am, Nicole. At least I hope to God you don't."

When I was finished, I listened to the silence on the line for twenty long seconds. When she spoke again, her anger was gone, replaced by a note of apology.

"You're right, Harry," she said. "I sorry. It's just that . . ."

"I know, don't worry about it. I'll think of something."

"No," she said. "I'll think of something. Larry and I'll put our heads together this weekend and we'll straighten it out."

"Thanks," I said gratefully. The pounding in my brain had moved from the back to the front, right behind my left eye. I shut it, kept the other open.

"Listen, I plan on leaving early on Friday afternoon," she said. "With any luck, I ought to be there in time for dinner. I could stop by the butcher shop on the way out of town. You have any requests?"

"A thick rib eye would be nice," I said. "And Nicole, please don't forget—"

"The green stuff." She laughed. "I already got it. Large economy size."

We hung up, and I padded out to the kitchen and started a pot of coffee, rummaged around in the refrigerator until I'd found a pound of bacon, a dozen eggs, and a half loaf of bread. While the coffee perked in my old percolator, I treated myself to a long hot shower and dressed. Then I cooked a huge breakfast, slicing peppers, onions, and mushrooms into the frying pan with the scrambled eggs and pulling a jar of homemade strawberry jam from the cupboard.

I was already late for work, so I decided another hour would hardly matter. As soon as the food was ready I piled it on a plate, put it on a tray with my mug and a handful of aspirin, and carried it out to the side porch, where I could sit in the shade and eat. A freshet whispered down the flank of the Snowies, and the air was full of pine. At the corral, Edna's old ponies were feeling frisky, chasing each other around in circles. The dog was in the yard, excavating an abandoned prairie dog hole. A couple of gray jays perched in a small pine tree near the porch, eyed my breakfast enviously. If I waited long enough, they'd eventually work up the courage to steal it right from the plate.

When the phone rang, I thought about ignoring it, and that's what I did for the first ten rings. When it persisted into twenty, then twenty-five, I cursed, threw a napkin over my plate, and trudged back into the kitchen.

"Starbranch," I answered.

"Mornin' Harry." It was Ken Keegan, who sounded every bit as tired and cantankerous as ever. "Did I get you out of the shower?"

"Nah, I was outside eating breakfast. What's up?"

"Well," he said, "I just got to work and found a report waiting on my desk that I thought you might be interested in."

"Yeah?"

"It's from the Platte County Sheriff's Office," he said.

Platte County borders my county to the northeast, and I'd met its sheriff, Glenn Oxford, on several occasions. We'd even cooperated on a couple of search-and-rescue operations in the Medicine Bow range during the spring and early summer. "What's going on with Glenn?" I asked.

"It seems a couple of fishermen were out on La Bonte Creek yesterday and found a body," Keegan said. "It was almost completely skeletonized, so it had to have been there for several months. Oxford found the guy's wallet, though. Man by the name of Emile Cross."

"And what," I asked, "would this have to do with me?"

"I don't know for sure," Keegan said. "But here's the deal. Emile Cross was a known rustler. Matter of fact, he'd been in and out of prison for it for more than twenty years. His probation officer thought he might have given it up, but looks like he may not have. His body was found on summer range, and he was armed.

From the damage to his skull, Oxford says it looks like he was killed by a single gunshot wound to the head."

"And you think this might have something to do with the McAfferty case?" I asked.

"It's a possibility," Keegan said. "I made a couple calls this morning, and came up with something fairly interesting. Cross was Ralphie Skates's cell mate in prison."

"And you think he may have gotten Skates involved with rustling afterwards?" I asked. "That they may have been working together?"

"Well, it's a theory, and it fits with what I was talking about yesterday."

"Saul Irons?" I asked.

"Exactly," Keegan said. "With him in the brush, rustling is a very unhealthy profession."

Keegan planned to spend the day in Platte County poking around the site where Emile Cross's skeleton had been discovered. There was no reason for me to go along, so we made arrangements to meet first thing the next morning and drive out for another talk with Saul Irons.

I decided to spend the day at my office in Laramie, reviewing the lab reports and interview notes my deputies had collected on the McAfferty killings, and was on my way out the front door when the phone drew me back into the house. It was Frankie Bull, calling to see if I could meet him for breakfast at Ginny Larsen's café in Victory before I left for the sheriff's department.

"Sorry, Frankie," I said. "You're too late by a half an hour. I already ate."

"Too bad," he said happily. "So why not stop on down and watch me eat? I'll buy you a cup of coffee."

"Is there some kinda problem?"

"Nah," he said. In the background, I could hear the clack of silverware and dishes, the hum of conversation, Ginny shouting at her short-order cook to hurry up with the damn scrambled eggs. "There's just a couple people asking for you this mornin'. Thought you might like to stop down and show the flag, that's all."

"Give me ten minutes," I said.

"Make it fifteen," he said. "Mike O'Neal's just starting to tell the story about the time he tried to land his plane with all those deer on the runway. If you drive a little slower, you'll miss the part where one of them hits the propeller."

Mrs. Larsen's Country Kitchen is Victory's nerve center. If townies want to read local news that's a week old, they pick up the *Laramie Boomerang* or the *Casper Star Tribune*. If they want to hear it while it's still news, they visit Ginny Larsen's, where most of the best gossip is common knowledge almost before it happens.

A ramshackle place that seems to miss most of the tourist trade, Ginny makes up for it by maintaining the undying loyalty and devotion of the locals. It's the kind of place where the chairs don't match and the walls are crammed with Ginny's awful watercolor paintings. But the food is fantastic, and cheap, and for most of us it's the bistro of choice. Before I was named sheriff, in fact, I ate most of my meals there, even when I was sick.

I've slowed down some lately, but I always look forward to the three or four meals I'm able to take there throughout the week, and I never miss chicken-fried-steak night on Wednesday.

Frankie Bull was perched on a stool at the counter when I got to the café twenty minutes later, getting set to dive into a huge platter of scrambled eggs, sausage, and blueberry pancakes. He waved when he saw me walk in the front door and motioned to the empty stool between him and Mike O'Neal, but it took me at least five minutes to make it to my designated seat.

Esther Campbell, the librarian at the Victory branch of the Albany County Library, was in the first booth and stopped me to remind me my library books were overdue again. I promised to bring them in, and we spent a few minutes discussing the latest mystery books she'd received. I asked her to reserve a couple and moved on to the next booth, where Pearl Cox and Carrie Wilson were huddled together over cups of tea. Carrie's eyes lit up as soon as she saw me.

"Harry," she said, her voice as shrill as a macaw's. "We were just talking about the Labor Day parade. You're going to be in it again, aren't you?"

I groaned inwardly at the thought. Each year, Pearl and Carrie, who comprise the entire ladies' auxiliary of the Victory Elks club, organize the community's salute to labor, a salute that includes perhaps the world's shortest and most boring parade. The procession travels the entire three-block length of Main Street and is over in about six minutes flat. But each year, the ladies' auxiliary strongarms the members of the Victory VFW, the Cowbelles, the Grange, and all the local politicians and dignitaries into riding the route on horseback, tossing candy to the twenty or thirty kids who happen to show up with their parents to watch the spectacle.

About halfway through the route the year before, the horse I'd been assigned, an ill-tempered pinto named Shorty, decided he'd gone far enough and started to buck. His acrobatics took me by surprise, and I landed on the pavement in front of the feed and seed store. Shorty ran home, and I limped the rest of the route on foot. It took weeks for the bruises to my dignity and backside to heal, and I wasn't anxious to give a repeat performance.

"We gonna be riding horses?" I asked.

Pearl and Carrie giggled mischievously. "Sure," Pearl said. "We think you should ride Shorty again. Last year the spectators said you two were the best part of the parade."

"Then forget it," I said gruffly. "If my participation depends on that mean-spirited nag, then Victory will just have to salute labor without my help."

Pearl looked like she'd already considered that sentiment. "Then how 'bout riding in Harley Coyne's new convertible?" she asked. "It's red. We'll put the top down. You can wave."

"Fine," I said. "I'll ride a convertible in your parade—on one condition."

"What is it?" Carrie asked.

"Give Shorty to the mayor." I grinned. "I think Curly and that horse are soul mates."

The ladies' auxiliary laughed and went back to their planning. I moved on to the next booth, spent a couple of minutes with Tom Clay and Carl Bonner, who'd opened a fishing guide operation on the Laramie River early in the summer. We discussed flies and casting approaches, and I made plans to go fishing with them one Saturday in September after the tourist season began to fade.

By the time I made it to the back of the café, where Frankie was nearly finished with his breakfast, I'd spoken with nearly everyone in the place, with the exception of Jay Sun, who was in one of his famous sulks. Sun, a widower who owns a local convenience store, was hunched in a booth by himself, glowering at everyone who walked by. I spoke to him as I passed, but he was too busy scowling to answer.

I took the stool beside Frankie and leaned across to Ginny, who was behind the counter with one of her breakfast specials—a big slab of cured Virginia ham, four scrambled eggs, about a half pound of O'Brien potatoes, and six pieces of toast—balanced in each arm.

"What's up with Jay?" I asked.

She rolled her eyes and delivered the specials to a couple of lumberjacks at the end of the counter.

"It's Harriet Fisher," she said when she came back. Harriet is the town's best beautician.

Ginny wiped her hands on her apron, brushed a stray wisp of brown hair from her face. "Jay claims he's in love, but Harriet won't go out with him anymore."

"Why not?" I asked. "Jay's a nice guy. He's polite, has his own business—"

"And pictures of his dead wife all over his house," Ginny said. "Harriet says she wouldn't mind having a fling, but she's not desperate enough to compete with a ghost."

I shrugged my shoulders and reached for a menu. I wasn't

especially hungry, but the smell of fresh cinnamon rolls coming from the kitchen was tough to ignore. Maybe I'd order one and just take a couple of bites, save the rest for lunch.

It took me a half hour, but I ate the whole thing while I visited with Frankie and Mike, made plans for a late-season elk hunt at Mike's camp near Sheep Lake. I've hunted every year since I moved to Victory, but I've never come home with an animal. For years, my marksmanship was the stuff of local legend, although it's my contention that I missed on purpose. This year, I didn't even plan to bring a gun. I'd let the real hunters hunt. I'd stay in camp, sleep late and cook. Feed bread crumbs to the prairie dogs and gray jays. Read a good book. Come evening, I'd light the campfire, pour the whiskey, and skin my pals at poker.

I could hardly wait.

When we finished our breakfast I paid the tab, and the three of us stood outside on the sidewalk for a few minutes in the warm morning sunshine. The day's first tourists had drifted into town and were cruising Main slowly, their faces curious and friendly as they peered through their windows at the locals, some of them waving as they passed.

Across the street in front of Jay's Hardware, Jay's son Billy was helping Gary Rogers load a new riding lawn mower into the back of his pickup. Fast Eddie Warnock, the town's only physician, and Ray Hladky stood on the sidewalk in front of the hardware store, inspecting Eddie's new car, a black Nissan with windows tinted so dark you couldn't see inside.

Frankie wandered off to help Carrie Wilson, who was done with her breakfast and cursing a parking meter that wouldn't take her coin. Mike left for his office in Laramie.

I pulled my keys from my pocket, unlocked the door of the Blazer, and was just getting ready to climb inside when a light blue pickup pulled into the space next to mine, it's old motor clacking like lug nuts in a washing machine.

"Sheriff Starbranch?" the driver called through his open window.

"That's me."

"Glad I caught you," he said. "Can you spare a couple minutes?"

I nodded that I could.

A skinny red-faced man with peeling skin on his nose and a battered John Deere cap pulled low on his forehead, he unfolded himself from the cab, knocked dust from the knees of his denim trousers, and stretched himself to his full height. He was about six foot two and maybe 165 pounds, his skin as rough and cracked as old leather.

He stuck a bony hand in my direction and I took it, felt the huge knobs of his knuckles, the thick calluses on his fingers. I winced from the pressure of his grip. I didn't recognize him as a local, but his pickup was sporting Albany County license plates and he was dressed in working cowboy garb, blue jeans threadbare at the knees and cuffs, a snap-button western-cut shirt with the sleeves cut off at the biceps, scuffed and patched cowboy boots with badly worn heels, and a wide belt with a huge silver and gold buckle.

"Will Jensen," he said. "Your office told me you were out here."

"Just on my way to Laramie," I said. "But if you tracked me down, it must be important. You havin' some trouble?"

"No trouble," he said. "I just thought we needed to talk."

I leaned back against the fender of the Blazer and waited until he went on. "I own the Rockin' J Ranch," he said. "The ranch next to Tess McAfferty's? I'm right on the eastern border of her property. We share water rights to Sailor's Creek."

"Yeah," I said. "A couple of my people were out there to talk to you, but they said you weren't home. I think they talked to your family."

"My wife and daughter," he agreed. "I've been in the high country bringin' my cattle down. Just got home this mornin'. My daughter said your deputies came out to talk to me last Monday, but they missed me by a few hours."

He paused, a frown crinkling the corners of his windburned mouth. "I heard about Colleen when I got home this mornin'," he said. "She and my daughter, Cora . . . They were friends."

"It's a terrible thing, Mr. Jensen."

"Used to come over on that mare of hers every weekend, and they'd barrel-race in my corral. Sometimes, I'd let 'em drive the pickup on the back roads around the house. Nice girl, Colleen. When my wife was sick, she called or stopped by every day."

Jensen's face clouded with the memory, and he looked away. I waited silently until he was ready to go on.

"Anyway," he said after some moments, "when I came in this mornin' . . . heard about the murder . . . heard your people had been around to see me, I called a couple of neighbors. You'd been to see them too."

"We were trying to find out if one of the neighbors noticed anyone at the McAfferty ranch Sunday evening. Nobody had."

"I didn't either, not exactly," he said. "But the more I got to thinkin' about what I did see, the more I thought I ought to let you know about it. It may not be anythin' that will help, but on the other hand . . ."

He had my full attention now. I pulled my notebook and a ballpoint pen from my shirt pocket. "Thanks for going out of your way," I said. "But why don't you tell me what you saw and let me figure out if it's important. We'll follow up."

"Well, that's the problem," he said. "Tess McAfferty is a good friend of mine, and I wouldn't want to say anythin' that would put her in a bad light." He hesitated, kicked the ground with the toe of his boot.

"But what?" I asked. "We know she had nothing to do with Colleen's murder. Do you think she had something to do with the killings of Ralphie Skates and Clarence Hathaway?"

"No, I don't," he said. "But I think she may know who did. Not for nothin' Sheriff, but I've had the feelin' all summer some-thin' weird was going on at her place. People comin' and goin' at odd hours. Drivin' her property late at night. And then last Sunday night . . ." He stopped again, uncomfortable with what he'd come to say.

"Go on," I urged.

"It was about seven o'clock," he said, "shortly after sundown. I was down in my lower fields checkin' some irrigation pipe, when I heard a vehicle workin' its way down an arroyo that links my ranch with McAfferty's. The driver might have been fishin' up Sailor's Creek on my property and waited until after dark to start home, so I didn't think much of it at the time. But now it strikes me he could also have been comin' out the back way of the McAfferty ranch to avoid bein' seen."

"Did you get a look at him?" I asked.

"Oh yeah," Jensen said. "I've got a big pole lamp down by that field, and he drove right underneath it. I saw him, all right."

"You can describe him?"

"I can do better than that," Jensen said. "I recognized him right away. It was that regulator some of the ranchers hired. Name of Irons. I argued against bringin' him in last spring, but some of the local cattle operations hired him anyway."

He looked me in the eye, and I sensed his uncertainty. It had cost him to say as much as he had, and there'd be a greater price for saying more. I tried to help him over the hump.

"You think Tess might be one of his employers?" I asked quietly. In the background, the police radio squawked and snapped.

Jensen shook his head vigorously. "I didn't say that," he said. "All I know is what I saw. It's your job to figure out what it means."

Jerry Slaymaker called my office late that afternoon.

I was still going over the interview notes we'd taken so far in the McAfferty investigation, and the sound of his voice hit me like a sap.

The last time I'd seen him was at his sentencing, the day the court consigned him to life in prison with no chance of parole.

As the jailers came to lead him away, Slaymaker looked in my direction, made a gun of his thumb and index finger. He fired it at my head and smiled, blew the smoke from the make-believe barrel.

Now he was out. And he had my number.

"Hello, Harry," he said. His voice was soft and well modulated, a thousand years old and as foul as mold. "You know who this is, don't you?"

"I know who it is, Slaymaker," I said. I rested my hand on the handle of my revolver, drew inappropriate comfort from its solid bulk. "What do you want?"

"I sense a certain anger in your voice, Harry." He laughed. "I'll bet you're not glad I'm out."

"You'll go back," I said. "It's just a matter of time."

"Maybe," he said. "But in the meantime, I just thought you'd like to know how I plan to use my freedom."

I didn't answer, listened to his breathing, the faint, electrically charged static from the long-distance connection.

"I'm gonna use it to close the books on an old grievance, Harry," he said. "You didn't play by the rules, you know. Does that ever bother you?"

"Rules?" I spat. "You asshole, Slaymaker. Get off my fuckin' phone."

"The lawsuit's bullshit, Harry. I just did that to piss you off. I'm looking for something more . . . subtle. Harry? You still there?"

I didn't answer.

"Did you really think you were right, Harry? Do you really think you saved somebody else's kid?" he asked. "I know what it is, Harry. I'll bet you think you saved your *own* kid."

"Don't you dare mention my family." My voice came out a choking rasp.

"What?" he said cheerfully. "I couldn't understand you. Must be a bad connection."

"I'll kill you," I whispered. "Don't even think about my family, or I'll kill you. I'll rip your fucking eyes out and piss in your skull."

Slaymaker just laughed.

Then the line went dead.

I came home that night to a dark and empty house. Sometimes I find that comforting, but that night the quiet seemed oppressive and sinister. I let the dog in and fed him a bowl of leftovers from the refrigerator, then I made myself some dinner, fried bologna and canned beans heated up in the nuke.

I'd spent the best part of the afternoon trying to reach Nicole, but she was in court. I left messages, and when she hadn't gotten back to me by six, I called the house.

No answer, but I had a good idea where she was. Nicole spends most summer evenings at the Little League baseball park, where she volunteers as a scorekeeper and announcer. If she'd gone straight to the park from work, she probably wouldn't be home until after ten. I'd have to wait until then.

In between calls to Nicole that afternoon, I'd retained the services of an attorney to represent me in Slaymaker's lawsuit, an old friend from Denver who used to work for the prosecutor's office but has gone into private practice. He told me to stay calm, since lawsuits move through the court system at glacial speed, and come see him sometime next month. In the meantime, his only advice was to stay away from Slaymaker and refuse to discuss the case with the press.

I'd also tracked down John Bruno, my old partner in the Denver Police Department. Bruno's still in homicide, and I thought he'd be interested to know that prison had not rehabilitated our friend, Jerry Slaymaker. I caught him on his way out of the office for his afternoon workout at the health club and told him about my conversation with Slaymaker, the implied threat he'd made against my family.

I asked him if he could have a talk with Slaymaker, let him know the police hadn't forgotten him.

"I'd dearly love to, Harry," he said. "But the boss won't let me within a million miles of Slaymaker. If I roust him, it'll be my ass."

He did agree to speak to the patrol commander and have a black-and-white take a few extra runs past my house at night for the next few weeks. It wasn't much, but short of going to Denver myself, there was little more I could do.

To pass the time until Nicole got home, I washed my dishes, took a long shower, and spent the next two hours trying to keep busy. It was an effort in futility. I couldn't concentrate, because my mind kept coming back to Sean McDonald, Jerry Slaymaker, and the not so veiled threat he'd made that afternoon against my children.

I picked up a novel but gave it up twenty minutes later when I realized I'd read the same paragraph at least a dozen times. I tried to tie a few trout flies, but I couldn't seem to remember the intricate knots or combinations of feathers and fur. Finally I just paced until the clock said it was time for Nicole to be home.

I dialed her number nervously, was relieved when she answered before the first ring ended.

"Hey, good-lookin'," I said. She was out of breath, and I could hear the kids in the background grousing over who's turn it was to put the frozen pizza in the microwave. "Just get home?"

"Yeah, Harry," she said. She sounded apprehensive, like she was expecting bad news. "Just a couple seconds ago. Is something wrong?"

"No," I said. "Have you packed to come up here tomorrow?"

"Not yet. I was gonna do it as soon as I got the kids settled. Why?"

"I've been thinking," I said. "Maybe this isn't the best time for you to visit after all. Maybe we ought to put it off a couple weeks."

"Something come up since this morning, Harry?" she asked. There was an edge of suspicion in her tone, and just a little anger. She remembered the old Harry Starbranch, who let lots of unexpected things come up to ruin our plans—the job, booze, women. Those wounds have started to scab over in the last months, but they're not completely healed.

I didn't know quite where to start, so I blurted it out all in a rush. Told her about Slaymaker's call, his reference to our children, his intention to even the long-standing score between us. I told her this might not be the best time to leave our boys alone, told her I'd leave for Denver that very minute if not for the murder investigation.

"You really think he'd hurt one of the kids?" she asked when I finished.

"I don't know," I said. "He's crazy, but I don't think he's that crazy. I asked the police to send a couple extra patrols around in the evenings."

Nicole was quiet while she thought about what she'd learned, and I gave her time to work it through. When she'd considered it thoroughly, she sounded determined in her judgment. "It's bullshit, Harry," she said.

"What?"

"I think his threats are bullshit. But it's real bullshit if he thinks he's gonna make us hide in our hole like a bunch of damn rabbits. I'm not gonna give him that much control over our lives. That's what he wants, you know?"

"Maybe," I said, "but—"

"I'm takin' the kids to my sister's," Nicole said. "They'll be safe there. Slaymaker probably doesn't even know she exists."

"Good idea," I said. "And then?"

"And then I'm coming to Victory, just like we planned."

# NINE

I set my wristwatch alarm for 5:00 A.M., and by the time the sun peeked over the Medicine Bow range around six-thirty, Keegan and I were already turning off the blacktop and onto the dirt road that led to Saul Irons's cabin on the Hardesty ranch.

With less than two hours sleep the night before, I felt trail-worn and logy, but my square-shaped friend was positively jubilant. He'd been more than happy to make the drive over from Cheyenne in the middle of the night and had arrived at the office in Laramie absolutely wired on black coffee and the Camel unfil-tereds he pulled one after another from the battered pack in his jacket pocket.

He looked even more rumpled and tired than usual, and he smelled like a barroom from all the smoke. The bags under his eyes had taken on a distinctly unhealthy-looking grayish cast, and his eyeballs were so bloodshot they looked like two eggs in a glass of buttermilk. After this was over, he'd need a long rest, but I figured he'd be all right for the time being.

On the drive up the Sybille, he kept the radio tuned to KOWB and sang along with every tune, doing particular disservice to Crystal Gayle and Dolly Parton. I tried to ignore him, but it was like trying to ignore a typhoon. When I could stand no more, I cursed and flicked the radio off. He reached over to turn it back on but stopped when he saw the look of menace in my own undoubtedly bloodshot eyes.

I swatted at the thick cigarette smoke in the car and cracked a window. The cool air stung my face and made my eyes water, but it seemed to shock my system back to a minimal level of consciousness. After a minute, I rolled the window down all the way, ignoring the dust that billowed around us like fog.

Keegan lit another Camel from the butt of his last. "We're almost there, Harry," he smiled. "Catch that bastard still in his nightie."

It was supposed to work like this: we'd confront Irons with Jensen's statement, ask him again about the deaths of Skates and Hathaway, ask him what he'd seen the night of Colleen's murder. He'd deny any knowledge, so we'd drag him back to town for interrogation, in handcuffs if we had to. Eventually, he'd tell us what we wanted to know.

My heart sank the minute we pulled up in front of the dark cabin.

Keegan slapped the wheel with his ham-size fist. "God damn it," he growled. "We missed him."

Irons's four-wheel-drive and horse trailer were gone from their parking places at the side of the cabin, and the front door was locked from the outside with a heavy padlock. The corral was empty, the horses absent, the railings bare of saddles and tack.

Keegan killed the engine and we creaked our way out of his government-issue Ford, closed the doors, and listened to the tick of the cooling motor.

A weather vane on the peak of the cabin roof gave a metallic groan as it rotated in the slight breeze, and two magpies squawked and jabbered as they fought over a prize morsel from a fifty-gallon barrel doing duty as a trash can. My nostrils filled with the smell of fresh manure and old hay, and my skin tingled in the early morning chill.

I waited for the Doberman to make an appearance, but he

148

didn't show. I imagined that wherever Irons had gone, he'd taken the mutt along.

"What now, podna?" I asked. Reaching into the back seat for my jacket, I shrugged it on, buttoned it halfway, and jammed my hands in the pockets.

Keegan shrugged. "Who knows?" he said, his face dark with disappointment. "I doubt if he filed a travel plan. He could be anywhere."

I pulled my blackthorn walking stick from the front seat and climbed the front steps to the porch, cupped my hands around my face and peered through the window. The cabin was a neatly kept one-room bunkhouse with a bed and overstuffed wing chair to one side, a small Franklin stove, and a rough wooden table. A Coleman camp stove sat atop a narrow counter on the far side of the table. Clean dishes were stacked neatly on a dish towel beside the stove.

There was a rifle rack on the wall behind the bed that held at least three weapons, but it was too dark inside to be certain what they were.

I glanced over my shoulder at Keegan, and he shrugged at my unspoken question.

"Why not?" he said. He reached down to pick up a grape-fruit-size rock, bounced it a couple of times in his hands, and lobbed it underhand to me.

It only took a second to break one of the small squares of glass near the top of the window. I used the rock to knock off the jagged remnants, then reached through and turned the latch. That done, I slid the window open, lifted my bad leg and climbed through the opening. Keegan was inside a moment later.

Irons was obviously a man who traveled light. In one corner of the room was a heavy punching bag suspended from the ceiling by a chain. A pair of black Justin boots stood at the foot of the bed. An old brown Stetson hat hung from a peg on the wall, along with a faded denim jacket and a heavy sheepskin winter coat. A stack of Louis L'Amour paperback Westerns and a couple empty packs of

Blackjack sat on a nightstand beside the bed. A battered leather suitcase rested on the floor, filled with carefully folded shirts, jeans and underwear, a heavy cable-knit sweater.

I picked up one of the boots and studied the sole. My deputies had made casts of footprints found on a small rocky hill the morning after the killings, and from them we'd been able to determine that the man who made the footprints wore size 10 cowboy boots outfitted with badly worn riding heels. There were half soles on the boots, which meant the original soles had been replaced, maybe more than once.

The boots in my hand were size 10, but the heels and soles were the originals, still in good shape. These were Irons's dress boots, and I tried to remember what kind of footwear he'd worn at our meeting. I recalled boots that had seen plenty of miles, but I hadn't paid attention to the particulars.

I put the boots down and moved to where Keegan stood before the rifle rack, a grim scowl on his face. The two weapons stored there, a small chain through the trigger guards, were standard sporting hardware—a semiautomatic .22 and a twelve-gauge Browning shotgun. Conspicuously absent was the heavy artillery. Wherever Irons had gone, he'd taken his 7-millimeter and the .22-.454 along for company.

Saul Irons claimed to be nothing more than an amateur archeologist, treasure hunter, and sometime prospector. Maybe his activities were confined to those gentle pursuits, but he carried enough firepower to drive the Brits from Ireland.

You had to wonder why.

The thermometer on the dash said it was 97 degrees by the time I turned onto the dirt road to the McAfferty ranch around one o'-clock. Keegan had dropped me off in Laramie about an hour before, and I'd jumped in the Blazer without stopping at my office and boogied down the highway toward Rock River. Shimmering heat waves rose from the hard-packed roadbed, and though my window was down, I couldn't rest my arm on the frame because it was too hot to touch.

A hundred yards along I hit the brakes to avoid a mature rattlesnake coiled in the middle of the road, but I squashed him flat because I hadn't been paying enough attention to my driving. I'd been rolling along, trying to figure out where Saul Irons had gotten to and wondering how I'd ask Tess McAfferty about her connection to the man. There's no law to prevent livestock growers like Tess from hiring the equivalent of a private security guard to reduce losses of inventory—in this case yearling cattle and horses—but in the past, stock detectives have sometimes crossed the line between lawful deterrence and highly illegal extermination. Maybe Irons hadn't stepped across that boundary yet, but Keegan, a man whose instincts I trusted, believed otherwise. If Irons had, and it could be proven, Tess and the other people who paid him would likely face a few criminal charges of their own. Hiring a man to commit murder is still considered one of your major felonies, even here in the West. And that being the case, I didn't imagine any of them would be eager to shoulder their share of the blame and confess all.

As it turned out, I needn't have worried, because the McAfferty ranch was deserted. The old Jeep and the pickup were still in the driveway, but Tess's Honda was nowhere around. The gate to her front yard was latched and padlocked, and the drapes were drawn. The wind sock at the corner of the porch snapped in the afternoon breeze, and the porch swing creaked on its rusty chains.

I dropped the transmission into low and began to ease down the steep grade toward the corral. A half dozen yearling cattle penned up in the enclosure heard the rumble of the engine and looked up just long enough to satisfy their bovine curiosity before they dipped their snouts back into the cool water of the stock trough. A blaze-faced colt who shared the corral was less complacent; he lurched away from the water and galloped to the other side of the corral, where he turned, nostrils flaring, and whinnied out a note of challenge, watching me with his ears back, ready to bolt. I killed the engine, walked over, and folded my arms on the sun-bleached railing of the corral.

The rickety pine planks moaned as I rested my weight against them, and the eerie noise spooked the pony again. This time, he tried to jump the fence, but he caught his front leg between a couple of planks and raised an incredible ruckus before he could disentangle himself and run around the corral some more.

Checking my revolver to make sure it was seated in the holster, I went back and pulled a couple of evidence bags and my walking stick, canteen, and sunglasses from the front seat of the Blazer. Then I shuffled off in the direction of the small hill fifty yards south of the corral where we'd found and cast footprints the morning after the killings. The hill would have provided natural cover and a clear line of sight for anyone firing at Ralphie Skates and Clarence Hathaway. We hadn't found anything there the first time around, but I wanted a second look.

The small stream on my right burbled merrily, and a tepid breeze ruffled the prairie grasses as I tramped the parched ground and picked my way through the sandstone and shale scattered on the hillside. The top of the hill was bare, and the glare of the sun off the cracked white clay hurt my eyes, even through the dark lenses of my glasses. A prairie dog poked his head from a burrow dug at the center of the crest, chittered angrily when he saw me, and disappeared underground.

A hawk perched majestically atop a telephone pole took flight at my approach, not out of fear, it turned out, but because he'd seen a mouse scrambling through the rabbitbrush alongside the bank of the stream. He attacked silently in a steep dive, his huge wings spread to catch the current. Then he pulled out, wings flapping powerfully, his luncheon clutched in his razor-sharp talons.

After spending twenty minutes scouring the top of the hill in a fruitless search for something left behind by Irons, I sat down and spent another fifteen minutes studying the maze of gullies and washes that feed Sailor's Creek. If Saul had been atop or behind that hill when he killed Ralphie and Clarence, he left the area on foot, since we'd found no fresh vehicle tracks nearby the morning after the murders.

Jensen said he saw Irons leave the Rocking J at around seven Sunday evening, which fit the time of death Bowen established for young Colleen, Skates, and Hathaway. If Irons had been on this hill at about five P.M., he would have had more than enough time to follow one of the arroyos or gullies to the place he'd left his vehicle on the Rocking J and cross paths with Jensen at seven.

The immediate problem was to prove Irons had been on the McAfferty ranch the night of the killings. The long-term problem was to find out what brought him there, and what he'd done once he arrived.

I pushed myself to my feet and came down off the hillock. My bad knee complained with every step, and it was slow going through the heavy sagebrush and dried buffalo grass. Fifty yards from the hill, the mouth of the first arroyo opened. Another opened twenty-five yards from the mouth of the first. There were a half dozen others within a hundred yards of that.

It would have taken me a month to check them all, walking from their mouths to their heads, so I took a wild guess and entered the first one I met. It was a dead end, the gully petering out in a wall of shale and clay less than a quarter mile from its mouth. I walked back to where I'd started and began to work my way up the second wash.

I went the first hundred yards and then began to move more slowly, on my hands and knees at times, looking for any sign that a man had come this way. Coming to a bend in the gully choked by huge granite boulders, I picked my way over the rocks and dropped down onto a bed of fine sand. The sand was smooth, unmarked save for wildlife sign—mouse tracks, the two-toed print of a mule deer, the S-shaped mark of a passing snake.

It had been six days since the killings, plenty of time for Mother Nature to erase any human sign, but I took my time and was careful anyway. I found old bottle caps and ancient shotgun shell casings, the dry skin of a bull snake, shed sometime in the summer and left behind, magpie feathers, and bits of broken glass. There were no footprints.

The beige sand gave way to fine bentonite-laden soil, the surface broken by occasional clumps of parry oat grass and squirreltail. The walking there was easier, and I followed the gully eastward as it angled gradually uphill until I came to a place where the grade became more severe, the path strewn with loose shale and boulders.

At that point it felt more like I was climbing a ladder than walking, and there were several places where I had to stop, lift my bum leg upward to the next rung, grab hold of a rock or root, and haul my fat ass forward. I was sweating profusely; rivulets of stinging moisture ran down my hairline and into the corners of my eyes. I stopped and took a long swig of lukewarm water from the canteen, longing for a cigarette.

It took me over an hour, and I was nearly at the top of the gully when my foot slipped on the face of a granite slab and I landed in a tangled heap at the base of the rock. I cursed mightily, pushed myself up onto my hands and knees, and rolled over on my butt to take stock of the damage. I'd torn the knee of my trousers, scraped my elbow, and whacked my cheek on a rock, but nothing was bleeding profusely or obviously broken, except for the nail on my right index finger, from which a crescent-shaped hunk was missing. Wincing, I shook my hand to get the blood flowing again and stuck the wounded digit in my mouth.

I was sucking away when my gaze happened to land on the soft earth at the base of the rock. There was a small depression in the ground at the edge of the slab about the size of a small teacup in diameter, the edges softened by wind and gravity. I got back down on my knees and crawled over, lowered my face until it was inches away from the depression. On the far side of the little hollow, under the lip of the granite and out of the weather, was the clear imprint of a boot sole. The depression, at the edge of the rock and exposed to the elements, had been made by the heel.

154

Whoever made the track had done exactly as I had, placed his right foot at the base of the rock and put his left up on the granite slab to climb onto it. I don't have the tracking skills of Frankie Bull, but even I could make a rough estimate of when the print had been made. We hadn't had much rain and only moderate wind, so it was conceivable the footprint could be three days old, maybe as old as six. Someone had come out of the McAfferty ranch on foot within the last week, and there was a good chance that person had been involved in the killings.

With a growing sense of excitement, I climbed to the head of the arroyo as quickly as possible. It wasn't far, and when my head popped over the rim, I quickly scrambled out onto a flat table of land that stretched for twenty or thirty yards before it dropped off in another swale.

I hurried across the even ground, stopping at the edge of the next ravine. The banks were lined with gumweed and cactus, and a game trail led from the top to the floor of the swale, where a sagging barbed wire fence ran along the bottom. My nose caught the rotten stench of sulfur and decayed plant life, and I realized that this gully was the home of an underground seep, not enough water to create a flow, but more than enough to keep things moist and rotting.

I inched my way down until I was almost at the fence, which I figured must mark the property line between the McAfferty ranch and the Rocking J. My feet sank in the smelly alkali muck just below the surface, making a sickening plopping sound as I pulled them free. I tried not to gag from the smell, held my breath as long as possible between gulps of oxygen.

The top strand of barbed wire was loose, and I probably could have pushed it down and stepped over, but since the bottom strand was also slack, I decided to hold that strand to the ground with my foot, lift the top strand over my head, and step through the opening. As I held the wire above my head and bent over I felt a barb prick the back of my shirt. I bent lower until it was free and swung my torso through the gap.

The cuff of my pants caught on the bottom strand of wire as I stood up, and I was paying so much attention to getting myself free without tearing my trousers again I almost missed it, the blue and black foil package nearly obscured by a thatch of dried grass. When my leg was unsnagged, I bent down, gingerly pushed the grass aside.

"Hello!" I said. I smiled as I reached down with a bandana to preserve possible fingerprints and held my find to the sunlight. An unopened package of Blackjack licorice gum. Its bright and shiny foil had not been exposed to the elements more than a few days, had likely been dropped very recently by someone going through the barbed wire fence in the same way I had.

Who dropped it?

I didn't know for absolute no-doubt-about-it-Your-Honor positive, but there were only a couple of people I ever knew who chewed that black, disgusting crap.

One of them was Aunt Hattie, who died over twenty years ago from choking on an overly ambitious bite of barbecued pork.

The other was Saul Irons.

At four o'clock that afternoon, the county prosecutor sat on the edge of his barge-size walnut desk, blew his nose in an expensive silk handkerchief, and let me know exactly what he thought of my plan to arrest Saul Irons for suspicion of murder.

"You're fucking joking!" Walker Tisdale snorted. "You've got a witness who can only place him several miles away from the killings and a pack of gum, and you think that makes a murder case? What's going on with you Harry? Is this Slaymaker business getting to you or what?"

I'd dropped the gum package off at the office as soon as I got back to Laramie and assigned a deputy to drive it over to the state lab in Cheyenne immediately. I wanted to see if the fingerprints on the package matched the prints from when Irons was arrested for killing one of his own patrolman in Flagstaff. If I got lucky, I had two good bits of circumstantial evidence, and I was sure that I could find the real thing with only a little more time.

"I'll have the reports back on the prints on the gum package in a couple of hours," I said. "If they belong to Irons . . ."

Tisdale shot his cuffs and looked over at the full-length mirror on the wall to catch his stately reflection. The great-grandson of one of the biggest cattlemen in the state during the late 1800s, Walker came from a long line of Republican ranchers turned politician, and at thirty-eight he already had his eye on a seat in the state Senate, maybe would eventually make a run for governor. That meant he never did anything that had no potential for advancing his political career, never took chances in his personal life, never took a case to court he wasn't one-hundred-percent certain he could win or at least plead to his advantage.

"Fuck the gum package," he said. "So you find Irons's prints on it. So what? It proves nothing, Harry. And neither, I might add, does your eyewitness's testimony. All any of this means is that he was on Tess McAfferty's ranch at some point in the not too distant past, and that he was in the general area of the killings last Sunday night. Tell me this; you got any way to tie him to Skates or Hathaway?"

"No," I admitted.

"Any murder weapon?"

"No."

"Bullets? Bullet fragments."

"No. At least nothing big enough to link to a specific weapon."

"You got any way to prove he ever *saw* the other people involved in the killing of the McAfferty girl? That he could identify them? That he might be able to testify against them?"

"No."

"You got a witness who can place him on the McAfferty ranch Sunday night, and not just near it?"

"No."

"Then you got shit, Harry. Why you wasting my time?"

The morning papers were waiting on my desk when I got downstairs, and one of my treacherous underlings had circled the most important front page stories—the ones about me—in red grease pencil to make sure I didn't miss them. I queered the plan by dumping the whole stack in the trash.

Then I got on the phone in hopes of catching C. J. Fall between stakeouts, or brandings, or castrations, or whatever it is a brand inspector does all day.

I wanted to ask him if he could put his ear to the ground and find out which of the God-fearing, law-and-order-voting ranchers in the county might have gotten together over a nice breakfast of sausage biscuits and cream gravy and decided they should hire Saul Irons to maim and slaughter rustlers.

I also wanted to find out if he'd learned anything about Bobby Snow and whether the missing McAfferty livestock, or Bobby's missing stock trailer, had turned up at any of the kill plants under his surveillance.

Fall wasn't home, but at least this time he'd remembered to turn on his answering machine, so I left him a message asking him to call me at my farmhouse in Victory later that evening. Failing that, I told his machine, I'd be at Colleen McAfferty's funeral on Saturday morning and maybe I'd see him there.

It was just a few minutes shy of five o'clock on Friday night, and the administrative section of the office was shutting down for the weekend. Through the open door I could hear one of the secretaries, a late-thirty-something bottle blonde, tell her pal, a twenty-something court reporter from upstairs who'd recently divorced her husband, that maybe they ought to check out the rock 'n' roll down at Shooter's Saloon that evening.

"I can't stand that heavy-metal garbage myself," the secretary said. "But at least most of the men there are young enough they aren't worried about gingivitis."

Their laughter faded as they made their way out the front

door of the office and headed off for the weekend, high heels clicking like castanets on the industrial-strength tile floor. I poked through the mail and the incident reports for the previous couple of days, satisfied that the county hadn't exploded in my absence.

There'd been a minor brawl at the fairgrounds between some tourists from Indiana and a couple of bronc riders working the rodeo who got bucked off before their eight-second rides were over, and who didn't take kindly to catcalls from the peanut gallery. The tourists escaped the encounter unscathed, but one of the cowboys claimed he'd suffered a chipped tooth when the wife of one of the noisy tourists whacked him with her bottle of Evian water.

Other than that, it had been business as usual. Two deputies broke up a keg party of college and high school kids in West Laramie. An intoxicated Basque sheepherder was arrested for driving on the sidewalk in front of the university president's house. A couple of cross-country motorists had broken down near Sevenmile Creek on I-80 and the husband, a seventy-one-year-old Mormon from Ohio on his way to the LDS temple in Salt Lake, had suffered heat stroke while he changed a tire. The deputy's report said the old gent was treated and released from Ivinson Memorial Hospital.

I hadn't seen my undersheriff on the way in, so I dialed Pajak's extension to see if he'd heard from the deputy who'd driven the Blackjack gum package over to the DCI lab in Cheyenne.

"He phoned about twenty minutes ago," Pajak said between sniffles. A chronic hay fever sufferer, he's allergic to nearly everything that grows in Wyoming. I suppose I should have felt some sympathy for him, but he'd been acting so testy lately I couldn't drum any up.

"And?"

"And what do you think?" he said grumpily, as if the answer was obvious. "They got a clear print, plugged it into the FBI's computer network, and got a match right away. Saul Irons. No doubt about it. That make you happy, Harry?"

"Happier than I was a minute ago," I said. "I still want to talk to the man, though. Why don't you send out a bulletin to have him brought in if any of our people happen to run across him? Make sure our guys understand he's wanted for questioning only."

"You're the boss, Harry," Pajak said, sarcastic emphasis on the word *boss*. "You want us to call you if we find him?"

Fuck you Nicky, I thought uncharitably. I am the boss. Best you remember it. "Yeah, do that," I said. "I should be at home most of the evening."

I hung up and spent the next twenty minutes signing pay vouchers and bills, and my eyes strayed more than once to the newspapers that poked out of the trash can. I knew it would ruin my night if I gave in and read them, but I was drawn to them like a fat hog to a slop bucket. Lots of people in the public eye swear they never read anything that's written about them, especially if what's being written is bad news, but it's my experience those people are incorrigible liars.

My willpower had just about evaporated and I was using the toe of my boot to edge the trash can close enough to reach without getting up when a sharp rap on the frame of my open door made me jump at least six inches in my chair. It was Larry Rawls, who still wore his dark glasses and sported pie-size sweat stains under the armpits of his wrinkled uniform shirt. His face was dark with fatigue and five o'clock shadow, his wiry frame sagging at the shoulders. Bogie in *The African Queen*.

"Got a minute, Sheriff?" he asked, as if he couldn't see I'd been sitting there with nothing better to do than play footsie with a wastebasket.

"Just a minute," I said. I pushed the tantalizing newspapers back to their original location at the side of the desk. "As you can see, I was in the middle of some high-level administrative paperwork."

Rawls laughed and sprawled his long frame on the railroad bench, lit a cigarette and sucked in a hungry mouthful of smoke. He flicked his spent match at the trash can and missed.

"Shit," he grumbled.

"Tough day?" I asked.

"Not so tough," he said. "But plenty boring. I've been helping out on the Snow stakeout. Took over about one o'clock and sat out there all afternoon. You know, Harry, there isn't a damn shade tree for fifty miles around the place I was parked.

I smiled. "That's why they call it the plains, Larry. If there were shade trees everywhere, they'd call it the forest. You see anything worth mentioning out there?"

"Yeah, I saw plenty. Jackrabbits. Eagles. Magpies. Prairie dogs. Coupla antelope that walked right up to the car."

"But no Bobby Snow?"

"Oh, yeah, him too," Rawls said, making me pay a little for my teasing.

"And what, Deputy Rawls, was our man doing? Was he butchering stolen cattle? Digging a grave in his back yard?"

"Nope," Rawls said. "He was packing up. Took him about an hour, but he loaded his pickup with camping gear and took off with a couple saddle horses in a little stock trailer."

"Which direction?"

"Toward Laramie," Rawls said. "I followed him into town, but I got stuck behind a red light on Third Street and lost him. I think he was headed south on Highway 287."

"Toward Tie Siding?" I asked.

"Yeah, maybe," Rawls said. "Maybe down to Colorado. All I know is, wherever he was going, it looked like he was planning to be gone for a good long time."

"That figures," I grumbled. "Sometimes, you look at all the out-of-state plates on Main Street and it seems like everyone in the world is trying to think of a way to get to Wyoming—until I get interested in them, and then they can't wait to get out."

# TEN

My landlady, my ex-wife, and the mutt were all waiting for me on the back porch when I got back to Victory about six-thirty, the dog gnawing on a soup bone and the women gathered around the barbecue. The grill, upon which they'd obviously just dumped about a half gallon of lighter fluid before chucking on a match, shot three-foot flames, and they'd pulled their lawn chairs back to avoid getting their eyebrows singed.

An open gallon jug of cheap burgundy sat at their feet, and they drank the vile stuff from the mason jars I keep around for iced tea. Judging from the twinkle in Nicole's eyes and the fact that Edna was smoking one of her nasty little cigars in public, I figured they'd been at the sauce for at least an hour.

Edna, who was dressed in knee-high rubber fireman's boots, coveralls, and an oversize orange Denver Broncos T-shirt, gave me a tipsy little wave and toasted me with her fruit jar when I clumped up the steps. The mongrel looked up long enough to see who I was, then burrowed himself under Nicole's chair, the bone clamped between his enormous paws like I planned to steal it.

"It looks like you met my new roommate," I said as Nicole pushed herself up from the chair and came across the porch to give me a full-contact hug and a not so perfunctory kiss on the lips.

Barefoot, she wore a white cotton shirt tied beneath her breasts and an old pair of blue jeans cut off so high the white cotton pockets peeked out from beneath where she'd hacked off the legs. Her long auburn hair was pulled back in a thick braid, tied with a black velvet ribbon. As she stood there on her tiptoes, the tip of her tongue traced my upper lip. I closed my eyes, smelled her musky perfume, and felt the warmth radiating from her slender body like a hardwood fire in a Franklin stove.

I felt an unmistakable stirring in my groin and came up for air, looked over Nicole's shoulder at Edna, who watched us with unabashed, lecherous interest. Grinning sheepishly at Edna, I wrapped my arms more tightly around Nicole's waist.

"You two keep that up," the old woman cackled, "and I'm gonna have to go in to the vet and get my pacemaker recalibrated."

Nicole pulled me by the hand toward the lawn chairs. "Sorry, Edna," she laughed. "It's just that—"

"Yeah, yeah, it's been a long time," Edna said. "But how long, though? Two weeks? Three? For me it's thirty years, kiddo. It ain't nice to tease an old lady who's livin' on memories."

"Oh be quiet, you old harpie," I said, and kissed her on the top of the head before I reached down to fill a jar of my own. "You wore out two husbands. Give someone else a turn in the saddle."

If Nicole was getting tanked and gabbing it up with Edna, then it was pretty clear she wasn't worried about the boys. When I asked her, she told me the two little boys were safe at her sister's, and her brother-in-law was on the lookout for trouble. Robert was camping with friends in Estes Park. She'd warned our oldest boy, now eighteen and six two, 190 pounds, to keep his eyes open. He'd scoffed at first, she said, then turned solemn. He wondered if he should stay with Sam and Tommy and help keep them safe. Doing the job I should have been doing.

"Christ, I'm a hell of a dad, aren't I?" I asked.

Edna stirred at that and snorted, tossed the butt of her stogie on the coals.

"Here you are," she said. "Good food, good drink, and all you can do is talk about the kids. You might as well be married."

She handed me her mason jar. "Just half a glass," she said.

When I picked up the green wine bottle, I saw I'd seriously underestimated the length of their happy hour. The jug was half empty, which meant they'd had about a quart apiece. I decided I'd better feed 'em quick or they'd start singing old Big Bopper songs. I went over to the table at the side of the porch, picked up a plate of sliced cheese, crackers, and vegetables, brought it back and passed it around.

"I like him," Nicole said around a mouthful of carrot. "He's really sweet."

I assumed she was talking about me. "Why thanks," I said.

She wrinkled her forehead, shot a which-planet-did-this-moron-come-from? look in Edna's direction. "Not you, Harry," she said. "The dog. I like the dog. What's his name?"

I looked down at the animal in question. Still guarding his bone, he glared at me and growled viciously, the fickle bastard. He'd like me well enough when it was just him and me and I was his only ticket on the gravy train. But now, with women around to moon over him, I looked like competition.

"*Pendejo,*" I said testily. "It's Spanish. Literally translated, it means pubic hair."

"You name him?" Nicole asked.

I nodded, grinning.

"Well no wonder he doesn't like you," she said. "I'm gonna take 'im home to the boys. But I'm gonna tell 'em his name is Blackfoot, and don't you ever tell 'em different."

"Good," I said. "I hate dogs anyway, especially that one."

She and Edna shared a conspiratorial smile, and the old woman creaked her way to her feet. "All that talkin' wore me out," she said. "Think I'll take myself home and plug in a Sylvester Stallone."

"Stay for dinner?" I asked.

"Nah," she said, and gave me a peck on the cheek. "You two need to be alone, and I already ate. Old people like to eat early, you know. Keeps 'em regular. I'll see you in the morning."

"You bakin' cinnamon rolls?" I asked.

"Of course, you damn mooch," she said. "It's Saturday, ain't it? I'll leave a pan on your kitchen counter, if you leave the door unlocked."

With that, she shuffled off across the driveway. Her oversize boots made a curious sucking noise with every step.

"She loves you, Harry," Nicole said as the old woman disappeared around the corner of her house.

"I know," I said. I took a sip of the wine. It was noxious stuff, so I poured the contents of my jar into the driveway and started into the house for a cold Coors. "I usually have that effect on women. Especially ones who are old enough to have traveled in covered wagons."

"I mean it," Nicole said. "She doesn't get along very well with her own family, you know. She told me before you came home that if it hadn't been for you, she figures they would have forced her into a nursing home two or three years ago. And if that had happened, she says, she'd be dead by now. You're her family, Harry. Her real family."

"Bull-oney," I said, as gruffly as I could. "One of these days you and I'll be in a nursing home and that old crow will still be living out here alone, cleaning the stables and throwing hay to those geriatric nags. I can't stand it when she gets all mushy like that."

With that pronouncement, I fetched myself a beer and a spare, hung my Blackhawk on a peg behind my bedroom door, and changed into a pair of cutoffs, a T-shirt with a leaping cut-throat trout on the front, and a pair of electric blue flipflops.

While the coals burned down to the appropriate tempera-ture, Nicole and I sipped our drinks and caught up on our lives, our kids, and our jobs. Her long legs were stretched from her lawn chair to mine, her bare feet rested on my thigh. Her toenails were red, and I wondered idly when she'd started to polish them. Somehow the image of her with little cotton balls between her toes was downright amusing. Maybe tomorrow, I thought, I'd ask if she wanted me to paint them for her. Maybe I could catch her right after she got out of the shower, before she had a chance to . . .

". . . but the coach said he didn't care if Tommy did have a dentist appointment. He'd missed practice, so he couldn't play in the game."

"What?" I said. "I'm sorry, I kind of drifted off."

"I said Tommy couldn't play in the game because he got benched. I wanted to complain to the Little League's board of directors, but Tommy said if I did that he'd be so embarrassed he'd just quit the team."

"You want me to call this guy?" I asked.

"And do what?"

"Tell him if he benches my kid again, he'd better be wearing a cast iron cup."

"Sure, right," she said. She swung her legs off mine, sat forward in her chair. "Just jump right in and straighten things out. Jesus, Harry, if that isn't just like you, I don't know what is. If Tommy doesn't want me to call the league, you think he's gonna feel better if you threaten his coach?"

Christ on a crutch, I thought, these winos are touchy. "Just a joke, Nicole. Just a joke."

"Well, it's hard to tell with you sometimes," she said huffily. With that, she marched off into the house a bit unsteadily to get the steaks from the refrigerator and put some music on the stereo. She picked one of my favorites, Ry Cooder's *Bop 'til You Drop,* the album where Jim Keltner plays drums and Bobby King sings backup soul. And as Ry warmed up his hot slide guitar, I took the plate of thick rib eyes she carried back outside and busied myself doing manly things at the grill to keep from shooting off my mouth and getting myself in trouble.

We ate our meal on the porch as the sun set over the Laramie Plains, Nicole wrapped in one of my old cardigans to ward off the early evening chill. In the yard, the mercury vapor light kicked on as dusk settled, and the bug zapper had a field day with a late-season hatch of moths. We lit a hurricane lamp, sat side by side and brushed shoulders like a couple of honeymooners. I put a mason jar to her lips and held it while she sipped wine. She fed me bites of blood-rare steak.

We got pleasantly high and did not talk about murder, rape, Jerry Slaymaker, or elections. And when we finished, we carried the dishes inside, wrapped our arms around each other's middles, and danced to almost an entire side of Willie Nelson's *Stardust,* her breasts pressed against my chest, her head nestled on my shoulder. Our bodies barely moved as we swayed in time to "Georgia."

At some point during that song, my fingers found the buttons on her blouse. I undid them carefully, untied the knot, and pushed the cotton shirt away from her shoulders. Slowly, I slipped it off her arms—her skin looked pale blue in the moonlight—reached down to pop the snap on her cutoffs.

She smiled as she unzipped my shorts. "This is kinda one-sided cowboy," she said. "How 'bout we both play?"

Fine with me. I closed my eyes and rose to my tiptoes as I felt myself beginning to respond.

Remember this moment, Starbranch, I thought, because it's as good as it gets. You've got exactly what you want. And a chance to keep it.

As long as you don't screw it up.

Again.

We didn't even get to the green stuff until after two in the morning, and after that I slept so soundly I didn't hear Edna when she let herself in around seven and left a half dozen monstrous cinnamon rolls on the kitchen counter for our breakfast. Nor did I hear Nicole when she padded out of the bedroom about seven-thirty, fed and watered the mutt, puttered around the kitchen brewing coffee, and left for her morning jog.

I did hear her, though, when she breezed into the bedroom an hour or so later singing a Randy Travis tune off key at the top of her lungs. It was almost impossible, but I ignored her good humor and buried my head under the pillow. She retaliated by throwing open the curtains and pulling the covers off the bed, which left me naked from the neck down.

She thwacked the bottom of my foot. "Time to get up, Harry," she chirped. I tried to kick her. Missed. "We need to be at that funeral by eleven thirty."

I refused to open my eyes. "So go way 'til ten," I grumbled. "Jesus, aren't you hung over? You *should* be hung over."

"Nope, Harry. You worked that poison right out of my system."

Cautiously, I opened one sleep-encrusted eye and looked up at her. She stood at the foot of the bed, disgustingly healthy-looking. Her hair was pulled back in a tight ponytail, her cheeks were pink, and she was wearing a hot pink spandex something that appeared to have been applied to her body with a spray gun, Ray-Ban sunglasses with a safety strap, running shoes, pink socks, and a pink terrycloth sweatband.

I couldn't help but notice she looked damn good in spandex, taut, lean, and curvy. I patted the empty side of the bed. "C'mon back here," I said. "Let me peel you outta that suit before it cuts off the circulation to your brain."

"No way, podna. Get your ass outta the sack. A good breakfast and you'll feel like a new man." She took a long look at me, shook her head in mock disapproval. "A brisk walk, wouldn't hurt either," she said. "Looks like you could use some exercise."

I groaned, reached for a water glass on the nightstand, raised my head and washed away the worst of the gumbo. I hadn't consumed much beer the night before, so my head felt reasonably intact. I diagnosed my malady as acute sleep deprivation and total bodily exhaustion. Exercise would only make me more tired, and what was the point of that? I whined, pointed at my bad leg, tried to sound pitiful. "I can't go power-walking on this. I can't even go half-power walking."

"Bullshit, Harry," she said. "You've come to depend on that walking stick of yours, but you don't need it. At least, you wouldn't if you'd take the time to build up your leg muscles and loosen up that knee."

I groaned and sat up, but my head started to swim so I lay back down and threw my arm over my face.

"What's the matter, Slim?" she asked. Kicking off her shoes, she sat down on the bed, pulled her knees to her chest, and wrapped her arms around them.

"I'm old," I croaked, "and you made me that way."

She laughed. "Nah, nature did that. Nature and chicken-fried steaks." She scooched her bottom across the bed until she got close to me, rubbed her hands against my thigh, began to knead the muscles of my leg with her strong fingers. "Does it hurt?" she asked.

"Some," I admitted. "But it's getting better. On days when I don't have to get out of bed, I hardly notice it at all."

"You gotta work it, Harry. Make it strong," she said. "Remember what your physical therapist told you? Fifteen minutes of stretching exercises a day, followed by a half hour of strenuous exercise. You been doing that?"

"Not always," I admitted. "I exercise, but—"

"But when it comes time to exercise that leg, you find an excuse to avoid it, because exercising hurts. I know how you are, Harry. You don't like pain, and for some reason you think if you ignore it long enough your body will just rejuvenate itself."

"Horseshit."

"Oh is it? Tell me this, Harry. How long has it been since you went to the dentist?"

"Six months," I said.

"Come on," she said. "How long really?"

I avoided her eyes. "Two years," I said. "I don't like drills."

"And how long since you've been for a physical?"

"I was in the hospital last winter," I reminded her.

"Right, because you're so goddamn stubborn you wouldn't listen to your ski instructor and stay on the beginner slope. Had to be a big strong he-man and sneak onto the intermediate before you even know how to snowplow. It's just lucky you only got hurt as bad as you did, lucky you didn't tear that stinking leg all the way off."

"I made out a lot better than the other guy, the one I rearended," I said. "I think I killed him. Aren't they supposed to signal or something when they turn?"

"That's beside the point," she said impatiently. "The point is how you take care of yourself. How long since you went to the doctor just for a checkup? How long since you saw a doctor when you weren't being wheeled into the emergency room?"

"Three years," I said. "Maybe a little more. I don't like needles, I don't like doctors, and I especially don't like the part where he pulls on a rubber glove. But that doesn't mean I'm afraid."

"I didn't say you were afraid of anything. I just said that given the option, you'll avoid doing what's good for you, if doing what's good for you is uncomfortable or inconvenient. It's sort of an overriding tenet of your personality."

She was right, and there was no point in arguing. I creaked my way out of bed and sucked down a few cups of strong coffee while Nicole scrambled eggs and made toast.

We ate our breakfast on the back porch, and afterward we shared a hot shower and washed each other's backs. Then, wrapped in a thick white towel, Nicole disappeared into the bedroom to dress for Colleen McAfferty's funeral service.

I sat in the kitchen naked, drank coffee and munched one of Edna's cinnamon rolls, listened to Nicole sing to herself as she dried her hair and put on makeup. A nice breeze came through the screen doors and windows, drying the droplets of water on my back and legs and bringing little goose bumps to the skin on my forearms.

In the days when we were still married, I liked to watch Nicole get ready for work in the morning or a date on Friday night. I liked the look of concentration on her face when the applied her lipstick, liked the almost feline pleasure she took in brushing her long hair, liked to watch her wriggle into her pantyhose, slip a dress over her head and smooth it over her hips.

These days, however, that little intimacy is one she denies me. Perhaps it's because she thinks we've grown too far apart to allow me a glimpse at such a personal and private activity. Perhaps she's a little sensitive because at thirty-nine, it takes her a little longer to achieve her self-imposed standard of beauty than it did when she was twenty-one. Whatever her reasons, I miss that harmless marital voyeurism and was tempted to tiptoe up to the bedroom door, open it a crack, and sneak a peek at my sweetheart in her skivvies.

Instead, I opened the *Laramie Boomerang* to the sports page and caught up on my favorite baseball teams and players. Of all major league sports, baseball is best, and I find my general mood over the summer months closely tracks the level of excitement generated by the major league season. I was halfway through the statistical roundup when my concentration was broken by the jangle of the phone. I folded the paper in a rough approximation of its original shape, swallowed the last bite of cinnamon roll and picked up on the fourth ring.

"Starbranch here."

"Mornin' Harry," C.J. Fall said. "Got your message on my machine and thought I'd better call you before I went out in the field."

"You're not going to Colleen McAfferty's funeral?" I asked.

"I'd like to, but I can't," he said. "I've got a case coming to a head out near Carbon County, and I think I might be able to wrap it up today. If I do, it's something you might be interested in."

"What's going on?"

"I'd rather not say too much right now," he said. "I'm at a pay phone at Foster's. It might have something to do with Bobby

Snow, though. If it does, I'll let you know first thing."

"Do that, C.J.," I said. "I should be around here most of the afternoon. And if not, I'll leave word at the office where I can be reached."

"Good," he said. "I'll try to call tonight, but it might be late."

"C.J.?"

"What is it, Sheriff?"

"I've gotta ask you a question. The DCI thinks some Albany County ranchers may have gotten themselves a hired gun to work as a range regulator down here, man by the name of Saul Irons. You heard anything about that? Any idea of who might be signing his paycheck?"

There was a long pause on the other end of the line, the sound of dish carts banging through the restaurant in the background, the blare of a semi's air horn in the parking lot outside. "I've heard of Saul Irons," he said noncommittally. "He's outta Flagstaff, isn't he? Had some trouble down there a few years back with one of his patrolmen?"

"That's him," I said. "Right now, though, he's living in a cabin on the old Hardesty ranch. At least he was."

"That's funny. I checked some brands out there a couple weeks ago, and the foreman never mentioned him. And what do you mean, he was?"

"Just that. He was there early in the week, but when I went out there looking for him yesterday he was gone. I put out a bulletin, but apparently he hasn't turned up yet. At least, we haven't found him."

"And from what I've heard through the grapevine, you won't unless he wants to be found," Fall said.

"So what do you hear, C.J.? You think my friend at the DCI is right? You think we've got a paid killer wandering around the sagebrush country looking for rustlers to whack? You think some of these local stockgrowers are paying him to do it?"

"I haven't heard that," he said. "But I suppose it's possible.

It's happened other places, so I wouldn't be surprised to see it here."

"But why?" I asked. "What makes them think they can be vigilantes, C.J.? Why would they take that kind of chance?"

"They might do it," he said, "because the stakes are high. It's like I told you, Harry, there's big money to be made rustling. Remember that seven grand you found at Ralphie Skates's house? That was rustling money. And one successful rustler means lots of ranchers come up puny when it's time to total the profits. Most of them just can't stand the losses, not if they want to be in business next year, or the year after that. And if that was Ralphie's take for a few days' work, imagine what kind of losses we're talking with a whole gang operating."

"But you guys do a pretty good job."

"Not good enough," he said. "Brand inspectors been working this country for over a hundred years, and we haven't stopped rustling. In fact, the best we do is slow it down some. We're like city slickers on a coyote roundup, Harry. Unless we're really lucky, we only catch the dumb ones."

# ELEVEN

If you counted the kids in the choir, there were over three hundred fifty people at Colleen McAfferty's funeral service, so many that the pews were filled to capacity and the back of the small church was standing room only.

The closed mahogany casket rested on its wheeled stand at the front of the church, covered by a blanket of mums, carnations, lilies, and roses by the hundreds. Dozens of expensive arrangements sent by well-wishers cluttered the area in front of the pulpit. The organist played "Amazing Grace," and the voices of the choir were true and sweet as they sang the heart-wrenching old-time gospel hymn.

Tess, dressed in a black knee-length dress, black hose, and black pumps, sat in the front row with her parents, who'd arrived the day before from Ohio. Her father was a frail old man in his late sixties with jowly cheeks, a red nose with the kind of bulging veins that indicate a heavy drinker, and a fringe of white hair around the edges of his bald head. Her mother, heavyset and with a ruddy complexion, looked like she came from hardy peasant stock and was obviously the strength in the family. A woman in her late twenties or early thirties who shared Tess's hair coloring and facial structure, sat at Tess's left, dabbing her eyes and nose with a hand-kerchief.

Across the aisle were Tess's in-laws, the family of the husband who'd been killed six years before. There were several members of the McAfferty clan present, most of them, I imagined, down from the family ranch outside Sundance. The men were dressed in their best western clothing, the patriarch and the young men in good wool-blend western coats, matching pants, and expensive boots. The women wore subdued cotton dresses and jackets in grays and black.

Behind the families, about a hundred high school kids were clustered in a group, most of the girls red-eyed from tears, the boys looking uncomfortable, but quiet and attentive.

Townspeople from Laramie, neighbors from around Rock River, friends and other relatives filled out the remaining seats, and ushers quietly guided latecomers down the outsides of the aisles.

Nicole and I arrived too late for a seat, so we found a place to stand at the back of the room near the doors. I scanned the crowd and saw lots of familiar faces. Curly Ahearn sat with Frankie and Frieda Bull in the middle of the pews. Sally Sheridan from the *Casper Star Tribune* and a young reporter from the *Boomerang* whose name I couldn't remember sat together in the last pew, notebooks open and felt-tipped pens poised. Most of the Albany County judicial community was in attendance, including Walker Tisdale and what looked like his entire prosecutorial staff.

Coroner Jim Bowen, who looked even more mournful than he had during our last visit, was wedged in at the end of a pew with an incredibly fat woman on one side and a fidgety teenage boy on the other. I caught his eye when he turned around to look over the late arrivals, and he gave me a sad wave before he faced forward again.

When the hymn was finished, the minister, a distinguished man with a full head of silver hair, a fine nose, and pale blue eyes, took the podium, placed his hands on the sides, and looked out over his audience for a full minute before he began the service. The Reverend Coleman Samuelson has served the First Christian congregation in Laramie since he graduated seminary school in the fifties and had known many of the people there that morning since they were children.

He looked at Tess, smiled a gentle and compassionate smile, then scanned the faces of the high school kids who'd come to say good-bye to their classmate. He welcomed those in attendance, led us in a prayer, then looked down for several long minutes, as if thinking of what he would say.

"I married Colleen McAfferty's parents in this very church," Samuelson began. "And when Colleen was born a year later, I visited her in the hospital before her parents took her home.

"In the years that followed, I watched her grow, and came to love her as one of my own. I saw her perform in our Christmas pageants. I taught her in Sunday school. When she was a little older, I baptized her. When she was older still, I spoke with her often about the sorts of things that trouble young people as they prepare to take their rightful places in the world.

"As well as any person here, I knew Colleen McAfferty as a fine and decent young woman. And when her mother asked me to speak for her today, I spent many hours trying to decide what Colleen might have wanted, had she planned this service. Knowing and loving her as I did, I believe that she would have wanted not for us to be saddened or wounded further by what we say and do here today, but for us to find a way to help her friends and loved ones come to terms with their sadness, perhaps even find something constructive and useful in her death. That's why I'm going to address most of my remarks not only to her family, but to her classmates, many of whom may be attending their first funeral this morning, most of whom have never had to face life after one so young and vital is taken from them in such a tragic, cruel, and senseless manner."

The crowd's attention was riveted on Samuelson, who spoke

without written notes, his clear, strong voice tinged with a Texas drawl. Beside me, Nicole took my arm, leaned against me for support.

"Since Colleen McAfferty's death," he continued, "I have felt many of the same emotions I imagine most of you have felt. At first, I felt a burning anger. And with that anger, I felt the thirst for vengeance, the desire to inflict upon those persons responsible worse suffering than they could ever imagine. Like an Old Testament prophet, my sense of justice cried out, 'An eye for an eye, a tooth for a tooth!'—as if that would even the scales and heal the rents in my heart and soul."

Many in the congregation nodded that they too had considered vengeance, and from the front of the church where the McAfferty clan was gathered came a murmur of agreement. Samuelson held their gazes, waited until they were quiet again.

"But vengeance is a two-edged sword," he said. "A sword that not only cuts one's enemies but cuts those who wield it as well. In the end, anger, the thirst for vengeance, are destructive emotions. We think they will destroy that which we perceive as evil, but instead they destroy what is good in us.

"Knowing Colleen as we did, we must ask ourselves if she would have taken comfort in the knowledge that our anger at her death, our thirst for revenge, whether we take that revenge or not, had cost each of us a measure of our humanity. That it had not lessened our bitterness or our rage but had instead placed a greater, longer-lasting burden on our souls."

Samuelson paused to allow those in the audience to consider his question. "She would not have wanted that," Samuelson said finally. "She loved too much to have wanted something so destructive. She would not have wanted her memory forever associated in our minds with anger. Instead, I believe she would have wanted something better, better for her friends and those she loved. I believe she would have wanted her memory to stand for something positive, something healing, something pure and wholesome.

"Yesterday morning," he said, "I was approached by a group of local businessmen and friends of Colleen's from her school. They came with a check for ten thousand dollars, with which they propose to establish a scholarship fund in her name, to be used to further the educations of Albany County high school students who might not otherwise have the opportunity to receive a university education. I agreed that this fund could be administered through the auspices of the church, and that I would lend my support to see that this initial endowment is increased until our goal of at least one hundred thousand dollars is met. I would like to invite Colleen's mother, Tess, to sit on the panel that awards scholarships from this fund, and I would like to invite any of the rest of you here today to take part in our venture as well.

"Nothing we can do or say will bring this young woman back to us. But perhaps through the work of this scholarship program, she will reside with us in spirit through the rest of our lives."

With that, Samuelson read a passage from Ecclesiastes, led the congregation in a prayer for Colleen, and motioned to the choir, whose members sang "Wind Beneath My Wings" while Colleen's classmates walked haltingly up to the casket and placed trinkets and remembrances on its lid. A photograph. A single rose. A favorite book. A pair of white gloves. A class ring tied with a red ribbon.

By the time the song ended, the knot in my throat was so tight I could barely breathe, and hot tears burned my eyes.

It was sad.

Nicole and I followed the funeral procession to the McAfferty ranch outside Rock River, stood in the crowd and listened as Samuelson said a last prayer over the coffin, watched as they lowered Colleen McAfferty's remains into the shady ground beneath a giant cottonwood.

Then we followed the crowd back to the ranch house, where women from the church had coordinated a sit-down luncheon in the yard for everyone in attendance. We filled our plates but ate sparingly, seated at the same table as Tess's father-in-law, Cyrus McAfferty, and two young McAfferty men someone told me were brothers of Tess's husband.

When we'd finished our meal, Nicole gathered up an armload of plates and disappeared into the house, presumably to help out in the kitchen. I stayed at the picnic table with the men and looked around for Tess, but she was nowhere to be seen, so I sipped the last of my tea and looked down the table, where the McAfferty men were hunched over in conversation.

". . . stay down here and keep an eye on things for us."

It was Tess's father-in-law, old man McAfferty, speaking, but he shut up as soon as he saw I was listening. Two younger McAffertys watched me curiously, and there was a long and edgy silence during which all of us pretended we didn't notice a thing. I got the feeling all three of them wished I would go away and mind my own business so they could speak freely again.

Across the yard, Will Jensen talked to Kelly Furlong, a stockgrower who owns the C-Bar-C Ranch on the other side of Rock River. They both had plates of food balanced in their hands and stood up to eat. Both of them looked exceedingly uncomfortable in their dress clothes, and Jensen had draped his polyester jacket across the back of a nearby folding chair and rolled his sleeves up to his elbows. There was a faded tattoo on his forearm, and half moons of perspiration darkened the armpits of his light blue shirt. I thought about questioning him again while I had the chance, see if he'd remembered anything else about his encounter with Saul Irons. I decided this wasn't the best time, since it would probably make him nervous to be seen speaking to the law.

"I've been looking for Tess," I finally said to old man McAfferty, who jumped a little at the sound of my voice. "I'd like to give her our condolences before we leave."

He looked at me for a long moment, as if I wasn't speaking a language he could understand. When he finally started to answer, the words caught in his throat. He cleared it noisily. "She's in her bedroom," McAfferty said curtly. "Broke down right after the burial. Her parents are in there with her, and by now maybe the doc's there too. Don't think we'll be seein' her again this afternoon, but I'll be glad to give her your message."

"Thanks," I said. For a man who'd just buried his grand-daughter, he handled his grief stoically. There were dark circles under his eyes, and his complexion was a bit sallow, but he'd shown no outward sign of his pain all day, even at the end of Colleen's service, when nearly everyone else—including me—had shed real tears. Not that his reaction is unusual. In the West, many of our daddies taught us that real men don't cry, ever. But I also know that the hurt is the same, whether you show it to the world or keep it to yourself. I tried to reach out in the best way I knew.

"That was a fine service today, Mr. McAfferty," I said. "I think Colleen would have been proud."

"Proud?" he asked. "What makes you say that?"

His question caught me off guard, and it took a couple of seconds to shift my mental gears.

"Well," I said tentatively, "I think what Samuelson said had an impact on everyone there. I want you to know that we're doing everything we can to find the other men involved in Colleen's murder. But nothing we do will change the fact that she's gone. I think she would have been proud that even after we bring these guys to trial and put them away, this scholarship program means her life will be remembered, that it will stand for something positive."

McAfferty didn't answer, but the cold look in his eyes said that he disagreed.

"I also believe," I said, "that Colleen would have agreed with Samuelson about the destructiveness of anger, that thirst for revenge he talked about. I don't think she would have wanted the people she loved to carry that in their hearts. Do you?"

McAfferty looked into his drink. He closed his eyes, and his fingertips drummed the top of the pine table as he wrestled with his thoughts. Looking up at the young McAfferty men watching him, he answered me in a voice that was icily calm and packed with barely subdued menace.

"Let me tell you a story," he said. "In 1907 a traveling drummer stopped by the McAfferty homestead one spring evening and asked if he could stay the night. They let him stay, gave him some food and a nice place to sleep in the barn. But later that evening, when one of the young McAfferty women came out to feed her horse, he raped her. Raped her, knocked her unconscious, and took off."

I nodded for him to go on.

"The next morning," he continued, "they found that girl and brought her around, but of course by that time the drummer was long gone. So they followed him. Caught him about fifteen miles from the homestead, riding like hell. One of those McAfferty boys roped him and pulled him off his horse." He looked at me.

"And?"

"They took their revenge," McAfferty said simply. "They pulled out their hunting knives and cut off his prick. Then they tied a rope around his ankles, tied the other end to a saddle horn, and dragged that bastard through the sagebrush and cactus until he was dead.

"The man on the horse was my grandfather."

McAfferty described the gruesome scene—the killing of a human being, albeit a despicable one—with no more emotion than he'd describe squashing a spider, and the effect was chilling. "What are you saying?" I asked. "Are you saying you're going after these people on your own? Why the hell would you tell me something like that? You know who I am, don't you?"

"I know who you are, Sheriff. All I'm sayin' is that the McAffertys have always birthed their own, they've raised their own, taken care of their own, and buried their own. And when we have to find justice for our own, we damn sure take care of that too."

"And you believe Colleen would have approved that? That she would have wanted to see blood on your hands?"

"Colleen was a McAfferty," the old man said, as if that explained everything. "That's exactly what she'd expect."

After that, the atmosphere at the McAfferty table grew even more chilly, so I left them alone and tried to mingle. I won't say that the ranchers and cowboys clustered in small groups around the front yard were unfriendly, but almost everywhere I stopped, I got the feeling people knew something I didn't and weren't anxious to include me in their discussions. Several conversations that seemed spirited and intense as I approached suddenly turned to sedate ruminations about the weather and the price of hay as I came within earshot.

It made me uneasy and a bit self-conscious, to tell you the truth. So when I'd spent long enough feeling unwanted and out of place, I decided it was time to track Nicole down and head on back to Victory. If we hurried, there'd still be plenty of daylight for a leisurely horseback ride, an early prime-rib dinner at the Trail's End, and maybe even a little dancing to the jukebox at the Silver Dollar.

I excused my way through the mourners still gathered around the lunch tables and walked through the open door and into the living room. Tess's father reclined on the couch, his collar open, a wet washrag over his eyes. Her physician, Helen Aruna, was at the other end of the couch, leafing through a copy of *Vanity Fair*. Her mother, sister, a few McAfferty women, and three or four ladies from the church were in the kitchen, where some of them dried pots and a couple more loaded the dishwasher.

Nicole was not with them, nor did I see her in the dining room, where yet more volunteers wrapped big plates of leftover cold cuts and desserts in tin foil to be frozen. When she saw me standing in the living room with my hat in my hand, the church volunteer who seemed to be the field marshal of the food operation, a stout woman in a sleeveless blue dress and sensible shoes, held her finger to her lips and pointed at Tess's father, who by this time was snoring softly.

I whispered Nicole's name and the woman pointed down the

hall toward the bedroom door, came over to where I stood and took me by the arm.

"Your wife is talking to Tess," she whispered. "After the funeral service, they seemed to hit it off right away. Tess was riding the ragged edge, and your young lady seemed to calm her down. I think Nicole is staying in there with her till she falls asleep."

I told her I understood, said that when Nicole was finished she could find me at the Blazer.

"You're in a hurry?" she asked.

"No, no hurry," I said, not too convincingly it seemed, because she smiled and gave my elbow a gentle squeeze.

"Why don't I just go in and take a peek?" she said. "At least tell her you're here?"

I started to protest, but by that time she was already on her way down the hall. She turned the bedroom doorknob quietly and slipped inside the dark room. She was back in less than a minute.

"Tess is sleeping," the woman said. "Nicole says she'll be along as soon as she tucks her in."

When my ex-wife finally turned up at the vehicle a half-hour later, she looked like a wilted flower. I had the windows closed and the air conditioner running, the radio tuned to KOWB. Nicole folded her long legs into the cab, kicked her shoes off, and bent over to let the cool air from the vent wash across her face. I reached over to knead the tight muscles of her neck.

"Mmm," she said, leaning into me. "That feels good."

"I'm sorry," I said. "I didn't mean for you to get dragged into that."

"It's no problem, Harry," Nicole said. "She's hurting and she needed someone."

"But why you?" I asked.

"I don't know," she said. "I really don't. But do you remember when my father died and all the relatives came to the house after the service for the wake?"

"Yeah, I remember."

"Well," she said, "I locked myself in my bedroom that afternoon because I couldn't bear to have one more of them tell me how sorry they were, because every time they said it, it was like . . . I don't know. It was like they were making me feel that pain all over again, like every one of their expressions of sympathy was a fresh cut. At one level, I knew they were there for me, but on another I knew that if I stayed around trying to keep a stiff upper lip, I'd go completely crazy.

"I had to get off by myself. So I locked the door, took all my clothes off, and spent the afternoon reading Elmore Leonard. I'm sure they thought I was very rude."

"So you were Tess's Elmore Leonard?" I asked. "Her diversion?"

"Something like that, I guess. She doesn't know me very well, so I suppose there isn't the same emotional baggage as there is with family and friends. Whatever it was, we talked for a while, and then she asked me to stay until she fell asleep."

I put the Blazer in reverse, began to back out. In the front yard, the church ladies had taken all the food away, but it looked like many of the guests were settling in for an extended stay. Groups of men gathered around the tables, sat in twos and threes on the grass. Women had made themselves comfortable in lawn chairs and on the porch swing. A group of kids had started a pickup game of baseball in the meadow near the corral.

I nodded at the hangers-on. "I hope she gets some rest," I said. "It looks like it's gonna be a long night."

"That's what we figured," Nicole said. "So I invited her out to your house later this evening. I thought she might need a break."

"She's coming?" I asked. I expected to hear that Tess had declined.

"You don't mind do you?"

"No, of course not," I said, surprised that Nicole felt the need to ask. "But what will we do?"

"Well," she said, brushing my cheek with a kiss, "maybe we

could just get her drunk and let her stay the night. Might do her a world of good."

Call me moody, but I've always found there's nothing like a funeral to put a damper on a summer day. But in spite of the somber pall that dogged us all the way back to Victory, Nicole and I managed to squeeze some life out of the afternoon.

Although Edna's nags are as friendly as a couple of puppy dogs most of the time, they have an uncanny ability to sense when it's my intention to strap saddles on them and make them work. On those occasions, they snort and run off to the end of the pasture, glaring balefully and pawing the ground, and it takes me a half hour or better to get close enough to slip halters around their heads.

That day it took a little longer, because I'd run out of sugar cubes, but I finally managed to catch the hay burners while Nicole traded her funeral clothes for a pair of blue jeans, cowboy boots, and a tank top that left very little to the imagination. She topped it off with a beaten-up straw Stetson, under which she tucked her long auburn hair, and a pair of old deerskin gloves with the fingers cut off.

She hopped aboard the mare while I adjusted the cinches on the gelding's saddle, lifted my bad leg into the stirrup, and hefted myself up. The horse grunted and farted as I settled into the worn leather saddle. His body was too wide for me to sit comfortably on his back, and as we worked our way down to the gate that leads out of the pasture, moving at the horses' maximum speed of about three miles an hour, I reconciled myself to the thought that by evening I'd be so saddle sore I'd need a whole jar of Bag Balm just to stand up.

For the moment, though, it was nice to amble along, the pleasant smell of horse and prairie in our nostrils, the sun warm and soothing on our backs. We rode to the boundary of Edna's property, up a little mesa and down the other side to Antelope Creek, a tiny spring-fed stream that meanders through the flatlands before it eventually reaches confluence with the Little Laramie near Victory Valley. We didn't talk much, lulled by the gentle rhythm of the animals' gait and the metronomic sound of their hooves on hard-packed ground.

We rode down the creek along a deer trail for three or four miles, past two of the four pools deep enough to support trout on a year-round basis, past a stand of willows where an industrious beaver busily chomped through the trunk of one of the small trees. When he saw us, he scurried into the creek, swam to midstream, slapped his tail against the water in warning to other beavers that may have been within earshot, and disappeared below the surface. I waited for several minutes in hopes he'd pop his head out of the water again and give us another slap but gave up when it became apparent he had no intention of putting on a show for the likes of me.

To the north, the foothills of the Snowies rose from the prairie bed, a painter's palette of browns, greens, grays, and reds, the sides of the hills sprinkled with red bouquets of Indian paintbrush and aromatic horsemint. We jumped a family of pronghorns bedded down in one of the small draws of their namesake creek, and they bounded off, the white rosettes of their rumps providing counterpoint to the burnt vegetation of the prairie.

To the east, the Laramie Plains were a flat ocean of brown stretching more than twenty miles, the horizon broken by the dark green slopes of the Medicine Bow range. Overhead, a high ribbon of clouds blew along in the jet stream. The contrail of a jet bisected the sky from north to south. I nudged the gelding along, resisted the pull of my heavy eyelids. It's not a real good idea to fall asleep while you're riding a horse, not unless you don't mind pulling cactus barbs from your privates with a pair of pliers.

At Arapaho Bend, we stopped, tied our horses to some chokecherry bushes with long tethers, stretched our bodies out in the tall grass along the streambank, and munched the snack of cheese and fruit Nicole had packed in her saddlebag.

Then, we made love. Slowly. Tenderly. Fragrantly. Nicole riding me gently while the horses grazed and the meadowlarks sang a Rocky Mountain serenade.

All in all, I'd call it a Kodak moment.

Tess McAfferty pulled into my driveway a little before ten, shortly after Nicole and I had returned from a heavy dinner of extra-rare prime rib at the Trail's End. She was driving her little Honda Accord and had brought a twelve-pack of Olympia, several cans of which she'd apparently finished on the drive from Rock River to Victory. I looked out the door when the light from her headlights swept the living room, saw her extricate herself from the small car and make her way to the foot of the porch steps, weaving a little. Dressed in the same black dress she'd worn at the funeral, she'd shed her hose and carried a pair of open-toed sandals in one hand and the beer in the other.

Nicole—barefoot herself and wearing her red dress, my favorite—slipped by me and out the door to welcome our guest and help her carry her things inside. The women hugged briefly in the glow of the yard light, then Nicole draped her arm over Tess's shoulders to guide her up the two steps to the front porch.

"Hello, Harry," Tess said as soon as she was seated on the couch and Nicole had taken her beery offering to the refrigerator. "I thought I'd take your wife up on her invitation. I needed to get away from the house, and the drive out here helped more than I'd imagined. I feel like a wrung-out dishrag, you know? All those people, they want to give something—support, understanding, help around the house. But it seems like they also want something in return. They want to share my grief, and I don't know if I'm ready for that."

"You have a lot of friends, Tess," I said lamely. "I'm sure they understand."

"My boyfriend didn't," she said. "I finally sent him home a

couple of hours ago. He was trying so hard to help, to give me some comfort, but . . ."

She looked down at the floor and began to weep softly. Wiping a tear away with the heel of her hand, she took a long pull of beer and began to search through her pocketbook for her smokes. When she found them she put one in her mouth, fumbled with her butane lighter, held the trembling flame to the tip of her cigarette.

She bent forward on the couch, wrapping her arms around her stomach. "It hurts," she said softly. "I miss her so much it hurts."

It had been my intention to question her about Saul Irons and what I'd learned from Will Jensen, but I realized then was not the time. Tess McAfferty had come to my home to find a temporary haven, and it would have been cruel to deprive her of refuge. Tomorrow, I decided, would be soon enough for that unpleasantness.

When Nicole had finished in the kitchen, she padded back into the living room with two shot glasses and a bottle of bourbon. She placed the sour mash on the coffee table and filled the glasses. Then, she sat next to Tess on the couch, tucked her legs beneath her, and gave me a look that said it was time to disappear.

I obliged, excused myself to the spare bedroom and found an old movie on the portable television. With that comforting noise in the background, I spent the next two hours tinkering with my hobbies.

I cleaned and oiled the .54-caliber black powder Hawken rifle I use to slaughter coffee cans and paper buffalo silhouette targets whenever Curly Ahearn and I decide it's time for the latest installment of the world's longest-running sharpshooters' grudge match.

I read a couple chapters from my favorite Terry Johnston mountain man novel.

And when I was sufficiently relaxed, I sat down behind the jeweler's magnifying glass at my fly-tying bench and churned out the dozen Starbranch specials I'd promised more than two months before to Danny King, a detective in the Laramie Police Department with whom I've developed an effective barter system over the years. Each year, I supply King with a stock of Starbranch specials—an ugly black representation of a stonefly nymph that trout are unable to resist—and take him along on a couple of fishing expeditions. In return, he does me the odd law-enforcement-related favor and keeps me abreast of the latest gossip in the department.

I'd just finished snipping the excess thread off the last knot when I looked up to find Nicole in the doorway, leaning her weight against the doorframe.

"Hi, sweetie," I said. "I was just about—"

She put a finger to her lips and motioned for me to follow her to the living room, where Tess was curled up on the couch. The bottle of bourbon that still sat on the coffee table was down about a fourth, and there were a half dozen empty beer cans scattered around to keep it company. Tess might have been drunk when she fell asleep, but for the first time in a week she looked peaceful, her hands tucked beneath a pillow, her breathing deep and regular.

"We'll just let her stay there," Nicole whispered. "She's in no condition to drive home."

I nodded my agreement and we quietly went about tidying the room. I took the beer cans and the whiskey bottle to the kitchen so Tess wouldn't have to see them when she woke up. Nicole pulled my afghan from the closet and tucked it around Tess.

I was just reaching to turn off the living room light when the first bullet smashed through the door and blew the glass from a Jim Bama print—his painting of Bob Edgar at the burial of Gallager and Blind Bill—hanging on the far wall.

The thunderous report of the rifle followed it a split second later, but at first my brain refused to register what was happening. I was still staring at the neat round hole in Edgar's forehead when the second round crashed through the Sheetrock paneling and showered us in a spray of debris.

Nicole screamed as I threw us both to the floor but got control of herself immediately and scrambled across the room to where Tess was sitting up, her eyes wide with incomprehension and terror. Nicole grabbed her by her dress and jerked her to the carpet, crawled over her body and yanked the light plug from the socket.

Three more rounds punched through the living room wall, and one blew in the picture window as I hugged the floor of the room and tried to remember where I'd left my revolver. It was in the bedroom, hanging from a peg on the door. I stood up, hunched my back, and lunged toward the bedroom, banged my knee on the ottoman and tumbled in a heap. Broken glass cut through the back of my shirt, stung my back, and when I put my hands down to push myself up again, more of it sliced the palms of my hands.

I had just regained my feet when another slug hit the front door, knocking it from its hinges. I dived, rolled into the bedroom, and ran my hands up the heavy door until I felt the leather holster. Yanking it down, I tore the safety strap free and rolled back into the living room.

In the light coming through the window and door from the mercury vapor lamp in the yard, I could see Tess and Nicole wrestling on the carpet. Tess struggled to break free and Nicole was trying to hold her down. Another bullet crashed through the Sheetrock.

"Get out of here!" I hissed. "Keep low and get to the back of the house!"

Through the front door I saw the blue and orange muzzle flash as the shooter fired again. Most likely he was parked on the roadway into Edna's property, about seventy-five yards a-way—too far to pick specific targets out in a dark house, but plenty close to hit anything or anyone who exposed himself in the well-lit yard.

Crawling to the picture window, I held the .357 in both hands and drew a bead on the yard light. I squeezed the trigger and the big gun bucked in my hands, throwing a six-foot blue flame from its bore. The yard light winked and went out with an electric sputter as I tried to blink the afterimage of the muzzle flash from my eyes.

I figured I had about three seconds to act before whatever advantage I'd gained by plunging us into darkness was lost, before the shooter's eyes had time to adjust to the change in light. Bellowing like a bull and with the Blackhawk still clenched in a two-handed grip, I hit the screen door like a lineman, rolled across the porch, and came up on one knee, sweeping the barrel across my field of vision.

In the distance, the assailant's weapon belched fire again, and I heard the slug thwack the side of the house. I used his muzzle flash as a target and emptied my revolver. Then I stood and ran for the Blazer, where I keep a twelve-gauge shotgun loaded with deer slugs in a front-seat stand and an old World War II .45 automatic in the glove compartment.

I threw open the door, hit the glove compartment button and pulled the .45 free, racked a round into the chamber, and turned to empty the clip at the bastard trying to kill me. All I saw was the cherry glow of his taillights as he fishtailed away, his motor whining as his tires fought for traction on the loose gravel. In seconds he was out of range, howling down the dirt road toward the highway leading into Victory.

"Cocksucker," I growled. I raced around the Blazer to the driver's-side door. I planned to chase him down, run him off the road, and make him suffer. There was enough adrenaline pumping through my veins to jump-start a corpse, and my heart thundered in my chest.

I was trying to jam a key in the ignition when the sound of a woman's horrified scream came from the interior of the house.

"Oh, Jesus!" she cried. "She's hurt, Harry! She's hurt!"

I didn't know whose voice I heard, but it sounded desperate.

I threw the keys on the seat, stuck the .45 in my waistband, and jumped from the Blazer, taking one last look in the direction the shooter had fled. With a growing sense of horror and urgency, I stumbled up the porch steps and through the front door, fumbling around for the switch to the living room's overhead light.

The two women were still on the floor. They'd been trying to get out of the line of fire, just like I told them, but they hadn't been fast enough. Tess held Nicole's limp body in her arms, rocked her gently as she caressed her face. She appeared unhurt, but in the harsh light, Nicole was a study in scarlet.

Red dress. Red hair. Red blood washing her pale white face.

# TWELVE

It bounced off? What do you mean it bounced off?"

"What can I tell you, Sheriff?" Dr. Nancy Kim said. She collapsed on one of the blue Naugahyde couches in the patients waiting room at Ivinson Memorial Hospital in Laramie. Her legs were so short they didn't quite reach the floor, which made her look a little bit like a child, an impression of bloodstains on her jacket dispelled immediately. "It hit her head at an oblique angle and bounced off. It's a good thing, too. Otherwise, she'd probably be dead. As it is, all we have to worry about is curing her headache."

The massive jolt of adrenaline her body provided during the shooting sobered Tess up in record time, and together we'd wrapped Nicole in a sheet, carried her from the farmhouse, and driven her the thirty miles to Laramie faster than the speed of light. Nicole had not regained consciousness fully, but by the time we hit the blacktop she was moaning and her eyelids fluttered like butterfly wings. The hair on the left side of her head was soaked with blood, and blood collected in huge pools on the seats, running down the seams in rivulets to spill onto the carpet. When we finally arrived in Laramie, Tess was covered in gore from trying to stop the bleeding and had wide swaths of it streaked across her face.

As soon as we pulled up they'd taken Nicole away, her arms dangling lifelessly from the sides of the gurney, and we'd paced the waiting room for over an hour while Dr. Kim, a petite Korean who was that night's physician in attendance, looked her over and decided that instead of severe brain trauma, we were basically dealing with a glorified shaving nick.

I was so relieved by the news that I felt like breaking into one of my patented Scandinavian jigs but decided that would be unseemly. Instead, I picked Dr. Kim up in a bear hug and waltzed her around until she tried to push her way out of my arms. Then, we sat back down on the ugly couch so she could give me her expert medical opinion on why my wife was still alive.

Kim shrugged her tiny shoulders. "Damned if I know what happened," she said. "Maybe it was only a bullet fragment that hit her. Maybe the bullet broke up when it came through the wall. Maybe she was only hit by some debris. Whatever, it looked worse than it was because head wounds bleed so badly, but it really didn't do anything more serious than give her a nasty gash, a bruise, and a concussion."

"Any danger there?" I asked.

"Some," Kim said. "I'm gonna keep her in the hospital overnight for observation. Losing that blood made her a little woozy, and she has a little temporary memory loss, but I don't think it's too serious. Still, it won't hurt to be sure. The hardest part is going to be keeping her awake. With concussions, we can't let them sleep for at least twelve hours."

Down the hall, I could hear Nicole arguing strenuously with someone that she for goddamn sure was not going to walk out of the examining room in a gown that left her backside exposed, and they'd better give her clothes back or she'd stay where she was until the year 2049.

Kim chuckled when it became apparent the nurse in charge

was not going to win, not now, not ever. "Of course her hard head may have helped more than anything."

"It runs in the family," I said, smiling broadly. "Can I see her?"

"Sure, but not too long." Kim said. She stood up, stretched her back, and shuffled off toward the coffee machine at the nurses' station. Across the room, Tess McAfferty talked on a pay phone. She finished her conversation and hung up as soon as she saw me stand.

"I heard the good news, Harry," she said. "I'm so glad."

"Me too," I said. "They tell me I can see her for a minute. You mind?"

"Take as long as you like," she said. "I just called the house, and they're sending one of the boys in to pick me up. I'll come out and get my car tomorrow or the next day, if that's all right with you."

"No problem," I said. "I could have someone drive it out to your ranch if you like, though. It might be easier for you."

"Nah, don't bother," she said, shouldering her pocketbook. "I won't need it." She pecked my cheek and turned toward the exit, took a couple of steps before I stopped her.

"Tess?"

"What is it?" she asked, turning back. There were fatigue lines on her forehead and around her mouth. Her eyes were bloodshot from stress, the aftereffects of the booze, and lack of sleep.

"Be careful. Whoever did this is—"

"Still out there. I know," she said. "But so am I, Harry. I'm still out there, too."

Nicole sat up on the edge of her small bed, dangling her legs over the side as she examined herself in a small hand mirror she'd commandeered from somewhere. Despite the fact that there was still a good deal of dark congealed blood in her hair and the left side of her head was covered in a large gauze bandage and plenty of white tape, she looked better to me than she'd ever looked before. I threw my arms around her and pulled her close, buried my face against her neck. She tolerated it for couple of minutes, then gave me a pat on the shoulder and pushed me away to arm's length.

"You'll get blood all over you," she said.

I pulled away, shook my head in disbelief. "Give me a break," I said, pointing at the bloodstains that already covered my shirt and pants. "Who gives a damn if I get a little more blood on myself? It's the least of my worries right now. I thought you were . . ."

"Well I'm not, Harry," she said. "As a matter of fact, I'm not even hurt very badly. It's no big deal. The big deal is I can't remember exactly how I got here, or what happened to put me here. You wanta fill me in?"

I hiked myself up to sit beside her on the bed. "All right," I said. "What's the last thing you remember?"

She pointed to a crop of insect bites on her thighs. "This afternoon," she said. "I remember screwing around out in the woods where there were too many mosquitoes. After that, it's a blank until I woke up with Nancy Kim's face about six inches from mine. At the time she was stitching my head."

I laughed, poured her a glass of ice water from the little pitcher on the bedside tray. "Well," I said, "you invited Tess McAfferty over and the two of you got so stinking drunk you fell down and whacked your noggin on the side of the coffee table. For a while there, we thought you were a goner."

She frowned, grabbed my forearm and squeezed until it hurt. "Bullshit, Harry," she said. "I heard a couple of the nurses talking about a gunshot wound. If that's what this is, you damn sure better tell me."

So I did, the whole thing, starting from the time Tess showed up until we pulled up at the door of the hospital.

"I was afraid I'd lost you," I said when I was finished. "I was scared."

Nicole took my hands in hers and pulled me around to face her.

"Well you didn't," she said. "You almost lost me once, podna. It ain't gonna happen again. And speaking of which, I think it's time you got me out of here. We have unfinished business at home."

"It might be kind of crowded," I said apologetically. "At this moment, I figure there are at least ten people at my house, digging around in the walls for bullets. The place looked like a Beirut hotel when we left. God only knows what it'll look like when they're finished."

"Did you see 'em, Harry?" she asked, and looked down at the butt of the .45 still stuck in my waistband. "Did you see who did this?"

"No," I said. "He was too far away. He was driving a pickup, though. I know that much for sure."

"Perfect," she said. "He was driving a pickup. So are three quarters of the postpubescent males in Albany County, Sheriff. I'm glad you've at least narrowed it down that far."

"I'll get 'em," I assured her. "There are a lot of pickups around, but not that many of them with bullet holes. I couldn't have missed every time, could I?"

"I don't know," she smiled. "I've heard a lot of your deer hunting stories."

"I missed those deer on purpose!" I protested. "What's the point of hunting if you've gotta shoot something? When I want to hit something, I hit it."

She smiled and lay herself down on the bed. Her face had grown even more pale and she took deep breaths, as if trying to ride a wave of nausea.

"You okay?" I asked, reaching down to stroke her forehead.

"Yeah, I'm fine. Just a little queasy." She closed her eyes, placed her hands on her stomach. "I think I need to sleep."

"That's exactly what you don't need," I said. She looked at me questioningly. "Doc says you gotta stay awake for at least twelve hours. But you still have to stay quiet."

"Shit."

"I know," I said. "But it won't be that bad. They're taking us to a private room in a few minutes, and when they do, I'll tell you all my best stories. Have you heard the one about the time I was surrounded by Sioux warriors on Crazy Woman's Creek? It was the summer of 1873—"

"Oh no you don't," she said forcefully, and made an effort to push herself back up to a sitting position. I put my hand on her shoulder and guided her back down, but she rallied enough to keep on ordering me around. "I've already been shot. I don't need to be tortured into the bargain." She chuckled weakly. "You get out of here right now and give those deputies of yours a hand. Come get me tomorrow at checkout time. I'll be fine till then."

It was after 4:00 A.M. when I made it back to the farmhouse and found a place to park among the gaggle of sheriff's department vehicles scattered across the front yard. Frankie Tall Bull's Victory Police cruiser was in my regular parking place at the side of the house, and lights burned next door at Edna's.

I shut the engine down and got out, heard the sound of raucous laughter through the open door. Great, I thought, their boss almost gets himself killed, his ex-wife is in the hospital, his house is shot to shit, and these bums think it's hilarious.

Yeah, I was tired. And it made me cranky. I slammed through what was left of the front door. "Fuck it," I swore, "just fuck it," and threw my hat across the room toward the hat rack like a Frisbee. It missed, cartwheeled out of the living room and into the kitchen.

Larry Rawls and the others were in various stages of repose around my living room, most with cups of coffee and a few with sandwiches from my kitchen. Bull had his big feet on the coffee table and had helped himself to a diet soda and the leftover prime rib from our dinner at the Trail's End. Frankie watched my hat roll out of the room and laughed, but Rawls and the rest jumped up, looking embarrassed.

"Something funny?" I asked, looking at the huge holes they'd dug in my walls. They'd helped themselves to my provisions, but I also noticed they'd cleaned up the worst of the bloodstains from the carpet. "Something I missed?"

My deputies couldn't have said shit if they'd had a mouthful, but Frankie took a big slug of soda and assumed the job of designated speaker for the group. "Well, yeah, as a matter of fact, there is," he said. He glanced at the assembled deputies, who were trying not to smile.

"Rawls was just telling us about a strange call he went on this morning. You know Carla Morin, tends bar out at the Oregon Trail in West Laramie?"

"Yeah," I said. I pictured Carla in my mind. Mid-forties. Hair the color of a naval orange. Big thighs. Wore T-shirts with slogans that are derogatory to people from Colorado, Texans, politicians, gays, or anyone of the male persuasion. Her favorite: THE MORE I KNOW ABOUT COWBOYS, THE MORE I LOVE MY VIBRATOR. "What about her?"

"Deputy Rawls answered a call this morning from one of Carla's neighbors," Bull said. "Said Carla was out chasing one of the neighborhood kids around her yard with a broom, beaning him every chance she got."

"Was she?" I asked. I motioned to Bull to scoot over so I could share some space on the couch.

"Oh, yeah," Frankie said. "But you tell it, Larry. It was your call."

Rawls looked around the group and laughed, leaned forward like he was telling his favorite joke. "Well, I got there and there's Carla, whacking this little kid. The kid's screaming, covering his head, Carla's yelling that he better mind his own fucking business or she's gonna kill 'im.

"I ask her why she's picking on the little guy, and it turns out the reason is she's been on the phone that morning to her boyfriend, the boyfriend she's not married to. But she's talking to 'im on her cellular phone."

"Oh, no." I chuckled, leaned back on the couch. "He didn't . . ."

"Sure as hell did," Rawls said. "The kid's been picking up her cellular calls on his CB radio for weeks now. But today, he taped a really juicy one—and played it back for Carla's husband as soon as he got home from work."

I laughed. "God. No wonder she was trying to kill him." It felt good to release a little of the tension, even if it was only for a second. "What is this little kid, the Son of Satan?"

"Nah," Rawls said. "He was just getting even because Carla ratted him out for shooting pop bottle rockets at her laundry last Fourth of July. Said that on account of her, he'd been grounded for most of summer vacation."

"You restored the peace, I take it," I said.

Rawls patted his shirt pocket. "That I did," he said. "I took the tape, too. You wanna hear it? She's a phone tease, Harry. Worse than one of those dial-your-fantasy babes."

"No thanks," I said, reaching for a Coors from one of the six-packs they'd raided from my refrigerator. I screwed off the cap, took a long satisfying sip.

"We called the hospital, but they said you'd already left," Frankie said. "They told us Nicole was sleeping. We're glad she's all right, Chief."

"Thanks," I said, and looked up at the gaping holes in my wall. "I appreciate it. You guys find anything out here? Any brass out on the road?"

Rawls pulled a plastic evidence bag from the briefcase at his feet, tossed it in my direction. "No brass, but we'll get this to the lab in Cheyenne as soon as it opens," he said. The bag was heavy, filled with bullet fragments, shards of copper jacketing and mushroomed lead.

"Looks like most of this is useless," I said. "It's so deformed, there's no way of telling what it came from. I'd say a hunting rifle, though. How 'bout you?"

"Yeah." Rawls smiled, reached down for a second bag. He tossed it over and I caught it. There was a single slug in this one, the jacketing intact, the soft lead of the nose only slightly deformed. "I'd say they're hunting slugs, all right. And I'm betting they're from the same rifle that fired that one."

"How did this baby make it in such good shape?" I asked.

He stood up to reveal a large hole in the seat cushion of my La-Z-Boy recliner. "Pure luck," he said. "The slug came through the screen door and hit the chair. I figure the cushion slowed it down some, because when it exited the back of this thing and hit the wall, it landed in decent shape."

I studied the lethal-looking round through the plastic, and although I couldn't see them with the naked eye, I knew the lab would be able to find the distinctive lands and grooves on the slug. And those markings could match the bullet to the specific weapon it was fired from.

Frankie pointed at the bullet. "I don't know, Harry," he said. "But unless I miss my guess, I'd say that came from a seven-millimeter. I use the same caliber for elk hunting, and I load my own ammunition. That slug looks awful familiar."

"It does to me, too," I said. "I've got a Remington seven-millimeter in the bedroom. It's a popular weapon, Frankie."

"Yeah, it is," he said. "You see 'em everywhere."

He was right, of course. As a matter of fact, I'd seen one just a few days before. Saul Irons was loading it at the time.

We put out another be-on-the-lookout bulletin for Irons and a few of us sat around the living room until after the sun came up, listened to the radio traffic on a portable unit, and unwound. It was quiet in Albany County that night and nobody was moving, least of all Irons.

Around five thirty, Edna finally gave in to her curiosity and came over to assure herself that Nicole and I were all right. Frankie had spoken to her earlier, but as usual, she wasn't about to believe anything until she saw it for herself. When she was satisfied that we were among the living, I sent her off to feed her horses and sent the deputies home to get some rest.

When everyone else was gone, Frankie stretched himself out on the couch and put his big hat over his eyes. I noticed he hadn't taken off his pistol or his pigsticker and realized he was hanging around because he thought I might need protection.

"Does Frieda know where you are?" I asked. "You want to call her?"

"Nah," he said. "I like her to think I'm out with another woman once in a while. Keeps her on her toes."

While he tried to snooze, I made a pot of strong coffee, got myself a hot shower, and munched down a handful of No-Doz. When I was dressed in fresh clothes, I sat at the kitchen table with my mug and tried to figure out why Saul Irons would want to kill me. Problem was, I couldn't think of a single reason.

I knew he'd probably heard I'd put out a bulletin on him. I imagined he was aware that Keegan and I had tossed his house.

If his contacts in the law enforcement community were good enough, he might have learned I'd found a witness to place him on Will Jensen's ranch the night of the killings. He might even have heard I'd found his fingerprint on a pack of Blackjack gum.

But Saul Irons had been a cop plenty long enough to know that kind of evidence for the useless crap it turns out to be in a courtroom, and my possession of it just didn't seem enough to push him over the edge. Nor was the fact that I was proving to be a minor complication in his life.

I waited until a few minutes after six and dialed Keegan's home number in Cheyenne, let it ring a dozen times.

"Keegan here," his sleepy voice answered. He sounded like he was hiding a rock crusher in his larynx.

"Ken, it's Harry. Sorry to call so early but—"

"Did you find him?" Keegan broke in. "I sure as hell hope so, 'cause I looked all day yesterday."

"No, it's not that," I said. "It's about Nicole. Someone shot her."

Keegan didn't respond for a long moment. "I'm truly sorry, Harry," he said finally. "Is she . . ."

"She's fine," I said. "Coming home today, as a matter of fact. The doc says it's no big deal, but she was very lucky."

"Thank God," he said.

"I already have."

"Then tell me what happened. And start from the beginning."

So that's exactly what I did. I told him about finding Irons's fingerprint. I told him about my conversation with C.J. Fall. I told him about the funeral. I told him about Tess McAfferty's visit. I told him about the gunner who'd shot up the farmhouse. I told him about rushing Nicole to the hospital. And I told him my initial assumption that Irons had put her there.

When I finished, he didn't respond, and I let him think in peace. I heard the flick of his Zippo lighter as he lit his first smoke of the day. "It wasn't Irons," he said. There was absolute certainty in the statement, and I was curious how he could be so sure.

"Okay, Ken. It wasn't Saul Irons. How do you know?"

"Let me ask you this," he said. "You said the shooter was about seventy-five yards out. In the dark, probably using a high-powered scoped rifle to shoot at targets in a well-lit room. You figure that's a tough shot, Harry?"

"No," I said. "It's an easy shot."

"Could you have made it?"

"Of course."

"You think Saul Irons could have made it?"

The answer was obvious. The man was an expert marksman. He could have made the shot with a bag over his head.

The person who ventilated my house, on the other hand, had missed more than a half dozen times.

"I get the point," I said. "If Saul Irons had been out there, all three of us would have been dead. Unless he was sending us some kind of warning."

"I don't know, Harry," Keegan said. "I suppose I know Saul Irons as well as anybody, and that just doesn't feel right."

"Stranger things have happened, Ken," I reminded him. "To both of us."

"You're right," he sighed. "But I still don't think it was Saul. It's gotta be somebody else."

"Who?"

"I can't tell you that, Harry, but I've got a feeling you'll find out, and those bullets your deputies found will prove it."

"In the meantime I'll keep looking for Irons," I said. "He might not be the man who tried to kill us, but I still want to talk to him."

"Me too," Keegan said. "I'm looking forward to that conversation a great deal."

I called Dr. Kim about seven and caught her just as she went off shift. She sounded exhausted but told me Nicole was resting comfortably and was in absolutely no danger.

"But she's still groggy, and I don't know if she'll even be back to normal by the eleven A.M. discharge time," Kim said. "Why don't we just let her stay where she is until she feels strong enough to navigate on her own power? I'll have the floor supervisor call your office, and you can come and get her then."

That sounded fine, so I rousted Frankie and told him to go home for a couple hours of shut-eye. I imagined he'd ignore me and catch a few winks in the office instead, because Victory was waking up by that hour and he'd want to be around to make sure nobody threatened public safety by ignoring the town's only stop-light or double-parking in front of Ginny Larsen's café while they ate their waffles.

When he was gone, I called Nicole's sister to check on the boys, assured her that there was no reason for her to hop in the car and drive to Laramie because Nicole would be home safely by Sunday night. Then I drove back to Laramie in the sort of stupor you find yourself in when you've been up all night and know you're facing another long day.

I turned on the radio as the Blazer nibbled highway at about fifty but had trouble concentrating. In addition to my mental leth-argy, my physical self felt like it was moving in slow motion, my hands, arms, and feet disconnected from the neural messages that set them in motion.

As I passed through the Big Hollow oil field, a vanload of churchgoers on their way home from Sunday services in Laramie strayed a couple inches over my side of the center line coming out of a turn. No big deal, but I overcompensated, tried to give them more room, and almost drove myself into the barrow pit.

I stopped, leaned my head back on the headrest and closed my eyes, waited until the spinning sensation in my brain dis-sipated.

The smart thing would have been to turn the motor off, re-cline the seat, and snooze right there by the side of the road until I was alert enough to drive the rest of the way into town. But I knew that in spite of the wisdom of that course of action, there was way too much caffeine percolating through my system from the No-Doz and coffee to permit sleep. I eased back onto the highway and crawled the rest of the way into Laramie, my hands gripping the wheel like a nervous kid with a brand new driver's license.

It was a quiet Sunday morning in town, the streets empty of business traffic. I drove down Third, turned left on Grand Avenue, and pulled into the parking lot at the courthouse building. It was empty save for a few sheriff's department vehicles, and Walker Tisdale's lonely-looking Lincoln in his reserved space.

The sheriff's office operates with a skeleton crew on Sundays, so the only people in the waiting area were the dispatcher and Bill Wachtel, a deputy who was sitting with his feet up on an empty desk when I came in, reading the color comics section of the *Denver Post*. He tried to fold the funnies up as soon as he saw me coming through the door, but I smiled and waved to let him know he wasn't in hot water.

"What's happening troops?" I asked the dispatcher, who hurriedly tried to hide the copy of *The First Wives Club* she'd been reading when I came in.

"Absolutely nothing," she said sheepishly, handing me the call sheet clipboard. Besides the fireworks at the Starbranch house, there'd only been a half dozen calls since midnight, mostly of the cowboy-got-too-drunk-to-drive-home-but-tried-it-anyway variety.

Nobody had spotted a bullet-riddled pickup truck anywhere in the county, in spite of the fact that every deputy on the road had been looking for it since shortly after midnight.

As I turned to collect Saturday's mail from my basket, she said, "Oh, yeah, Sheriff. Walker Tisdale called down here about a half an hour ago and said if you showed up he'd like to see you in his office."

I remembered seeing Walker's Lincoln in the lot and wondered what brought him to the salt mine on Sunday, a day he usually reserves exclusively for golf at Old Baldy. "He say what he wanted?" I asked.

"Nope," she said, and picked up her novel. "He wouldn't share that kind of information with a grunt like me, now would he?"

I shook my head in agreement, resigned to spending a few unpleasant minutes in Tisdale's company, and turned toward the staircase up to the third floor.

"Sheriff?" the dispatcher called as I hit the second step.

"What is it?"

"We just wanted you to know," she said. "We're glad you

weren't hurt. And we're glad your wife's gonna make it, too."

I walked as slowly as I could up the two flights of stairs, the heels of my boots echoing through the empty halls. With each additional foot of elevation, the temperature increased in the poorly insulated old building. I thought about my prisoners in the fourth-floor jail and wondered if the air-conditioning would make it through the summer.

The door to Walker's office was open, so I let myself in and wandered through his waiting room, knocked lightly on the open door to his inner sanctum. Tisdale, whose prematurely silver hair looked like it had been sculpted in granite, wore a magenta and orange polo shirt, lime green knickers, and the kind of floppy hat made popular by Brooklyn pimps in the twenties. He sat behind his huge desk, chomping a cigar while he thumbed through a stack of papers.

C.J. Fall, who was in one of two leather wing chairs across from Tisdale's desk, his Stetson balanced precariously on one knee, looked like he'd been ridden hard and hung up wet. His normally meticulous starched white shirt was wrinkled, sweat-stained, and dusty. There was mud caked on the knees of his jeans, and his boots were scuffed to a dull matte brown. He had a severe case of hat hair, and to judge from the dark bags under his bloodshot eyes, I wasn't the only one in the room who'd missed a night's sleep.

I nodded to the prosecutor. "Nice outfit, Walker," I said.

He looked down at his knickers, knocked off an imaginary piece of lint, and smoothed a couple of imaginary wrinkles.

"You really think so?" he asked hopefully, grinning broadly around the cigar.

"Nope," I deadpanned. "How ya doin', C.J.?"

Fall let a trace of a smile cross his chapped lips, but it disappeared as soon as Walker glanced in his direction. "Sittin' up and takin' nourishment," he said. "But that's about all."

I sat while C.J. told me he'd heard about Nicole, and I spent a few minutes telling him about the attack on my house the night before, my feeling that it might have been Saul Irons behind the gunsights, but maybe not. I asked him if he could press his sources a little harder, since our be-on-the-lookout had so far come up puny. He agreed to make the calls.

Walker scowled like he'd just had a bite of tainted meat as he listened to the exchange. He shuffled his stack of papers noisily, tapped them into a perfectly squared stack. I tried to ignore his displeasure at being left out of the conversation, but Walker Tisdale isn't the sort of fellow who'll let you ignore him for long.

"Listen Starbranch," he said when he was sure I wasn't going to ask the reason for his summons. "I called you up here because C.J. thought you ought to be informed of a little something we've got going."

C.J. thought? I looked questioningly at Fall. He shrugged his shoulders, rolled his eyes. Walker had not mentioned the shooting, nor did he afford me the courtesy of showing even minimum interest in my ex-wife's health. Vintage Walker. What an asshole.

"That's decent of you, Walker," I said sarcastically, and turned to face Fall, using body language to shut Tisdale out of the circle. "What's up, C.J.? This have something to do with that Carbon County business you mentioned yesterday morning?"

"It does," Fall said. "You remember me telling you about Wayne Carney? Runs a rustling operation on the Carbon County line?"

I thought back to our conversation at the El Conquistador, remembered Fall's mention of Carney as one of the bigger rustlers in the area. "Yeah," I said. "I remember."

"I busted him last night," Fall said. "Caught him red-handed with a truckload of yearlings he was trying to get out of state. Pretty slick little operation, too. He'd only been taking a couple of animals from each ranch he hit, so the ranchers either wouldn't notice the loss or might write it off as due to natural causes. He kept 'em on his ranch until he had a truck full, then he shipped 'em to Oklahoma. He loaded a shipment last night, and we took him just before he crossed the state line into Nebraska."

I thought back to the jail roster, which I'd checked briefly, along with the previous night's call sheet, when I came into the office. I hadn't seen Carney's name on the roster. That meant he wasn't being held in my jail, which is usual procedure whenever C.J. makes a collar.

"Where is he?" I asked.

"We didn't want anyone to know we had him," Fall said. "So we tucked him away at the university police department's holding facility. They didn't have any other guests, so he's got the place to himself."

It smelled like there was a deal cooking somewhere, and I was curious what it had to do with me. I nodded to show C.J. I was interested and waited for him to go on.

"It took Wayne Carney about three seconds after I put the cuffs on for him to realize that he was looking at a minimum of ten years in the pen," Fall continued. "And it took him about two more to realize he couldn't do the time without losing everything. His ranch is mortgaged to the hilt, and there won't be anybody to make the payments if he's busting rocks in Rawlins. His wife left him a couple of years ago and took the kids. She's back temporarily, but I don't imagine she's the kind to keep the home fires burning for a decade while her man's away. And then there's his quarter horse herd. Nice blood stock, and it provides a bit of money. He'll lose that too if he goes away."

"So he wants to make a deal," I said. "But what's he got to give?"

"Well, that's where you come in," C.J. said. "Carney claims to know for a fact that Bobby Snow hired Ralphie Skates and Clarence Hathaway early last spring to steal cattle and horses with him. Says he'll testify to that effect if we cut him some slack."

I sat forward in my chair, gripped my knees eagerly. "Can he put Snow with them at the McAfferty ranch the night Colleen was killed?" I asked.

"He says not. Says he was in jail at the time. Which we know is the truth.

"Damn."

"Exactly," Fall said. "But it might not be so bad after all. He says Snow trusts him, since they're in the same business. And he doesn't think it would be too hard to get him to talk about what happened at the McAfferty place."

"He's agreed to wear a wire?" I asked.

"Agreed to it?" Fall laughed. "To stay out of jail, Wayne Carney would stick a wire up his ass and walk on his elbows. Hell, he's practically begging to."

Which explained why Walker Tisdale was at his office in his golf clothes on a Sunday morning.

As the county prosecutor, he had to approve any deals like the one C.J. was talking about. If it worked, he'd get most of the credit for solving the murder of Colleen McAfferty, a fact that gave me a little twinge of professional jealousy. But tell you the truth, I didn't give a shit who got the credit as long as the case was cleared.

"There's one problem," I said. "Bobby took off the other day, loaded down like he planned to be gone awhile. One of my deputies followed him but lost him here in Laramie. He was heading south, but we've got no idea where."

"Carney says he can find him," Tisdale cut in. "No problem."

His inflection told me he'd meant to cut me just a little for making fun of his clothes: a crook like Wayne Carney could find Bobby Snow with no trouble, whereas I couldn't do it, not even with the resources of my whole department.

"Then why the hell doesn't he just tell us where Snow is?" I asked crossly. "So we can pick him up ourselves."

"First," Walker said, ticking it off on his fingers, "that wouldn't help us make our murder case, now would it? We want Snow on tape talking about murder before we arrest him for some chickenshit rustling thing. You see that, don't you Harry?"

I glared at Walker but held my tongue.

"Second," he continued, "he won't tell us where Snow is because that's his leverage, what he brings to the bargain. We're gonna do it, Harry. That part's a done deal. Asking you up here was just a courtesy call."

As far as Walker was concerned, I was dismissed at that point. I looked at C.J., who studied the mud on the knees of his jeans.

"Can I talk to him?" I asked. "I've got at least three bodies, three active cases. He could be a material witness, even if he didn't see the shootings."

"We don't think that's a good idea at this time," Tisdale said. "We don't want to make him any more nervous than he already is."

I couldn't believe that Tisdale would cut me out entirely. Even if he couldn't stand me personally, our offices had to maintain a decent working relationship, and there'd been plenty of times I'd gone the extra block to accommodate him. Still, that's what it looked like he was trying to do. I felt the blood rise in my face as a wave of anger washed over me. I tried to control it, but only because I could see that Fall was embarrassed and I didn't want him to think I held him responsible.

"You will let me know if you turn up anything germaine to my investigations, won't you Walker?" I growled. "Or will I have to read about it in the papers?"

"Oh, we'll call you." Walker smiled. "First thing. You've got my word on it."

I pushed myself out of the chair, let go an expletive deleted or two, and steamed off in the direction of the office door.

"Harry?" C.J. called just as I reached the outer office.

"What?" I asked impatiently, turning back to look at the old man.

"You've got my word on it too."

Nicole finally got around to calling me a little after noon, but when I got to the hospital about fifteen minutes later, she wasn't in her room, she was in the lobby with my campaign manager, Larry Calhoun, and his sulky daughter, Tina.

Instead of the bloodstained red dress she'd worn when I rushed her to the emergency room the night before, Nicole was dressed in a black pantsuit with a wide black belt, new black flats, and a floppy oatmeal-colored straw hat that hid the bandages on her head.

"You like it?" she asked, standing to let me admire her ensemble. "Tina picked it out for me on the way to the hospital."

Tina, as usual, tried to pretend none of us existed and didn't acknowledge the implied compliment. Outfitted in her usual Doc Martens, ripped jeans, and heavy-metal T-shirt, I noticed she'd lost twenty pounds or better since the last time I'd seen her, and she'd traded in her mousy blond hair for hair the color of a cherry-flavored Tootsie Pop. She looked at Nicole, shook her head as if she would never understand adults, and picked up a copy of *Cosmopolitan* to peruse while we talked.

I didn't answer Nicole's question, but I did take a seat on one of the waiting room couches, where I planned to stay until they got around to telling me what was up. It took about twelve seconds.

"Nicole called me about an hour ago and asked if I'd mind coming down to talk to her," Larry said by way of explaining his presence. He had a guilty look on his blocky face, and I knew they'd been up to something I wouldn't like. "We've been talking about your campaign."

I groaned and leaned back on the couch, closed my eyes and rubbed my temples with my fingertips. Nicole sat down beside me, gave me a few wifely pats on the thigh. She wore a fresh dose of perfume, but not her usual fragrance. Must have borrowed some from one of the nurses, I thought.

"Sounds to me like your campaign is dead in the water, baby," she said. "And Larry tells me you won't even help him row for shore."

I glared at Calhoun, who'd apparently gotten past his case of the guilts and now looked at me in friendly earnest.

"You think this is really the time to talk about it?" I asked Nicole. "You just got out of the—"

"I'm fine," she said. "And as far as I can see, this is the best time in the world to talk about it. Baldi is eating you up with this Slaymaker business, Harry, and if we don't do something right now, it's gonna be too late. I know that. Larry knows that. You know it too, but you're just too damn stubborn to admit it. So the question is, how are we gonna help you save your career?"

"What do you two want me to do?" I asked. "Call Jerry Slaymaker and ask him to forgive me? Let bygones be bygones?"

"Of course not," Nicole said. "But we think you should go on the offensive."

"And how will I do that?"

"By calling your own press conference for tomorrow," Calhoun said. "Get the media together and tell them you arrested Slaymaker on the best evidence available at the time. Tell them you did your job and a jury agreed. Tell them how lucky we are to finally have DNA testing. Tell them that without it, an innocent man might have spent his life in prison. Then tell 'em how close you are to making an arrest in Colleen's case. See if we can't divert everyone's attention."

I couldn't believe what I'd just heard.

"Have you both gone crazy?" I asked. "Slaymaker is guilty, for God's sake. You think telling people he was innocent is gonna make me look good the next time he kills someone?"

"No," Calhoun said. "It won't. But it would make you look better in the minds of a bunch of people who count right now. And in the meantime, I wish you'd stop insisting he's guilty. You're the only person in the world whose saying that these days, Harry. It makes you sound like a fanatic."

"Well he is guilty, damn it," I said. "He killed that boy, pure and simple. Besides, my lawyer says I shouldn't talk because there's a pending lawsuit."

"That's bullshit," Calhoun said. "Since when have you ever listened to the advice of lawyers?"

I shrugged my shoulders, set my jaw, and crossed my arms defensively across my chest. "What about his threats against the kids?" I asked Nicole. "Do we just forget that, too?"

She shook her head, laid her hand on mine. "Did he actually say he was gonna hurt the boys?" she asked.

"Well, no," I admitted. "But I understood what he meant well enough without—"

"Then maybe you're overreacting, reading more into what he said than was there. And even if you're not, are you gonna come with me to Denver this afternoon and make sure nothing happens?"

"I can't, Nicole," I said.

"Then the best thing you can do is get your life together and bring us up here," she said. "Solve the case and win the election, Harry. Until then, we'll stay at my sister's if we have to. It's only a few weeks."

I stood, turned my back to them, watched cars pulling up in the hospital parking lot, a gardener pruning the lilac bushes around the entrance, a robin pulling worms from the ground.

"You're not gonna give an inch on this, are you?" Calhoun asked.

I didn't answer.

He slammed his briefcase shut.

"Then find yourself another campaign manager," he said. "I only work with winners."

# THIRTEEN

I tried to get back on Nicole's good side while we drove back to Victory, but I think I might have had a better chance if she'd been able to hear me over the Reverend Stony Hank Tilton and his Baptist Revival Choir, live and direct from the campus of his personal Bible college in Norman, Oklahoma, which she'd tuned in on the radio at full volume.

Nicole, a devout Methodist, was engrossed in Stony Hank's sermon not because of anything Stony had to tell her, but because she'd made her mind up to ignore me. And once she starts down that rocky trail, she never looks back until enough time has passed to make her forget what made her mad in the first place. From past experience, I figured that would be at least Wednesday, by which time she'd have been back home in Denver for three days and I'd have been left to stew in my own juices for seventy-two miserable hours.

Not only would she not speak to me in anything beyond grunts on the thousand-mile drive home, she held her tongue while she packed her clothes and refused to even discuss it when I suggested I should probably drive her home to Denver in her car and then catch a late flight back to Brees Field in Laramie.

She tossed her suitcase in the trunk, slammed the lid. "I'm

fine, Harry," she said. "But I think we have a real medical curiosity going on here, kind of like one of those sympathetic labor pains guys get when their wives have a baby. Except in this case, I got shot in the head and you're the one who suffered brain damage."

I stood on the porch like an idiot while Nicole steamed over to Edna's house to say good-bye, watched while the two of them hugged in my landlady's back yard. I was still standing there, waving forlornly, when Nicole hot-rodded out of my driveway and down the dirt road, her rear wheels spitting gravel as she blew me a motorized raspberry, the dog giving me the evil eye through the back window.

When I was sure she wasn't going to have a change of heart and come back, I hung my head and went inside to see what I could do about my poor house. Not much, as it turned out.

There were cardboard panels taped over the broken windows and great holes in the Sheetrock where my deputies had dug bullets and bullet fragments out of the walls. My cherished James Bama print was a total loss. My favorite chair was in critical condition, and my couch was beyond hope. Don't even mention the front door.

I figured I faced a seven-hundred-dollar repair bill, minimum, even if I did most of the carpentry work myself. But even that wouldn't make me whole again. While Sheetrock, paint, recliners, and secondhand sofas are in plentiful supply, I'd never be able to replace the Bama.

I shuffled out the back door to the toolshed, found my skill saw, hammer, nails, and a couple panels of Sheetrock left over from the time I tried to redecorate my kitchen, dragged it all inside—and promptly abandoned the project entirely.

As a man with your average-size macho complex, I like to imagine myself up to any home repair project that presents itself. In truth, though, I'm all thumbs when it comes to anything more complicated than hanging a picture. In a flash of self-awareness, I realized that if I tried to do the repair job myself, I'd probably end up sawing my home in two. Best thing, I figured, was to hire myself a carpenter and pay him whatever exorbitant fee he required to do the job.

Since no self-respecting carpenter works Sundays, however, that meant I had an entire Sunday afternoon to kill.

I flipped through the channels on the television, gave up when the only choices were a golf tournament in Palm Springs, a rerun of an old *Partridge Family* episode, candlepin bowling from somewhere in Massachusetts, and coverage of a bass-fishing tournament in Florida.

Then I ambled aimlessly around the house for a half hour, picked my dirty laundry off the floor, cleaned up in the kitchen, and made my bed. Nicole had left a pair of hose and a blouse on my dresser, and I held the blouse to my nose, smelled the traces of her perfume and wished not for the first time that day that I wasn't such a jackass. The opened jar of minty green Kama Sutra Pleasure Balm rested on the nightstand, and I tucked that away in the top drawer of the stand, remembering the way it tingled when Nicole rubbed it on my . . .

Well, never mind where she rubbed it. Point is, by the time I finished my housekeeping chores I was beginning to feel low, mean, and fairly sorry for myself. It was attitude adjustment time, time to get my ex-wife off my mind, time for an afternoon at the Silver Dollar. A few pleasant hours of drinking beer, arguing with Curly Ahearn and flirting with Lou McGrew. Around dinnertime, I might even get myself a double-greasy cheeseburger and a heaping order of sizzling onion rings. Top it off with a nice fat Roi-Tan.

As a great American named Pogo once said, "A woman has only acumen, but a good cigar is a smoke."

I read an article a while back in one of the sporting magazines about this company in the Midwest that caters to the widows of hunters who are having trouble deciding where to dispose of the dearly departed's ashes. For a nominal fee, this company will take the earthly remains of the the former hunting enthusiast, load them into shotgun shells, and fire them at the animal or over the location of the widow's choice.

Personally, I think that sounds ridiculous, but I wouldn't mind having my ashes poured out of a beer bottle and spread on the dance floor of the Silver Dollar Saloon, since it's one of my all-time favorite places on Earth.

In the years after I first moved to Victory and took over as chief of police, I spent so much time in the Dollar it could have qualified as my legal place of residence.

Since I've been back together with Nicole, I've cut back on my drinking to the point that Mayor Curly Ahearn no longer believes my patronage alone will put his kids through medical school. But I still spend a lot of my spare time at the place, sipping a few beers, relaxing in front of the large-screen television, and taking the pulse of my home community. In the West, saloons have more in common with the pubs of Ireland and Scotland than they do with those art deco fern farms on every street corner in more "sophisticated" urban areas. Out here, our saloons, at least the real ones, are communal gathering places, the places where we come not necessarily to get drunk, but to make connections with our friends and neighbors, exchange information, and make the important decisions of our communities.

You can't be a lawman in a town like Victory, or anywhere in Wyoming for that matter, without being on intimate terms with the local watering holes, and for my money, the Silver Dollar is about the best of the bunch.

Not that it's any great shakes in terms of ambience. The window decorations are mostly neon beer signs, the clocks are all supplied by whiskey companies, and the posters usually feature buxom women with beer logos on their string bikinis. Stuffed animal heads occupy nearly every available square inch of wall space and there are pickled eggs in gallon jars of vinegar behind the bar, a threadbare pool table, and an old Wurlitzer jukebox with the original Ernest Tubb version of "Walking the Floor Over You." The place reeks of stale cigarette smoke and spilled beer, the booths are held together by silver duct tape, and most of the tables are made level by means of matchbook strategically placed under one or more of their legs.

It is, in other words, a dump. But it's my dump, and I spend as much time there as I can.

That Sunday, the afternoon crowd was light when I came through the heavy oak front doors. A double brace of cowboys played a game of eight-ball, and three hungry-looking hands from the Victory sawmill were gathered around a table, ostensibly watching a hockey game on the big-screen television but actually more interested in the two young women perched on stools near the jukebox. The women, who looked like they might be students from the university, showed no interest in their brawny blue-collar admirers but seemed to enjoy playing grown-up, smoking long cigarettes, sipping whiskey sours, and preening in the back-bar mirror. Harv Thompson, a loan officer at the First Rocky Mountain National Bank in Laramie who commutes to work from his home in Victory, was by himself at the end of the bar, sipping one of the mayor's special extra-large Margaritas, dubbed a "Quart-a-Rita" by His Nibs, from a salted glass the size of a wash-basin.

Curly, who wore a Colorado Rockies cap backwards on his bald head, was behind the bar, mixing up another batch of the high-octane green concoction. His face lit up in a huge smile when he saw me making my way to the bar, but he had to yell to make himself heard over the hideous grinding noise his blender made as it slushed the ice in the drinks.

"Looks like I win the pool," he hollered at Lou McGrew, who was also behind the bar, filling individual ketchup squeezers from a gallon can.

She set the ketchup down. "Shit," she said. She took her purse from the backbar, dug around until she found a wrinkled dollar bill, and threw it in Curly's direction. It fluttered through the air like a leaf and drifted to the floor. The mayor grabbed it and stuffed it in his shirt pocket, an extremely satisfied grin on his round face. "I always lose these pools," Lou groused. "I don't even know why I bet."

Wobbling precariously on his perch, Harv Thompson pulled a crumpled dollar bill from his front pants pocket and winged it in the mayor's direction.

"Did I come in in the middle of something?" I asked while Curly poured me a diet cola over crushed ice, set me up with a napkin.

"No," he laughed. "You came in at exactly the right time. For me at least."

I looked down the bar to where Thompson was happily licking salt from the rim of his glass, but he was no help. Nor was Lou, who was done with the ketchup and had headed for the walk-in cooler to get fresh mixer. "Good," I said. "Now why don't you let me in on the joke?"

"No joke," he said. "Only a friendly wager. We all knew Nicole was going back to Denver this afternoon, and we just had a little pool over how long it would take you to get tired of hanging around the house by yourself and show up here. Lou said three hours. Harv said you'd turn up by dinner. I said less than an hour, so I won. Jesus, Harry, do I know you, or what?"

At the end of the bar, Harv cackled drunkenly at the mayor's humor, toasted me with his nearly empty glass. "Less than an hour!" he beamed.

"Shut up you old wino," I told him, "or I'll throw your ass in jail as soon as you try to go home. You aren't planning on driving, are you?"

"Nope, I'm walkin' home," he assured me with the what-me-drunk? ultrasincerity most heavy drinkers adopt when they don't want to admit they're crocked. Unfortunately, it came out sounding like "Noopimmawakkinhoe," which gave his game away.

I looked questioningly at the mayor. "How many has he had anyway?"

"Don't worry," Curly whispered, and pointed at the fresh

blender full of Quart-a-ritas, "I quit putting tequila in those a long time ago."

While Lou made a swing through the barroom picking up empties and taking orders for refills, I brought Curly up to speed on what had happened the night before at the farmhouse, Nicole's visit to the hospital, and the reason she'd left in a huff. He listened intently, sipped his Margarita, and nodded occasionally, not necessarily in agreement but just to let me know he was following the conversation. When I finished, he gave me one of the condescending half smiles he usually reserves for drunks who've just forgotten the punchline to their umpteenth consecutive joke.

"She's right, you know," he said.

"Right? What's she right about?"

"Baldi," Curly said. "You've got to go on the attack. Call a damn press conference and do exactly what Calhoun said. Deny planting the evidence. Thank God for DNA testing. Thank God Slaymaker wasn't given the death sentence, so at least he can live out the rest of his life a free man. You might not like it, but it'll take the wind out of Baldi's sails for a while."

"I won't do it," I said. "The man's guilty."

"Says you."

"Yeah, says me—and I'm the one who should know, Curly. Jesus, are you doubting me now too?"

"No I'm not doubting you, Harry. I'm your friend, and I'm just looking out for your best interests."

I suppose I could have let the whole thing drop at that point, but I began feeling fairly guilty for being less than honest with my friend. If Curly Ahearn couldn't handle the truth, I reasoned, then nobody could. And I needed to get it off my chest.

It started coming out before I could think twice. "I tampered with the evidence, Curly," I said miserably. "I found it in his basement without a search warrant and planted it in his trash. I justified it in my own mind because I knew he was guilty and there was no other way to get him, but if I admit it now . . ."

"Oh, Jesus," Curly said. "No wonder you don't want to talk about this thing. The sheriff admits he used tainted evidence to put a man in prison for life? Bad public relations, Harry. Very bad. Not to mention expensive. How much is he suing for?"

"Ten million," I said. "But you know what, Curly? I'd do it again tomorrow if that was the only way I could get him off the streets. I'd do whatever it takes."

"So would I," he said. "And so would every parent in this county. That's irrelevant. What's immediately relevant is Tony Baldi. What are you gonna do about him?"

"What do you mean?" I asked irritably. "I'll tell you the same thing I told everyone else. I'm not gonna do a damn thing. I won't get up there and lie about the evidence, and I won't say I'm glad Slaymaker's out of jail. It wouldn't be right, Curly, and if that means I lose the election, so be it."

"Just my luck," Curly moaned, and slapped his bar rag on the counter. "I live long enough to finally see someone who's got what it takes to be a good sheriff in this county, and he turns out to be a goddamn bleeding-heart moralist. You say Slaymaker was guilty? Fine, he's guilty, and I don't give a shit what you had to do to put him behind bars. But that's not important now, Harry. It was ten years ago! What's important is your career, which you are doing your best to flush down the stinking toilet. Listen to Calhoun and Nicole, Harry. Call the friggin' press conference!"

I slammed my glass of cola on the bar so hard most of it sloshed over the sides and spun around on my stool to sit with my back to the mayor, my arms folded across my chest. "Asshole," I muttered.

"Who's the asshole?" Curly asked, leaning across the bar so I could hear him better while he yelled. "Is it my fault a goddamn redneck Republican is gonna be the next sheriff of Albany County? Is it my fault a man I respect and admire won't lift a finger to save his own reputation? Is it my fault you're mad at all the people who care about you, just because those people want to give you some good advice? Does any of that make me an asshole?

How about Nicole, Harry? Does it make her an asshole, too?"

I spun back around and glared at him, squeezed my glass until my fingers turned white. But Curly wasn't finished yet.

"Christ, it's almost like you want to lose, Harry," he said. "Is that it? Because if that's the case, there are simpler ways of doin' it. You just call Baldi and say I quit. That easy enough isn't it, Harry? You've had plenty of practice."

Before I could give my best friend a well-deserved punch in the nose, Lou plopped a tray of empties on the counter at the barmaid's station, rapped her knuckles on the bar to get our attention.

"You guys need a referee?" she asked.

"Nah, we're done talkin'," Curly said, stomping off in the direction of the walk-in cooler, talking to himself as he went. " 'It wouldn't be right.' Give me a fuckin' break!"

I looked down the bar at Harv Thompson, who was grinning like a maniac. "Asshole!" he said, pointing in Curly's direction. "I been sayin' it for years!"

A man with more pride might have gone home at that point to lick his wounds, but I didn't do that. I stuck around and drank sodas, watched the game, and glowered at Curly every time he walked by.

Around six I switched from diet cola to beer, moved down the bar to the stool next to Harv's, and let him sucker me into a liar's poker marathon. Thanks to the mayor's virgin Quart-a-ritas, he'd sobered up considerably since I first came in and had regained enough of his wits to beat me out of fifteen bucks, the last time on a hand I was sure was a bluff. Nobody gets lucky enough to find five aces on a dollar bill he just "happens" to have tucked away in his wallet. Nobody but Harv Thompson.

That day, Harv's wife Margarite was visiting relatives in Torrington, which explained why he was at the Silver Dollar instead of at home painting the fence or mowing his yard. Besides, he pointed out, he needed a little rest and relaxation after the week he'd had, testifying in a trial in federal court in Cheyenne on behalf of an oil company that had borrowed several million dollars from his bank and lost most of it drilling dry holes. The oil company, which was being sued by lots of its investors, was trying to explain where the money went and was having trouble making the opposing attorney clear on some of the concepts.

"The dumb son of a bitch has me up there on the stand, and he's got the oil company's expense reports for the last year, and he's asking me if I think some of these purchases are justified, since it was my bank that loaned out the money," Harv explained. "And he looks down at one of the items and reads out, in this real officious voice, 'It says here, Mr. Thompson, that Lucky Shamrock Oil spent over one hundred fifty thousand dollars last year on doghouses. Did you think that was a wise use of the money, Mr. Thompson? That's a lot of dogs to be living on one oil rig.'"

Harv shook his head to emphasize the point he'd been trying to make, that communicating with this East Coast attorney was just about as easy as speaking with a two-headed purple alien fresh from planet Neptune. "I had to tell him a doghouse isn't where dogs live, it's where the rig hands go to get out of the weather," Harv said. "It brought down the house."

We laughed about the stupidity of lawyers in general and of this one in particular, and then Harv asked me about Nicole. I assured him she was fine and spent a few minutes telling him all I could about the murder cases, which wasn't much more than he could have picked up in the newspapers.

"Well, I guess it doesn't surprise me much," he said when I'd finished.

"What doesn't surprise you?"

"That some of those ranchers have gone out and gotten themselves a hired gun," he said. "A lot of 'em are ridin' the ragged edge of solvency. In the last year alone, I've had to initiate fourteen foreclosures. There isn't a one of 'em who wouldn't feel the loss of some of their yearlings, and in some cases, the loss might be enough to push 'em over the rim."

"How about Tess McAfferty?" I asked, signaling Lou for a

fresh Coors for myself and another cup of coffee for Harv. She blew me a kiss and made a face at Curly, who'd ignored me for the better part of two hours. "Is she one of the ones in trouble?"

Harv fidgeted on his seat and drummed his fingers on the bar. I knew why he was uncomfortable. Like a doctor, a lawyer, or a psychiatrist, he's usually happy to discuss almost anything in general terms, but he considers it a breach of confidence to talk about the financial dealings of specific people, even to a cop. Sometimes especially to a cop. "I don't know," he said. "She's been a good customer of mine for lots of years."

"Look, Harv," I said. "This is just between us, you've got my word on it. My problem is, I think she might be one of the stock-growers paying Saul Irons's salary, and I haven't been able to figure out why she'd do that, unless she feels like she doesn't have a choice."

"You wouldn't tell her I talked to you?"

"Nope."

"I wouldn't have to testify, ever? I've had enough of that lately to last a lifetime."

"No, I'll forget we ever talked," I promised. "Understand me, Harv. I'm trying to help these people. We both know they're good folks who may have gotten themselves into something a lot more sticky than they ever intended. At the bottom of it, you and me both want the same thing, to see 'em through this unpleasantness safely. And if you know something that might help me do that . . ."

He chewed on that for a while, sipped his coffee and lit a fresh smoke. Finally coming to a decision, he leaned over and spoke to me in a tone low enough that nobody else could hear.

"Yeah," he said, "Tess is one who's in trouble. She managed to pay the interest on her notes last year and the year before that, but she hasn't made a payment on the principal for almost three years. I've worked with her as long as my board of directors will let me, but if she doesn't make a payment this year . . ." He shook his head as if the possibility was too painful to bear. Unlike a lot of other bankers of my aquaintance, Harv actually likes most of the people he does business with, and it shows.

"She could lose the ranch?" I urged him on gently.

"Yeah," he said, and held up thumb and forefinger about an inch apart. "She's this close."

"Close enough that the loss of a few cows could make the difference?"

"A few cows?" he asked, genuinely surprised. "Who said it was a few cows? Last year she lost over fifty. That's more than thirty thousand dollars, Harry. This year she's lost more than thirty yearlings already, and there's still two months until she ships. And we haven't even mentioned the horses."

I hadn't imagined her losses had been so great. And if her neighbors had lost livestock in similar numbers . . .

Harv brought me back from my mental calculations. "You know what she makes for profit in a good year?" he asked.

"No," I admitted.

"A hell of a lot less than thirty thousand dollars," he said. "That's why I could understand it if she and some of the others out there decided they had to take drastic action, like hiring this Irons fellow. They're fighting for their lives, Harry, and it doesn't look like they've got much chance of winning if they keep fighting fair."

I arrived home a little after nine to find my house dark save for the little message light blinking on my answering machine. Two calls, one from Nicole, terse and to the point, the other from Ken Keegan.

"I made it home fine," Nicole said. "But if you need to get in touch with me in the next few days, you'll have to call my sister's. Talk to you later." *Click.*

Keegan's recorded message was nearly as brief, but at least he didn't sound angry.

"You'll like this, Harry," he said. "I came into the office today to get the lab reports on Emile Cross a little early, and even though he was pretty badly decomposed, guess what they found in the dirt next to his body? A pack of Blackjack gum. Does that sound like coincidence to you? It doesn't to me, either. Call you tomorrow. And Harry, don't start acting like the Lone Ranger on this, huh? If you get anything going, give me a call, day or night."

What was this? Maybe Irons had placed that package of gum next to Cross's body after he killed him as a kind of calling card, the same thing Tom Horn used to do when he placed a flat rock under the heads of his victims. Maybe, though, my imagination was just running away with me. Maybe Emile Cross was one of the two or three people in the entire western United States who really liked black gum.

I stayed on the line and tried to call Keegan's home like he'd suggested, but the phone rang half a dozen times before his machine finally picked up and informed me that neither he nor his wife was available at that particular moment. I hung up without leaving a message, tucked the receiver between my shoulder and jaw, and dialed Nicole's sister's house in Denver.

My thirteen-year-old nephew Judson answered and informed me that, yes, Nicole and the boys were staying with him for a while, but no, they weren't home right then. They were out at a late doubleheader and weren't expected back until around midnight. Did I want to leave a message? Because if I did, he'd have to go and find a pencil.

"Just tell 'em I called when they come in," I said.

"Sure thing, Uncle Harry," he promised.

I racked the receiver, took a quick tour through my mail, and started thinking about food. I was disappointed that I'd missed Nicole and the boys, but since I hadn't eaten all day, I was also hungry. Problem was, there were no decent leftovers in the refrigerator on account of the fact that my deputies had raided it. As a last resort, I pulled a cast iron frying pan out of the cupboard and made myself a fried egg and onion sandwich slathered with Miracle Whip and melted cheese, holding it over the kitchen sink to eat.

Then I pulled on a pair of sweats and my bathrobe, popped the tab on a can of Coors, and surfed channels on television. There was nothing on but a rerun of *Murder, She Wrote,* so I left the picture on, turned the sound completely off, and glanced at it occasionally while I got my gun cleaning kit, reamed the barrel of my .357 with a bore brush, and rubbed the metal surfaces with a rag soaked in gun oil.

Around eleven I checked the locks, turned out the lights, and tucked myself into bed with a good mystery, *Chinaman's Chance,* by Ross Thomas. I've read it about a dozen times, so I don't feel the need to read it chronologically any more, I just skip around to my favorite parts until I'm too tired to read.

It must have worked better than usual, because when the ringing phone brought me out of a deep sleep, I opened my eyes to find the bedside lamp still burning, the book still gripped in my hands, and a horrible crink in my neck.

"Shit," I grumbled, squinting at the alarm clock. Twelve thirty. Maybe Nicole had gotten my message after all.

"Starbranch," I croaked. I flipped a light on but immediately turned it off again because the bright lights hurt my eyes.

"Sheriff?" a male voice asked.

"Yeah?"

"This is Larry Rawls. Did I wake you?"

"No problem, Larry. What's up?"

"I thought you'd want to hear this as soon as possible," he said. "I got a call about a half hour ago to respond to a shooting at the Woods Landing Bar. That's where I am now."

"Someone hurt?"

"Dead," Rawls said. "Man by the name of Wayne Carney. He's lying about three feet away from me. Shot through the forehead."

Wayne Carney, I thought anxiously. The rustler C.J. Fall and Walker Tisdale had let out of jail that very morning. The man they hoped would wear a wire to incriminate Bobby Snow.

"Have you secured the area?" I asked quickly. "How about suspects?"

"Yes and yes," Rawls said. "The shooting happened just as the bar was closing, and besides the bartender, Carney and the suspect were the only people in the place. We've got the doors locked now, so there's nothing else to secure."

"And what about the suspect?" I asked.

"Took off before I got here." Rawls said.

"Who was it?" I asked, wide awake and buzzing with anticipation. "Bobby Snow?"

"Nope, it wasn't Snow." Rawls said. "I hope you're sittin' down, Harry. The killer was Saul Irons."

# FOURTEEN

Thirty minutes later, I sat at a table in the Woods Landing Bar across from Mickey Sloane, the bartender, who sipped bourbon and branch while he explained how Saul Irons had laid the muzzle of his .357 between Wayne Carney's eyebrows and blown his brains all over the dartboard and beer posters on the back wall of the saloon.

Outside, James Bowen and the ambulance crew from Laramie waited for us to finish our discussion, and a growing crowd of curious townies milled around the parking lot, drinking beer and listening to country music on their tape decks.

In Woods Landing, a small ranching community in the foothills of the Medicine Bow range about fifteen miles southeast of Victory, shootings are the kind of news that travels fast, and most of the locals had beat me to the scene. I imagined that someone had intercepted the police traffic on his CB radio and called a few friends, who each called a few friends . . .

Sloane pointed to the far end of the room, where several small tables were clustered around a pool table, a few video poker machines, and an ancient Pac-Man game. "They were sitting back there talking," he said. "And the next thing you know, Carney starts yelling motherfucker this, cocksucker that. He stands up, knocks his chair over. And then Irons stands up, too. He's got a pistol in his hand. Points it between Carney's eyes, and BAM!"

The object of our discussion, sporting a neat round hole in the center of his wide forehead, was on his back amid a tangle of chairs, broken beer glasses, and ashtrays. His empty eyes gaped at the ceiling fan, and a dark burgundy stain puddled behind his head on the hardwood floor. He wore a sidearm, an automatic that looked like a Browning 9-millimeter, but it was still snug in the leather holster on his hip.

Irons, by contrast, had carried a snub-nosed .357 in a standard shoulder rig.

Just a couple of good old boys, out for a night on the town and dressed to kill. Not unusual in the backwaters of Wyoming, where there are no restrictive gun laws, and you can carry a weapon almost anywhere, as long as it's not concealed. We do, however, frown on using that weapon on another human being once you arrive.

"How long had they been here?" I asked.

"Carney came in around six-thirty and started drinking," Sloane said. "Had a sandwich around eight. Shot a few games of pool with some of the guys. Drank a little more."

"What about Irons?"

"He came in about ten thirty. Acted like he might have come here to meet Carney. Bought a couple rounds of beers, and the two of them sat back there talking until everyone else had gone home."

"What were they talking about?"

"I wouldn't know," Sloane said. "The jukebox was going most of the time, so I couldn't hear."

"Did you overhear anything when you went to wait on their table?"

"Nah," he said. "Irons came to the bar to get their drinks. It didn't look like either of them was particularly upset. Just seemed intense, you know? Had their heads together, talking low."

"How did the trouble start?"

"I couldn't say," Sloane said, and took a long sip of his bourbon. He winced, reached for a pack of smokes and lit one. "I was behind the bar, stocking the coolers and getting ready to close. In a few minutes I figured I'd have to tell them it was time to leave. I was bent over the cooler filling the Bud when I hear Carney start yelling. Cursing mostly, but also mad about something Irons had said. I think he said something about stealing, but I couldn't be sure."

"Was Wayne drunk?" I asked.

"If not, he was pretty damn close," Sloane said. "He'd had maybe ten beers, couple of bourbons. I probably shoulda cut him off."

"He was packing a weapon, Mickey," I said. "Why didn't he use it?"

"I have no idea," Sloane said. "When I looked up, his hand was coming down like he might have been reaching for his pistol. But I didn't have the best angle, so I couldn't say for sure."

"What happened then?"

"After that, it went faster than I can tell it," Sloane said. "I was looking at Wayne, and by the time my eyes went back to Irons, he already had his pistol in his hand. Leaned forward across the table, put the muzzle a few inches from Wayne's head, and pulled the trigger. Dropped him like a sack of manure."

"And then what happened?" I asked. "You've just witnessed a shooting, and the killer is standing there with a gun in his hand. Did Irons say anything to you then?"

"Yeah, he did," Sloane said. "I was scared shitless, but all he did was tell me I'd better call the police. Then he got himself a shot of whiskey—which he paid for, by the way—walked out the door, and drove off in that old pickup."

"The Chevy?"

"Yeah, that's it." Sloane said.

"Which direction?" I asked.

"South, I think," Sloane said. "Maybe toward Jelm Mountain.

And beyond that the Colorado border, just nine short miles away, I thought glumly. By now, Saul Irons could have lost himself in the emptiness of the Roosevelt National Forest, or he could have taken Highway 125 southwest toward Walden and gone from there over Rabbit Ears Pass into Steamboat Springs. Either way, if he'd crossed the state line it would take an extradition proceeding to bring him back.

My best hope was that he'd stayed in the Jelm Mountain area, although that only narrowed it down to around two hundred square miles or more of virtually uninhabited country just on the Wyoming side of the line.

"Send out an all-points bulletin on Saul Irons right away," I told Rawls. "Suspect last seen driving south on Highway 10 or possibly 125 in a 1989 blue and white Chevy four-by-four pickup. Wanted for first-degree murder. You've got his physical description."

Rawls went to the the front door, put his hand on the brass knob.

"And Larry," I said after him.

"What is it, Sheriff?"

"They should consider him armed and dangerous."

Rawls smiled grimly, looked at Wayne Carney's body, whose three sightless eyes still gawked at the ceiling fan. "Yeah," he said. "I suppose they should."

Keegan arrived from Cheyenne a little after six-thirty, his suit so rumpled it looked like he'd worn it in a steam bath. I'd phoned him at home and gotten him out of bed, and he was anxious to help coordinate the search for Saul Irons, which so far involved the county sheriff's office, the Department of Criminal Investigation and the highway patrol.

Two of my deputies had taken off in a single-engine Cessna at first light and were flying the back country between Jelm Mountain and the Colorado border on the off chance Saul had stayed on the Wyoming side of the line and was camped somewhere out in the open.

I had a half dozen additional deputies on the ground working the maze of back roads between Woods Landing and Boswell, and I had roadblocks on both Highway 10 and Highway 230, the only blacktop road into Colorado. In that state, the Jackson County Sheriff's Office was watching the main roads, although we'd been informed that because of a flu outbreak, they were down to half staff. We'd also notified Fatty Winston's office in Carbon County to be on the alert in case Irons slipped through one of the many giant-size holes in our net and wandered over the mountains and out of my jurisdiction.

Around eight, Keegan and I got tired of hanging around the Woods Landing Bar and hopped in the Blazer for a run up Jelm Mountain, atop which sits the University of Wyoming's huge infrared telescope, an amazingly complicated piece of equipment the university's outer space nerds use to chart the farthest reaches of space through the heat signatures of heavenly bodies.

The mountain itself is a ruthless hunk of ground, home to mountain lions, elk, mule deer, and bald eagles, accessible only by Sno-Cat for a good part of the year. In summer, the ground is clear of drifts, but even then the maze of canyons and draws along the slopes and the steep grade of the mountain make it torturous country to travel on foot.

If you're looking for a place to hide between Woods Landing and the Colorado border, Jelm Mountain is as good as any, and although the pilots had come up empty on their initial flyovers, there was still a chance we might come across Irons on the ground. We knew he was hauling his little string of saddle and pack horses when he left the Hardesty ranch, and since he wasn't pulling a horse trailer when he left the scene of the killing, that meant he'd left the horses somewhere. Maybe he had the animals picketed at a camp nearby.

It wasn't much of a plan, but it was the best one we had at

the moment, and both of us needed to get out for a breath of air and to clear our heads.

Keegan's government-issue Ford sedan is no good on washboard dirt roads, so we were in the Blazer with the windows rolled down. The Laramie River burbled on the west side of the highway, and the bright morning sun warmed the sagebrush hill country to the east. A half mile from the turnoff, we had to stop while a local rancher moved a herd of white-faced Hereford yearlings across the highway to another pasture, the Wyoming version of a traffic jam.

"So how do you read it, Harry?" Keegan asked as he peeled the wrapper from his second pack of Camels in the last few hours. He tapped one of the unfiltered smokes from the pack, double-back-flipped it into his mouth, and snapped open his battered Zippo lighter.

Drumming my hands impatiently on the wheel while the cowboys urged the languid cows to step brightly, I said, "I've got a few thoughts, and none of them make me very comfortable." I rolled my window up against the dust raised by a thousand hooves but rolled it back down as soon as I realized dust was preferable to being trapped inside a closed automobile with a cloud of Keegan's cigarette smoke.

"First of all, there's no way on God's earth Irons just 'happened' to come across Wayne Carney at the bar last night. He followed him there, Ken, which means he somehow found out Carney had been let out of jail so he could help Walker Tisdale make a rustling and murder case against Bobby Snow. I think Irons wanted the same thing from Carney that we did, information about Snow's operation and whereabouts."

"You think he got it?" Keegan asked. "What makes you think he's looking for Snow?"

"That's two questions, Ken," I said. The last of the cows had finally crossed the blacktop, so I eased the transmission into drive, steered through the cow flops the animals had left behind, and continued up the mountain. The motor hesitated slightly when I pressed the accelerator. Time for a tune-up.

"First, I don't think he got the information he wanted, since Carney wound up dead. And second, since everyone believes Irons was hired to take rustlers out of the game, it makes sense he'd be interested in Snow, who is known as one of the biggest livestock thieves in the county."

"All right, I'll buy that," Keegan said. He pointed to a cattle guard leading from the blacktop to the dirt road up Jelm Mountain lest I miss my turn. I nodded that I saw it, slowed the Blazer, and eased us across the guard. The vibration from the steel rails made by biceps shake like jelly. "But how did he find out Carney had been picked up in the first place? Or that he'd gotten out? That implies he's got a decent source of information."

"It wasn't my people," I assured him. "As far as I know, I'm the only one in my department who even knew Carney had been taken into custody. They tucked him away in the university police department's jail facility. Tisdale and C.J. Fall handled the whole thing."

"So it might have been either of them," Keegan said. "From what you've told me about Fall, I doubt it was him. But Tisdale?"

I shrugged my shoulders. "I don't know what he could have gained by doing that, but maybe. It might have been someone on the university police force, too. When you come to think about it, it could have come from a lot of places."

He made a sweeping gesture toward the mountain ahead of us. "Which means," he said, "that we're probably wasting our time up here. I don't think he's been camped on Jelm Mountain, since there aren't any phones, except at the observatory. And for someone to have fed him information about Carney's release—"

"They would've had to call him on the phone," I finished for him.

"Oh, well," he said, "we weren't doing anybody any good sitting around that barroom at eight in the morning. I guess it won't hurt to drive to the top and look around."

We passed most of the twenty-minute drive up the remainder of the mountain in silence that fit us like a pair of old boots.

Keegan smoked and watched the scenery as I negotiated the switchbacks on the narrow dirt track. A couple hundred yards from the top, we turned off at a wide spot in the road, pulled our binoculars out of their cases, and got out to scan the terrain between Jelm Mountain and the highway into Woods Landing. We spotted a small herd of mule deer creeping down a draw toward the river, a ranch hand repairing a barbed wire fence, and a couple of sleek gray coyotes hunting rabbits on Pollock Draw, but no Saul Irons.

"I suppose it could have happened just the way you said, Harry," Keegan said, the binoculars pressed to his eyes and his latest Camel unfiltered dangling from the corner of his mouth. "But there's something that keeps bothering me. I know Saul is plenty capable of killing, but I don't think he's ever been stupid about it. And this thing with Carney was a stupid killing."

"Because there was a witness?" I asked.

"Precisely," he said. "He had to know that killing Carney in public like that would bring charges, that he'd end up in jail because of it. I can see Saul taking Carney out—the man was a rustler after all—but it's more his style to do it on some lonesome dirt road in the middle of nowhere, somewhere the body won't even be found for months. Shooting Carney like this . . . He could wind up on death row, and it's like he just doesn't care."

"So what are you saying, Ken?" I asked.

"I don't know," he said. "There's something strange going on, but I can't put my finger on what it is."

"Maybe not so strange," I said. "He's done something like this once before, hasn't he? With that cop who worked for him. The one he shot."

"Yeah, he did that one in public too, but he didn't run off afterwards. He stayed around to explain he'd shot the guy in self-defense."

"Maybe he didn't think anyone would buy it if he tried telling the same story again," I offered.

"Maybe," Keegan agreed. "You heard what the bartender

said, though. Carney might have been going for his gun, he might not have. Would you buy self-defense?"

"I might—once," I said. "But twice? In such similar circumstances? I don't think so, Ken. He put himself in these situations, after all, and he went in armed. He had to have a good idea how they could come out."

"Then you think Carney's killing was premeditated?" Keegan asked.

I nodded. "Murder one. Your buddy could face death by lethal injection."

The only car in the parking lot at the observatory was a geriatric Volkswagen beetle, and we pounded on the front door until the weedy grad student on duty that morning finally got around to answering. No, he said, he hadn't seen anyone coming up the road in a blue and white Chevy pickup, but then he wouldn't have, since he'd had his eyes glued to the telescope's infrared readouts pretty much continuously since midnight the previous evening.

Which might have explained his swollen, bloodshot eyes. Then again, he might have been in there smoking a little reefer while he waited for his replacement to drive out from Laramie and spell him.

I think the latter was the more likely explanation, since the kid took one look at our badges and guns and refused to open the front door more than a crack lest we wanted to come in and visit. And he was visibly relieved when we thanked him, got back in the Blazer, and cranked the overheated engine up for the ride back down the hill.

Since Irons was still among the missing when we got back to the Woods Landing Bar, Keegan decided to drive out to Saul's cabin on the Hardesty ranch on the off chance he'd holed up there after the shooting.

I left Rawls in charge of the manhunt and drove to the sheriff's office in Laramie, where I checked myself into a vacant jail cell and caught a few hours' sleep.

I woke around noon, my back sore from the lumpy mattress and my head full of cobwebs. I showered in the guards' locker room, got back into my sweaty, wrinkled clothes and grabbed myself a ham and cheese sandwich from the cart the trustee was using to serve the lunchtime crowd of scofflaws in the county slam. Then I went downstairs to my office, checked the call sheets, and signed myself out for the afternoon.

If anybody in Albany County knew where Saul Irons had gone after he killed Wayne Carney, I figured it would be his employer. It was time to brace Tess McAfferty.

I drove out Highway 30 toward Rock River, the sun blistering the asphalt roadbed, shimmering waves of reflected heat rising from the baked ground like spirit mist. To the east, the flanks of Iron Mountain broke the horizon, the walls of a granite fortress that guard the grasslands of the high plains.

The Union Pacific Railroad line follows Highway 30 all the way to Walcott junction, and for fifteen miles between the city limits of Laramie and the ghost town of Bosler, I raced a ponderous freight train, over a hundred empty coal cars, making good time on the return leg of its journey from the Midwest to the strip mines around Hanna. With the window down, the train sounded like rolling thunder on the steel rails. I pushed the accelerator to the floor and the speedometer inched up to seventy-five, then eighty. As I passed the last diesel engine and took the lead, the engineer gave his air horn a mighty blast and waved good-bye.

I made good time into Rock River, where I slowed to the posted speed limit for the two-block ride through town. There were fifteen or twenty cars parked in front of the auction barn and a couple of pickups in front of the town's only bar, where Willie Nelson's voice drifted through the open screen door. It looked dark inside, and cool, and I toyed with the idea of stopping by on my way home for a diet cola over crushed ice with a slice of lime.

Maybe one of those Tombstone Pizzas they heat up in the nuke. See what the townies had to say about the recent spate of killings in their neck of the woods.

I punched it at the edge of town and burned asphalt until I came to the turnoff to the McAfferty ranch, where I eased off the highway, cut my speed to under ten miles an hour to avoid raising a cloud of dust, and worked my way up the washboard toward the ranch house.

When I reached the spot where Colleen had been buried on the bank of the stream two days before, I pulled off the bumpy road, drove a few yards past her fresh grave, and tucked the Blazer away in a small grove of willows and aspen where it couldn't be seen from the road. There was no marker on Colleen's grave yet, but the freshly turned earth clearly marked the dimensions of the coffin. The air smelled of decaying flowers; the hundreds of carnations and lilies that had been strewn over the gravesite, their petals wilted and brown from two days in the desert sun. An animal had been digging at one end of the grave, probably a badger, but he hadn't gone too deep. I kicked the dirt back into the hole he'd made and tamped it down with the sole of my boot.

Then I went back and pulled my binoculars from the glove box, locked the doors, and began to work my way through the grove of aspen toward a bend in the stream where I'd have a view of the ranch house. I don't know what I hoped to gain by spying on Tess before I announced my arrival, but it's always interesting to see how people act when they don't think anybody's watching, especially if those people might have something to hide.

The deadfall in the grove tangled around my feet, snapped and popped with every step. The supple branches at face level got in their licks too, stung me a couple good ones across the cheek when I pushed through the undergrowth. There are some people of my acquaintance—Frankie Bull comes to mind—who can walk through that stuff without making a sound, but I'm not one of them. When I walk through the woods, it sounds like a herd of Cape buffalo tromping through the brambles, the only difference being that Cape buffalo don't swear. This disability makes me a lousy deer hunter, but I've seldom found it a severe problem when I'm sneaking up on people, especially if the people are several hundred yards away and likely to be indoors.

At the edge of the grove, I had a clear view of the McAfferty ranch house, and beyond that, the corral. I scrunched down in a clump of sagebrush, poked my head through the branches, and brought the binoculars up to my eyes.

The ranch house was at least a hundred fifty yards away, but the high-power Bushnells made me feel like I was in the front yard—right next to the two young McAffertys I'd met at Colleen's funeral. I looked up to make sure the sun's rays weren't coming from a direction that would reflect off my lenses and give me away, then adjusted the focus on the binocs, sharpened the image until I could see the razor stubble on their windburned faces.

The McAfferty boys were good-looking specimens, T-shaped, with wide shoulders and narrow hips, hard-bodied ranch kids with the kind of taut, ropy musculature that doesn't come from lounging around the house eating potato chips and watching MTV.

The older one, who I judged to be in his middle twenties, was dressed in a new pair of blue jeans, good boots, a high-crowned Stetson, a black western shirt with pearl snaps, and a polished silver slide on his bolo. He stood in the driveway, leaning against the fender of Tess's pickup, anxiously twirling a set of keys on his index finger. It was the look of someone who's always the first one ready to go anywhere and used to waiting around for the rest of the crew.

His brother, a blunt-nosed kid of nineteen or twenty with a blond bandito mustache and a tattoo of a coiled serpent on his forearm, was bare-chested. He sat in the front porch swing, pushed himself back and forth with the toes of his boots while he flipped the pages of a magazine. His clean shirt, hat, and corduroy dress jacket hung from the arm of a bronze plant hanger on one of the porch supports. He too was ready to travel, but he obviously didn't want to wrinkle his dress clothes and so wouldn't put them on until the last minute. From time to time I could see his lips move and his easy smile as he spoke to his older brother.

Eventually the older McAfferty took off his jacket, climbed the porch steps, and made himself at home in the swing beside his brother. He pulled a can of chewing tobacco from his shirt pocket, tucked a chaw in his lower lip, and offered the snoose to his younger brother, who helped himself and went back to reading. The older brother leaned back in the seat, tipped the brim of his hat down over his eyes, stretched his long legs, and folded his hands on his stomach.

I watched him nap and his kid brother read for a good hour, the sun baking my back and a cloud of gnats buzzing around my face, before the screen door opened and Tess came outside. She was dressed in the feminine version of the outfits worn by the McAffertys. Jeans that fit considerably more snugly than theirs, good boots, straw hat, and a white Western shirt tied under her bosom, exposing her navel.

In one arm she carried a green and white cooler, which she sat at the edge of the porch. In her other was an object about thirty inches long wrapped in a gray wool blanket.

When he saw her, the younger McAfferty boy jumped up from the swing, lifted the cooler, and held out his free hand for whatever was wrapped in the blanket. Tess shook her head and tucked it more securely under her arm, strode purposefully down the porch steps, and yanked open the driver's-side door of the vehicle. As she folded herself behind the wheel, the blanket wrap fell away and the bright sun glinted off the polished barrel of a sawed-off pump shotgun with a black pistol grip.

Tess frowned, pulled the ugly weapon inside the cab, and laid it at her feet. Then she started the engine and began to back up, her rear wheels kicking up a spray of sand and gravel, and the lethargic McAffertys barely had time to grab their clothes, hop in, and slam the door.

She turned the pickup around and came racing down the

242

road toward the place where I was hidden, the vehicle moving too quickly to keep it in focus. I laid my binoculars on the ground and dropped to my stomach in the brush, waited until I heard the noise of her motor pass and begin receding down the road.

As soon as I figured it was safe, I jumped up and ran back toward the place where I'd hidden the Blazer, cursing the damn underbrush and my stiff muscles every step of the way. Climbing in, I fumbled for my keys and jammed them in the ignition. The engine cranked for a long time before it finally caught; the motor coughed and sputtered as I backed out from under the canopy of trees, yanked the wheel right, and gave it the gas until I was turned around and headed in the right direction. Then I put my foot to the floorboard, holding on to the wheel with one hand and snapping my seatbelt with the other.

It looked to me like the McAfferty clan was goin' huntin'.

And if I wanted to tag along, I needed to haul a little ass.

# FIFTEEN

There was a time shortly after I moved to Victory when I went to visit a friend in Casper, and one morning the two of us decided to drive to his summer cabin near Elk Mountain and do a little fishing. We left Casper a little after eight in the morning, made the long ninety-mile drive through Shirley Basin and Medicine Bow, turned West toward Hanna, passed the big strip mines, and finally crossed Interstate 80 south of Elmo.

The whole time we were on the highway, I had the feeling something odd was happening, but I couldn't put my finger on what it was. Finally, as we passed Halleck Creek, it hit me: we'd traveled over 120 miles on one of the state's major highways and in the whole distance we hadn't seen another vehicle going in either direction. That's the way it is out here sometimes, which explains why it's sometimes nearly impossible to follow another car without being spotted.

If the traffic is light, as it was as I set off after the McAffertys, there's no place for a pursuer to hide, especially if the vehicle in question is a green and white sheriff's department bruiser with a conspicuous light bar on top.

When I got to the highway, I scanned the blacktop toward Laramie until I spotted the McAffertys' pickup about a mile down the road. I let them put another half mile between us and then goosed the Blazer onto the asphalt.

There was no trouble keeping up. Once the Blazer gets over the initial shock of being spurred into forward motion and gets the bit in its mouth, it flat eats highway. I radioed the office to let them know we were heading their direction and asked the dispatcher to post a road deputy somewhere off Highway 30 where it crosses the city limits. If I was going to lose the McAffertys, that's where it would be, and I wanted someone on hand to track them between the time they entered town and the time I got there a couple minutes later.

It's thirty-seven miles from Rock River to Laramie, and at the rate she was traveling, Tess would make the entire trip in less time than it takes to boil coffee. A fast-moving bank of billowy gray rain clouds had moved in from the east, and a light sprinkle fell on the thirsty plains. The storm would pass in a matter of minutes, but I turned on the wipers, grimacing when the first pass did nothing more than streak the glass with a muddy, translucent film.

We drove out from under the storm in less than three miles into bright sunshine, the air fragrant with the clean, after-rain smell of sage and evaporating moisture. I pulled the mike from its stand and raised dispatch in Laramie. Yes, they said, a deputy was in place just over the city limits and two more in unmarked cars were waiting on Third Street to follow Tess if she came through the downtown area. I told them not to stop her for any reason, just keep her vehicle in sight and let me know where she was heading.

Tess was cruising at over ninety miles an hour when she hit Laramie, and she immediately cut her speed back to the limit. I crossed the border a minute later, but by that time, my deputies told me Tess was already several blocks down the road, waiting for a stop light on the corner of Third and Clark. When the light turned green, a deputy reported that she turned right on Clark and was headed over the railroad bridge into West Laramie.

Since there was no way she could see me behind her at that point, I hit the lights and the gas, made it to the corner in a few seconds. I had to put my right front wheel on the sidewalk to pass a car full of students at the red light, but I blew through the intersection, turned the emergency lights off and picked her up again as she passed the old Wyoming Territorial Prison. I radioed my deputies to back off and followed the McAffertys past Foster's Country Corners, the West Laramie Fly Shop, and the mobile home parks off Harrison Street. When she hit the junction of Highways 130 and 230, she flashed her right directional, turned onto 130 toward Victory, and stepped on the accelerator. Less than a mile past the city limit sign, she had her pickup doing ninety again.

I had an idea where we were going, but I wouldn't know for sure until we were several miles down the road. From the city limits it's pretty much a straightaway for the entire thirty-mile trip to Victory, and Tess took advantage of the light traffic to make time.

So far, I didn't think anyone in the McAfferty vehicle had noticed they were being tailed, but just to make sure, I let them put another quarter mile between us, which made it difficult to keep them in sight. Also, I was nervous about how much gasoline I had left. I was down to about a quarter tank, enough for about seventy-five miles of driving.

I shouldn't have worried. We passed the Big Hollow oil field and Hatton reservoir, but shortly after her pickup crossed the Little Laramie, I saw the flash of Tess's brake lights as she slowed down and made the left turn into the entrance of the T-Bar, Bobby Snow's ranch.

I wasn't surprised by her destination, but it did present me with the same dilemma my deputies had faced over the past few days as they tried to keep watch on Bobby's movements. There was no way I could follow her down the dirt road to his house without being seen, which meant I had to settle for parking across the highway behind some old railroad buildings and watch the road from there. That way, I'd know when she finished her business at Bobby's, and I'd be close enough to hear gunshots, if that's what she'd come for. It was better than nothing, but from that position I wasn't able to see what she was doing at the house. If I wanted to do that, I'd have to sneak closer on foot.

I scanned the ridgeline that forms the northern boundary of the T-Bar and saw what I was looking for about a quarter of a mile away, a flat mesa overlooking the little hollow where Bobby's house stood. It looked like a relatively easy walk, and from the top I'd be able to look down on his house and corrals. If I kept to the little gullies that scored the side of the mesa, I might even make it to the top without being noticed.

I locked the Blazer, checked to make sure the .357 was secured on my hip, slung the binoculars over my neck, and crossed the highway. At the barbed wire fence that marks the eastern boundary of Snow's ranch, I climbed through the fence without getting snagged and followed the bank of the Little Laramie to the foot of the mesa. It was a seventy-five-yard climb to the top, and my feet slipped constantly on the loose shale scree. I was in the bottom of a gully, bent over so I wouldn't be visible, and even using the walking stick for purchase it took me a good ten minutes to scramble to the top. I caught my breath, pulled my hat off, peeked over the lip of the wash, and brought the binocs to bear on the ranch buildings below.

Tess's pickup was parked near the aspen grove where I'd come upon Bobby and his lover, but aside from a couple of derelict pickups and some haying equipment, her's was the only vehicle in sight. The older McAfferty boy stood at the door to the barn, trying to open it. Tess and the other McAfferty kid were at the corral, looking over a couple of sleek buckskin quarter horses. From the top of the mesa, I could hear the hinges on the barn door screech when the older McAfferty finally got it open, but Tess and the younger brother only glanced up briefly when he slipped inside.

Two minutes later he came out again, hollered something to

Tess and his brother at the corral, and the three of them trudged up to the front porch, peered in the windows, and tried the front door.

It was locked.

Tess and the younger McAfferty waited on the porch while the other McAfferty boy made a quick circuit of Bobby's house, tested the windows and the side door. He found nothing open, and the three stood on the porch for several minutes, apparently arguing over what they should do next. Finally Tess ended the conversation, emphatically punching the air. She came down off the porch and went back to her pickup, slipped inside and started the engine while she waited for the McAffertys to saddle up.

By the time they were backing out of the aspen grove, I was already scrambling back down the hill, although I judged I probably wouldn't make it to the Blazer in time. I was right. Tess had driven from Bobby's house back to the highway as I was still coming down the hill, and by the time I was at the mouth of the arroyo, she was a mile down the blacktop. I hit the highway at what for me passes as a dead run, putting my hand to my eyes and scanning the road south. I saw her pickup about two miles away, gobbling asphalt toward Laramie.

I ran to the Blazer and radioed dispatch to have a deputy follow her again when she got back to town. Then I hopped into the driver's seat, fishtailed onto the blacktop, and tried to make up for lost time.

By the time I got to Laramie less than fifteen minutes later, I figured Tess was only a few minutes ahead of me, although I'd been too far behind on the highway to keep her pickup in sight. The Blazer—which to my knowledge had never been pushed to a hundred miles an hour—was threatening to go into cardiac arrest. I held the steering wheel with one hand and fumbled for the mike with the other, opened the channel, identified myself and asked for Tess's location. I had a response as soon as I released the transmit button. My guys had her in their sights, they said, but they didn't know what I wanted them to do next.

"Where is she?"

"She just turned off 287 at the entrance to the fairgrounds," a deputy said. "You want we should follow her?"

"No, break away," I said. "I'll take it from here. Dispatch?"

"Yes, Sheriff?"

"How many deputies do we already have out there working the crowd?"

"Three," the dispatcher said. "Four if you count the dog."

More than enough to keep me out of trouble, I thought as I turned right on Third and sped off in the direction of the fairgrounds.

Turns out I was wrong.

I parked the Blazer in the parking lot of the fairgrounds and looked for five minutes without spotting Tess's pickup in the throng of cars in the three-acre lot. I stopped one of the parking attendants, who directed traffic from the saddle of a tall black gelding, flashed my badge, and asked if he'd seen the pickup I was looking for. He hadn't, so I followed a family of tourists—Dad in Bermuda shorts, white socks, and black loafers, Mom in a fluorescent running suit, and the kids in wrinkly shorts and T-shirts—out of the dusty parking lot, past the ticket booth, and up the ramp to the grandstand.

In July we have a real honest-to-God pro rodeo in Laramie, Laramie Jubilee Days, which for three days draws the best talent from the Professional Rodeo Cowboys Association's membership. The rest of the summer we have a sort of minor league amateur rodeo two nights a week to keep the tourists happy.

That night was one of the amateur nights, but you couldn't have told that from the enthusiasm of the crowd. With fifteen minutes until showtime, the stands were already three quarters full, and more people were still pouring up the ramps. Those already seated shifted their fannies on the hard bench seats, flipped through their programs, glanced expectantly across the expanse of arena to the bucking chutes on the far side. The air was thick with a weird amalgam of scent—suntan lotion and perfume from the tourists, livestock musk, dust, and hay, the aroma of hotdogs, popcorn, and beer.

For several moments I stood at the top of the ramp and scanned the crowd, ignoring everyone not wearing traditional western clothing. There were still hundreds of people trudging up the walkways looking for their seats, and my eyes stopped a dozen times on groups of fans whose dress resembled the McAffertys'. I finally spotted them in the middle of the grandstand, about thirteen rows up. They paid no attention to the swirl of humanity around them but watched the chute area through binoculars.

I fell in behind a family of five and started working my way up the walkway, stopped a couple of rows beyond the McAffertys and took a seat behind them and fifteen feet to the left. When I was seated and as comfortable as I was going to get, I called for one of the vendors to pass me a soda and a couple of hot dogs, smothered in mustard and chopped onion, and ate while I waited for the grand entrance and the start of the fandango.

If you've been to a few rodeos, you know they all follow a fairly set pattern. A bunch of cowgirls and cowboys ride in carrying flags, and everybody in the audience stands while the cowpersons ride around the arena and someone in the announcer's booth plays a recording of "The Star Spangled Banner." Their patriotic duty done, everybody sits back down in the hopes they'll get a chance to see something dangerous, preferably bloody.

They're seldom disappointed.

First up are the bareback bronc riders, whose job it is to hang on to a thousand pounds of seriously pissed-off horseflesh for eight seconds. It doesn't sound so bad until you consider that they have to ride with one hand in the air, have nothing to hang on to with the other but a hunk of rope, and have to spur the horse every time he jumps in order to score points. For my money, bareback bronc riding is the premiere event in rodeo, because it's the purest. Whenever I see a cowboy in the bucking chute taking a deep seat and a short rein as he waits for that gate to open and all hell to break loose, there's a split second when I'd give anything I own to trade places with him. To be a great human athlete aboard a great animal athlete, one on one, skill against skill alone. Then the gate opens, the horse sunfishes, his front legs collide with earth hard enough to compress vertebra, and before the cowboy can begin to regain his balance, the horse is airborne again.

After the bareback riding comes one of the less dangerous competitions, barrel racing maybe, where women race quarter horses around fifty-gallon drums in a cloverleaf, or bulldogging, where a cowboy dives off the back of a horse at full gallop and wrestles a steer to the ground. I once saw a guy bulldog a steer without hands. No shit. He did it by biting the animal on the nose until it just gave up and fell over. I'm not making that up.

Next comes saddle broncs: same idea as bareback, except the cowboy has a saddle with stirrups and has to spur more.

Then it's calf roping, my least favorite rodeo sport because I've seen too many animals hurt in the process. I usually go for a beer during that part of the rodeo.

Sometimes, they follow calf roping with another roping event, like team roping, where one cowboy ropes a critter's head while the other ropes his heels. Maybe they even have a couple of audience participation events, like a kids' calf scramble or a ladies' ribbon roping.

Finally comes the event everyone remembers—bull riding, the Indy 500 of rodeo, perhaps the most dangerous sport on earth. It might not be that much harder to stay aboard a 1,500-pound, red-eyed, spinning, slobbering Brahma bull for eight seconds than it is to stay on a bucking bronc. But at least your average bronc is born without horns, and even if he had them, his temperament would discourage him from coming back to use them on you after he bucked you off. I've seen it happen more than once, and on one sad occasion I saw a cowboy die when the bullfighters, cleverly disguised as clowns, were unable to distract the enraged beast from his goal of crushing the young man's rib cage with his hooves and disemboweling him with the tip of his horn.

The grand entrance began as twilight settled over the Laramie plains, the cowgirls dressed in brightly colored western outfits and matching hats, circling the arena with the various flags, the cowboys spiffy in freshly starched shirts and crisp denims, all of them mounted on good quarter horse stock. We stood as the American colors passed, held our hats over our hearts while someone in the announcer's booth played a scratchy recording of the national anthem.

The grand entrance finished, the McAfferty clan settled in, and we all watched the bareback bronc riders. The McAfferty boys consulted their programs to see who was up next on what horse, discussed each short ride as it ended. I leaned back on the hard bleachers and kept one eye on the McAffertys and the other on the action, listened to the constant twangy patter of the announcer.

For the next hour and a half, the McAffertys stayed put, watching the rodeo, munching hot dogs, laughing occasionally as they talked amongst themselves. Then, as the last calves and tourists were ushered out of the arena after the scramble, they stood up and began to make their way down the aisles. Instead of turning toward the exit, however, they let themselves through the gate into the walkway that leads around the arena to the chutes and stock pens and disappeared into the darkness beyond the illumination of the bright stadium lights.

I hustled down the aisles after them, let myself through the gate and began to walk as quickly as I could toward the bucking chutes. A breeze from the north picked up a haze of dust from the arena and sent it whipping in my direction. The fine particles of dirt clung to my teeth, stung my eyes and made them water.

In the arena, the first bull rider broke out of the chute gate and the crowd suddenly quieted as the Brahma planted his front hooves in the earth and whipped his hindquarters in a savage arc. The cowboy spurred in a desperate attempt to rack up points on his ride. At the end of eight seconds, the crowd erupted in a thunderous wave of applause as the cowboy jumped off the leaping animal's back, landed on his feet, and walked nonchalantly back toward the chutes, and the clowns and cowboys on horseback tried to distract the animal and herd it out of the arena before it could cause trouble.

The chute area is off limits to spectators, and my passage was halted at the entrance gate by a burly cowboy with a soggy cigar in the corner of his mouth and a RODEO SECURITY badge pinned to his sweat-stained shirt. He gave my sheriff's badge and sidearm a curious look and opened the gate to let me through.

"Did you just let three other people through here?" I asked.

"Yeah, Tess McAfferty and a couple kids," he said. "Told me they needed to come back here and look at some bucking stock. Is there a problem?"

"No, no problem," I said, peering over his shoulder in an attempt to find the McAffertys in the mob of cowboys and arena hands working the chutes. They were nowhere to be seen. "I just need to talk to them. Which way did they go?"

He shrugged his shoulders and hooked a thumb in the general direction of the chutes and holding pens. "That direction, I guess. I wasn't paying much attention."

I entered the little fenced-off area where cowboys prepare for their rides. The small group of young men waiting for their bulls to be called paid me little attention as I took up a position at the edge of the nearest chute. From there I had a perfect view of the arena directly in front of the eight bucking chutes, the tops of the chutes themselves, and a bit of the stock-loading area behind the announcer's booth.

I leaned against a wooden fence post and tried to make myself invisible as cowboys worked their way down the roster of the night's bulls. Some of them stayed aboard for the whole eight seconds and scored well, most failed to make it to the buzzer. I hadn't seen Tess or the young McAffertys since they left the grandstand, and I wondered where they could have gone.

Beside me a young cowboy pulled a rosin-soaked glove from his kit bag and slipped it on his riding hand. He walked to the back of the chute and climbed to the top of the railing, swung his long legs over the top rail, and looked down at the bull waiting in the chute, a nasty-looking black Brahma cross with a huge muscled hump, red eyes, and horns the size of sabers. Carefully he lowered himself onto the animal's back. The bull snorted and banged its sides against the railing as the cowboy began to wrap the rosined braid of the bucking rigging around his riding hand. When he was finished, he used his free hand to pound his riding hand closed, tucked his knees into the bull's hide, and nodded for the arena hands to open the gate.

With an explosion of muscle and fury, the bull burst from the chute, kicked his back legs straight in the air, twisted his body, and came down at an angle stiff-legged, landing so forcefully I could feel the impact through the ground beneath my feet. Immediately the bull kicked, sunfished, and began a clockwise spin. The cowboy hunched close to the bull's back, wedged his right leg behind the bull's shoulder, and raked his left spur over the bull's neck. Four seconds into the ride, the bull suddenly planted its front legs in the dirt and came to an abrupt stop. The cowboy's forward momentum threw him dangerously off balance, and he was still unsteady as the bull, muscles bulging beneath the slack hide, erupted in another spin, this time counterclockwise, its head close to the ground, its back legs reaching higher with every kick.

It was too much for the young cowboy, who tumbled from the off side of the bull as the animal snorted and blew. My heart leapt into my throat as I saw that the cowboy's hand was still caught in the bucking rigging. He dangled from the bull's shoulder, fighting desperately to free his trapped hand as the bull spun to the right, its horns almost raking its own rib cage in his enraged attempt to gore the terrified cowboy.

Two rodeo clowns ran at the bull's head, waving their arms and trying to distract the animal's attention, while a third grabbed at the rigging, tried to free the cowboy's hand. The bull swung to his left and ran at the nearest clown, dragging the cowboy along as it charged. Then it stopped, turned its horns inward, and raked the cowboy's chest. He screamed, tried to push his body away from the horns but could not get out of reach. His shirt was torn and blood leaked from a long gash below his right nipple. The bull spun again, slammed the cowboy against the railing of the chute. The young man's body went limp. His feet dragged the ground and his head bounced pitifully from side to side with each horrendous lurch of the bull's 1,800-pound body.

I pulled my .357 and tried to draw a bead on the bull's forehead, but he was moving so quickly I was afraid to fire for fear I'd miss and hit the cowboy instead. Unless something happened in the next second, I knew I'd have to take the risk.

Suddenly, as my finger tightened on the trigger, two cowboys leapt from the top railing of the bucking chutes and darted into the arena. One of them slapped the bull between the eyes, lunged to the left, and rolled from the slashing horns. As the animal lowered its head to charge, the cowboy who had slapped the beast rolled under its legs, stood quickly, and grabbed the unconscious cowboy around the chest as his partner unwrapped the rigging and freed the cowboy's hand. Then, carrying the cowboy between them in their arms, they dived to the ground, shielding his body with their own.

As the clowns and pickup men coaxed the bull from the arena, I followed a group of at least a dozen cowboys who raced from the bucking chutes toward the two men huddled around the unfortunate rider, who was already beginning to regain consciousness. The gash inflicted by the bull's horns looked superficial, and there were no other life-threatening injuries apparent at first glance.

Over the loudspeakers I heard the announcer's down-home voice assure the crowd that the rider's wounds were not serious. He thanked them all for coming to the Laramie River Rodeo, "the rip-snortinest amateur rodeo in America," and invited them to come again. The crowd rose in a standing ovation as the stadium lights in the arena went down, plunging us momentarily into relative darkness before the lights in the grandstand came up.

I tried again to pick out the McAffertys in the chute area, but it was too dark there and all I could make out were the indistinct shapes of people milling around, the cherry glow of their cigarettes as they smoked and laughed and relaxed after a long day's work. As we trooped through the well-tilled ground of the arena back toward the chutes, I fell in behind a pair of long-legged cowboys I'd watched earlier in the saddle bronc competition, listened with half an ear as they cursed the bull that had injured their friend.

"He pulls that goofy crap every time they turn him out of the chute," one of them grumbled. "I warned Gary he liked to spin one way for a while and then change directions. Guess he wasn't ready for it."

"Ain't no gettin' ready for that shit," the other said. "That bull's a mean sumbitch. I hear they want him on the pro circuit."

The first cowboy chuckled. "That oughta make Snow happy."

I hurried ahead a couple of steps, grabbed him by the elbow.

He turned, saw the light from the grandstand reflecting off my badge. "Somethin' we can do for you, Sheriff?"

"Maybe," I said. "I just heard you mention Bobby Snow in connection with that last bull. What's he got to do with it?"

The cowboy was surprised at my ignorance. "He owns most of the bucking stock in this rodeo. Everybody knows that, Sheriff."

Suddenly the reason the McAffertys had attended the evening's performance was clear. Since he hadn't had much luck as a rancher, I knew Bobby Snow contracted bucking stock to area rodeos, and there was no reason the people who ran the Laramie River show wouldn't be among his clients. When the McAffertys had failed to find him at home earlier that afternoon, they'd simply driven in to try him at the office.

It was so simple, I should have thought of it myself.

"You boys haven't seen Snow around here today, have you?" I asked.

"Sure," one of them said. He pointed to the far end of the bucking chutes. "He was down there watching most of the performance." Then he hooked a thumb in the direction of the holding pens behind the bucking chutes. "Last I saw him, he was headed back there to tend his stock."

Which explained why Tess had spent so much time scanning the chute area with her binoculars.

I pushed by the cowboys and hurried to the end of the chutes, let myself through the arena gate, and worked my way through a knot of cowboys and their girlfriends at the side of the small grandstand. Then I walked as quickly as I could to the livestock holding area. The holding pens, thirty or forty in number, were six-foot-high wooden enclosures about twelve feet wide by twenty feet long, each filled with rodeo livestock—calves, bucking horses, and steers, packed a dozen to the pen. The bulls were each given their own enclosures, to keep them from fighting.

With the exception of a couple of mercury vapor lamps on tall poles at either end of the holding area, it was dark in the pens, almost surreal. The air was hot, sticky and oppressively thick with the scent of livestock sweat, hay, and manure. Behind the wooden railings of the pens, I could barely make out the shapes of the animals. The night, however, was alive with their sounds: the bawling of the cattle, the whinnying of a horse as he kicked the slats of the fence, the snorting and farting of the bulls.

I climbed up to stand on the top rail of a pen full of docile steers, where I could see most of the holding area. At the end closest to the bucking chutes, two cowboys on horseback were herding a cluster of cattle up a ramp and into the trailer of a huge semi.

There was no one moving in between the pens in my area, but at the far end of the holding area I saw a man hurrying down a walkway through the shadows. At each intersection he stopped, glanced briefly right and then left, and moved on.

As he came to a third intersection, he stopped and turned, and the light from the mercury vapor lamp illuminated his profile, the stubby nose and long golden mustache.

It was one of the McAfferty brothers.

I yelled for him to stop but there was no way he could have heard me over the din of the livestock. Even so, he turned back in the direction he had been traveling, breaking into a run. At the end of the walkway he turned left and disappeared from sight.

I climbed down from the railing and followed him. One hand brushed the butt of my Blackhawk with each step, the other clutched my blackthorn walking stick like a club. It took perhaps thirty seconds to make it to the place where he'd turned, and I wasn't prepared for what I found as I came around the corner.

The older McAfferty boy lay face down in the dirt with one arm tucked under his torso and the other pointing straight ahead of his body, like a swimmer taking a long forward stroke.

Tess McAfferty rode Bobby Snow's back like a cougar, held one arm around his throat while she pummeled his head with her other hand.

Despite his burden, Bobby and the younger McAfferty circled each other like seasoned boxers, crouching, their fists cocked.

The younger McAfferty feinted with two quick left jabs. Then he closed, threw a loopy overhand right at Snow's head. Bobby blocked it easily with his left, followed with a straight right of his own that connected with McAfferty's nose. It broke with a crack that I heard above the noises of the animals, and the young man dropped to his knees. Bobby finished him with a terrible kick to the chin with his booted foot that sent the young man sprawling backwards.

As Bobby drew back his leg to kick him again, I shouted for him to stop and drew my revolver.

Neither Tess nor Bobby paid me the least attention. Tess concentrated on crushing Bobby's skull with her bare fist and Bobby tried desperately to peel her other arm from around his Adam's apple with one hand as he jabbed the elbow of his free arm into her rib cage.

Had I been paying more attention to what was on either side of me than to the mayhem ahead, I probably would have seen the

258

man who stepped out of the shadows at the side of one of the stock pens before I had already passed him and it was too late.

As it was, the first I awareness I had of him was a dark blur of movement in the corner of my eye. I slowed, began to turn my head, saw the axe handle he was already swinging in my direction.

There was a horrible crunch that reverberated through my cranium. A bright light flashed behind my eyes.

And the entire universe went black.

# SIXTEEN

It's a fairly strange experience, regaining consciousness after you've been knocked loopy. I don't know where your soul goes while you're senseless, but wherever it is, it's black and silent and empty, and you float there like some sort of disembodied brain in an endless sea of tepid ink.

Then, as you start to awake, your subconscious first begins to notice sounds, voices that drift aimlessly like the music from a distant transistor radio while you're napping on the beach. Time has no real meaning, but later you gradually begin to feel—the hard ground, the way the rocks dig into your back, bumps, bruises, cramps, the way your tongue sticks to the roof of your mouth. And finally, you're fully sentient, trying to remember what happened, how you got there, quietly assessing the damage before you commit yourself to anything strenuous, like opening your eyes.

When I began to come around that night in the stock pens, my headache measured about 9.5 on the Richter scale, the sort of banger you only get from a half a bottle of tequila, beer chasers, and a triple-brandy nightcap. Trouble was, I couldn't remember drinking anything, which frankly scared me shitless. Blackouts, after all, are one sure sign of alcoholism, right up there with putting vodka on your cornflakes and sneaking a flask of gin into the grade school Christmas pageant.

I was almost relieved, therefore, when I opened my eyes to find that I wasn't in bed with some shopworn barmaid whose name I didn't remember. I was lying with my head in Tess McAfferty's lap.

Tess stroked my cheek with her rough fingers. She smiled when she saw I recognized her and leaned back wearily against the wooden railing behind her. Her bottom lip was split, and a slender trickle of blood dribbled down her chin. She had the beginning of a tremendous shiner around her left eye, and her disheveled hair was shot through with bits of hay and leaves.

"You've got one hard head, Harry." She smiled, then winced, touching her bloodied lip. "I think he broke his axe handle on it. Can you move?"

"Who was it?" I asked.

"One of Bobby's crew," she said. "I didn't see him either, until he whacked you. Big flat-nosed guy. Cigar stuck in the corner of his mouth."

Ray, the man Frankie Bull had punched the day we visited Snow's ranch.

I groaned, nodded, and pushed myself up on one elbow. Bad plan. My stomach rolled as soon as my head was vertical, and I'm afraid I couldn't move fast enough to completely miss the legs of her jeans. She rested her hand gently on my back until I was through, then helped me lie back down.

A few feet away, the older McAfferty boy was also sitting on the ground with his back against a railing, mumbling angrily and holding his right hand to his face. Beside him, his brother stood watching us, his fists clenched at his hips. The blood from his shattered nose covered the bottom half of his face.

"How 'bout you?" I groaned, looking up at Tess. "Okay?"

"I'll make it," she said, and nodded in the direction of the others. "And so will they. They always thought they were ten feet tall and bulletproof. Gettin' their butts kicked might have caused some temporary realignments of their handsome faces, but if there's any permanent damage, it's only to their egos."

The boys glared at Tess, but I imagined their gruff demeanor was only camouflage for their embarrassment. "Hi, boys," I croaked. "I wouldn't worry if I were you. As you can see, it happens to the best of us."

The younger boy spat a glob of blood in the dirt and turned away so we couldn't see his face. He was young enough that I suspected he was fighting back tears. It's never an easy thing for any man to take a beating, especially when there's three of you and only one of him.

"Bobby?" I asked. "Where is he?"

"Long gone," Tess said. "I lasted about three seconds after you went down. Then he punched me in the mouth and I was out too. When we all came around, the boys wanted to go after him, but we couldn't leave you here. We'll catch up with him again."

When my internal scales reached a tenuous equilibrium, I sat up, took a deep breath as the banging in my head reached crescendo and waited patiently until it had receded to vibrato. Cautiously, I ran my fingers along my temple, over the golf-ball-size lump that sprouted just inside my hairline. They came away sticky with coagulated blood, but the flow had already stopped. With considerable effort, I used the railing of the pen for support and tried to lift myself to a standing position. Halfway up, the younger McAfferty took hold of my elbow.

"Have you two met?" Tess asked when I had stopped wobbling.

I nodded. "At Colleen's funeral. They were with your father-in-law." I held my hand out to the blond young man, who took it warily. "But I'm afraid I didn't get your names."

"Angus McAfferty," he said. "Tess's brother-in-law."

"And that," Tess said, pointing at the older brother, who was still sulking, "is Andrew. They stayed after the funeral to help out."

I looked around until I saw my Stetson, picked it up, dusted it off, and tried to jam it on my head. The goose egg increased the size of my head by at least two hat sizes, so the hat didn't fit, and besides, it hurt. I took it off and held it loosely in my right hand while I looked around the holding area to see if my deputies or anyone else was in hailing distance. It looked like the McAffertys and I were alone.

"Why don't you wait a few minutes before you try to go anywhere, Harry?" Tess said. "I'd hate to have you pass out again. You really ought to have a doctor look at your head pretty soon, though. In case you've got a concussion."

"Why don't you three come with me?" I asked. "Looks like you could do with a doctor too."

"Afraid not," she said. "We've got to get back to the ranch. We're tough, Harry. We'll be okay."

If Tess was interested in how I happened along just as she and her brothers-in-law were getting their clocks cleaned by Bobby Snow, she didn't show it. Instead, she looked like she was in a hurry to get somewhere else. She stood, ran the back of her hand along her split lip, brushed the seat of her pants, and motioned for the boys to follow her. "Come on, Harry," she said. "We'll walk you as far as the parking lot."

I grabbed her elbow as she began to turn away, pulled until she faced me again. "Not yet," I said. "We need to talk. It's time you answered a few questions."

She started to protest, but I cut her off. "You can start by telling me why you came here tonight looking for Bobby Snow."

"We didn't," she said. "We just came out to watch the rodeo."

"Bullshit, Tess," I said roughly. "First, you went to Bobby Snow's ranch and then you drove in here like you were chasing the devil. I know it because I've been following you all afternoon. I even saw you put the shotgun in your car."

She watched my face for a full ten seconds, but the whole time she watched, something was growing hard inside her. When she spoke, there was tempered steel in her voice. "Well, as you can see, the damn gun didn't do me a bit of good, because I didn't have it when I needed it. Won't happen again, though, Harry. I promise."

"Why were you after him, Tess?"

"Because he's one of the people who killed my daughter," she said flatly. "I know it. You know it. But you aren't doing anything about it. I'm tired of waiting."

"Tess, we're building a case."

"And what do you have, Harry?" she spat. "Nothing, that's what you have. You've got no evidence. No witnesses. How you going to catch him?"

"We'll catch him," I said. "But in the meantime, I can't have people like you taking the law into their own hands."

"You don't really have a choice," she said. "How are you going to stop us? Arrest us? For what? For confronting a man who's been stealing livestock from me and every other honest rancher around Rock River for over a year, a man who was one of the men who killed my daughter? Are you going to arrest us for getting ourselves beat up, Harry? You think the courts will hold any of that against us? I don't."

She held her arms out, wrists together. "Cuff me and take me in if you're going to, Sheriff. If not, I'm going home. I suggest you do the same." With that, she spun on her heel and walked away, touching Angus McAfferty on the shoulder as she passed. With a last look in my direction, Angus turned to follow her, Andrew close behind.

As they entered the shadows between two stock pens, I called her name. She stopped, turned slowly until she faced me again. In the pen behind me, a bull scraped his horns along the wood, pushed his weight against the railings. The old boards creaked and popped.

"What about Saul Irons?" I asked. "What do you think the courts would say about him? I don't know all the details yet, I can't prove anything, but I think you hired him and he's committed murder on your behalf. I'll arrest you for that, Tess, and I'll put you in prison. Your best hope is to call him off now, before he kills someone else. Have him turn himself in."

Even in the blue light that reflected off her face from the half-moon and the mercury lamps, I could see her weariness, but also her grim determination. "I don't know who you're talking about, Sheriff," she said. "I don't think I've ever heard the name."

"You've heard it, all right," I said. "He's wanted for the murder of Wayne Carney, but I also know he's been on your property. I think he was even there the night Colleen was murdered. Will Jensen saw him coming out of his place that night, and I tracked him from an area near your corrals to Jensen's. If nothing else, I need to talk to him to find out who he saw out there."

"Don't know the man," she said firmly. "But I'll tell you this: Saul Irons, Bobby Snow, you—it sounds like a lot of people have been sneaking around on my property lately." She cocked her head in the direction of the McAfferty boys, who waited behind her in the gloom. "You be careful if you come out that way again, Harry," she said. "I'd hate for one of us to mistake you for a prowler."

The next morning, I woke to the smell of frying bacon and coffee coming from my kitchen. Groggily I rolled over and pulled the alarm clock from the nightstand, held it close to my eyes. Nine-thirty.

I sat up, touched my fingers to the side of my head. The swelling was down, but the goose egg was still tender, and there was dried blood in my hair. I'd stripped myself naked before going to bed, so I rummaged around in the pile of clothing on my dresser until I found a clean pair of blue jeans. I pulled them on and padded out into the kitchen, grimacing when I passed the mirror.

Frankie Bull and his wife Frieda stood with their backs to me at the counter, chopping onions and green peppers on a cutting board. Frankie used his huge Bowie knife, while Frieda used a paring knife she'd found in one of my drawers.

From the back, they're an incongruous couple. Frankie, his long braid reaching the middle of his back, towers over his wife, who weighs all of ninety-eight pounds and stands about five-three. She wore a flowered sundress, hose, and white pumps. Frankie was decked out in his leather motorcycle vest, and hammered silver armbands. His mirrored sunglasses were pushed up on his head, and he had a .44 mag on his right hip.

Underneath the heady aromas of the bacon, coffee, and onions, I caught a faint trace of Frieda's perfume. It smelled of wildflowers and spice. She giggled as she cut the last of the onion, wiped a tear from her eye, and reached up to gently brush its twin from Frankie's cheek. He bent down to kiss her cheek, and I waited until he was finished before I cleared my throat and pulled a coffee mug from one of the wall pegs.

"Good morning, Harry," Freida said brightly. She took my cup and filled it with steaming coffee. "Why don't you sit down and drink this? We'll have breakfast ready in a flash."

I took the coffee to the table, held the cup to my nose to savor the smell, and took a cautious sip. It was scalding, but it washed away that evil gumbo in my mouth and jump-started my nervous system.

"To what do I owe this unexpected pleasure?" I asked when I was sufficiently caffeinated to form a coherent sentence. At the stove, Frieda used a long fork to move bacon from the frying pan to a plate covered with a paper towels. Frankie cracked eggs into a mixing bowl. In his huge hands, the eggs looked like marbles.

"I called your office around eight," he said. "And they told me what happened last night. We just figured you could use a decent meal, that's all."

I stood, walked across the kitchen, and pulled the phone receiver from its cradle. "Give me just a minute," I said. "I should call in."

"No need," he said, beating the eggs to a froth. "They figured you'd be late, and besides, there's nothing new to report. Your people looked all night and didn't find Bobby. And Ken Keegan has fifteen DCI agents looking for Saul Irons. No luck so far. They think he might have gone down to Colorado, maybe on to New Mexico. You mind if I put on some music?"

I said I didn't mind at all, so Frankie lumbered out to the living room and thumbed through my record collection, cursing softly to himself the whole time. "Johnny fucking Paycheck," he grumbled. "Who buys Johnny fucking Paycheck?"

When he came back to the kitchen, the first strains of Van Morrison's album *Common One* were playing softly in the background. Frankie shrugged his shoulders as Frieda looked up from her cooking.

"Best I could do," he explained. "No Bach. Not even a Strauss. And you can plumb forget Vivaldi. Looks like we're amongst the heathen, darlin'. Gird up your loins." He pointed to the knot on my temple. "You see a doctor about that?"

I shook my head.

"Didn't think so," he said. "Want me to call someone?"

"I'm all right," I said. "It looks worse than it is."

"Did you see who conked you?" he asked. "Anybody you recognized?"

I told him I hadn't seen the man, but Tess said it was Bobby's hired hand, Ray. Then I told him about following Tess most of the previous day, about her visit to Snow's ranch, about the fight in the stock pens with Snow and about my confrontation with her afterwards. I talked a bit about Wayne Carney and told him how frustrated I was becoming with the whole thing.

He munched thoughtfully on a piece of buttered toast as Frieda set dishes of scrambled eggs, crisp bacon, and O'Brien potatoes in front of us. "So what're you gonna do?" he asked. I suddenly realized I was ravenous, and I heaped my plate full, forked scrambled eggs into my mouth.

"I dunno," I mumbled. The food was wonderful. I swallowed greedily, scooped up another forkful and held it in front of my mouth. "It's apparent that Tess is the common denominator between both Bobby Snow and Saul Irons. We'll keep up our manhunt for Irons and we'll keep looking for Snow, but neither of those guys are gonna make it easy to find them if they don't want to be found. I think my best chance is getting Tess to lead us to one or both of them. The only problem is how I'm gonna get her to do it."

He nodded his agreement, stuffed a whole piece of bacon in his mouth and chewed. "Sounds like as good a plan as any," he said. "Anything I can help with? I could watch Bobby's ranch if you like. There's not a hell of a lot happening in Victory, so I've got the time."

"Fine," I said. "But remember that his place is out of your jurisdiction. If you see anything—"

"Don't worry, I'll get on the horn right away."

We finished our meal in silence, cleaned up every last scrap food, and carried our plates to the counter. I started to run water in the sink, but Frieda waved us back to the table to drink more coffee while she washed the dishes.

"Listen, Harry," Frankie said tentatively. "You've already got plenty to worry about, and I hate to be the one who brings you more bad news, but . . ." He shifted his considerable weight and pulled a piece of folded newspaper from his back pocket, frowned as he tossed it on the table. "That was in this morning's *Star Tribune*," he said. "I thought you should see it before you went into town."

I set my cup down and picked up the article, gingerly unfolded it and smoothed it flat on the table. The porous newsprint had absorbed enough moisture from Frankie's body that the ink was smudged, but it was still plenty legible.

Under a two-deck headline reading COUNTY PROSECUTOR ACCUSES STARBRANCH OF INCOMPETENCE, Sally Sheridan's story quoted Walker Tisdale as saying that my office had so badly bungled the investigation of the murders of Colleen McAfferty, Ralphie Skates, and Clarence Hathaway that he had been forced to take an active

268

hand in the proceedings by releasing Wayne Carney from jail. And once he was released, Carney had met a "tragic" end at the hands of Saul Irons, another of the many people my office had failed to bring to justice. I couldn't believe what I was reading.

> "For several months, I've heard rumors about this administration's lack of leadership, its moral shortcomings and general ineptitude," Tisdale told the *Tribune*. "Until now, however, I've held my tongue because they were only rumors.
>
> "But I can no longer remain silent. I released Wayne Carney from jail against my better judgment because Sheriff Harry Starbranch convinced me that Carney would provide important evidence and promised that he would be protected. As we now know, the sheriff had no intention of fulfilling his promise. Wayne Carney's death is the direct result of near criminal neglect on the part of the sheriff's department, and just one more indication of the pitiful level of incompetence to which it has sunk. The voters of Albany County deserve better, and it is my sincere hope that they will make their displeasure known at the polls this November."

The slimy bastard was lying in a desperate attempt to cover his own ass. Not only had he made the decision to release Carney, he'd done it without consulting me, and C.J. Fall was a witness. I promised myself Tisdale wouldn't get away with it.

I wadded the story into a tight ball and threw it to the floor. My cheeks burned, and I felt decidedly light-headed. Frankie was inscrutable, but Frieda dried her hands on a dish towel and came and laid them gently on my shoulders. "I'm sorry, Harry," she said. "We thought you should probably hear it from us."

"Thanks, I guess," I said, and leaned back in my chair. The food felt heavy in my stomach, and there was a bitter taste in my

mouth. I wished for the first time in over a week that I had a cigarette. Either that or a double shot of bourbon. "I just don't know
what to do about this thing. Ignoring it certainly doesn't appear to
be working."

I looked at Frankie, who had taken out his knife and was
paring his fingernails. "You have any suggestions?" I asked.

"What I'd do if I were you, I'd go in there this afternoon and
kick their asses," he said. "Fucking place is a nest of vipers."

"Sure," I said sharply. "And then what?"

"Come back to Victory where you're appreciated," he said
simply. "Come home."

There was a lively conversation going on in the office when I
slammed through the front door forty-five minutes later, but it
died instantly.

The dispatcher looked at me over her shoulder and then
turned back to her equipment as if she'd been trying desperately
to raise one of the road deputies for the last hour without success.
A couple of road deputies and a maintenance man from the jail
were standing in front of the soda machine, laughing at some joke,
but their group broke up as soon as they spotted me, and they
scurried off in different directions.

The receptionist tried a halfhearted smile. The color flowed
in her cheeks, and her hand shook perceptibly. "Good morning,
Sheriff," she said. "It's good to see you."

I smiled at her, pulled my mail from the basket, and went
down to my office, where I closed the door and punched in
Walker's extension on the phone. No luck. Walker had gone to
Cheyenne to watch the closing arguments in a murder trial and
then to an appointment with his chiropractor. He wasn't expected
back until the next morning, so I left a message with his secretary
and tried to catch C.J. Fall at home.

No luck there either.

My frustration complete, I leaned back in my swivel chair

and put my feet on the desk. Outside my basement window, I could hear the light breeze ruffle the leaves of the big shade trees as their dappled shadows danced across the glass. Held together with a paper clip and placed to the left of my phone were at least a dozen pink message slips that had come in the previous day. Idly I picked them up and sorted through the stack. Three messages from Sally Sheridan at the *Star Tribune,* two from the police reporter at the *Laramie Boomerang,* four from Larry Calhoun with the word *urgent* underlined three times in red, one from the chairman of the Albany County Democratic Party, one from Ken Keegan, and the rest from people whose names I didn't recognize.

I threw all of the messages in the trash except Keegan's, sorted through the mail, and took a quick look at my in-basket, which was stuffed full of requisitions, incident reports, and time sheets. Halfway down, I came across a sealed manila envelope with my name on the front marked CONFIDENTIAL.

I slit it open with my Swiss Army knife and found a terse note from Calhoun explaining his attempts to reach me the previous day. Included with the handwritten missive were the results of Calhoun's latest preelection voter survey, and the numbers weren't exactly encouraging. As a matter of fact, if his sample was representative of the 12,000 or so registered voters in Albany County, the only people planning to vote for me in the election were three or four close friends, one old man in the nursing home who said he'd vote for the devil himself, as long as he was running on the Democratic ticket, myself, and Calhoun—although from the way he'd been acting lately, I figured he was sitting on the fence.

Well shit, I thought, I was lookin' for a job when I found this one. Maybe going back to Victory wouldn't be so bad after all. Tell the truth, I'd had just about enough politics to last a lifetime, and fall is a fine, crisp and shining time in the mountains, as long as you wear plenty of blaze orange so the hunters don't mistake you for a moose. Maybe I could even use my spare time to learn something useful, get Frankie to teach me how to cook Japanese, for example, maybe take a Berlitz course and learn to speak French.

Nicole wouldn't like it much that I'd gone back to being nothing but a small-town cop, but if she really loved me, she'd get used to the idea. She'd have to, have to accept me for what I am. If she couldn't, well . . .

I struck a match to the poll results and dropped the burning paper into the the trash, waited until it was nothing but ash. Then I spent the next half hour going over the latest cost overrun figures on the new jail and toying with the notion of calling Fast Eddie Warnock, who's been my physician for the last few years, and asking him to give me a stress test. I'd been feeling a strange tightness in my chest all morning, and naturally I was thinking heart trouble. Then again, it might just be indigestion. Yep, I thought, and decided I'd wait to call Eddie until next week. Maybe the week after.

I stood up and wandered down the hall for a cup of coffee, brought it back to my desk along with the morning papers. On the off chance that she'd come home for lunch, I called Nicole at the house in Denver, but the phone rang fifteen times before Robert finally picked up. Sorry, he explained, but he'd still been in bed and no—before I even asked—no, he hadn't found a part-time job. He had, however, signed on as lead singer in a band called Gangrene, and they were scheduled to play a gig in two weeks at the Holiday Inn. Did I want to come down and watch?

"I didn't even know you could sing," I said, genuinely surprised at this heretofore unrevealed talent. "Where did you learn to do that?"

"It isn't really singing," he admitted testily. "More like yelling. I can make my voice sound real growly."

"Do you think lots of people will come to dance?"

"Shit, Dad," he said, "this isn't a dance band, for Christ's sake. We play for people in the mosh pit."

"The which?"

"The mosh pit," he explained, obviously exasperated beyond patience. "Mostly people just slam into each other, and once in a while they pass somebody's body hand to hand over their heads. It's the big thing now, Pop. You never heard of it?"

"No, of course not. Up here, we'd call something like that a brawl. Is it dangerous?"

"Oh forget it," he said. "You probably wouldn't like it anyway. I'll tell Mom you called."

I started to ask him if he'd given some thought to coming up for a weekend before school started in the fall, but he'd already hung up. I listened to the wires crackle for thirty seconds and wondered dejectedly whether Robert and I would ever have a normal relationship again.

Putting the receiver back in its cradle, I scanned the front page stories in the newspapers, reread Sally's story in the *Tribune.* The *Boomerang,* whose reporter isn't quite as aggressive as Sally, treated me a little better, but the hometown newspaper made up for it on the opinion page with an editorial demanding my immediate resignation and urging the county commission to appoint Nicky Pajak, who the writer said had "proven his professionalism and integrity through twenty years of unblemished service to Albany County," sheriff until the election.

I've got to tell you, I was feeling a little sorry for myself by the time I finished the papers. Maybe the thing to do, I thought, was take the rest of the day off, get out my fly rod, and spend a little time on the Laramie River. Stop at the Trail's End on the way home and treat myself to a huge blood-rare porterhouse and a bottle of good wine. Maybe drop by the Silver Dollar after that and see if I could convince someone to dance.

The ringing phone snapped me back from the depths of self-pity.

"Starbranch," I answered.

"Harry, how the hell are you?" It was Keegan's voice, and he sounded unaccountably chipper. "Not so good, I reckon, after the beating you took this morning in the rags."

"I've had better days," I admitted. "What can I do for you, my friend?"

"It's not what you can do for me," Keegan said. "It's what I can do for you."

"Yeah?"

"Yeah," he said. "I just got off the phone with Sheriff Hawkins up in Casper. You remember him?"

I said I did, had roomed with him at a law enforcement conference in Cheyenne the year before.

"Well, one of Hawkins's deputies found something this morning he thought we'd be interested in. Asked me to pass the message along to you."

"What did he find?"

"You remember that livestock trailer Bobby Snow reported stolen the day after the McAfferty killing?"

"Yep." I leaned forward eagerly.

"They found it at the bottom of a gully on Poison Spider Road outside of Casper. Blood all over the floor. Says he doesn't know yet, but it might be human. They're having it tested."

I absorbed what he'd told me and grinned. "If the blood matches Clarence Hathaway's," I said, thinking out loud, "and the tread marks match the casts we took at the ranch—"

"We're a lot closer to having enough evidence to arrest Bobby for murder," Keegan said, completing the thought.

"He filed a stolen-property report on that trailer," I said. "Claims it was taken before the killings."

"I don't buy that," Keegan said. "Do you?"

"Of course not," I said. "I think whoever killed Colleen and Ralphie Skates loaded that truck with Hathaway's body and the stolen McAfferty livestock, hauled ass until they got to that rest area at Elk Mountain, and dumped Clarence there."

Keegan grunted to show he was following me.

"At that point," I said, "I think they transferred the animals to another vehicle and someone drove Bobby's livestock trailer up to Casper and ditched it. Whoever did that went to a lot of trouble to make sure we wouldn't find that trailer for a long time. Probably figured we'd never find it."

"Out on Poison Spider that's a distinct possibility. That's some tough real estate," Keegan agreed.

"Did you ask Hawkins to make some tire impressions of the stock trailer?" I asked.

"Yeah," Keegan said. "They're sending us a photo and blood samples by courier. Ought to have 'em both by tomorrow morning."

Suddenly I was feeling more optimistic about the case than I had since it started. As soon as Hawkins sent us the blood samples and the photo of the tire impressions, Keegan could run them through the DCI lab. If the blood samples matched the samples taken from the sagebrush at the McAfferty ranch and the samples taken during Hathaway's autopsy, and if the tire casts matched those we'd taken at the murder scene, we had the foundation of a strong case against Snow. It wouldn't be enough evidence for a conviction by itself, but I was confident it was a giant step in the right direction.

I realized I hadn't heard a sound from Keegan's end of the phone line for several minutes. "You awake?" I asked.

"Yeah," he mumbled. "Why?"

"I was just thinking," I said. "Fatty Winston hasn't sent me a copy of the autopsy report on Hathaway yet, and he stalls every time I call him to ask for it. One of us needs to get it from him, and to make sure he includes samples of Hathaway's blood and pubic hair."

"You want me to call him? Pull a little rank?" Keegan asked.

"Nah, I'll try again before I go home tonight," I said. "Have one of my deputies drive over to Rawlins and pick everything up tomorrow."

"Anything else?" Keegan asked.

"Maybe," I said. "The lab report on Colleen McAfferty said they found pubic hairs on her body and clothing from at least two people besides Skates, and semen from at least one more, maybe others."

"Yeah?" Keegan said, perking up.

"Skates was a secretor," I continued, "and they matched his blood type and sperm diaphorase with semen found in Colleen's vagina. But they also found semen in her body from at least one other person. You think that based on the evidence in the trailer we could get a judge to order Snow to provide us with pubic hair and semen samples as part of a search warrant? It we got those, we could put the pubic hairs through your lab and have the FBI run DNA tests, see if Snow's semen matches the semen found in Colleen's vagina."

"That'd nail the son of a bitch," Keegan said happily. "Yeah, I think a judge would do that for us—and I know just the judge to ask. I could have a warrant for us by ten tomorrow morning."

"Good."

"Then," he said happily, "all you have to do is find Bobby to serve it." Before we hung up, I told Keegan about the events at the rodeo the night before, how I'd been bushwacked by one of Bobby's hands.

"We'll find him," Keegan said tautly, "even if we have to call out the National Guard and scour that damn county inch by fucking inch."

# SEVENTEEN

I spent the rest of the day coordinating the search for Bobby Snow and Saul Irons and killed so much time driving washboard roads my kidneys felt like they'd been stomped on by that big, fat professional wrestler who wears a diaper—Yakuzuma? Montezuma? Anyway, they hurt like hell, and all for nothing. By late afternoon when I stopped back at the office to catch the road deputies checking in at the end of shift, we were still empty-handed on both counts.

It was like Irons had been sucked up by space aliens and had taken Snow along for the trip, although the people in charge of the fairgrounds were as anxious to find Bobby as we were. Snow had left several broncs and bulls in the fairground pens and was scheduled to bring some others for rodeo performances over the next few days. He'd never abandoned livestock before and he'd never failed to meet his obligations to provide bucking stock.

I put Snow and Irons at the top of the list of priorities for the night shift, saw the deputies off, and sat in my office with the lights turned out and the doors shut as the courthouse closed down for the day. Outside on the lawn a couple of young boys tossed a Frisbee back and forth and a couple of secretaries from the court offices upstairs had kicked off their shoes and spread a picnic supper—fast-food chicken in a cardboard bucket and a thermos jug of iced tea—in the shade of a huge maple tree. Two young men with their suit coats slung over their shoulders, impoverished attorneys from the public defenders office, stopped for a minute to chat with the women. They left dejectedly a few minutes later when it became apparent the women weren't going to invite them to sit down and share a bite of dinner. I didn't blame them for trying however. The smell of the ladies' fried chicken through the open window made my mouth water, a condition that caused me to remember I hadn't eaten since breakfast.

The repairmen had started on my house that morning, and I was anxious to see how long they'd be around to disrupt my life, so I called the carpenter I'd hired to oversee the project on his mobile number. He answered on the twelfth ring and told me he was sitting in my driveway at that very moment.

"It was no big deal, Harry," he said. "A little plaster, a little paint, a new door, coupla windows. Couldn't do anything for that picture, though. Too bad. Jim Bama's my favorite. We're all finished though. Have the place cleaned up and be gone by the time you get home."

"How much?" I asked.

"This gonna go on your homeowner's insurance?"

"Why?"

" 'Cause if it is, I'm gonna have to charge you nine hundred bucks."

"And if it isn't?"

"Six hundred," he said. "Not as much paperwork. I won't have to wait for the money."

I quickly calculated the balance in my checking account, whistled through my teeth in dismay. It looked like I'd be eating plenty of macaroni and cheese for the next few weeks, and forget that new pair of sharkskin cowboy boots I'd been eyeing at Corral West Ranchwear. I'd have to settle for getting my old pair resoled—again.

"You can deduct five bucks for the six-pack of beer we just

borrowed from your refrigerator," he offered helpfully.

"Send me a bill for six hundred," I told him, "and consider the beer a bonus."

He laughed. "Thanks," he said.

I started to tell him good-bye but he broke in. "Harry?"

"Yeah?"

"I almost forgot. Some guy called for you a couple times while we were working. Said his name was Slaymaker."

The muscles in my stomach contracted. "What did he want?" I rasped.

"Nothin'," he said. "Just said to tell you he was thinking about you. That's all."

I hung up and went back to the window, watched the young women munch chicken and wiggle their toes in the grass while I tried to get the image of Slaymaker's face out of my mind. It didn't work. I began to feel trapped, to feel the walls of the office closing in. I felt like I was careening down a mountain with no brakes and wished, not for the first time in recent days, that I could just get out of town. Call my ex-wife and have her drive with me to Jackson Hole for a few days. Stop at the hot springs in Thermopolis on the way up and soak our bones in the warm mineral water. Ride the Screaming Mimi. Check in at the Antler Motel in Jackson Hole. Catch a performance of the Teton Music Festival. Do some buckle polishing at the Wort Hotel or the Million Dollar Cowboy Bar. Make love with the windows open, our bodies cooled by a pine-scented breeze coming down the wood-and-granite slopes of Grand Teton.

Maybe when this business was finished, I thought wistfully, we'd have time for a late-summer visit to the north country. Take a whole week and do it right. If the boys wanted to come along, that would be fine too. They were old enough to have a motel room of their own, so Nicole and I would still have our privacy—as long as we made sure their room was on the opposite side of the motel from ours.

At five thirty I finally broke down and called Calhoun, but he didn't answer, so I left a message on his machine. After that I returned Sally Sheridan's call at the *Star Tribune,* and my luck held. She wasn't in the office either, so I left a message with the receptionist. Same with the cop reporter for the *Boomerang* and the chairman of the county Democratic party, both of whom I knew full well left the office for home around five. I left messages on their work machines but didn't bother trying either at home.

Before I left the office, I tried C.J. Fall's home number to tell him we'd found Bobby's stock trailer and see if he'd had any luck finding out where Tess McAfferty's missing livestock had gone.

Whoever had driven the trailer from the McAfferty ranch to Poison Spider Road was either a suspect in my case or a witness. So was the person who drove the livestock to the slaughterhouse after it had been transferred from Bobby's trailer at the rest area at Elk Mountain where we'd found Clarence Hathaway's body.

It had always been a long shot that one of Fall's snitches would identify either of them when they sold the stolen livestock at any one of a dozen or more far-flung slaughterhouses. But on the premise that a long shot is always better than no shot, I kept my fingers crossed.

Unfortunately, Fall wasn't home either, and I didn't feel particularly optimistic he'd get the message I left on his machine.

"This thing's been actin' up," his recorded voice told me. "Leave a message anyway. I hope I get it."

I asked him to call me at home when he got in that evening and told him not to worry about the hour, since I'd probably be up late.

My responsibilities more or less met, I signed out and drove back to Victory in the gathering dark.

Once on Main Street, I drove by the big steakhouses and the Silver Dollar to check the action. It looked like a quiet night. Fifteen or twenty cars in the parking lot at the Trail's End, a similar number at Gus Alzonakis', six or eight lined up at the curb in front of Curly's saloon.

Satisfied that my town was tucked in for the night, I stopped at Ginny Larsen's Country Kitchen for a platter-size chicken-fried steak smothered in cream gravy with mashed potatoes and corn on the cob, and a manly slab of homemade apple pie for dessert.

Then I made my way out to the farmhouse, checked the repairs, tied a half dozen stonefly nymphs, and crawled into bed around eleven with a new novel, one of those popular fairy tales where a good lawyer—like *jumbo shrimp,* one of the most amusing oxymorons in our language—beats a bad system.

I was asleep ten minutes later.

I woke about two thirty to the sound of a light rain falling against the eaves. My bedroom drapes billowed in the prairie breeze like the folds of a white cotton skirt.

I'd been having an especially good dream starring a vaguely familiar-looking woman who could suck the chrome off a trailer hitch, and for a couple of minutes I cursed my luck at having awakened before the payoff. Then I tried to will my spirit back to dreamland, on the off chance I could pick up where we'd left off.

No use.

I spent the next half hour lying in the dark with my eyes closed, my hormones and brain revving with that weird kind of psychosexual turmoil that usually means I won't be falling asleep again unless I have sexual intercourse or engage in some kind of strenuous exercise involving barbells.

I'm not a big fan of self-abuse, and only crazy people lift weights in the middle of the night, so around three I gave in to the inevitable and got up, showered, and fixed myself a pot of strong coffee.

The gentle storm had already ended, so I took my steaming mug outside and stood there naked as I watched the shadows of the cloud cover break up to reveal the night sky and a billion stars. The half moon cast an eerie silver light across the porch, making my fishbelly white skin gleam with an almost otherworldly incandescence.

I looked, I imagined, like a big, middle-aged, naked ghost, and I was glad I didn't have fainthearted city neighbors who might have gotten up in the wee hours to answer the call of nature and been shocked to death by such a horrible apparition. If Edna Cook saw me out there, I figured she'd probably just take it in stride and write my appearance off as a visit from the shade of an Indian, an old-time cowpuncher, or her dearly departed husband. She's close enough to the spirit world herself, she wouldn't get too worked up about a visit from a harmless specter.

My coffee finished, I took the cup inside, washed it, and set it on the drainboard to dry. Then I creaked my way into a fresh set of clothes, strapped on my Blackhawk, and pulled my car keys from their peg on the wall. I filled a thermos with the remainder of the coffee, then rumaged around in the refrigerator until I found the ingredients of a barely edible lunch—two hard-boiled eggs, expiration date unknown, a mushy apple, and a couple heels of bread which I used to make a peanut butter and Miracle Whip sandwich. I jammed my repast in a brown paper bag, switched off the lights, and left, careful not to slam the door when I got into the Blazer.

It was fifty miles to Tess McAfferty's ranch. If I hurried, I'd be there an hour before sunrise.

I saw four cars on the road during the entire fifty-minute drive from my house in Victory to the turnoff to the McAfferty ranch, three long-haul truckers pulling heavy loads of drainage pipe and a club-cab pickup with a Union Pacific Railroad logo heading out of the sleeping town of Rock River.

At the dirt road turnoff to Tess's ranch, I doused the headlights, thankful that the moon was bright enough to show me the outlines of the road. I cut my speed to under ten miles an hour in order to avoid making a racket and crept down the washboard track until I came to the grove of trees near Colleen's grave where I'd hidden the Blazer on my last visit. Cautiously, I nosed the vehicle into the trees, letting it coast to a stop so the brake lights wouldn't give me away.

I stuffed my binoculars and provisions into a nylon ruck-sack, eased out of the car, and stood quietly while my eyes adjusted to the darkness. The scent of decaying flowers had given way to normal prairie smells—the bitter odor of aspen bark, the clean smell of pine sap, tangy sage. I heard the chirp of the crickets, the rustle of the breeze through the leaves in the upper branches of the trees, the hoot of a night-hunting owl, the tick of the motor as it cooled, the sound of my own breathing.

When I could see well enough to make out the shapes of the trees and the undergrowth, I began to pick my way through the bush at a snail's pace. I couldn't use my flashlight, so I had to feel my way along with my feet and the tip of the Blackthorn walking stick, gingerly testing my footing with each step to avoid stumbling. I'd had plenty of trouble navigating the undergrowth in broad daylight; in the dark it took me almost a half hour to reach the edge of the grove where I'd watched the McAffertys the day of the rodeo.

I concealed myself in the same clump of sagebrush, felt around in the rucksack until I found the binoculars, and brought them to bear on the ranch house and corrals. In the corrals, I could see the dark shapes of livestock, a horse standing quietly against the fence, the outlines of a half dozen cattle around the water trough. The house was dark, without even a porch light to break the gloom. I sensed without knowing why that it was empty.

I tried to focus on the parking area at the side of the house, but the shadow of the building made it almost impossible to see anything. Straining my eyes, I finally made out the shapes of the old Jeep and Tess's Honda.

The pickup they'd driven when I followed them to the rodeo was gone.

Briefly I toyed with the idea of going closer to do a little snooping but gave it up when I imagined how difficult it would be to explain myself should Tess come back unexpectedly. Besides, I had no clear idea what I was looking for.

The luminous dial of my watch said it was five-thirty, which meant the sun would be up in less than half an hour. Cautiously, I moved from the sagebrush to a nearby aspen tree and sat down, resting my back against the trunk. Confident that my presence would not be detected, I poured myself a cup of coffee from the thermos, peeled the shells from the hard-boiled eggs, and ate my snack.

In the east, the sky began to lighten with the false dawn, and the noise of the crickets gave way to the song of birds—the distinctive call of the meadowlarks, the melodic chirps of jays, the cawing of magpies. I closed my eyes and listened, opened my senses to the waking prairie. When morning comes on the high plains, it comes quickly. Darkness gives way to a thousand shades of gray. Indistinct shapes take form, assume soft-focus definition. The brightest colors are pastels, gradually increasing in vibrancy as the first bright rays of the sun broach the horizon.

I heard the motor of the vehicle long before I saw it, the throaty rumble of the pistons. It was approaching from the broken canyon land beyond the corrals, and soon I could see the glow of its headlights reflecting off the rims of the arroyos as it neared the ranch house.

Five minutes later Tess's green pickup emerged from the mouth of a wide ravine parallel to the draw I'd followed on my walk to Jensen's ranch. When the vehicle was in the open, the driver killed the headlights and drove cross-country to the corral, then up the small hill to the parking area beside the ranch house.

The doors opened, I saw the glow of the dome light. There were three people in the pickup—Tess McAfferty behind the wheel, Angus McAfferty in the middle, Andrew riding shotgun. They piled out of the cab, slammed the doors, and stretched their legs and backs before going to unload their gear from the back.

Angus hefted a cooler and carried it to the porch as Andrew filled his arms with rucksacks and jackets. Which left Tess to carry weapons, the shotgun and two high-powered hunting rifles with scopes. She rested them against the wall beside the front door, fumbled with the key, and held the door open as the McAfferty boys carried the gear inside. A moment later I saw the faint yellow glow of the kitchen light through the window. I focused the binoculars on the kitchen window, above the half curtains. At the counter, Tess made coffee. Angus was at the stove cracking eggs into a skillet. Andrew, yawning luxuriously, was pulling mugs and plates from a cupboard.

I sneaked back to the Blazer while the McAffertys were busy at their breakfast, started the engine, drove slowly back to the highway, and headed toward Laramie.

I wanted to be at the office early so I could finish my business in time to catch a few hours sleep before sundown.

It appeared the McAffertys had become nocturnal hunters. To find out what they were hunting, I'd have to do the same.

# EIGHTEEN

Ken Keegan was eating a breakfast of Egg McMuffins at my desk when I walked into my office around eight thirty. It was my plan to stake out the McAfferty place come nightfall, and I'd decided to spend the daylight hours at the office running down other leads. As always, I was glad to see him.

Keegan's blue suit coat was draped over the back of my chair, the knot of his tie was pulled away from his open collar, and his sleeves were rolled up to his elbows, exposing muscular forearms hairier than your average chimpanzee's. There was a coffee stain on his shirt pocket and his hair looked like he'd combed it with a hay rake. If this was how he looked first thing in the morning, I felt sorry for his wife.

He grinned when I came through the door, stood up and started to clear away the remains of his meal. "Sorry," he mumbled through a mouthful of food. "I didn't think you'd be in this early."

"Stay put," I said, taking my own bag-o'-breakfast to the railroad bench. I took the wrapper off my McMuffin, opened the sandwich, and slathered one half of the English muffin with grape jelly. Then I put it all back together again and took a hungry, lip-smacking bite.

"Grape jelly?" he grimaced. "Why the hell would you put grape jelly on one of these things?"

I licked a purple blob of escaped jelly from my finger. "Why not?" I asked. "I like the way the flavors mush together."

"Gross," he said. He threw the rest of his own sandwich in the trash. "But I guess it's about what I could expect from a guy who puts ketchup on macaroni and cheese."

I swallowed the last of the muffin, opened the sip-lid on my cup of coffee and washed it down. "Is there a business-related reason you're here so early?" I asked. "Or did you drive all the way over here just to criticize my eating habits?"

"I've been on the job since six," he said. He took his coat from the back of my chair and reached into the inside pocket to remove a folded sheaf of papers. "I wanted to get here first thing and give you these."

I wiped my hands on a napkin and opened the papers. On top was a search warrant for Bobby Snow's house and a court order to obtain a sample of his blood and pubic hair.

After that was a one-page report from the DCI's evidence lab stating that the blood found at the side of Tess McAfferty's corral the morning of the murders matched the blood found in Bobby Snow's livestock trailer. The tire casts from the corral also matched the casts we'd brought back from Casper.

That meant Bobby's livestock trailer had definitely been at the McAfferty Ranch the evening of the killings. It looked like the noose of evidence was beginning to tighten around Snow's neck. I had a circumstantial case I thought a decent prosecutor might be able to sell to a jury. All I needed was a smidgen of hard evidence—a single shred—that put Snow himself at the McAfferty ranch the night of the killings, and I'd have enough to nail him. I smiled and laid the warrant and lab reports on the desk.

"That's the good news," Keegan said.

"And the bad?"

"The bad news is Fatty Winston screwed up again," he explained. "I was on the phone to his office about a half hour ago, but I couldn't get hold of Fatty 'cause he just left on a month-long vacation, a salmon-fishing expedition up the West Coast from Oregon to Alaska with a couple of pals."

I wondered what kind of person would want to be cooped up for a month on a motor boat with Fatty Winston. "Must be nice," I said dryly. "What'd he mess up this time?"

"Hathaway's autopsy," Keegan said. "I haven't seen the actual document yet, but I pulled rank and got one of his deputies to tell me what it said."

"Which is?"

"Which is everything we already knew," Keegan said. "He was killed with a high-powered weapon. He was hit by one round that took out most of his chest. Lots of internal damage. No slugs found in his body. No scorching or powder residue to indicate he was shot from close range. Wounds were immediately fatal. Death was between five P.M. and seven P.M. the day before, same as Ralphie. Hathaway's body was transported from the place of death to the place we found it and blah blah blah."

"There's nothing there to suggest who killed him?"

"Nope," Keegan said. "We weren't very lucky in that regard with either Skates or Hathaway. We aren't gonna solve this one on the basis of evidence from the scene."

"Was there any evidence that Hathaway had recent sexual contact?" I asked. "What about pubic hair samples? Are they sending those over with the report?"

"Winston's deputy said the autopsy report doesn't mention evidence of sexual activity. Fatty apparently didn't tell the coroner that we thought it was important, so nobody checked," Keegan said. "And Fatty didn't bother to request pubic hair samples."

"What do you mean?" I asked incredulously. "Why not?"

"Fuck if I know," Keegan said. "You'll have to ask Fatty when he gets back. I do know this: Hathaway's blood type matches the type found at the corral and in the livestock trailer."

"He was type O, Ken," I said unenthusiastically. "So are more than half the people in the world. Even if Fatty didn't request hair samples, doesn't the coroner keep them just as a matter of course?"

Keegan gave his big shoulders an exasperated shrug. "We're talkin' Carbon County here, Harry," he said. "Who knows what they do as a matter of course. At least Fatty's office is sending over a blood sample from Hathaway with the report. We'll run it through our lab, break it down. Who knows, maybe something will pop up."

"It won't tell us conclusively whether Hathaway raped Colleen McAfferty," I said.

"No, it won't," Keegan agreed. "It'll narrow it down some, but we may never know for sure. Unless we have the FBI run DNA tests."

"That could take months," I groused.

"I imagine it will," he agreed. "With both Hathaway and Colleen dead, it won't be a top priority. Now, if we get a sample of Bobby's blood, that'd be a different story. In that case, we're only talkin' weeks."

"In the meantime, I want pubic hair samples from Hathaway's corpse," I said. "Let's exhume him, it's not too late."

"Yes it is."

"Why?"

"Because he wasn't buried," Keegan said, and looked at his watch. "His mother had him cremated. About twenty-four hours ago."

Keegan brought his cupped hands to his mouth and blew across them. "Ashes to ashes," he said. "Dust to fucking dust."

After Keegan left my office around nine thirty to check in with the DCI agent who was coordinating the statewide search for Saul Irons, I assigned another deputy to drive over to Rawlins and pick up a copy of Clarence Hathaway's autopsy report and his blood sample. Then I called Rawls into my office and placed him in charge of executing the search warrant for Snow's ranch house until I could come out around noon and take over myself. Of particular interest, I told him, were financial records, phone records, money, anything that might tie him to Hathaway, Skates, Wayne Carney, Emile Cross, or Tess McAfferty. I also wanted to have a look at any weapons he'd left at his house.

"What should I do if I find guns?" Rawls asked.

"We'll take 'em over to Cheyenne and have the DCI run ballistics tests," I said.

He shook his head to indicate he didn't understand. "But we don't have any bullets from the murders to check them against," he said.

"I know that, Larry," I said. "But that doesn't mean we're *never* gonna have 'em."

He chuckled, jammed his hat on his head, and adjusted his Sam Browne. "One more thing, Sheriff," he said on the way out.

"Yeah?"

"Frankie Bull called here about a half hour before you came in, and since you weren't here, I talked to him. Apparently, he's been watching Snow's ranch house."

I nodded, waited for him to go on.

"Frankie says there hasn't been a soul at Snow's since he started hanging around," Rawls said. "But what happens if Bobby shows up while we're there?"

"Same as you'd do if he showed up here," I said. "Arrest him for assault on a police officer, clap him in irons, and bring him in. By that time maybe we'll have enough to tack on an accomplice to murder charge, just for good measure."

I spent the next hour doing administrative chores, paying bills, opening bids for the heating and cooling system at the new jail, finishing the paperwork on prisoner transfers and on reimbursements for prisoners we were holding for other law enforcement agencies. I'd told the secretary at the front desk to hold my calls and not to disturb me unless it was a dire emergency, so I was a bit surprised and annoyed when the door burst open and C.J. Fall walked in, followed closely by the secretary, who was still telling him he'd have to wait in the reception area.

"Sorry, Harry," he said by way of explanation, "they said you were busy, but I didn't have time to wait."

I gave him a cool nod and gestured toward the bench. "No problem, C.J.," I said. "Take a load off."

The secretary left apologetically and Fall folded himself onto the bench, set his sweat-stained hat on his knees, and leaned forward. When he spoke, he spoke with such quiet earnestness that I could barely hear him.

"I'm sorry I didn't get back to you last night," he said. "I've been out of town for a few days, and just got the message you left on my machine this morning."

"Vacation?"

"Don't I wish," he said. "Actually, I've been down in Fort Worth, poking around the slaughterhouses. Real sad situation. The Japanese and the Belgians have stepped up their demand for horseflesh, so the slaughterhouses are full of strong, healthy animals, a lot of them thoroughbreds with plenty of good years left in them. It really chaps my ass to see them out there in the pens waiting for the bolt."

"Couldn't their owners have sold them to someone besides the slaughterhouses?" I asked.

"I suppose so," he said. "There's a few friends-of-the-animals types trying to adopt some of the better horses. But the truth is, these ponies are worth more as food than they are as riding stock. Damn, it makes me want to become a vegetarian."

I sat back and thought about what it would be like to go into a first-class European restaurant and order a pony porterhouse, medium rare, and decided I'd rather save my money and get a plateful of well-marbled beef right here at home.

Fall broke my reverie by pulling a pouch of Red Man from his back pocket and jamming about a half pound of chew in his cheek. I declined when he offered me a wad, explained I'd rather inhale my nicotine than jaw it, and at any rate I'd gone cold turkey recently and couldn't afford to backslide.

He waited until his tobacco was settled nicely and came to the real reason for his visit. Opening the old leather doctor's bag he carries around for a briefcase, he rooted around in it until he found what he was after, a handful of carbon copies held together by a paper clip. He unfolded the papers, straightened them on his knee, and laid them on top of my desk.

I scanned the top sheet, saw what looked to be a long list of sales records. The letterhead at the top identified the company as the Texas Meat Packing Company, wholesalers of beef, pork, and horse meat. I stopped reading halfway down the first page when I realized I couldn't understand the code.

"What do we have here, C.J.?" I asked, puzzled by the long columns of weights and prices.

"About two hundred hours of work," he said. "If you look at the top of page five, you'll see an entry for a horse sold four days ago, and a buyer's code. It's circled in red."

I turned to the page he indicated and saw that on that day a horse weighing 1,014 pounds had been bought from a seller identified by a numerical code for the price of 62 cents a pound, live weight. The owner's numerical code was listed next to the sale price.

"It don't say so there," Fall said when I was finished. "But that horse belonged to Colleen McAfferty. One of my people recognized her brand when she was in the holding pen."

I felt a rush of anticipation as I scanned the rest of the pages. In the ten copied pages, there were three more circled entries, steers bought to a seller with the same numerical code as the person who sold Jezebel.

"Jess's missing cattle?" I asked.

"The same," he said. "We did a little looking—well no, we did a hell of a lot—and found out the man with that seller's code is a fella named Swenson. Max Swenson."

"Never heard of him."

"No reason you woulda," Fall said. "He's outta the Kaycee country up north. Got a little ranch up there. We arrested him late yesterday afternoon."

"Where is he now?" I asked.

"Johnson County Jail, up in Buffalo," Fall said.

"Can I talk to him?" I asked eagerly. "I'd like to find out how he wound up selling McAfferty livestock. Maybe he even had something to do with those killings. If we hurry, we could hop in the Blazer and be up there by—"

"Hold on, Harry," Fall said, his square jaw working the chaw. He spit a long stream of juice into my trash can, wiped his lips with the back of his hand. "You can talk to him if you want, but there's really no reason. I pretty much covered everything we want to know."

My heart pounded in my chest, and my tongue was dry. I had to force my next words from my mouth. "Was he there when Colleen was killed?"

"He says not," Fall said. "Says he picked up that livestock out at Elk Mountain. Said it was delivered by Snow and one of his hands, man by the name of Ray Bolton, and all he did was drive it down to Texas and sell it for Bobby. Said he'd been doing the same thing for the last year. That's Bobby's owner code on the packing house records."

I stared at the numbers until the digits started to swim, not quite able to believe our luck.

"Will this hold up in court?" I asked.

"With Swenson's testimony and the subpoenaed payment records from the packing company, it will," Fall said. "They made their checks to Swenson, but Swenson turned right around and paid Bobby with personal checks."

"Did Bobby endorse 'em?"

"A whole stack of 'em," Fall said. "A little over two hundred thousand dollars' worth in the last eighteen months. None of it reported to the IRS as income, by the way."

I laughed out loud, pounded my fist on the desk.

"Turns out they're a buncha dumb shits," Fall chortled. "Every last one of 'em."

I thanked C.J. profusely and danced around the office with the packinghouse records as soon as he'd left. Then I jammed them in my pocket, straightened my tie and bounded up the stairs.

Walker's Tisdale's secretary said the great man was in, but he wasn't to be disturbed on account of the fact that he was busy writing a lecture for a class he'd agreed to teach over the summer at the university's law school. Come back in the afternoon, she said, he might have a few minutes of free time then.

She turned her back to me and returned to her typing, so I just walked around her desk and barged through Tisdale's door. I found the prosecutor with his feet up on his desk, not hard at work on an educational treatise as advertised but holding a copy of *Playboy* open to the centerfold.

Today, instead of golf togs designed by Toodles the Clown, he was wearing an expensive dove gray summer-weight suit with teeny black pinstripes, a midnight black Oxford shirt, and a silk tie just a shade darker than his jacket. Given his finely sculpted silver hair, the comparison between Tisdale and John Gotti, the Dapper Don, was nearly irresistible.

"I know, counselor," I said as he looked up, shock, then irritation registering on his face. "You just buy it for the articles."

He looked past me to his secretary, who'd followed me in and was waiting impatiently to escort me back out. "Damn it, Claire," he snapped, jamming the magazine in a desk drawer, "I said no—"

"It wasn't her fault, Walker," I said. "She told me you were busy, but I ignored her."

Claire nodded her head in eager agreement, nervously brushed a strand of hair from her face.

Walker glowered at me, then at his browbeaten employee.

294

"All right," he told her brusquely. "That'll be all. I'll see the sheriff as long as he's here, but after that I'm not to be disturbed. Do you understand?"

She said that she did and disappeared as silently as a wraith. I closed the door to the office, took a seat in one of the leather chairs in front of Walker's desk, and did my best to ignore his glare by concentrating on picking nonexistent lint from the leg of my trousers.

"Look, Harry," Walker said, "if you've come to talk about that newspaper article, I don't think we have anything to dis—"

"I don't give a shit what you told the papers, Walker," I said, looking up. I gave the imaginary lint a flick in his direction. "I just consider the source."

"Meaning?"

"Meaning that personally I think you're a two-faced, arrogant, ambitious, lying, prick shyster bastard," I said. I made sure to enunciate each word slowly and clearly, in as level a voice as I could manage.

For about three seconds, Walker looked like I'd punched him in the breadbasket. Then he started to sputter. "You get out of here right now!" he stammered, rising shakily from his chair. "No goddamn boozehound is gonna come in my office and—"

"Sit down, Walker," I said, and stood up, reached across his desk, and pushed him back into his chair. "That's what I think personally. Professionally, I've got my doubts, but you still have your uses. I need something from you, counselor. Wanna hear what it is? I think you're gonna give it to me before I leave here."

"Not a goddamn chance, Starbranch. I told you I want you—"

"I know what happened to Colleen McAfferty, at least most of it," I interrupted. "If we cooperate with each other, there's still a way for you to come out of this looking like a champ."

Walker was still angry, but at least the promise of glory, deserved or undeserved, made him indecisive about throwing me out. He sat back in his chair and gave me his most intimidating scowl in an effort to regain control of the situation. I grinned, pulled a toothpick from my shirt pocket and cleaned my canines.

"You've got ten minutes," he said petulantly. He shot his cuffs to reveal a gold Rolex. "Starting now."

It didn't take quite that long.

Eight minutes later, Walker and I were on our way down the hall to Judge Willitson's chambers.

We had to listen to a half hour of the judge's fish tales, but a half hour after that, I was on my way back downstairs to my office. In my hand were warrants to arrest Bobby Snow and Ray Bolton for numerous crimes, but primarily for their roles as accomplices to the murder of Colleen McAfferty. They were also wanted for several counts of rustling, and Willitson, in an unexpected show of generosity, had convinced Tisdale to upgrade the charge for attacking me at the rodeo from assault to attempted murder.

If Tisdale convicted the pair on all the counts we had so far and didn't plea-bargain, Bobby Snow and Ray Bolton would grow to be old men at the state pen in Rawlins.

Much better than nothing, I mused, but not nearly as satisfying as the punishment they'd get in a perfect world—a five-minute ride on an old-time electric throne, the hot current flowing full-tilt boogie. I'd seen Colleen's body. I knew what she'd suffered. Snow and Bolton deserved to fry.

Bobby Snow's barn was a huge affair with double sliding doors large enough to drive a tractor through. The air was thick with the smell of hay, manure, and cut grass and the odor of gasoline, diesel, old leather, and saddle soap.

The barn itself was a lot cleaner than a lot of houses I've been in. The stalls had been mucked out and the dirt floors raked, although the stalls still smelled of horse dung and sweat, scents that soak into the very wood fibers after a few years and never leave. Outside the Dutch door of the last stall someone had hung a 1985 calendar featuring a blonde in the bottom half of a string bikini posed seductively against the tire of a John Deere tractor. Below that were tacked a dozen photographs of a black quarter horse mare that had just given birth to a blaze-faced foal. No telling how old the photos were.

I was poking around the shop area at the back of the barn while Rawls and two other deputies searched the tack room and the stalls.

At the door of the barn were two large cardboard boxes filled with papers and ledgers we'd taken from a locked filing cabinet in Bobby's spare bedroom—financial records from the ranch operations, check stubs, and personal records of everything from Snow's Visa bills to the warranty of his washing machine. I hadn't seen anything that tied him to Skates, Hathaway, or the McAffertys, but I planned to haul both boxes back to Laramie and pick through the contents at my leisure.

Beside the boxes, the remainder of Snow's personal arsenal rested against the white walls of the barn—an old .410 shotgun, a lever-action .30-30, a tube-fed .22, and a couple of well-worn handguns. As soon as we finished our search, I'd have one of the deputies drive them over to the DCI for testing. None of them smelled like they'd been fired recently, but I still wanted to make sure.

I was just starting to climb the ladder leading to the hayloft when Rawls came from the tack room holding a purple gym bag.

"Hey Sheriff," he called. I came down off the ladder and turned around just in time to catch the bag as he tossed it in my direction. "I think I found something you're gonna be very interested in."

I caught the bag, unzipped it, and peered inside. At one end of the bag was a worn leather wallet that was bent at the corners and split at the seams. The edges of several pieces of paper peeked from the bill compartment. I pulled it out, holding it gingerly between two fingers.

Rawls was so excited he looked like a man-size whippet straining at the leash. "It belongs to Clarence Hathaway," he said.

"Driver's license, credit cards, the address of a massage parlor in Denver."

Clarence hadn't had been carrying a wallet when his body was found at Elk Mountain. He'd been tentatively identified from his prison photo, and later his mother had positively identified his corpse.

I dropped the wallet back in the bag and began sorting through the rest of the contents—dirty clothes, toiletries, a well-thumbed copy of *Hustler*. At the bottom of the bag were two other items, a gold high school ring and a silver pocket watch.

I pulled out the ring and held it to the light. The stone was blue, set beneath the gold crest of the local high school. Small numbers at the sides of the stone identified the year the owner graduated, 1975. Beside that were the initials C.H. The same year and initials were engraved on the back of the watch.

"Why would Snow keep that stuff?" Rawls asked incredulously.

"I don't know," I shrugged. "Maybe he didn't know it was there. On the other hand, maybe he thought there was still some credit on Clarence's card. Maybe he wanted to pawn the ring in one of those we-buy-gold places in Cheyenne. Who knows why people do anything, Larry? I guess we'll have to ask him."

I grinned wickedly, clapped Rawls on the back. Then I tucked the gym bag under my arm and walked out of the barn, happier than I'd been in days. Truth was, no matter how the items came to be in Bobby's possession, they were strong links in the growing chain of evidence binding Snow to the murders of Hathaway and Colleen McAfferty.

As soon as I found him, Bobby's ass was mine.

When I got back to the office in Laramie late that afternoon, I needed rest, but I didn't feel like sleeping in a jail cell again. So I appropriated one of the cots in the jail infirmary, closed the drapes on the examining room, and dozed until after six.

I woke to the smell of the TV dinners we were serving that night to the inmates. The steamy aroma of roast beef and gravy made my stomach rumble, and I groggily remembered I hadn't eaten since breakfast. Not eating was beginning to be a habit, and if I kept at it I guessed I could quit worrying about the extra pounds I was carrying around my middle. I pulled my boots on and tracked down the trustee who was serving the dinners, took one for myself, brought it back to the infirmary, and left it on the bed while I performed some minimal ablutions. I splashed cold water on my head and ran a comb through my hair, but I couldn't do a thing about the thatch of stubble on my face. Without the badge, I thought, I'd look exactly like most of the winos in my care.

I ate the TV dinner without tasting it, which is the best you can hope for with that kind of food. Then I went back downstairs to the department to gather the ordinance I figured I might need that night.

In a black nylon gym bag with the Wyoming Law Enforcement Academy logo on the side, I put my binoculars, gloves, flashlight, matches, a light jacket, some candy bars, and a half dozen cans of soda. I had a full chamber in my .357 and twenty additional rounds on my belt, but before I zipped the bag I threw in a box of hollow-point cartridges for the Blackhawk, just to be on the safe side.

Then I let myself into the room where we store our heavy artillery.

A couple of years ago the previous sheriff had cadged a 9-millimeter Heckler & Koch submachine gun from the National Guard, and we still keep it around in case Wyoming is ever invaded by drug dealers or Russians, like in that movie *Red Dawn*. We also have a half dozen Harrington & Richardson M14s and a Colt M16 that I obtained from the same source when I was toying with the notion of building a special response team, a notion I'd abandoned because the department couldn't afford the specialized training.

None of those weapons, however, were outfitted with night scopes, so I settled for a twelve-gauge pump shotgun loaded with double-ought buck, the same weapon all of my deputies carry in their cruisers. The equivalent of one of those point-and-shoot cameras they sell to photographic idiots, the twelve-gauge isn't a sexy weapon. It's short and squat and ugly. But loaded with double-ought buck it'll stop a grizzly in his tracks at close range, or anything else I might encounter on the prairie at night.

I racked the slide a couple of times to make sure the action was smooth, then I loaded the fat rounds into the magazine, clicked the safety on, and put a spare box of ammunition in my bag.

On the way out I stopped by the dispatcher's desk to tell her I'd probably be away from a radio or phone for the rest of the night. She looked puzzled, but I didn't offer to explain, just told her I'd check in before her shift ended in the morning.

Out in the parking lot, I saw that rain clouds were building to the east behind the Medicine Bow range. It would be raining in Cheyenne, I thought, but with any luck the front would break up before it crossed the divide. Just to be safe, I dashed back inside and grabbed a yellow rain slicker and threw it along with the rest of my gear in the back seat of the Blazer.

Then, with darkness settling and KOWB blasting Creedence Clearwater's "Bad Moon Rising" from the speakers on my radio, I pointed the nose of the Blazer toward Rock River and Tess McAfferty's ranch.

# NINETEEN

It was nine-thirty and fully dark by the time I squatted down at the base of the familiar tree to resume my nocturnal vigil of Tess McAfferty's ranch. The bank of rain clouds hadn't made it over the mountains after all, so the sky was clear and inky black. The moon wasn't up, but the heavens were dotted with the pinprick twinkle of stars. A chill wind blew down from the mountains to the north.

Laying the shotgun across my knees, I opened my nylon gym bag, popped the top of a can of soda, and peeled the wrapper from a Payday candy bar. I didn't need the binoculars to see that all the hens were in the McAfferty roost. The four-wheel-drive pickup they'd driven the night before was parked at the side of the house, and so were Tess's Accord and the old Jeep. Yellow light from the living room and kitchen streamed through the windows, and I could see the flickering blue light of a television.

I finished my candy bar and focused my binoculars on the living room window. Angus was on the couch, bare-chested and barefoot, his head propped on throw pillows as he watched something on TV. Andrew lounged in a reclining chair at the side of the couch, engrossed in a magazine. I could see Tess at the kitchen table, a mug of something at her side as she concentrated on a stack of paperwork. Now and then she'd pause, put her pen in her mouth thoughtfully, mull her problem for several quiet moments, and then resume her work.

All in all, it looked like a quiet night on the old homestead.

I tried to make myself as comfortable as possible, dug a little hole in the soft earth for my fanny, found a log to use as a footrest. I bunched my jacket into a passable pillow and leaned back against the sturdy aspen tree. At that moment, the McAffertys showed no signs of going anywhere, but it was still more than eight hours until dawn. Despite my general fatigue, I promised to stay awake in case they changed their minds.

I kept my promise for about two incredibly boring hours. Drifted off, woke with a start about one-thirty. It took me several seconds to remember where I was and another thirty seconds to work the kinks out of my neck, back, and legs. Then I stood and scanned the front of the house.

The vehicles were still in the yard, but the lights inside the house were out. The McAffertys were probably sleeping, just like me.

I relieved myself in the bushes, opened another soda, and sat back down—and promptly dozed off again, this time dreaming a strange dream about a bumbling high school buddy who showed up at my farmhouse trying to sell a trunk full of stolen car-stereo equipment. Problem was, it was all eight-track paraphernalia, the kind nobody's used since the days of Jimi Hendrix. I was trying to explain that in order to be a successful thief you have to steal stuff people want today, not what they wanted twenty-five years ago, when the report of a slammed door jolted me back to reluctant wakefulness.

Groggily I looked at the luminous dial of my watch. The blurry hands said it was a little after two. When my eyes were able to focus better, I picked up the binoculars and looked at Tess's house. A thin sliver of moon had come up while I slept, and it provided enough light to see the three forms quietly moving back and forth from the front door of the house to the pickup. One of the McAfferty boys carried the same cooler he'd carried the night before. The other carried jackets and rucksacks. Tess came last with the weapons. She placed them carefully in the bed of the pickup and said something to the boys.

The dome lights came on for a few seconds while they quietly mounted up, and then I could hear the whine of the starter and the low rumble of the engine as it came to life. Tess let it warm up for a minute or so, then eased the old transmission into gear, backed around, and started not toward the highway but toward the interior of the ranch, the direction they'd come from early the previous morning.

They didn't use their headlights, but I watched the dark shape of the truck as they eased down the hill to the corral and around the loading chute and started off cross-country toward the broken canyon land and grassy foothills that made up the lion's share of Jess's ranch.

I knew I should follow and do it quickly, but I wasn't quite sure how to go about it. The easiest and quickest way, of course, would have been to run back to the grove beside Colleen's grave where I'd parked the Blazer and drive after them.

I wouldn't be able to use my lights, though, so I stood a good chance of either getting stuck or missing their trail in the darkness. Besides, if they stopped and got out of the pickup, they'd surely hear me coming.

The best bet, I realized, was to follow on foot. That way, I reasoned, I'd have a better chance of tracking them, and it would be easier to move undetected. It was all uphill to the fence that marked the boundary between the McAfferty ranch and Will Jensen's, but I'd walked it before, and although that had been in daylight, felt confident I could do it again in the dark. If I found them, I could jump into a patch of brush and watch, something I couldn't do in my vehicle. And if they outdistanced me, I wouldn't have lost much but my effort.

I felt good as I shouldered my gym bag, settled the shotgun under my right arm, and trudged off toward the mouth of the arroyo the McAffertys had entered. It was easy going for the first quarter of a mile across the flat ground between the corral and the mouth of the canyon. The backbone of the heat spell had been broken, and the air was crisp, cool enough for the jacket if I sat still but not as long as I kept moving. The night was full of cricket song, the murmur of the creek that ran through the valley, and the whisper of the breeze in the prairie grass. I stopped every fifty yards or so and listened for the sound of the McAffertys' truck, which I could still hear working its way up the draw.

It wasn't difficult to follow their trail once it left the flats and began to head upcanyon; the four-wheel-drive's big tires had left deep imprints in the sandy soil, clearly visible in the faint moonlight. Since I'd left the blackthorn walking stick behind, I walked slowly, both to conserve my breath and so I wouldn't stumble, my eyes scanning the rocky terrain ahead and the deepening canyon walls at my sides. I traveled that way for a half an hour, until I figured I was halfway to the top of the canyon, and then I sat down on flat boulder to rest.

I strained my ears but could no longer hear the sound of their vehicle, which meant they were either too far away—which I doubted, because I'd left right after they did, and they'd been traveling slowly—or they'd stopped. From here on out, I thought, I'd have to be especially quiet, since I didn't want to stumble over any of the armed clan in the dark. My throat was dry, so I opened a can of soda and drank deeply. Then I ate the last of my candy bars and stood up to move on.

It took me several seconds to realize what had changed while I'd rested. The crickets had stopped singing, and that meant something had made them stop.

I searched the canyon ahead, could see nothing but the white sand reflecting moonlight, the massive outlines of boulders, now and then a tangle of downed timber. Above me on the rim of the arroyo, the sage looked black and foreboding, and for a moment I thought I could see the outline of an animal crouched between two bushes. I climbed halfway up the bank for a better look and finally realized that what I'd believed was an animal was only a smaller bush growing between two larger ones. Breathing a sigh of relief, I made my way gingerly back to the bottom of the arroyo, then started off again.

I heard the click just as I came to the next bend in the canyon.

It was a small metallic sound, definitely manmade, and it came from the rim of the canyon above me. I stood as still as I possibly could, tried to will myself into invisibility, watched the rim of the arroyo. I thought I heard the scrape of footsteps and the sound of breathing, ragged panting, the sound of an animal that has exerted itself in the heat.

I waited for five minutes, slowly set the gym bag on the ground and released the safety on the shotgun. As far as I could tell, I was in the worst possible position if the person I believed was hiding just beyond the rim of the canyon meant me harm. I couldn't rush up the side of the canyon without him hearing me coming. I'd be a clear target as soon as I poked my head out of the draw. Nor could I hope to make a decent stand of it in the bottom of the gully unless whatever was up there made a boneheaded blunder, like popping up in range of my scattergun. I didn't think that was likely.

My only real choice was to keep moving, either upward toward the McAffertys or back down the way I'd come. I chose to go up and moved out at a determined pace. I didn't try to hide the sound of my progress, and my boots made dry, scraping noises in the sand. Branches and leaves hissed and cracked as they brushed against my trousers. My breath came in loud gasps, and I imagined the sound of my pounding heart could be heard for a half mile.

I saw him about thirty yards later, but only for a second as he stood at the top of the canyon on the lip of a little ravine carved by erosion. His was a large shape, a little darker than the blackness surrounding him. I sensed his movement more than saw it, and then he was gone.

Startled, I ducked down behind a boulder on the far side of

the arroyo and laid the barrel of the shotgun on the flat top of the rock, curled my finger around the trigger, and waited.

Nothing.

Cautiously, I flipped the safety on, picked up the bag, and moved on up the canyon, crouching low.

I walked for ten minutes through increasingly rugged country, picked my way over rocks and deadfall. The McAffertys had left a clear trail of broken branches and tire tracks in the sand, but the farther I traveled up the arroyo, the narrower and more brush-choked it became.

I found their vehicle around the next bend, parked with its nose in a stand of juniper and sage.

The pickup was locked and the windows were up. I laid my hand on the hood, which was still hot, pulled my flashlight from the bag and switched it on. In its beam I soon found their tracks, the trail leading away from the truck and up a small ravine.

As I climbed the steep ravine, my feet slipped on the loose shale, created small rock slides that sounded like hail on a tin roof. Once I stumbled and slid a dozen feet back down the hills, digging my heels into the earth while I held the shotgun aloft to keep it from becoming fouled with grit.

When I came to a stop, I realized I'd lost both my flashlight and the gym bag, so I crawled on hands and knees until my fingers found the smooth nylon of the bag. I couldn't find the light, though, so I planted the butt of the shotgun in the dirt and hauled myself back to my feet.

A few minutes later, winded and sweating profusely, I poked my head over the lip of the ravine.

The Doberman waited a few yards away, a growl rumbling in his deep chest.

Beside him, sitting with his back against a fallen log and holding a rifle pointed at the center of my chest, was his master.

"He doesn't care much for guns," Saul Irons said cordially. "Why don't you drop yours and put your hands out where I can see 'em?"

When I'd relieved myself of the shotgun and my Blackhawk, Irons called the Dobie off with a hand signal. The animal hesitated for a second, just long enough to let me know he was backing away under protest. Then he lay down by Irons's side, his big head resting on his paws. I couldn't see his eyes, but I could feel them watching my every move.

"Sit," Irons said.

For a second I thought he was talking to the dog, then I realized he meant me. I lowered myself to the ground and crossed my legs Indian style. Irons was wearing his old scuffed boots, blue jeans, a black T-shirt, and a black leather vest. There was what looked like a .357 Colt in a leather holster on his right hip, a long-bladed knife in a beaded sheath on his right. A weathered gray Stetson with a rattlesnake band was pulled low on his forehead. His back was toward the moon and his face was veiled in shadow, but I could clearly see the muzzle of his rifle trained on my midsection.

"Your leg botherin' you?" he asked. "You were limpin' a little on your way up the canyon."

The phantom stalking me in the canyon. "How long have you been following me?" I asked.

"Since you left the ranch house. I didn't know who you were until just a few seconds ago," he said.

"Glad you didn't shoot," I said.

A soft smile played across Irons's face. "Me too," he chuckled. "That wouldn't do, would it? Don't know how I'd ever explain that one. Just in case you're wondering', Harry, you're in no danger. I don't intend to harm you—unless you do something incredibly stupid."

Given the fact that he had just disarmed me at gunpoint and was still pointing a rifle directly at numerous organs vital to my continued well-being, I wasn't completely reassured. "Then why the gun?" I asked. I pulled my bum leg into a more comfortable position. "Why'd you take mine?"

His smile widened.

There was no use being coy. "You're under arrest, Saul," I said. "For the murder of Wayne Carney. We might as well be clear about that."

He gave me a no-big-deal shrug of his wide shoulders. "Least of my worries, Harry," he said. "But before we go too far along this trail, I want to get one thing straight. I'm not goin' to jail, because I didn't murder Wayne Carney. I shot him in self-defense."

If it hadn't been for the fact that I didn't want to startle the dog, I think I actually might have laughed. As it was, I trapped the sound in my throat, so what actually came out sounded like a cough. Irons pretended not to notice.

"He was goin' for his gun," he explained, not at all offended by my response. "I outdrew him, that's all."

I snorted again. What the hell did he think we were talking about? Gunfight at the OK Corral? "You're gonna have a hell of a time getting a jury to believe that one," I said. "His pistol was still in the holster."

Irons shrugged. "He was slow. I'm not. But it really doesn't matter whether a jury will believe it or not. Like I said, I'm not goin' in."

A note of finality in his voice told me not to push the issue any more just then, so I leaned back on my arms and looked around. We were in a wide, sage-choked swale, very near the place where I'd crossed the fence line that separated the McAfferty and Jensen ranches. The McAffertys must have come that way after they abandoned their pickup, but I didn't know where they'd gone after they reached the top. Maybe onto Jensen's ranch, but maybe they just followed their own side of the fence line over the top of a little ridge a few hundred yards to the north.

Irons rested the rifle on his knees, reached into his vest pocket and pulled out a pack of gum. He unwrapped a stick and put it in his mouth, chewed thoughtfully for a while and offered the pack in my direction. I shook my head. He smoothed his long mustache with the tips of his fingers. "Mind if I ask what you're doin' out here?" he asked.

Well yes, as a matter of fact, I did mind. "How 'bout if I ask you the same thing?"

He thought for a few seconds, then rested his hands on the stock of the weapon. He didn't point it at me again, but we both knew he could raise the barrel and fire in plenty of time to stop me if he wanted to. At that range, he couldn't miss. "Fair enough," he said. "I suppose I'm doin' the same thing you are, lookin' for the McAffertys. Difference is, they're waitin' for me. You, I think, will come as something of a surprise."

"You're working for them," I said. It wasn't a question.

Irons laughed softly, just to let me know I couldn't get him that easily. "If I told you I was workin' for Tess, it would cause problems for her, wouldn't it?" he asked.

I agreed that it could.

"Then let's say I'm just a concerned citizen," Irons said.

It was as close as he was going to come to admitting he'd been hired as an enforcer by Tess McAfferty, but I let it pass without comment, shifting my weight on my arms.

"You didn't tell me why you're here, Harry," he said finally. When I didn't answer, he said, "Let me guess. You think Tess will lead you to Bobby Snow. You're doin' a little guardian angel work of your own."

I picked up a small stone and chucked it into the dirt at the tip of my feet. Beside Irons, the dog raised his head at the movement. I chucked another stone. A low growl rumbled in the dog's throat.

I had no reason to lie and something to gain by telling the truth: his cooperation. "Tess led me to him once before," I said. "It seemed possible she'd do it again. Where is she?"

Irons was quiet for several minutes, considering what I'd said. Eventually he came to some sort of personal decision, nodded, and crooked his head to the north. "If you follow her fence line over that little hill for about a half mile, you'll come to small valley with a windmill, a stock trough, and some haystacks. The only way you can get to the place on foot from her ranch is the way you came. If you go by car, there's a Jeep trail that will take you there through the back end of Jensen's property. That's where she's keepin' the bait."

I was surprised, and it came through in my voice. "Bait?"

"Yearlings," he said. "About twenty of them. They figure considerin' the remote location, it'll be too much for Bobby to resist. Of course, someone had to watch the ranch house for a while after they left. That's where I came in."

I was beginning to get a bad feeling. "What do they plan to do if they catch him?"

"In the immortal words of Ted Kennedy," he said, laughing, "they'll drive off that bridge when they come to it."

I didn't think he was all that damn funny. "Someone's gonna get hurt," I said angrily.

Irons matched my anger with his own. It cracked like lightning, swift and intense, lethal at close range. "No shit, Harry?" he spat, and brought the rifle up again, training it on my heart. "People are gonna get hurt?" He punched the air with the barrel of the weapon. "People have already been hurt. This thing didn't start yesterday, you know."

I recoiled, my brain backpedaling at the unexpected force of his reaction. I was blowing it. "I didn't mean—"

He waved me off, looked away. I gave him a minute to calm down while I collected my own thoughts. When I saw his muscular shoulders relax a little, I pressed forward. "When did it start?" I asked. "When Colleen McAfferty was killed? Do you know what happened to her, Saul? Does Tess? Did Tess hire you to kill Bobby Snow for her? Or just to help her catch him so she can do it herself?"

I leaned toward Irons anxiously, but Saul gave no indication he'd even heard me. He looked up to check the progress of some high clouds across the inky sky, reached over to scratch the dog between the ears. "That's a lot of questions, Harry," he said. There was no promise in his voice that he'd provide answers. He went back to watching the clouds, scratching the watchful hound.

"Come on, damn it," I said. "I'm not your enemy. We're on the same side here."

He smiled faintly. "Is that why I'm under arrest?"

I threw some more stones in the dirt. Dusted my hands off in frustration. "We're on the same side when it comes to Colleen McAfferty's murder," I said. "When it comes to protecting Tess."

He lowered the barrel of the rifle almost imperceptibly. "If I tell you," he said, testing the water, "would you consider—"

"No deals," I cut in. "You'll have to answer for Carney whether you help me or not."

His face hardened. "And as I told you, I have no intention of goin' to jail for that, so we seem to be right back where we started."

So we were. Almost. The last few minutes had convinced me there was no way I could make Irons talk if he didn't want to. They'd also convinced me the man didn't want to shoot me, probably wouldn't unless I threatened him physically. At least that's what I decided to bet.

"Then there's no sense in talking any more, is there?" I asked. He mumbled something, but I didn't hear what he said. I pushed myself to my feet, dusted off the seat of my britches. A growl rumbled in the dog's throat when I turned my back on Irons and began walking slowly in the direction of Tess McAfferty and her "bait." I'd taken almost a dozen steps when I heard the lethal, metallic click as Irons flipped the safety on the rifle. He was locked and loaded, the only thing standing between me and the great beyond was a twitch of his finger. I hoped the fucker didn't sneeze.

"That's as far as I'd go if I were you," he said softly. There was no doubt or hesitation in his voice, and I could almost feel his finger taking up a few pounds of pull on the trigger.

I stopped walking, stuffed my hands in my pockets. "You won't do it," I said with as much conviction as I could muster. My heartbeat was accelerating, and I could feel cold beads of sweat on my forehead. "You won't kill me, Saul. Not in cold blood." I put my head down and took another step.

"Harry?"

I stopped, choked back the acid taste of fear that was settled on the back of my tongue. "I've got to go help them, Saul" I said. "They're amateurs. Not like you and me. Not like Bobby Snow. I don't think you'll kill me for trying to do my job. But before I go, I'll tell you what I think happened. You stop me if I'm wrong."

He didn't answer. I pressed on. "I think Bobby started hitting ranchers in this area late last summer, hitting 'em hard," I began. There was a slight trembling in my legs. I willed it to stop. "For a while, the livestock owners did just what they were supposed to. They reported the thefts to C.J. Fall's office. They filed claims on their insurance. But Fall doesn't do much on-site surveillance, and even if he did, the chances he'd catch a rustler in the act are pretty slim. He told 'em he'd watch the kill plants and the feed lots, but nothing much came of it. In the meantime, the insurance companies started getting suspicious of the ranchers."

I took a deep, deep lungful of air, listened to the breeze riffling the sage. Behind me, I could hear Irons's measured breathing, the panting of the dog.

"All right, Sheriff," he said, his voice almost a whisper. "So far, so good."

I collected my thoughts before beginning again. "Most of these folks are on shaky ground, nothing unusual about that," I said. "But when a livestock owner gets in trouble, he sometimes starts reporting losses he didn't have so he can collect the insurance. If that happens often enough, the suits at the insurance company start thinking fraud. The folks around here didn't want that to happen, so they just stopped reporting their losses and . . ."

I paused. Lowered my voice an octave. "And hired their own regulator," I said. I hesitated for a beat. "That would be you."

I turned to face him, saw that the barrel of his rifle was still pointed at me. The muzzle looked a mile wide, the bore as black as eternity. A cloud passed in front of the moon, and for a moment Irons was in shadow, but I thought I saw a glint of white. Was he grinning?

"It worked when their granddaddies hired Tom Horn," he said. "When you get right down to it, not that much has changed out here in the last hundred years."

I tried to dull the sharp edge of sarcasm in my voice, but it came through anyway. "So your job was to keep the riffraff out," I said. "Scare 'em out of the country, if they'd scare."

Irons shrugged noncommittally.

"Like Emile Cross," I said. "We found his body, you know. It looks like you scared him to death."

"Never met the man," he grumbled.

I clucked my tongue to let him know I didn't believe him. His face was a mask. "Fuck you, Harry," he said. He stood, still aiming the rifle from the hip. "I don't think we've got much to talk about after all. It's about time for me to fly."

There were fifteen long feet between me and the weapon. In order to get it, I'd have to cover the distance between us and get it away from him before either he or the dog had time to react. A fine plan—if my goal was to commit suicide. I had to come up with an alternative. When none presented itself, I resorted to what I do best: talking.

"You didn't scare Snow," I said. "As a matter of fact, I figure when Snow found out the ranchers had hired you, it just made him mad. I think he kept hitting around here, even on the McAfferty place, just to let you and everyone else know he could do whatever he damn well pleased."

I meant my words to hit Irons like punches, but they rolled off him like raindrops. He held the muzzle of the rifle steady on my gut.

"I would have gotten him," he said matter-of-factly. The dog sensed some change in his master's voice, looked like he wanted to take a bite of meat from my body. I balled my fists and cocked my arms. If the cur came for me, I'd break his nose before he could rip out my throat. At least I'd try.

"But you didn't get him, did you?" My adrenaline was pumping, maybe from anger, more likely from fear. I took a step toward him. The dog curled its lip, exposing long white canines. Growled. "Not in time to save Colleen." My voice came out in a rasp.

For a split second, a flash of pain crossed his features, but it didn't stick. Before the sound of my words had truly died, Saul was back to his old stoic self. "That one was below the belt, Harry," he said quietly. "I gave you more credit than that."

I squatted down on my haunches, my old knees crying out in pain. He cradled the rifle in his arms, reached down again to scratch the dog between the ears. I pushed on with my questions. There was nothing else I could do. "Tell me about it," I said plaintively. "Was Bobby there?"

Irons was back to ignoring me, and I waited without an answer. "Come on, Saul," I said when I could stand it no longer. "You can tell me. What can it hurt?"

Irons looked up from the dog. He watched my face, taking my measure. Finally he nodded almost imperceptibly, pointed to a place about thirty yards away. He'd made his decision. "I guess there's no harm in tellin' you, Harry. You probably deserve it, and there's not a hell of a lot to gain by keepin' it to myself.

"Besides," he said, "you think you know the rest of it anyway, don't you?"

I shrugged my shoulders, picked up a handful of dirt and let it sift through my fingers.

"That's what I thought," he said. "I guess I'd better make sure you have it right."

He was making me a gift I was happy to accept. I smiled inwardly, waiting quietly for him to go on.

"I was walkin' range the evenin' she was killed, checkin'

314

things out," he said finally. "I was just over there, in fact, when I heard the shots."

"From the ranch?"

"Yeah, two of them, about thirty seconds apart. I ran to the top of the canyon mesa overlookin' the ranch and used my scope to pick out those people in the corral."

"Colleen was already dead?"

"Probably," he said. "If not, she was dead a few minutes later. At the time, though, I didn't know it was Colleen. I thought it might be Tess. They must've already loaded Clarence into the stock trailer, but Ralphie was still lyin' in the corral. I jacked a round into the chamber and took a shot at one of the guys loadin' the livestock. But it's over eight hundred yards from where I was to the corral. Too far for a sure shot, even for the .22-.454. Maybe I misjudged the bullet drop, the wind."

"Whatever," he said sadly. "I missed."

I could imagine his rage and frustration, the bitter tang of impotence. "I suppose it got their attention."

"That it did," he said bitterly. "They took off like a bunch of damn jackrabbits."

I nodded for him to go on.

"I came down the hill as fast as I could."

"But only as far as that little hill near the corral," I broke in.

Irons looked surprised at what I knew, so I explained. "I followed your tracks back here from where you stopped on the hill," I said. "Even found a package of that gum. You were parked on Jensen's ranch. But why didn't you go into the corral?"

"I used my binoculars, and I could see they were both dead," he said tightly. "I recognized Colleen, and I could see that Tess wasn't home. I didn't want to go into the corral, because I didn't want my footprints around. The last thing I wanted was to become a suspect in her murder."

I didn't buy that explanation, couldn't imagine him simply leaving those bodies on the ground, walking away. "Why didn't you try to find Tess?" I asked. "Why not call the police?"

Irons was a study in determination and self-assurance. "There wasn't a damn thing I could do for Colleen, and I didn't know where Tess had gone," he said hotly. "I figured I could do the most good goin' after the men in the stock trailer. So I hurried back to my pickup and went after 'em."

"You went to Snow's ranch?"

"Yeah," he said, "but no luck. They weren't there. After that, I drove over to Rawlins in case they'd gone on I-80. Turns out they did, and they dumped Hathaway's body at Elk Mountain on the way. But I guess I was too far behind them. By the time I got back to the McAfferty ranch the next mornin' your deputies were already here, so I didn't bother to stop."

My own anger was returning as he spoke, not because I didn't believe him, but because Keegan and I had come to him for help early in the investigation, and he'd denied any knowledge. If he'd told me the truth the first time I asked, I could have closed the books and never broken a sweat. Bobby would have gone to jail, Wayne Carney would still be alive, and Saul would not have been facing a charge of first-degree murder. "What I still don't understand," I said, "is why you didn't just come forward with what you knew. It looks like you even encouraged Tess to go after Snow herself, Saul. You were a cop once. Didn't you trust us to put this thing to rest?"

"It wasn't that we didn't trust you," he said. "We did. But tell you the truth, we all wanted to catch him before you did, catch him somewhere lonesome. Tess wanted that most of all, and that's why she hasn't been especially cooperative. She didn't want you to get him before she did.

"I don't think you blame her, either, Harry," he said. "You're a father, you can imagine what it's like."

I could imagine that only too well. If I were in Tess's shoes, I wouldn't want the police involved either. I'd hunt the bastard down and kill him with my own hands. I'd make it my life's work.

I couldn't admit that to Irons, though, so I said nothing. And in my silence, he found his answer.

"You want some coffee?" he asked. "I've got a thermos in my saddlebags."

I said I did, and Irons turned and disappeared into a thicket of sage, leaving the rifle behind. From the brush I heard the snuffle of the horse he had tethered there, heard him speaking softly and reassuringly to the animal. The dog still watched me warily, but I realized that if I wanted, I could probably reach the shotgun in time to kill it.

I didn't try, though, just sat quietly until Irons returned and poured two cups of coffee. I took the one he offered, inhaled the fragrant steam, and sipped gratefully. Cowboy coffee, black and freshly brewed, strong enough to make my nerve endings tingle. I drank half a cup and rested the speckled enamelware mug on my knee.

It was almost five, and the sky was lightening in the east, the horizon a thin, pulsing line of diffused light. I was chilly, so I opened the gym bag and pulled out my jacket. The synthetic outer shell kept the breeze out, and the cotton lining felt cozy and warm.

"Tell me about Carney," I said. "How'd you happen to meet up with him at Woods Landing?"

Irons blew a wreath of steam from the surface of his coffee. "I got a call from someone who told me he was being released."

"Who would have done that? Someone from the district attorney's office? The university police?"

"Doesn't matter," he said. "All that matters is I have some friends in Laramie, and one of 'em knew I was lookin' for someone who could take me to Bobby Snow. I just showed up at the university police station around the time they let Carney out and followed him to Woods Landing. From there on, it was just a matter of convincin' him I was a greater health hazard than Bobby Snow.

When he was persuaded, he told me almost everything I wanted to know."

"Such as?"

"Such as what happened the night Colleen was killed," Irons said.

"How'd it go down?"

Irons held his hands out, palms upwards. "Snow was feelin' arrogant, wanted Tess to know I couldn't protect her if he felt like takin' her livestock," he said. "He saw her in town late that afternoon, so he called his boys to head out to her house and start loadin' stock. He drove out from Laramie to meet 'em, but by the time he got there, Colleen was already dead. At that point, the crazy son of a bitch flipped out. Shot Skates and Hathaway on the spot. Christ, Ralphie didn't even have time to hitch his pants."

"Was he angry they'd killed her?" I asked.

"That I don't know," he said. "I suppose we'll have to ask Bobby."

"Yeah," I said, "I guess we will. We'll have to ask him who shot up my house, too. You wouldn't know anything about that, would you?"

A dark scowl crossed Irons's face. "You think that was me?" he asked stiffly.

"For a while I did," I said. "Keegan changed my mind."

"I don't know who popped your house, Harry, but Keegan's right, it wasn't me. He knows I wouldn't have missed. Not from that distance."

"I suppose not," I said. "You sure didn't miss Carney. Why'd you kill him, Saul?"

"Couldn't be helped," he said. "He told me everything I wanted to know, except where Bobby was. He balked when I said I wanted him to take me to him, started cursin', stood up and went for his gun. The rest you already know."

I finished the coffee, wiped my mouth. "Except for where you've been hiding," I said.

"I've been camped right here on Tess's ranch," he said.

"Plenty of room to get lost in, if you're of a mind to get lost. I guess now, though, I'll have to move on. Too bad, too. I sure would've liked to finish this business first. I like to have a sense of closure in my life, Harry. Don't like leavin' things undone."

He got to his feet and went to the place I'd dropped the shotgun and my Blackhawk. With quick, practiced motions, he emptied the revolver's chamber, jacked the pump on the shotgun until the magazine was empty. He picked up the ejected rounds, tossed them into the bushes, and laid my weapons back on the ground.

"I'm gonna take off now," he said. "Go see how Tess and those young McAfferty boys are doin'. Then I'm gonna get my truck and head down the road. Maybe I'll go to Mexico. I hear it's nice down there this time of year. Mezcal. Lotsa fresh shrimp. And hot, Harry. I like it hot."

He picked up the rifle, gave the muzzle a casual wave in my direction. "Do yourself a favor, podna," he said. "Don't bother comin' after me. Just turn yourself around and head back down the hill."

As I pushed myself to my feet, the cartilage in my knees cracked like popcorn. I winced, stomped my boots to restore my circulation. The Doberman sat up expectantly, licked its chops, and let out a short, frustrated whine.

"I can't do that, Saul," I said. "You killed a man in front of witnesses, and it doesn't matter whether I believe you or not. You've got to stand trial."

Saul's lips curved in an icy grin. "Don't press your luck, amigo," he said. "I don't think you'd like the result."

After Irons and the Dobie melted away into the dense thicket of sage, I slowly reloaded my revolver and the shotgun with ammunition from the gym bag. Then I sat down on a flat boulder and watched the sun rise while I tried to decide what to do next.

In the thicket I could hear the muffled sounds as Irons prepared his horse for travel, the creak of old leather, the animal's grunts and snorts as Saul tightened the cinch, the snap of branches and twigs as the horse shifted its weight. He kept up a constant patter as he worked, the hallmark of a man whose most constant companions in the bush have four legs.

I wondered how long it had been since Saul Irons sat down to dinner with a woman, or just had a beer and burgers with some pals at the neighborhood saloon. I wondered how long it had been since he played a game of back yard catch, touch football. How long since he'd spent an hour in the company of anyone who wasn't somehow involved with his profession, someone who wasn't a cop, a crook, or a cattleman. How long since he'd done anything as simple as walking into a greasy spoon for breakfast without being stared at by people who knew his background and feared him because of it, avoided by people who didn't but sensed in him something dangerous and barely restrained.

I felt a twinge of pity for Irons and the isolation he'd chosen since the day he shot a fellow cop in Flagstaff, and I realized that I was drawn to him in the same way Keegan was drawn. I liked him, liked his taciturn manner, his strength and self-reliance, his utter self-confidence.

But there was a dark side to Saul Irons I didn't like, and it was because of that dark side, the side that led him to murder, that I had to take him in.

I didn't want to try it by myself, however. Down deep, every man knows his own limitations—or should—and I knew only too well that even though I'm a good shot and generally hit what I aim at, I was no match for Saul Irons in a one-on-one confrontation, shotgun or no shotgun.

With Irons on his way to meet up with the McAffertys, there was no longer any point in trying to follow them, since Saul would inform them of my presence. There was no point in attempting to change Saul's mind. And with the sun up, there seemed little likelihood that Bobby Snow would make an appearance.

My best hope of accomplishing anything of value was to get my butt back down the hill, radio Laramie for backup, and stop

Irons either on the McAfferty ranch or as he tried to leave. Maybe the office would even be able to reach Keegan in time for him to be on hand for the arrest.

Snapping the Blackhawk into my holster, I picked up the gym bag and the shotgun and I began walking back to the edge of the arroyo. I stopped at the rim and looked down. The rising sun bathed the valley below in soft golden light that turned the greens of the hay and alfalfa fields to the deepest emerald, a sharp contrast to the ravines directly in front of me, still in shadow. I squatted down, plucked a blooming prairie gentian, and brought it to my nose, closing my eyes and inhaling the aroma of its nectar, savoring it for a long moment. Then I tucked the fragile flower in my pocket.

I was snapping the button on my shirt pocket when the sound of the first shot echoed across the hilltops.

I stood and turned quickly in the direction from which it came, the place where Irons told me Tess and the McAfferty boys were watching their "bait." The first shot was followed almost immediately by two more, and then another, much louder, the hearty boom of a rifle. A second later, the rifle roared again.

I dropped the gym bag and began to run in the direction of the reports, barely aware of the sound Saul's Appaloosa made as it crashed through the brush and up the slight incline toward me, its hoofbeats hollow thuds on the sandy earth. I saw the animal's charging bulk in my peripheral vision and stopped when I realized a collision was inevitable.

But Irons drew the animal up in time; its front legs dug into the ground, spewing me with a cloud of dirt. I looked up at Irons, who reached toward me with an outstretched hand.

"Hop on, Harry!" he yelled. "I was too damn late the last time. It ain't gonna happen again!"

# TWENTY

We rode hard and I didn't fall off, but in spite of the Appaloosa's speed and Irons's grim determination, by the time we reached the top of the mesa overlooking the hollow where the McAffertys had set their trap for Bobby Snow, we were too late to save Angus McAfferty.

We dismounted, tethered the horse, and crouched behind a bank of shale and scrub cedar. Irons peered through the scope of his custom .22-.454, me through my binoculars. It was about three hundred yards to the bottom of the ravine-scarred bluff where the shots had been fired only minutes before.

"Son of a fuckin' bitch," Irons swore. "Tess and those boys must have tried to take Snow by themselves."

The sun had not yet cleared the hills to the east, so the hollow was still blanketed in gray shadow. Even so, there was enough light that I could see Ray Bolton and another man dragging Angus through the sagebrush by his legs toward the place near the water trough where two more men were loading bawling cattle into the back of a long livestock trailer hitched to Snow's pickup. Angus's arms bounced lifelessly, caught occasionally on the sage. His head lolled from side to side, and there was a dark stain on the front of his white shirt.

"Look there," Irons hissed. "Front of the pickup."

Training my binoculars where he indicated, I picked out the fuzzy shape of human forms. I adjusted the focus, and what I saw made my breath catch in my chest.

Bobby Snow, holding the shotgun I'd seen Tess load into her pickup, stood in front of a kneeling Andrew McAfferty. Tess sat leaning forward with her arms wrapped tightly around her stomach.

Andrew tried to get to his feet, but Snow grabbed the hair at the nape of his neck with his free hand and held the boy's head in place while he smashed a knee into his face. He let Andrew go and the boy fell to his hands and knees, his head swinging back and forth like a disoriented, wounded bull. Then Snow raised the shotgun butt first and slammed the wooden stock into the back of Andrew's head.

The boy collapsed in a heap.

Tess struggled to get up, but Snow grabbed a handful of her hair and dragged her over to Andrew McAfferty. He roughly let her go and then reached down and grabbed Andrew's hair, lifted his head so she could see his face.

A second later, we heard the echo of her scream.

Beside me, I heard the metallic sound of Irons's rifle bolt closing as he jacked a round into the chamber. He brought the scope to his eye, his finger resting lightly on the trigger.

"Can you take him?" I whispered.

"I don't know," he said. "It's a long shot. If I miss . . ."

He didn't have to finish the sentence. If he missed with the first shot, Snow might use Tess as a shield against the second. He might kill her out of spite. And even if Saul got lucky and killed Snow, there were four more rustlers to contend with. From where we were, there was no way we could protect Tess and Andrew—if he was still alive—from the survivors.

Tess was at Andrew's side, holding his head in her arms. Snow had moved away to help with the loading. There were more than a dozen cattle still to be herded to the trailer and loaded aboard, and they weren't cooperating. The rustlers tried to shoo them along with lariats, but the frightened animals bolted at every opportunity, loped away from the men and ran until they came to the barbed wire fence that marked the limits of their enclosure. If Snow intended to steal them all, it was going to take some time.

Irons raised the rifle and brought the scope to his eye again, flicked the safety off with his thumb.

I reached over and put my hand on the barrel of the rifle, pushed it down. "Don't," I said. "There's got to be another way."

Cradling the rifle in the crook of his left arm, he removed his Stetson and wiped his brow with the back of his hand. He looked at me for a long moment, taking my measure. "Can you shoot, Harry?" he asked. "Ever killed a man?"

I looked away, replayed the images of faces that still haunt my occasional dreams.

"Yes," I said. "And yes."

He nodded, reached out for the binoculars and used them to study the terrain between us and the hollow. Most of the ravines were shallow and exposed in places, but fifty yards to the north was the lip of a deep gully choked with scrub cedar, sage, and dwarf pine that scored the face of the bluff vertically, emptying a mere thirty yards from Snow's pickup. Irons scanned the ravine from top to bottom several times, then handed the binoculars back so I could look.

"We'll go in there," he said. "The sun's at our backs, so they won't be able to see us easily. We'll work down about halfway. See that big boulder with the pine at its base?"

I traced the course of the ravine with the binoculars. "I see it," I said. From the boulder to Snow's pickup it looked to be about a hundred yards.

"That's where I'll shoot from," he said.

"That might be close enough for you," I said, pointing to the twelve-gauge shotgun at my side. "But all I've got's a scattergun and a revolver. Neither one of 'em's good at a hundred yards."

"Doesn't matter," he said. "You're not gonna be usin' 'em."

"What?" I sputtered. "Then how the hell am I—"

Irons cut me off with a terse wave of his hand. "Listen, Harry," he said. "There's no way we're gonna take those guys by surprise, so we've gotta do it another way. Chances are, we aren't gonna get 'em all, even then. I've got an idea, but it's more dangerous for you than it is for me. You want to hear it?"

I scanned the hollow with the binoculars. Tess was still with Andrew, but Bobby and the rustlers had managed to load two more of the cattle. About ten to go. If we were going to try anything, it had to be soon. "I guess I don't have much choice," I said.

"Then here's what I want to do," he said. "We go together down to that boulder, then you go the rest of the way by yourself. When you get to the bottom, just walk right out in the open and arrest the bastards."

"You're joking," I said. "At best, they'll take my weapons away and go on about their business. At worst, they'll shoot me. How's that gonna help Tess?"

"It's a risk," he agreed. "We're just gonna have to bet they don't kill you right away."

"So they take my guns," I said. "Then what? I talk them into letting us all go? I've got to tell you, Saul, I don't think much of this damn plan so far."

"Then you create a diversion," he said. "Take at least one of 'em out. Maybe two. I'll get the rest."

"There are five people down there, for Christ's sake," I snapped. "What do I take them out with, Saul? Rocks? Sticks?"

He sat up, pulled the leg of his blue jeans above the top of his right boot. A metal clip held something to the inside of the boot. He pulled the object loose, palmed it, tossed it to me.

It was a tiny derringer, about three and a half inches long and cased in a small holster molded to fit the handgun's contours. I recognized the weapon as one of Dick Casull's five-shot .22 mags. The world's smallest handgun, it's accurate to around six feet.

After that, it's a crapshoot.

"With that," he said. "Tuck it down the front of your jeans. Stick it in your underwear. They might search you, but I doubt they'll pat your Johnson."

I laughed in spite of myself. "If they do, I just hope they don't pat it so hard this thing goes off."

Irons smiled faintly. "You agree then?" he asked.

"Well damn it, Saul, I don't have a hell of a lot of choice. But I've got two conditions."

He looked skeptical. "Yeah?"

"One," I said, ticking it off on a finger, "if this works, you go back to town with me this afternoon. I'll make sure you're treated fairly."

Irons's face darkened and his hands gripped the stock of his rifle tightly. "I told you, Harry, I—"

"Two." I held up a second finger. He cocked his head, nodded for me to go on. "Two. If this doesn't work, if those bastards kill Tess, if they kill me?"

"Yes?"

"Shoot every last one of 'em."

Irons's face cracked in what almost passed for a grin. "That some new kinda *rehabilitation* therapy, Harry?" he asked.

I shrugged my shoulders, took the derringer out of its holster, and tucked the weapon inside the waistband of my underwear. Then I crawled back from the lip of the bluff, stood up, and began walking toward the ravine.

"Harry?" Irons called softly.

I turned back. Irons was no longer grinning.

"I won't let 'em get away," he said. "Count on it."

We moved quickly through the upper reaches of the ravine, our movements hidden by the shadows, the vegetation, and the banks of the gully, which were higher than our heads in most places. We hunched over through the shallow stretches and moved through the exposed areas rapidly, careful not to trip over loose rocks or deadfall and give ourselves away.

At the boulder Saul peeled away and took up a position behind the rock, the barrel of his rifle resting on its crown. He took off his Stetson and set it carefully at his side, ran a hand across the short stubble of his hair. Then he waved me on.

We couldn't speak out loud, so I mouthed the words *Good luck.*

*You too,* he mouthed back.

From the boulder there was a clear line of sight to the hollow, and from that distance I could hear the bawling of the cattle in the livestock trailer and the cursing of the rustlers as they tried to catch the remaining stragglers. I waited until the men were all facing away from me and then moved out in a crouch.

Twenty yards downhill from the boulder where Irons was perched, the banks of the ravine became too shallow to hide me, even bent over as far as I could bend. I could see the mouth of the ravine, though, and the barbed wire fence that ran across it, part of the enclosure that held the McAfferty cattle. If I walked fast, it would only take seconds to reach the fence, but then I'd have to get through it, a time-consuming process, even in the best circumstances. I damn sure couldn't sneak through it.

Maybe I could will myself invisible, I thought. Worked for the Indians, didn't it?

Well, no, as a matter of fact, it did not.

I took a deep breath, stood upright, and began walking as rapidly as I could toward the fence. To my hypersensitive ears, the sound of my boots on the rocky bottom of the ravine was as loud as cannon fire, the hiss of the sage branches against my clothes as noisy as a steam whistle.

But luck was with me, at least for the moment. I made it to the fence without being seen and carefully set the shotgun down on the other side. Then I pushed the top strand of wire down as far as it would go and lifted my legs across. I picked up the shotgun, flipped the safety off, then reached down to release the safety strap on the Blackhawk's holster.

I've known men and women who can look death in the face without flinching. Soldiers who could calmly jam a fresh clip into their M14s while a dozen screaming Vietcong bore down on them, AK-47s blazing. Cops who can look down the muzzle of a pistol in the hands of a crazed speed freak, draw their own weapons, and fire without a millisecond's hesitation. Skydivers who can let go of the wing struts of an airplane thousands of feet from the ground, secure in the knowledge that the bits of flimsy cloth they carry on their backs will keep them from colliding with Mother Earth at Mach 1.

Unfortunately, I'm not one of them, and as I began to close the distance between the fence line and the place where Snow and his men were loading the last of the cattle, the knot of fear in my belly was painful in its intensity. I fought back the sudden urge to turn around and run for the relative safety of the ravine, tried to concentrate on the position of my adversaries.

Two of the rustlers were on the far side of the livestock trailer, trying to slip a rope around the neck of a terrified steer. Snow, his back to me and no longer carrying Tess's shotgun, watched them from the front end of the pickup. Ray Bolton was standing on the loading ramp of the trailer, using a cattle prod to encourage one of the animals inside to move to a more desirable position.

At least in the hollow it was easier walking, flat, with only an occasional thatch of buffalo grass to slow my stride. I wanted to look back over my shoulder to where Irons was hidden, just to make sure he was still in place, but I didn't. Just kept walking forward.

Tess saw me before the others. She looked up from Andrew's face and stared in my direction. I don't think she recognized me at first, or perhaps she didn't believe her eyes. But for a few long seconds as I covered the ground between us, her startled gaze never left my face. Then she shook her head violently and began to wave me away.

I held a finger to my lips, but it was too late.

"Harry," she screamed, "get out of here!"

At the sound of her voice, Bolton turned from the livestock trailer. He saw me and reacted quickly, drew the long-barreled pistol he carried on his hip and pointed the muzzle at my chest. Snow was there a second later. His own sidearm was still holstered. He shook his head as if he couldn't believe my stupidity, reached into the bed of his pickup and pulled out a bolt-action rifle with a scope. He worked the bolt and brought the barrel of the weapon even with his waist. At that distance, he wouldn't need to aim.

Beyond the truck I could see the other three rustlers hurrying in our direction. The steer they'd been leading broke away at a run, the rope dangling from his thick neck, it's end raising small mushroom clouds of dust whenever it touched ground.

I didn't look at Bolton as I walked past him, but I could feel him following me with the front blade of his revolver. I didn't think he'd shoot unless Bobby gave the word. At least that's what I was hoping.

I looked instead at Angus McAfferty's body, sprawled face down beside the rear wheels of the double-axled trailer. Dumped like so much human offal. Blood from the exit wound had soaked the back of his shirt and drawn a cloud of buzzing insects.

I didn't stop until I was beside Tess. There was a bruise on her cheek and her blouse was torn open at the bottom. Through the rent, I could see another black and ugly bruise on her rib cage.

Andrew McAfferty was in much worse condition. Bobby's knee had shattered his nose and smashed his upper lip against his front teeth. His face was a mask of blood, and more had soaked into Tess's jeans from the wound on the back of his head.

And those were just the injuries I knew about.

I knelt and placed my finger on his carotid artery, found a

strong pulse. Andrew moaned, coughed blood from his torn mouth.

I wiped it away with my fingers and looked up at Tess, startled by the intensity in her eyes.

Not pain. Not fear.

Hatred. Burning with blue flame, strong and pure.

"Don't," I whispered. "Not yet."

I don't know if she understood, because she didn't give me the slightest response. Just looked back down at Andrew's face, wiped the blood from his lips. Bent down and whispered into his ear.

I looked up at Snow, who was eight feet away, an amused smirk on his weather-beaten face. At that angle, the bore of his rifle, a .30-06 Remington with a thick rubber recoil pad on the butt and a good scope, looked like the doorway to eternity.

"I'll say this for you, Sheriff," he said. "You certainly have the knack for showing up at inconvenient moments."

Ray Bolton took the shotgun and my .357, but as Irons predicted, he didn't think to check the front of my pants when he patted me down.

When he was finished, he grabbed the back of my shirt and pushed me to the ground beside Tess. He was as ugly as ever, the ever present cigar butt hanging from the corner of his corpulent mouth. There was crusted mucus around the edges of the nostrils of his flat nose and he smelled like a garbage dump. He laughed like a maniac when I informed him that he and the rest of his pals were under arrest, and I couldn't believe what mirth did to his face.

Real horror show.

Snow put the rifle under his arm, pushed his Ray-Bans to the crown of his head, pulled off his cowhide gloves and jammed them in his back pocket. Then he fished around in the front pocket of his jeans until he came up with a paper-wrapped plug of chewing tobacco. He offered it to the man standing at his right, the man with the zipper scar across his forehead, whom I recognized from my first visit to Snow's ranch. Zipper shook his head, so Snow took the bone-handled hunting knife he wore in a belt sheath and cut himself a chaw. He filled his cheek with tobacco, tamped it down with his tongue. "A stand-up comedian," he said. "Guy comes down here, gonna tell us jokes. Thinks he's Jay fucking Leno."

Ray and Zipper chortled at Bobby's wit, but the other two rustlers didn't bother. Both dark with long black hair curling over their collars, they looked like they might be Mexican, maybe Basque. Both were armed with revolvers and hunting knives, and both looked like they knew how to use them.

Ray took the cigar from his mouth, spit a stream of brown saliva in the dirt just inches from my hand. "Where's Cochise today?" he asked. "He go back to the blanket?"

"He'll be along any minute," I said. "Kick your fat ass again."

Ray's foot lashed out before I could raise my arm to deflect it and the toe of his boot caught me in the left shoulder, knocked me on my back. I rolled away from him and started to come up. My shoulder felt like it had been whacked with a bat, and my arm gave way as soon as I put some weight on it. I crumpled face down to the ground, raised my head to see Ray cocking his leg for another punt.

"Cut the shit, Ray!" Bobby yelled.

Ray stopped in mid kick like someone had flipped his power switch. Anger smoldered in his porcine eyes, and he glared at me, his lips drawn back in a feral snarl, then at Bobby. "But this cock-sucker—"

"Forget it," Bobby said. "I don't want him all bruised up."

Ray backed off a couple paces, his fists balled at his sides. He wanted to hurt me, badly, and it took every ounce of his self-control to keep from doing it. The blood vessels in his temples throbbed. A crimson wave started at the place where his neck should have been and worked its way up his jowly cheeks. Parboiled pig. I pushed myself back up to a sitting position. Gave him the finger. He looked like he might actually explode.

Snow said something in rapid Spanish to the two dark-skinned rustlers and they turned and loped off toward the few cattle still loose in the enclosure. Zipper and Ray stayed with us. Snow squatted, planting the rifle butt first in the ground for support.

"Those boys are gonna be finished here in just a few minutes," he said. He looked at Tess, reached over and touched a strand of her hair. Eyes and nostrils flaring, she jerked away as if his touch were acid. "And then I'm afraid we're gonna have to say good-bye to you folks, once and for all."

"You'll kill us," I said. The barrel of the derringer poked the muscles of my groin. I ignored it.

He smiled and nodded. "Don't see I have much choice," he said. "I hear I'm wanted for a variety of crimes, none of which I particularly want to answer for." He pointed at Angus McAfferty's corpse." And then, there's that. It was self-defense, of course. They shot at us first. But who's gonna believe it, Sheriff? You?"

Nope, not me. "You won't get away with it."

Bobby laughed, spat a stream of tobacco juice. "Well, maybe not," he said. "But I figure I'll do Ms. McAfferty and her young friend with your Blackhawk." He pointed to the bed of the truck, where he'd placed Tess's shotgun. "I'll do you with hers. It might not fool 'em for long, but by the time they get it sorted out, I'll be in Canada with those cows. Got me a little nest egg, so I just might stay. You know, buy a little ranch. Find a wife. Start a family. It's the immigrant's dream, Starbranch."

The sun had risen above the hills surrounding the hollow and was bathing us in bright yellow light. Although Irons was behind me, I knew that light would have driven the shadows from the ravine where he waited as well. He was exposed, and I knew I'd have to do something very soon. Trouble was, I couldn't figure how to pull it off. Unless you're a major league baseball player, you don't just reach down the front of your pants and grope yourself any time you feel like it.

Beside me, Tess lowered Andrew's head to the ground, put his hat on his face to shield him from the sun. She hadn't spoken since she called out to me in warning, but I knew she'd been listening, knew what Snow had in mind. If she was afraid, she didn't show it. Her eyes were on Bobby Snow like a rattler's on a mouse.

"One thing I don't understand, Bobby," I said. I was stalling for time, and he knew it.

"Yeah, what?" He brought the rifle up, rested it across his knees.

"Why'd you kill Skates and Hathaway?" I asked. "I've got the rest of it figured out, but not that."

"Because they killed my baby?" Tess asked. Her breathing was shallow and her question came out in a whisper.

Snow looked at her for a long count, smiled, revealing the black wad of tobacco tucked in the corner of his mouth. His hands tightened on the stock of the rifle. "No," he said, his voice taut, cutting. "I killed Skates because he strangled her before I had my piece. I did Hathaway because he was Skates's friend and I didn't trust him. In this bunch, woman, we share and share alike."

I remember the next few seconds only in flashes, scattered images of sound, movement, and gore.

I remember Tess's scream, loud and piercing as a banshee's, as she lunged for Snow, and the two of them tumbling to the ground in a heap. Snow rolled her beneath him and wrapped his hands around Tess's wrists, pinning her arms to the ground.

I remember the look of surprise on Snow's face when she brought her knee up sharply between his legs, remember his loud grunts of pain as he rolled off and doubled up in an attempt to protect his bruised privates from the kick Tess was aiming in his direction. I remember his heaving stomach as he tried to hold back the vomit that looked to be rising in his throat.

I remember grasping for the derringer, pulling it free, cocking the small hammer.

I remember hearing Bolton moving behind me. Remember dropping to an elbow, pointing over my shoulder and firing upwards into his face. I remember the incredible noise of the small weapon, as loud as a howitzer, the way the muzzle flash from the miniature pistol scorched my fingers, the way it kicked, bucked in my hand.

I remember the startled look on Ray Bolton's features as the slug from the .22 mag hit him just below the left eye, traveled upward through his skull, remember the small, bee-sting entrance wound. Remember the way his body felt when it fell across mine, pinning me to the ground.

He wasn't dead, and I remember the way he began to struggle and growl, to push himself up, one hand fumbling with the holstered revolver at his belt. I raised the derringer and shot him twice more in the chest at point-blank range. The muzzle flash scorched his shirt around the entrance wounds, and I remember the way the fabric smoked, remember the blast of foul breath that exploded from his mouth as he died.

I remember Zipper's confusion as he pulled his weapon, tried to decide whether to shoot me or Tess, who was still fighting with Snow. The way the muzzle looked when he finally decided to kill me first and swung the barrel of his gun toward my head.

I remember the way his body shuddered as Saul's bullet slammed the middle of his chest. He dropped his revolver, turned away, and took two painful, lurching steps before he crumpled.

I remember seeing the Latino rustlers on the far side of the enclosure crouched and firing wildly in Saul's direction, and the snapping reports of two more rifle shots, and they were down, too.

But most of all, I remember the look of righteous fury in Tess McAfferty's eyes when she threw herself on top of Snow—still incapacitated by her knee to the groin—and wrestled him onto his back. Remember the complete absence of pity on her face as she pulled the hunting knife from the sheath at his belt, held it in a two-handed grip, and plunged it into the hollow at the base of his throat.

By the time I'd extricated myself from Ray Bolton's corpse and found a weapon, Irons was out of the ravine and running toward us. There seemed to be bodies everywhere, and I swept the muzzle of the revolver around, looking for signs of movement. With the exception of Andrew McAfferty, whose arms were thrashing, the place was as still as a crypt.

I let the hammer of the derringer down, tucked the weapon in my belt, and went to where Tess was still sitting astraddle Bobby's chest. Her hands were still clenched tightly around the hilt of the knife, as if she were trying to hold him there, pinned to the ground. Blood had stopped spurting from his wound but still seeped out around the edges of the buried blade.

His hat and sunglasses had come off, and his sightless gray eyes seemed to scan the heavens.

I doubted he was headed that direction.

I reached down to take Tess's arm and help her up, but she pulled away, her gaze locked on the knife.

Slowly, reluctantly, she released the hilt. Dipped her index finger in his blood. Brought it to her mouth and licked it off. Smiled. His warm, sticky blood smeared her straight, white teeth.

She was stone crazy.

I heard the sound of Irons's footsteps behind me but didn't turn around.

"This is your fault, Saul," I said.

He laid his rifle across Snow's legs, took Tess by the arms, and lifted her to her feet. Her eyes never left Bobby's face.

"It was her choice," he said sadly. "What she wanted."

He turned Tess away from Bobby's corpse, toward me. I put my arm around her waist and she leaned against my chest. I could feel her trembling. Her body radiated white heat.

"Is it what she wanted, Saul?" I asked. I swept my free arm around, indicating the scene of carnage. "Do you think this is what she wanted?"

Picking up his rifle, he carried it to Andrew's side, squatted down to feel the boy's pulse. "I don't know the answer to that question," he said. "I suppose I never will."

He stood, slung the rifle on his shoulder, pulled his hat low on his forehead. "This one will be all right, but you'd better get him to a hospital. Her too. Use Bobby's pickup." He turned, took two steps in the direction of the ravine.

"Where are you going?" I said. I started to go after him, but Tess wrapped her arms around my waist, held me in place.

Irons stopped, pointed at the top of the draw. "My horse is up there," he said. "I'm gonna get my horse, Harry. And then I'm gonna disappear."

I let him walk for twenty yards before I moved. I pried Tess's arms from my waist, went to pick up Bobby's rifle, chambered a round. I brought the barrel up, felt the recoil pad firm against my shoulder.

"Saul!" I yelled. "Stop, now!"

He kept walking. I fired at the ground beside his feet. The bullet kicked up an explosion of dirt that showered his boots and the bottom of his pants legs, but he didn't stop. My hands were shaking badly as I chambered another round.

"Saul! Don't make me do this!" I looked through the scope, centered the crosshairs on his spine, took a deep breath to calm my frayed nerve endings and tightened my finger on the trigger.

Irons stopped, swung around and faced me. He was so close I couldn't get all his body in the scope, just his torso and head. Sweat ran down my brow, burned my eyes. I rubbed it away, brought the rifle to bear again and put the crosshairs on his heart.

Irons grinned.

Waved good-bye.

"It was self-defense, Harry," he hollered. "Carney was goin' for his gun. You have to believe that." He pivoted again and began walking. Back straight. Head high. Long legs eating ground.

I should have stopped him, shot him in the back if I had to. But I didn't. Perhaps I couldn't. He'd just saved my life. And two others.

I held the crosshairs on his back until he got to the mouth of the ravine. In seconds, he'd be in the gully and out of view. Gone, perhaps forever. I knew what I had to do, there was no other choice.

I lowered the barrel of the rifle. Set the safety.

And let Saul Irons go.

# TWENTY-ONE

The light of the mercury vapor lamp on the street outside Nicole's bedroom streamed through the venetian blinds, turning our skin an electric blue. She turned away from me, took most of the sheet with her. One tan leg stuck out from the tangle of bedding and she drew it toward her, curled herself into a ball. She'd been crying, and I reached over her shoulder, gently wiped a tear from her cheek.

"I can't do it, Harry," she said quietly. "I can't move to Victory with you. There's nothing for me there."

"Then we won't live in Victory," I said placatingly. "We'll live in Laramie and I'll drive to work every day. It's not that long a commute."

She shook her head, closed her eyes and bit her lip. "The town charter says the police chief has to live in the community," she said. "We've been over this a thousand times in the last few days."

And indeed we had. Two days after the deaths of Angus McAfferty, Bobby Snow, Ray Bolton, and the other three rustlers who'd been shot by Saul Irons on Tess McAfferty's ranch, I'd resigned my position as Albany County sheriff and dropped my bid for election. As I'd hoped he would, Curly had welcomed me back to Victory with open arms. He didn't give me the raise I asked for, but he kicked in an additional two weeks of vacation. I told him I wanted to use it up front and had been in Denver for the last ten days trying unsuccessfully to put my family back together. I was scheduled to go back to work the following Monday.

I'd tried to explain why I'd dropped out of the race, but Nicole had not taken it well. On one level, she understood that the spate of killings had taken an emotional toll that I was unwilling to ever pay again, and that I wanted to live a simpler life. She understood my unwillingness to subject myself to the political meat grinder that is your typical small-town election campaign. She understood it when I told her that when all was said and done, the only reason I ever really wanted to be sheriff in the first place was for her, not for me.

She tried to understand my ambivalence about law enforcement in general, at least the practice of law enforcement in a large organization where the responsibility sometimes weighs you down like a stone, where the line between right and wrong is often nearly indecipherable, and where optimism and self-assurance harden into cynicism, self-doubt, and self-recrimination with every passing year. I even think she understood it when I told her that as much as I loved her, I simply could not live my life according to her definition of success, a definition almost diametrically opposed to my own.

But she still believed that my decision to give up the job as county sheriff and return to my spartan existence in Victory was, at some level at least, a rejection of both her and the responsibility that a family represents. There was no way my job as police chief could support us, she pointed out. And even though I thrive on isolation and life at its slowest possible pace, I could not expect the rest of my family to give up the important things in their own lives to share my self-imposed exile. I wasn't ready for us to be together again, she said. Wasn't ready to make the compromises, the sacrifices. And until I was ready, she was unwilling to consider remarriage. For the time being, she said, we'd continue as we were. We'd date, see where it led.

We were both afraid it would lead nowhere.

"I'm sorry I let you down, Nicole," I said. When she didn't answer, I eased myself out of bed, went to the window, and peered through the blinds. A soft breeze rustled the leaves of the big oak tree in the front yard, and the air carried the petroleum scent of the spray the city uses to control mosquitoes. Across the room, I could hear Nicole weeping softly.

I pulled on a thick terry-cloth robe and padded out of the room, flipped on a light and continued down the hall, past the bedrooms where the boys were sleeping to the top of the stairs. The old stairs creaked as I descended, and the noise woke Blackfoot, who was curled up at the bottom. He looked up, making sure who I was, then laid his head back on his paws, watching me with some interest. In the weeks since he'd come home with Nicole and been adopted into the family, he'd filled out, put on weight. His black coat was lustrous and healthy, and the muscles in his haunches and shoulders rippled beneath his skin. Because of their friendly natures, Labrador retrievers aren't the best guard dogs in the world, but he was doing his best to overcome his pacific genetic programming.

Nicole and the boys felt safe with him in the house, but I was still uneasy.

Out of habit, I checked the locks on the front door and peeked through the heavy drapes covering the picture window. One o'clock in the morning, and the streets of Highlands Ranch, the suburban development where Nicole and I had built this house when we were still married, were nearly deserted. There was no traffic save for a lone jogger who clomped down the pavement through the pool of light cast by the streetlamp and disappeared into darkness. A collie running with him paused in my driveway to pee on the tire of Nicole's car and then loped off after his master. While I watched, the underground sprinkling system kicked on, filling the air with a fine mist which hugged the ground like a cloud.

I closed the drapes and picked my way through the living room to the kitchen, turned on the light over the stove, and pulled a half-gallon bottle of Rebel Yell bourbon from the liquor cabinet and a jelly glass from the dishwasher to drink it from. I poured until the glass was half full, considered the fact that my alcohol consumption in the last two weeks could not be explained away as social drinking. The old Harry Starbranch's response to stress. Maybe Nicole was right, I thought unhappily. Maybe I hadn't changed that much after all. Maybe I was searching for any opportunity to go back to my old way of life.

Yep, I was feeling sorry for myself again. Starbranch in his best Scandinavian funk. I briefly considered pouring the sour mash back and then thought no, the hell with it. If she doesn't want me, I'll do whatever I want. I filled the glass to the rim. Then I carried both the glass and the bottle to the dark living room and sank down on the couch.

The smoky whiskey burned the back of my throat, but the second it reached my belly its warmth began to spread, to deaden the knot of anxiety that had been residing there on a full-time basis for the better part of a month. I sipped again, tried to disregard the urge to sneak back upstairs and retrieve my .357 from the nightstand. These days, I never feel comfortable without it, even in my own living room. Especially at night.

When the whiskey began to work its magic, I balanced the glass on my stomach, put my feet up, and thought for about the ten millionth time in recent days about the way the McAfferty case had turned out.

I suppose I should have been happy. These days, instead of criticism, the newspapers are full of praise for my actions, are crediting me, in fact, with almost single-handedly bringing down the most vicious gang of cutthroats to roam the Laramie plains in a hundred years.

Rustling is at its lowest level in a decade, and Walker Tisdale has shown no inclination to bring charges against Tess and her neighbors for hiring a professional killer, a course Keegan has vociferously recommended. Tisdale says there's not enough evidence to link them with the Emile Cross killing, and none to the killing of Wayne Carney. He's probably right, but I suspect his reluctance is as much political as professional. The ranchers he would be prosecuting are bedrock Republicans for the most part, the type of people who put him in his current office and will vote him into the next one, and a prosecution would undoubtedly alienate most of Tisdale's constituency. Best to let it ride. Best to forget.

Strange, but in this at least, I agree with Tisdale. I'm letting a few things ride myself.

For starters, I never mentioned Saul's involvement in bringing Snow and his cronies down. Neither did Andrew McAfferty, who was unconscious for forty-eight hours. When he came to, he told investigators he remembered nothing after dinner the night before.

Neither will Tess, at least not right away. The nice people at the Midwestern psychiatric hospital where her family sent her after the shootout say she won't be ready for visitors for a long, long time, especially visitors who remind her of Colleen.

Saul Irons disappeared beyond the far horizon and no one knows where he went. Although Keegan is suspicious, he doesn't press. Just keeps going through the motions, trying to bring him to trial.

He hasn't called the whole time I've been in Denver. Someday, I know, he'll ask me about it. I'll tell him.

As I've said, it's difficult for me to lie.

I finished the whiskey in my glass and poured another to fill the emptiness in my gut, listened to the creaking and settling of the house. Over the *thwack-thwack-thwack*ing of the sprinkling system, I could hear a police siren in the distance, the sound of a big jet making its descent into Stapleton. I pulled my robe tighter across my chest, walked unsteadily to the television and clicked it on. I turned the volume completely down and flipped through the offerings until I found what I was looking for, an old Western starring John Wayne, Dean Martin, and Ricky Nelson.

Then I stumbled back to the couch, pulled an afghan over my legs, and drank myself to sleep.

The phone rang at four in the morning, hour of the wolf.

At first, I tried to ignore it, but its insistence finally pulled me from the fog. I sat up, cursed the banging behind my eyeballs, and stumbled to the wall phone in the kitchen, fully prepared to hear nothing but a dial tone when I picked up. In the last two weeks, there'd been over a hundred hang-ups at all hours on Nicole's line. Slaymaker, no doubt about it. We'd asked Mountain Bell to install a trap, but our request was still caught up in the company's red tape. According to them, telephone harassment has to go on for at least two weeks before it's officially considered harassment. We wouldn't pass that milestone until Monday.

I yanked the receiver from the wall. "Hullo," I grumbled. My mouth was sticky and foul, and I had trouble forming the word.

"Harry?" There was a lot of noise in the background—sirens, shouting—but I recognized the voice immediately. It was John Bruno, my ex-partner on the Denver Police Department. It was a horrible connection, and I realized he was using a cellular phone. "Sorry to wake you."

They say bad news always comes in the dark, and my mind was racing with possibilities, none of them good, all of them frightening. I struggled to force myself to concentrate. To breathe.

"Harry?" he said again. His voice sounded like it came from inside a metal shed.

"I'm here, John," I said softly. The lights upstairs were still out, and I could hear no noise on the upper floor. Neither Nicole nor the boys had been awakened by the call. I wanted to keep it that way. I reached out and grabbed the doorframe for support. "What is it?"

He hesitated, cleared his throat. "Jerry Slaymaker," he said finally. "I think you should come down here right away."

I dressed quietly, shrugged into a shoulder holster and made the seventeen-mile drive from Highlands Ranch to Five Points in a little over twenty minutes.

Traffic was light on I-25, but in Five Points, one of the city's toughest neighborhoods, there were still plenty of people on the pavement. Hookers and pimps drifted in and out of dimly lit saloons, johns cruised slowly down the neighborhood streets. At Downing and Twenty-sixth, I passed a patrol car, its blue lights flashing as two officers handcuffed a young black man who was spread-eagled across the hood of his car. An overweight woman with wide hips and a vodka bottle in her hand railed at the officers from the sidewalk, her curses loud and shrill.

Past Welton Street, I turned right off Twenty-sixth onto Emerson and followed it for a block and a half to the parking lot of the abandoned brewery, the former home of Rocky Mountain Lager, where Bruno had told me to come. As soon as I pulled off Emerson and into the lot, I was stopped by a patrolman wearing a blaze orange jacket and carrying a flashlight long and heavy enough to be considered a weapon. I rolled down the window and stuck my head outside. "I'm here for Detective Bruno," I called, and held my badge out for him to see. "He's expecting me."

The patrolman nodded and spoke quickly into his walkie-talkie, listened to the garbled response. He pointed to an open space at the side of the lot. "Park your car there and wait," he said. "Bruno will be over in a few minutes."

I did as I'd been instructed, pulling slowly into the space until the Blazer's nose was kissing the chain link fence that bordered the parking lot. Then I switched the engine off, and pocketed the keys. Pulling on a light windbreaker to cover my weapon, I got out and stood anxiously beside the rear bumper.

The far side of the macadam was a convention of police and emergency vehicles. The blue lights from a half dozen patrol cars cut the darkness, lit the brick walls of the brewery in bizarre, intermittent flashes, interspersed with the flashing red lights from two city ambulances with their emergency doors open.

As I watched, a team of three EMTs wheeled someone on a gurney up to the door of one of the ambulances. They folded the gurney inside, and two of the EMTs jumped in the back with the patient. The third slammed the doors shut, hopped into the driver's seat, and eased the ambulance through the tangle of vehicles. He gunned it as he passed me on his way out of the lot, his young face grim and determined as he turned onto the street and sped off in the direction of Denver General.

There were ten or twelve men and women clustered at the side of the building, but I was too far away to pick out Bruno. A few more were gathered in small knots around the vehicles, smoking, using the radio.

I waited for ten minutes before one of the people broke away from the scene and began ambling in my direction. As he closed the distance between us, I recognized Bruno's easy shuffle, the way he moved on the balls of his feet, always leaning forward as if he was walking into a stiff breeze. He was wearing civilian clothes, khaki pants, a polo shirt, high-top sneakers. He carried a revolver in a holster on his belt and a flashlight in his left hand. In its light I saw he'd grown a full, black beard since I'd seen him last, but he'd shed at least fifteen pounds. From broad shoulders his torso tapered to his waist, giving him the menacing T-shape of a weight lifter. His thick biceps strained the fabric of his shirt.

He held out his hand, and I took it, felt the power in his strong grip. He looked me up and down. Smiled. I suppose I looked like hell. "Hello, Harry," he said. "Long time, no see."

I looked past him to the group of people around the warehouse. "What's this, John?" I asked. "Why'd you bring me down here?"

He didn't answer, took me by the elbow and began walking me toward the action. "It's just something," he said as we walked, "that I thought you should see."

We weaved our way through the parked patrol cars, past the

flashing lights of the remaining ambulance, to the side of the brewery building, where three officers and an evidence technician were bent over a body lying on the pavement. The strobe light from the flash on the technician's camera lit their faces in harsh, white flares, bounced off the legs of the body on the ground. Through the men clustered around the body, I could only see its legs. Work boots. Denim jeans. The camera flashed again and I saw a hand, its fingers still wrapped around the hilt of a long hunting knife with a wickedly curved blade.

When they heard us approaching, the patrolmen and the evidence technician looked up, the technician nodding when he recognized Bruno. As if responding to an unspoken command, he and the patrolmen stood up, moved a step back from the body to let us through.

Bruno moved forward, clicked on his flashlight, and played the yellow beam across Jerry Slaymaker's malevolent face.

His eyes were open, and his thick tongue lolled out of the corner of his mouth. His belt was open. The front of his pink oxford shirt was dark with blood. More of it pooled at his armpits. A trickle ran from the corner of his mouth to his ear, disappeared in his thick thatch of mouse brown hair.

I felt like I'd been punched. My stomach turned. I choked back the bile, tried not to vomit. Sinking down on my haunches beside Slaymaker's body, I looked into the abyss of his sightless eyes. I had the feeling that Slaymaker was still alive, trying to reach across the gulf of death to grab me, drag me to him. Flinching, I stood, moved two long steps away from his corpse.

"You were right about him, Harry," Bruno said. He put his massive arm around my shoulders. "You were right about him all along."

I looked at Bruno in confusion, tried to read his face. "What happened?" I croaked.

Bruno turned me away and we walked slowly along the building. I sank down until I was sitting and rested my back against the bricks. Bruno sat beside me, lit a smoke, and offered the pack to me. My fingers trembled as I pulled one loose and waited while he lit it with his lighter. I sucked the smoke deep into my lungs, coughed, and inhaled again, forced it out through my nose. Hacked a couple more times. It tasted wonderful.

"It went down about three o'clock," he said. He pointed to one of the nearby patrol cars, where a young female officer was sitting with her back against the tire, her head cradled in her arms. "Officer Katie Haines there and her partner responded to a call of suspicious activity here at the brewery. They arrived on scene . . ."

He sighed, ground his smoke out on the asphalt. "And found Jerry Slaymaker over there at the side of the building. He was in the process of raping a six-year-old boy."

I balled my fists, cursed under my breath. Another one. It shouldn't have happened. If only I'd . . .

"He came at them with the knife," Bruno said, nodding at Haines, "and she shot the son of a bitch dead."

I remembered the ambulance that was pulling out as I arrived. "The boy?" I asked.

Bruno looked at the ground, shook his head. "Didn't make it, Harry. They were too late."

I leaned my head back against the warm brick wall of the building and looked up at the sky. The first light of dawn was rising in the east and the quarter moon rode low above the horizon. On the streets of Five Points, traffic was increasing. People on their way to work. People curious about the commotion at the brewery. I felt a sadness so profound it threatened to overcome me, but at the same time an unmistakable sense of relief. Jerry Slaymaker was finally dead. He'd killed his last child.

"Guess this makes that lawsuit he filed against you a moot point, huh Harry?" Bruno said. He stood up, dusted the seat of his trousers. "In every dark cloud and all that crap, right?"

"What?" I looked up at Bruno, who put his hands in his pockets and watched the ambulance crew load Slaymaker into a bag. "Chew that a little finer, John."

He looked down, smiled gently. "This sucks, Harry," he said. "It truly does. But at least you're off the hook."

"Is that why you called me down here?" I asked angrily. "Because of that fucking lawsuit?"

I stood, ground the cigarette under the toe of my boot, and began walking away.

"Harry?"

"What?" I growled.

"I didn't call you because of that."

I stopped, turned back toward him. He was pulling a piece of crumpled paper from his shirt pocket. He handed it to me. "I called you because of this."

I took the square of paper from him and unfolded it. He used his flashlight to illuminate the writing. At the top of the wrinkled sheet was my telephone number in Victory. Below that, directions to my house. I looked questioningly at Bruno.

"Found it in his glove box," Bruno explained. "You have any idea why he'd be carrying directions to your house?"

I did indeed, although it took a couple of seconds for it to fall into place. I felt my heart beginning to race. "Where's his car?" I asked.

Bruno pointed to the side of the parking lot where a red Ford pickup sat by itself under the canopy of a willow tree. "Over there."

I grabbed the flashlight from Bruno's hand, pushed by him, and stormed across the parking lot to the Ford. I clicked the light on and ran the beam across the tailgate, saw two small, slightly puckered spots right under the Ford logo where repairs had been made and painted over. Fumbling in my pocket for my folding knife, I flicked open the blade and began digging at one of the repairs.

"Harry?" Bruno said. "What are you—"

I shook my head and bent into my work, cut through the paint with the tip of the knife and found fresh body putty. When I twisted the blade the putty fell out in a plug, revealing a neat, round hole in the metal. Bullet hole. I hadn't missed the son of a bitch after all. Not completely.

I put my foot on the bumper, pulled myself up, and climbed over the tailgate into the bed of the pickup. Dropped to my hands and knees and scoured the bed of the truck with the flashlight's beam.

It took me a few minutes, but I finally found what I was looking for, behind the spare tire bolted to the wall of the bed. I held it between my fingers, felt its weight.

Bruno was standing at the side of the truck. "What is it?" he asked.

I handed him the deformed hunk of lead. "A bullet," I said. "I think if you have it tested, you'll find it came from my Black-hawk."

"What the fuck?" he said. "Harry, I think you'd better—"

"I put it there," I said. "Right after the bastard drove up to Victory and tried to kill me. Shot the shit out of my house. Almost killed Nicole. I busted a couple caps at him as he was driving away.

"Looks like I didn't hit exactly where I was aiming." I smiled grimly. "But I did shoot his truck."

"Why didn't you report it?" Bruno asked. "Didn't you know it was him?"

"Nah," I said. I clicked off the light and climbed out of the pickup, hopped down from the bumper. "I thought the shooter was someone else. But I'll tell you this, John."

He closed his hand around the slug, waited for me to go on.

"When you check Slaymaker's house, I think you'll find a 7-millimeter rifle."

He nodded.

"And it's my bet ballistics will match it to a bullet my deputies pulled from my living room wall. Lucky for me the prick couldn't shoot worth spit."

Across the parking lot, the EMTs had finished loading Slay-maker's body into the ambulance. They slammed the door and saddled up, passed us with the red lights flashing, but no siren. There was no hurry.

"So much for subtlety, asshole," I mumbled when it passed.

"What's that, Harry?" Bruno asked.

I spat on the asphalt at my feet. Welcome to hell, Jerry. Too bad I couldn't have sent you there myself. Saved Katie Haines the grief.

"Nothin' important John," I said, walking toward the Blazer. I blinked my eyes against the September breeze. "Nothin' at all."

I crossed the Wyoming line on Highway 287 south of Tie Siding and pulled off the highway onto a dirt road leading northwest toward the Medicine Bows. I was less than an hour from Victory and home, but I wasn't in any hurry. I rumaged around in my tack bag until I found my Victory Police Chief's badge, polished it with a bandana, and pinned it to my breast pocket. Then I popped the Chris LeDoux tape I was listening to out of the player and killed the engine, poured myself a cup of steaming coffee from my metal thermos, swung my stiff legs out of the cab, and went to lean my hip against the front of the vehicle.

The first hint of fall was in the air, the sunlight laced with that curious deep yellow tint that intensifies the browns and greens of the landscape and signals the changing of the season. The summer's heat was broken, and the air was crisp, chilled by a breeze down from the piney flanks of the mountains. The air smelled of sage and rich antedeluvian earth. I put my binoculars to my eyes, scanned the open country spread out in front of me as far as the foothills of the Snowies.

About a half mile across the flat prairie tableland, a pickup full of hunters was working its way toward a small group of prong-horns grazing along the lip of a draw—a nice buck and a half dozen does—but the animals heard them coming long before they could put themselves in rifle range. By the time the hunters made it to within three hundred yards of the draw, the animals were racing flat out, sixty miles an hour, heading toward Colorado. The hunters piled out of the cab and cranked off a couple of shots anyway. Their bullets were short of the mark, kicked up white puffs of dust twenty yards behind the running herd. Disappointed, the truck-hunting sportsmen racked their rifles in the cab, climbed back in, and drove off in the direction they'd come. They were driving slowly, taking their time, the man in the passenger seat using his field glasses to scan the grassland as they rolled. There were plenty of pronghorns in the county, and plenty of daylight left to shoot them in. Sooner or later, they'd come across some dumb ones and make their meat.

With my small herd of antelope safe for the time being, I spent the next half hour drinking coffee, scanning the sky for hawks and eagles, letting the sun warm my bones and the wind caress my cheeks.

Overhead, a group of mallards battled the air currents on their way down the wide valley between the Snowies and the Laramie range, heading south. They were a beautiful, bittersweet sight. By evening, I figured, they'd be flying over Denver. Over Nicole, my boys.

My eyes began to water. I dabbed the moisture away with my knuckles. Gone only a little more than an hour, and I missed them already, their absence a tangible ache in my body, a yawning gray emptiness in my soul.

We hadn't parted badly, Nicole and I. Simply inconclusively.

She'd followed me out to the driveway as I put the last of my gear in my car, barefoot in her robe, her hair held back by a wide turquoise ribbon, her eyes red and puffy from crying most of the night. She put her arms around my waist and pulled me close, held me for a long moment, her head resting on my chest.

"I think you still need a little more time to sort things out, Harry," she said softly. "Time to figure out what you really want."

I started to protest, but she held her finger across my lips. Then she pushed herself away to arm's length, pulled my face toward hers. Kissed my cheek. Her warm breath smelled of cinnamon toast. She smiled. "I've said this before, cowboy, and I'll say it again," she whispered. "When you do figure it out, pick up the phone. You know the number."

I felt a knot tightening in my throat. Brushed my lips across the fine red hair at the top of her head. "You'll be the first to know," I promised.

Trouble is, I have no idea how long that could take.

It's the $64,000 question, the central conundrum of my existence: What does Harry Starbranch want? I guess I don't know for absolute, dead-center certain. I suppose I never have. The damn list keeps changing.

But right now, on this lonesome September morning on the Laramie Plains, here's what I think.

Short-term, I want a platter-size chicken-fried steak, a cold beer, and some real mashed potatoes with cream gravy.

I want a couple of perfect days of fishing before snow falls. I want the Wyoming Cowboy football team to beat Air Force. I want to make enough money to pay a little more than the minimum on my Visa balance every month and to buy a new pair of Tony Lamas once a year. I want to go elk hunting next month and spend the whole week on Wagonhound Creek with my buddies, playing cards and sitting around a campfire without ever having to shoot an elk. I want Frankie Bull to teach me to cook at least one fancy dish. I want Ry Cooder to cut a new album and Jack Livingston to write another book.

Long-term, it's a little fuzzy.

I want to be a live-in father to my boys again, teach them to drive and tie a decent trout fly. I want to grow old and cantankerous with Nicole, like Kate Hepburn and Henry Fonda in *On Golden Pond*. I'd like to feel good about police work again, to believe a cop can make a difference without compromising himself or his idealism. If it's not too much to ask, I'd like to make peace with the ghosts of the men I've killed, and the victims I couldn't save.

Most of all, though, I'd like an answer to the question that's been dogging me since that bloody day on Tess McAfferty's ranch.

In 1984, I broke the law to put a killer in prison. This year, I broke the law to keep one out. I broke the law of my own free will, and I'd do it again. But was I right?

I hope I was. I don't know. Maybe I never will. I guess I should be thankful I can still look at my reflection in the mirror when I shave.

Until the case is remanded to a higher authority, that may have to do.